DREAMS OF A DARK WARRIOR

"Fast, ...engaging, and captivating ... The perfect getaway."
—Examiner.com

"Sex scenes so hot there is a danger the pages could spontaneously combust ... Still fresh, still thrilling ... Phenomenally awesome!"
—Love Vampires

PLEASURE OF A DARK PRINCE

"Consistent excellence is a Cole standard!"
—*Romantic Times* (4½ stars)

"There are few authors that can move me to tears. Kresley Cole is one of them."
—Book Binge

"Kresley Cole's Immortals After Dark series does not cease to amaze me."
—Love Vampires

KISS OF A DEMON KING

"Perennial favorite Cole continues to round out her Immortals After Dark world with kick-butt action and scorching passion!"
—*Romantic Times*

"Kresley Cole knows what paranormal romance readers crave and superbly delivers on every page."
—Single Titles

"Full of magic, mayhem, sorcery, and sensuality. Readers will not want to miss one word of this memorable and enchanting tale. The closer to the end I got the slower I read because I knew once the story ended I would be left craving more of this brilliant and emotionally gripping saga. . . . It is truly one of the most amazing tales Kresley Cole has ever released."

—Wild On Books

"Cole deftly blends danger and desire into a brilliantly original contemporary paranormal romance. She neatly tempers the scorchingly sexy romance between Sabine and Rydstrom with a generous measure of sharp humor, and the combination of a cleverly constructed plot and an inventive cast of characters in *Kiss of a Demon King* is simply irresistible."

—Reader To Reader

DARK DESIRES AFTER DUSK

"*New York Times* bestseller Cole outdoes herself. . . . A gem."

—*Romantic Times*

"Kresley Cole is a gifted author with a knack for witty dialogue, smart heroines, fantastic alpha males, and yes, it has to be said, some of the hottest love scenes you'll read in mainstream romance. . . . You're in for a treat if you've never read a Kresley Cole book."

—RomanceNovel.tv

"A wonderfully romantic tale of two people from the opposite sides of their immortal world. . . . Everything I had hoped it to be and so much more!"

—Queue My Review

DARK NEEDS AT NIGHT'S EDGE

"Poignant and daring. You can trust Cole to always deliver sizzling sexy interludes within a darkly passionate romance."

—*Romantic Times*

"The evolution of this romance is among the most believable and engrossing I've ever read. Cole's Immortals After Dark series continues stronger than ever with this latest installment."

—Fresh Fiction

BOOKS BY KRESLEY COLE

The Sutherland Series

The Captain of All Pleasures

The Price of Pleasure

The MacCarrick Brothers Series

If You Dare

If You Desire

If You Deceive

The Immortals After Dark Series

The Warlord Wants Forever

A Hunger Like No Other

No Rest for the Wicked

Wicked Deeds on a Winter's Night

Dark Needs at Night's Edge

Dark Desires After Dusk

Kiss of a Demon King

Pleasure of a Dark Prince

Demon from the Dark

Dreams of a Dark Warrior

Anthologies

Playing Easy to Get

Deep Kiss of Winter

KRESLEY COLE

lothaire

**SIMON &
SCHUSTER**

London · New York · Sydney · Toronto · New Delhi

A CBS COMPANY

First published in the USA by Pocket Books, 2012
First published in Great Britain by Simon & Schuster UK Ltd, 2012
This paperback edition first published in Great Britain by Simon & Schuster UK Ltd, 2012
A CBS COMPANY

1 3 5 7 9 10 8 6 4 2

Simon & Schuster UK Ltd
1st Floor
222 Gray's Inn Road
London WC1X 8HB

www.simonandschuster.co.uk

Simon & Schuster Australia, Sydney
Simon & Schuster India, New Delhi

A CIP catalogue record for this book is available from the British Library

ISBN: 978-0-85720-693-0
E-book ISBN: 978-1-84983-691-3

Printed and bound in Great Britain by CPI Group (UK) Ltd, Croydon, CR0 4YY

To Swede—a good sport, a great guy, and a remarkable husband. As I'm writing this, it's four in the morning Deadline Standard Time, and you're still at the desk with me. How can I surprise you with a dedication when you refuse to desert the command center?

ACKNOWLEDGMENTS

Thank you so much to my editor, Lauren McKenna, and my publisher, Louise Burke, both fantastic ladies who continually inspire me.

A special thanks to the Production team at Gallery Books—and to Nancy Tonik, for her patience with my "unique" way of doing copy edits and my eccentric attachment schemes.

Much love and many thanks to my incredible agent, Robin Rue.

Finally, thank you to my readers, for taking this leap with me and for all your wonderful support

EXCERPTED FROM THE IMMORTALS'
BOOK OF LORE . . .

The Lore

"*. . . and those sentient creatures that are not human shall be united in one stratum, coexisting with, yet secret from, man's.*"

- Most are immortal and can regenerate from injuries. The stronger breeds can only be killed by mystical fire or beheading.
- Their eyes change with intense emotion, often to a breed-specific color.

The Vampires

"*In the first chaos of the Lore, a brotherhood of vampires dominated by relying on their worship of logic and absence of mercy. They sprang from the harsh steppes of Dacia and migrated to Russia, though some say a secret enclave, the Daci, live in Dacia still.*"

- Each adult male seeks his *Bride,* his eternal wife, and walks as the living dead until he finds her.
- A Bride will render his body fully alive, giving him breath and making his heart beat, a process known as *blooding.*
- *The Fallen* are vampires who have killed by drinking a victim to death. Distinguished by their red eyes.
- Two vampire armies continue to war: the Horde, which is mostly comprised of the Fallen, and the Forbearers, a legion of turned humans, who do not drink blood directly from the flesh.

The Valkyries

"When a maiden warrior screams for courage as she dies in battle, Wóden and Freya heed her call. The two gods give up lightning to strike her, rescuing her to their hall and preserving her courage forever in the form of the maiden's immortal Valkyrie daughter."

- They take sustenance from the electrical energy of the earth, sharing it in one collective power, and give it back with their emotions in the form of lightning.
- Without training, most can be mesmerized by shining objects.

The Turning

"Only through death can one become an 'other.'"

- Some beings can turn a human or even other Lore creatures into their kind through differing means, but the catalyst for change is always death, and success is not guaranteed.

The Accession

"And a time shall come to pass when all immortal beings in the Lore, from the Valkyrie, vampire, Lykae, and demon factions to the witches, shifters, fey, and sirens . . . must fight and destroy each other."

- A kind of mystical checks-and-balances system for an ever-growing population of immortals.
- Occurs every five hundred years. Or right now . . .

PROLOGUE

Castle Helvita, Horde vampire stronghold
RUSSIAN WINTER, IN AGES LONG PAST

"What fresh humiliation does this day bring?" Ivana the Bold asked her son, Lothaire, as guards escorted them to the vampire known as Stefanovich—the king of the Vampire Horde.

And Lothaire's father.

Though only nine, Lothaire could tell his mother's tone held a trace of recklessness. "And why wake you?" she demanded of him, as if he could explain his father's rash ways.

The summons had come at noon, well past his bedtime. "I know not, Mother," he mumbled as he adjusted his clothing. He'd had only seconds to dress.

"I grow weary of this treatment. One day he will push me too far and rue it."

Lothaire had overheard her complaining to his uncle Fyodor about the king's "tirades and dalliances, his increasingly bizarre behavior." She'd softly confessed, "I threw away my love on your brother, am naught but an ill-treated mistress in this realm, though I was heir to the throne in Dacia."

Fyodor had tried to comfort her, but she'd said, "I knew I only had so long with him before his heart stopped its beating. Now I question whether he has a heart at all."

Today her ice-blue eyes were ablaze with a dangerous light. "I was meant for better than this." With each of her steps, the furs that spilled over her shoulders swayed back and forth. The skirts of her scarlet gown rustled, a pleasing sound he always associated with her. "And you, my prince, were as well."

She called him "prince," but Lothaire wasn't one. At least, not in this kingdom. He was merely Stefanovich's bastard, one in a long line of them.

They followed the two guards up winding stairs to the king's private suites. The walls were gilded with gold and moist with cold. Outside a blizzard pounded the castle.

Sconces lit the way, but nothing could alleviate the gloom of these echoing corridors.

Lothaire shivered, longing to be back in his warm bed with his new puppy dozing over his legs.

Once they reached the anteroom outside of Stefanovich's chambers and the guards began opening the groaning gold doors, Ivana smoothed her hands over her elaborate white-blond braids and lifted her chin. Not for the first time, Lothaire thought she looked like an angel of yore.

Inside, lining the back wall, was a soaring window of jet glass inlaid with symbols of the dark arts. The stained glass kept out the faint sunlight visible through the storm and made a fearsome backdrop for the king's chair.

Not that the towering vampire needed anything more to make him fearsome. His build was more like a demon's, his shoulders broader than a carrying plank, his fists like anvils.

"Ah, Ivana Daciano deigns to obey a summons," Stefanovich called from the head of his long dining table. Every night his eyes seemed to grow redder, their crimson glow standing out against the sand-colored hair that fell over his forehead.

The dozen or so courtiers seated with him stared at Ivana with undisguised malice. In turn, she drew her lips back to flash her fangs. She found these courtiers beneath her and made no secret of it.

Seated to the king's left was Lothaire's uncle Fyodor, who appeared embarrassed.

Lothaire followed Ivana's gaze to the seat at Stefanovich's right hand—a place of honor usually reserved for her. Dining plates littered with the remains of a meal were spread before it.

Occasionally, young vampires ate food of the earth, consuming it in addition to blood. Perhaps another of Stefanovich's bastards had come to Helvita to live amongst them?

Lothaire's heart leapt. *I could befriend him, could have a companion.* As the king's bastard, he'd had no friends; his mother was everything to him.

"'Tis late," Ivana said. "All should be abed at this hateful hour."

Fyodor seemed to be silently warning Ivana, but she paid him no heed, demanding, "What do you want, Stefanovich?"

After drinking deep from a tankard of mead-laced blood, Stefanovich wiped his sleeve over his lips. "To see my haughty mistress and her feeble bastard." The king stared down at Lothaire. "Come."

"Do not, Son," Ivana bit out in Dacian.

Lothaire answered in the same, "I will, to spare you." As ever, he would do whatever he could to protect her, no matter how weak he knew himself to be.

In her expression, anxiety for him warred with pride. "I should have known Lothaire Daciano would never cower behind his mother's skirts, even in the face of such a red-eyed tyrant."

When Lothaire crossed to stand before the king's seat, Stefanovich shook his head with disgust. "You still cannot trace, then?"

Lothaire's face was impassive as he answered, "Not yet, my king." No matter how hard he tried to teleport, he could never succeed. Ivana had told him that tracing was a talent that came late to the Daci—they had limited need for it in their closed kingdom. She considered Lothaire's inability yet another sign that he took after her more than after a mere Horde vampire.

Stefanovich seized Lothaire's thin arm, squeezing. "Too frail, I see."

Lothaire was desperate to grow bigger, to be as formidable as his warrior father, if for no reason other than to protect his mother. Not that Princess Ivana needed another's protection.

"By all the gods, you shame me, boy. I should have wrung your runtling neck at birth."

Lothaire heard these criticisms routinely, was used to them.

His mother, however, was not.

With a shriek, Ivana snatched up a carafe of blood, hurling it at Stefanovich. It shattered a pane of black glass just behind him, unleashing a ray of muted light.

The courtiers hissed, scattering throughout the chamber. The beam seared inches from Stefanovich's unmoving elbow before a day servant scurried to stuff the hole with a wadded cloth.

"My son is *perfect*." Ivana bared her fangs, her blue irises gone black with emotion. "Other than the fact that he bears *your* stamp upon his face. Luckily, he inherited his keen mind from my royal lineage. He's full of cunning, a mark of the Daci!"

Stefanovich too bared his razor-sharp fangs, his eyes blazing even redder. "You tempt my wrath, woman!"

"As you tempt mine." Ivana never backed down before him. Whenever Stefanovich struck her, she struck him back twice.

Ivana had told Lothaire that the Daci were coldly logical, ruled by reason. Apparently, Ivana the Bold was the exception.

Fierce as the blizzard raging outside, she even goaded Stefanovich to get his attention, lashing him with her barbed tongue whenever he stared off into the night. She had once admitted to Lothaire that his father dreamed of finding the vampire female who would eventually be his—Stefanovich's Bride, the one who would make his heart beat for eternity.

The lawful queen who would bear his true heirs.

Ivana smoothed her braids once more, so clearly struggling with her temper. "You mock your son at your own peril, Stefanovich."

"Son? I don't claim him as such. That boy will never compare to my true successor!" Another gulp from his tankard. "Of that I am certain."

"I am as well. Lothaire will be superior to any other male in all ways! He's a Dacian!"

Lothaire watched this exchange with deepening unease, recalling the warning his uncle Fyodor had once given Ivana: "Even Stefanovich can grow jealous of your knowledge and strength. You must *bend*, ere his love for you turns to hate."

Lothaire knew his uncle's warning had come true.

For Stefanovich looked murderous. "You believe your kind so much better than mine—"

A female drunkenly staggered into the room from Stefanovich's private chamber. A *mortal* female.

Lothaire's jaw slackened, and Ivana pressed the back of her hand over her mouth.

The woman was dressed as a queen, her garments as rich as Ivana's own. *She* was the one who'd dined at the king's right hand?

"A human?" Ivana's shock quickly turned to ire. "You dare bring one of those diseased animals into my home! Near my only offspring?" She strode forward to shove Lothaire behind her.

Though adult vampires were immortal, Lothaire was still vulnerable to illness.

"The human is Olya, my new mistress."

"Mistress!" Ivana cried. "More like a pet. Her kind live in dirt hovels, sleeping amongst their livestock!"

Stefanovich waved for the woman, and she coyly meandered over to him. "Ah, but she tastes of wine and honey." He turned to his brother. "Does she not, Fyodor?"

Fyodor flashed a guilty look at Ivana.

Pulling his pet into his lap, Stefanovich sneered, "You should sample her, Ivana." He bared the mortal's pale arm.

Ivana's eyes widened. "Taking blood straight from her skin! I would no more sink my fangs into a human than into any other animal. Shall I bring you swine to pierce?"

They were staring each other down, their expressions telling, but Lothaire couldn't decipher exactly *what* they were saying.

Finally, Ivana spoke. "Stefanovich, you know there are consequences, especially for one like you. . . ."

"My kind revere the Thirst," Stefanovich said, "revere bloodtaking."

"Then you revere madness, because that is surely what will follow."

Ignoring Ivana's warning, he punctured the woman's wrist, making her moan.

"You are revolting!" Ivana blocked Lothaire's view, but he was fascinated by this sight, peeking around her skirts. Why had she taught him never to pierce another?

Once he'd finished feeding, Stefanovich released the mortal's arm, then kissed her full on the mouth, eliciting a yell of outrage from Ivana. "That you drink from their skin is foul enough, but to mate with their bodies? Have you no shame?"

He broke away from the kiss. "None." He licked his lips, and the mortal giggled, twirling Stefanovich's hair around her finger.

"'Tis too contemptible to be borne—I will no longer!"

"And what will you do about it?"

"I will leave this savage place forever," she declared. "Now, slaughter your new pet, or I shall return to Dacia."

"Be wary of ultimatums, Ivana. You will not relish the outcome. Especially since you cannot *find* your homeland."

Ivana had explained to Lothaire why the kingdom of Dacia had remained secret for so long. The mysterious Daci traveled in a cloaking mist. If one abandoned the mist, the Dacian could never trace home on his own, and his memories of its location would fade.

With her first sight of Stefanovich, Ivana had lost her heart, following him back to Helvita, leaving behind her own mist, her family, her future throne.

"I will find it," she averred now. "If it kills me, I shall deliver Lothaire to the Realm of Blood and Mist, a land where civilized immortals rule."

"Civilized?" Stefanovich laughed, and the courtiers followed suit. "Those fiends are more brutal than I!"

"Ignorant male! You have no idea of what you speak! You can't comprehend our ways—I know this, for I tried to teach you."

"Teach me?" He slammed his meaty fist on the table. "Your arrogance will be your ruin, Ivana! Always you believe you are better than I!"

"Because—I—*am*!"

At that, the courtiers went silent.

Between gritted teeth, Stefanovich commanded, "Take back your careless words, or at sunset I'll throw you and your bastard out into the cold."

Lothaire swallowed, thinking of the fire in his room, his beloved puzzles atop his desk, his toys scattered over warm fur rugs on the floor. Life at Helvita could be miserable, but 'twas the only life he'd ever known.

Apologize, Mother, he silently willed her.

Instead, she squared her shoulders. "Choose, Stefanovich. The fetid human or me."

"Beg my pardon *and* seek amends with my new mistress."

"Beg?" Ivana scoffed. "*Never.* I am a princess of the Daci!"

"And I am a king!"

"Leave Ivana be, Brother," Fyodor murmured. "This grows tedious."

"She must learn her place." To Ivana, he ordered, "Beseech Olya's forgiveness!"

When the mortal cast Ivana a victorious sneer, Lothaire knew he and his mother were doomed.

ONE MONTH LATER . . .

"Stoke that hatred, Son. Make it burn like a forge."

"Yes, Mother," Lothaire grated, his breaths fogging as they trudged through knee-high snowdrifts.

"'Tis the only thing that will keep us warm." Ivana's eyes gleamed with resentment, as they had ever since Stefanovich ordered them to leave Helvita.

On that night, Lothaire had heard the smallest hitch in Ivana's breath, had seen a flare of surprise. She'd known she'd made a mistake.

But she'd been too proud to remedy it, to bow down to a human.

Not even for me.

All the court had gathered at the castle's entrance to watch Lothaire and the haughty Ivana cast out with only the garments on their backs.

To die in the cold. They would have perished long since had Fyodor not slipped Lothaire coin.

Lothaire's puppy had followed him, wide-eyed and tripping over its own paws, panicked to catch up with him. While Lothaire stared in disbelief, Stefanovich had seized the dog by its scruff, snapping its back.

To the sound of the court vampires' laughter, the king had tossed the dying creature at Lothaire's feet. "Only one of our pets will perish on this day."

Lothaire's eyes had watered, but Ivana had hissed at him, "No tears, Lothaire! You draw on your hatred for him. Never forget this night's betrayal!" To Stefanovich, she'd yelled, *"You will realize what you had too late. . . ."*

Now she absently muttered, "By the time we reach Dacia, I'll have made your soul as bitter as the chill trying to kill us."

"How much longer will it be?" His feet were numb, his belly empty.

"I do not know. I can only follow my longing for such a home as Dacia."

As she'd told Lothaire, her father, King Serghei, ruled over that realm, a land of plenty and peace. 'Twas enclosed in stone, hidden within the very heart of a mountain range.

Inside a soaring cavern a thousand times larger than Helvita stood a majestic black castle, circled by dazzling fountains of blood. The king's subjects filled their pails each morning.

Lothaire could scarcely imagine such a place.

"After all our wanderings, I feel we are close, Son."

That first night, as they'd wended through the terrifying Bloodroot Forest that surrounded Helvita, she'd feared Lothaire wouldn't make it through the freezing night. Again and again, she'd tried to teleport them to Dacia, only to be returned to the same spot.

He'd survived; she'd exhausted herself.

Now she was too weak to trace, so they plodded toward another village, one that might provide a barn to shelter them from the coming day's sunlight.

Unfortunately, each village teemed with filthy mortals. They always gazed at Ivana's beauty and the foreign cut of her clothing with awe—then suspicion. Lothaire received his share of attention for his piercing ice-blue eyes and the white-blond hair forever spilling out from under his cap.

In turn, Ivana ridiculed their unwashed, louse-ridden bodies and simplistic language. Her loathing for mortals continued to grow, fueling his own.

Each night before dawn, she would leave Lothaire hidden while she hunted. Sometimes she'd return with her cheeks flushed from blood, and triumph in her eyes. A slice of her wrist would fill a cup for him as well.

Other times, she would be wan and sullen, cursing Stefanovich's betrayal, lamenting their plight. One sunrise, as he'd drifted off to sleep, he'd heard her mumble, "Now *we* sleep with livestock, and *I* must drink from the flesh. . . ."

Ivana slowed, jerking her head around.

"Are they following us, Mother?" Humans from the last town had been more hostile than in any other, trailing after them, even into the wilderness.

"I don't believe so. The snow covers our tracks so quickly." She trudged on, saying, "It's time for your lessons."

During each night's journey, she instructed him on everything from how to survive among humans—"drink from them only if starving, and *never* to the death"—to Dacian etiquette: "outbursts of emotion are considered the height of rudeness, so naturally I offended my share."

And always she extracted vows for the future, as if she thought she'd soon *die?*

"What must you do when you are grown, my prince?"

"Avenge this treachery against us. I will destroy Stefanovich and take his throne."

"When?"

"Before he finds his Bride."

"Why?"

Lothaire dutifully answered, "Once his fated female bloods him, he'll become more powerful, even more difficult to kill. And he will father a legitimate heir on her. The Vampire Horde will never follow Stefanovich's bastard while his true successor lives."

"You *must* be utterly certain that the Horde will swear fealty to you. If your effort to claim the crown is unsuccessful, they will annihilate you. Wait until you are at your most powerful."

"Will I have to go red-eyed to fight him?"

She stopped, tilting her head. "What do you know of such matters?"

"When a vampire kills his prey as he drinks, he becomes more powerful, but blood stains his eyes."

"Yes, because he drinks to the quick, to the pit of the soul. It brings strength—but also bloodlust. Stefanovich has become one of the *Fallen*." She added vaguely, "And it will be all the more torturous. For him, in particular."

"Why?"

She gave Lothaire an appraising look, as if deciding something about him. "Think not of these things," she eventually said, making her tone light. "Never kill as you drink, and you will never have to worry about them."

"Then how will I . . ." He blushed with shame. "How will *I* ever be strong enough to slay Stefanovich?"

Ivana reached for him, pressing her frozen hands against his cheeks, raising his face. "Forget all you've heard from your father. When you are older, immortal males will tremble before you in dread while their females swoon in your wake."

"Truly, Mother?"

"You are perfectly formed and will grow to be a magnificent Dacian, a vampire to be feared. Especially once you become blooded." She peered up at the cloudy sky, snow dotting her face. "And your Bride?" Ivana met his gaze once more. "She will be incomparable. A queen that even *I* would bow down to."

He squinted at her to see if she jested, but her demeanor was earnest.

Lothaire hoped he found this female quickly. He knew that when he was completely grown, his heart would slowly stop its beat, his lungs their breathing. As he became one among the walking-dead vampires, he'd feel no need for females.

His uncle had once chucked him under the chin and said, "Just when you've forgotten how much you miss the cradle of a female's soft thighs, you'll find your Bride, and she'll bring you back to life."

Lothaire cared naught about bedding, but the idea of his heart stopping horrified him. He asked Ivana, "How long will it be till I can find her?"

She gazed away, saying in an odd tone, "I know not. It might take centuries. Outside of Dacia, female vampires grow scarce. But I do know that you will be a good and faithful king to her." Then she asked, "And what will you do when you possess the throne of the Horde?"

"Unite with your father, aligning the Daci and the Horde under one family crest."

She nodded. "Serghei is the only one you can trust. Not my brothers or sisters with their scheming and plots. Solely my father. And of course you can trust your Bride. But what of everyone else?"

"I'm to use and discard them, caring about none, for they matter naught."

She curled her forefinger under his chin. "Yes, my clever son."

They spent the next few miles in this manner, with her teaching him the intricate customs of the Daci as they tried to ignore the cold. A lowering sky threatened even more snow; dawn would claw through the dark in mere hours.

Lothaire shivered, teeth and baby fangs chattering.

"Silence," Ivana hissed. "The humans did follow." She scented the air. "Gods, their smell aggrieves me!"

"What do they want?"

She murmured, "To *hunt* us."

"Wh-where can we hide?" They were in a wide valley with high plateaus to the east and west. The mortals advanced from the north. Mountains loomed far to the south.

She gazed around despairingly. "We must make it to those mountains. I believe that is where we'll find the pass that leads to Dacia." She gave him a shove. "Now run!"

He did, as fast as he could, but the snow was too high on the ground, blinding bits of it raining down too swiftly. "We'll never make it, Mother!"

She snatched his arm and attempted to trace with him. Their forms briefly faded but wouldn't disappear. Gritting her teeth, she tried once more, to no avail.

Releasing him, she spun in place, searching for an escape—then stilled, listening. Her eyes shot wide. "Father!" she screamed, the sound echoing down the valley. "I am here! Your Ivana is here."

No one answered.

"Father!"

Mortals in the distance gave shouts as they neared.

"Papa?" She swayed on her feet, her expression . . . *lost*. "I know I sensed him and others."

So had Lothaire. Immortals of great power had been here. Why not rescue their princess?

Crimson tears slid down her beautiful face as she dropped to her knees. "We were so close." The proud Ivana began to dig into the snow, using her claws to stab through the permanent layers of ice.

Even as her claws tore off and her fingers began to bleed she continued digging. "How low I've been brought, Lothaire. When you remember me, recall not this."

With each handful of ice, a hole grew. "You are the son of a king, the grandson of a king. Do not *ever* forget that!" When the skin on her fingertips began to peel away, he tried to help her, but she slapped his hands, seeming nigh maddened. Finally, she pulled him into the small pit she'd made. "Come. Hide here."

"I must make it deeper, Mother. There's not enough room."

She whispered, "There's room enough. I'll make sure you're safe."

His eyes widened. She meant to fight them? "Trace from here alone," he said, though he knew she was probably too weak even for that.

"Never! Now, what are your vows to me?"

"Mother, I—"

She snapped her fangs, her irises gone black. "Your vows!"

"Take the life of Stefanovich. Seize his throne."

"Whom will you trust?"

"None but your father and my queen."

More tears dropped. "No, your queen alone, Lothaire. Serghei and the Daci forsook us this day."

"Why?"

"I led these mortals too close." She gave a sob. "He chose the kingdom's precious secrecy—over our lives. I am to pay for my brashness, for my lack of cunning. They make an example of me."

Panic flared within Lothaire. "How will I find you? What do I do?"

"Once the humans are gone, my family will come for you. If not, you'll do whatever it takes to survive. Remember all I've taught you." She shoved her sleeve up her arm. "Drink, Lothaire."

"Now?" He shook his head in confusion. "You cannot lose blood."

"Obey me!" She bit into her wrist. "Lean your head back and part your lips."

Unwillingly, he did, and she raised her arm over his upturned face, above his mouth. Her blood was rich, quickly warding off the chill.

She made him drink till the stream had ebbed to a trickle, till ice had formed on the wound. "Now listen. I will lead them away from you, distract them. They will take me—"

"Nooo!" he howled.

"Lothaire, listen! When they capture me, the need to protect me will rise up within you. You must ignore it and remain here. Ignore your instinct and rely on cold reason. As I failed to do with Stefanovich. As I failed to do a thousand times. Vow this!"

"You want me to hide? To not defend you against those creatures?" Embarrassing tears welled.

"Yes, this is precisely what I want. Son, your mind is the brightest I've ever encountered. *Use* it. Do *not* repeat my mistakes!" She gripped his chin. "You've one last vow to give me. A vow to the Lore that you will not leave this spot until the mortals are gone."

To the Lore? 'Twas an unbreakable vow! He wanted to rail, to deny her this. How could he not defend her?

She raised her chin. "Lothaire, I . . . *beg* you for this."

A proud princess of the Daci begging one like me? His lips parted in shock. Words tumbled from them. "I vow it to the Lore."

"Very good." She pressed a cool kiss to his brow. "I want you never, never to be brought this low again." Over his frantic protests, she began to bury him in the snow. "Become the king you were born to be."

"Mother, please! H-how can you do this?"

"Because you are my son. My heart. I will do whatever it takes to protect you." They met gazes. "Lothaire, anything that was worthy in me began with you."

He refused to believe this would be the last time he saw her, refused to tell his mother how much he loved her—

She whispered, *"I know,"* then cocooned him in snow.

Warmed by her blood, he lay huddled, quaking with fear for her. His eyes darted, seeing nothing.

Had she swept to her feet, sprinting back in the mortals' direction? In time, he heard her struggles from a distance, could feel the vibrations of a number of footfalls. What must be dozens of humans surrounded her. He clenched his fists, battling his frenzied yearning to save her.

Yet Lothaire was powerless—bound by his vow and undermined by his weakness.

His stifled yells of frustration turned to scalding tears when he heard the clanking of chains, her muffled screams.

The guttural sounds of men.

He'd been raised in Helvita under the wicked reign of Stefanovich; Lothaire knew what those mortals were doing to her.

As he fought not to vomit the precious blood she'd gifted him, he resolved that he *would* become one of the Fallen, preying on other creatures for strength.

He might grow mad with bloodlust; *never* would he be helpless again. . . .

What must have been hours later, her cries fell silent. Again, his eyes darted. He thought he caught a thread of smoke, then the scent of burning flesh.

Dawn. Her screams renewed.

As she burned, she yelled in Dacian, "Never forget, my prince! Avenge me!" Other words followed, but he couldn't make them out. Then unintelligible sounds . . . agonized shrieks.

To the sound of her screams, he sobbed, repeating his vows over and over, adding a new one.

"Burn the k-king . . . of the Daci alive. . . ."

"My sanity will fail me long before my will does. Luckily, the only thing more interesting than a madman is a relentless one."

—LOTHAIRE KONSTANTIN DACIANO, THE ENEMY OF OLD

"Me, a steel magnolia? Steel, my ass! [Laughing, then abruptly serious.] *Try titanium."*

—ELIZABETH "ELLIE" PEIRCE, EXPERT IN BOYS, REVERSE PSYCHOLOGY, AND LAW-ENFORCEMENT EVASION

"The difference between you and me is that my actions have no consequences for me. That is what makes me a god."

—SAROYA THE SOUL REAPER, DEITY OF BLOOD, SACRED PROTECTRESS OF VAMPIRES, GODDESS OF DIVINE DEATH

1

"S o you thought to exorcise me?" Saroya the Soul Reaper asked the wounded man she stalked by firelight. "I don't know what is worse. The fact that you thought I was a demon . . ."

She twirled the blood-drenched cleaver in her hand, loving how the man's widened eyes followed each rotation. ". . . or that you believed you could separate me from my human host."

Nothing short of death could remove Saroya. Especially not a mortal deacon, one among a group of five who'd come all the way out to this vile trailer in Appalachia to perform an exorcism.

As he scrambled a retreat from her steady march forward, he stumbled over one of the broken lamps on the floor. He tripped onto his back, briefly releasing his hold on the spurting stump that used to be his right arm.

She sighed with delight. Centuries ago, when she'd been a death goddess, she would have swooped down and sunk her fangs into the human's jugular, sucking until he was naught but a husk and devouring his soul; now she was cursed to possess one powerless mortal after another, experiencing her own death again and again.

Her latest possession? Elizabeth Peirce, a nineteen-year-old girl, as lovely as she was poor.

When the deacon met the dismembered corpse of one of his brethren, he gave a panicked cry, glancing away from her. In a flash, Saroya leapt upon him, swinging the cleaver, plunging the metal into his thick neck.

Blood sprayed as she yanked the blade free for another hit. Then another. Then a last.

She swiped the back of her arm over her spattered face as her demeanor turned contemplative. Mortals believed themselves so special and elevated, but decapitating one sounded exactly like a fishmonger beheading a fat catch.

Finished with the last of the five deacons, Saroya turned to the only survivor left in the trailer: Ruth, Elizabeth's mother. She huddled in a corner, mumbling prayers as she brandished a fire poker.

"I have vanquished your daughter's spirit, woman. She will never return," Saroya lied, knowing that Elizabeth would soon find a way to rise from unconsciousness to the fore, regaining control of her body.

Of all the mortals Saroya had possessed, Elizabeth was the prettiest, the youngest—and the strongest. Saroya had difficulty rising to take control unless the girl was asleep or weakened in some way.

A first. Saroya gave a sigh. Elizabeth should consider it an honor to be the form to Saroya's essence, the flesh and blood temple housing her godly vampiric spirit.

Saroya peered down at her stolen body. Instead, she'd had to fight Elizabeth for possession, was *still* fighting her.

No matter. After centuries of being shuffled into stooped, elderly men or horse-faced women, she'd found her ideal fit in Elizabeth. In the end, Saroya would defeat her. She had wisdom from times past and present, hallowed gifts—and an ally.

Lothaire the Enemy of Old.

He was a notoriously evil vampire, millennia in age, and the son of a king. A year ago, his oracle had directed him to her. Though Saroya and Lothaire had spent only one night together in the nearby woods, he'd pledged himself to save her from her wretched existence.

He might not have the ability to return Saroya to her goddess state. But somehow he would extinguish Elizabeth's soul from her body, then transform Saroya into an immortal vampire—circumventing the curse.

Saroya knew Lothaire would be hunting ceaselessly for answers.

Because I'm his Bride.

She gazed past Elizabeth's mother out a small window, finding the wintry landscape empty. Had she hoped that a massacre like this might have brought Lothaire to her?

How much longer am I to wait for him in this godsforsaken wasteland? With no word?

He'd talked of the legion of adversaries out to destroy him, of ancient vendettas: "If a vampire can be measured by the caliber of his foes, goddess, then consider me fearsome. If by the number? Then I've no equal."

Perhaps his enemies had prevailed?

No longer would she remain here. The Peirce family had begun chaining Elizabeth to the bed at night, preventing Saroya from killing, the only thing she lived for.

Reminded of her treatment, she turned to the mother. "Yes, your daughter is mine forever. And after I've slain you, I'll eviscerate your young son, then sweep through your family like a disease." She raised the cleaver above her, took a step forward—

Suddenly, black spots dotted her vision. Dizziness?

No, no! Elizabeth was rising to consciousness with all the finesse of a freight train. Every single time, she surfaced like a drowning woman held underwater, overwhelming Saroya.

The little bitch might reclaim control of her body, but, as usual, she'd wake to a fresh nightmare. "Enjoy, Elizabeth. . . ."

Her legs buckled, her back meeting the carpet. Blackness.

Heartbeat heartbeat heartbeat heartbeat—

Ellie Peirce woke to a mad drumming in her ears. She lay on the floor of her family's trailer, eyes squeezed shut, her body coated with something warm and sticky.

No words were spoken around her. The only sounds were the living room's crackling fire, her shallow breaths, and the howling dogs outside. She had no memory of how she'd come to be like this, no idea of how long she'd blacked out.

"Mama, did it work?" she whispered as she peeked open her eyes. Maybe the deacons had been successful?

Please, God, let the exorcism have worked . . . my last hope.

Her eyes adjusting to the dim, firelit room, she raised her head to peer down at her body. Her worn jeans, T-shirt, and secondhand boots were sopping wet.

With blood. She swallowed. *Not my own.*

Oh, God. Her fingers were curled around the hilt of a dripping cleaver. *I told them not to unchain me until my uncle and cousins got here!*

But Reverend Slocumb and his fellow members of their church's "emergency ministry" had smugly thought they could handle her—

Movement drew her gaze up. A fire poker?

Clenched in her mother's hands.

"Wait!" Ellie flung herself to her side just as the poker came slamming down on the floor where her head had been. Blood splashed from the carpet like a stepped-in puddle.

"You foul thing, begone!" Mama shrieked, raising the iron again. "You got my girl, but you won't have my boy!"

"Just wait!" Ellie scrambled to her feet, dropping the cleaver. "It's me!" She raised her hands, palms outward.

Mama didn't lower the poker. Her long auburn hair was loose, tangled all around her unlined face. She used one shoulder to shove tendrils from her eyes. "That's what you said afore you started snarlin' that demon language and slashin' about!" Her mascara ran down her cheeks, her peach lipstick smeared across her chin. "Afore you killed all them deacons!"

"Killed?" Ellie whirled around, dumbfounded by the grisly sight.

Five hacked-up bodies lay strewn across the living room.

These men had been lured all the way out here by her mother's imploring letters and by evidence of Ellie's possession: recordings of her speaking dead languages she had no way of knowing and photographs of messages in blood that she had no memory of writing.

Apparently, Ellie had once written in Sumerian, *Surrender to me.*

Now Slocumb's head lay apart from his other remains. His eyes were glassy in death, his tongue lolling between parted lips. One arm was missing from his corpse. She dimly realized it must be the one under the dining room table. The one lying beside the hank of scalp and a pile of severed fingers.

Ellie covered her mouth, fighting not to retch. The five had vowed to exorcise the demon. Instead, it'd butchered them all. "Th-this was done by . . . *me?*"

"As if you don't know, demon!" Mama wagged her poker at Ellie. "Play your games with somebody else."

Ellie scratched at her chest, her skin seeming to crawl from the being within. *Hate it so much, hate it, hate it, HATE it.* Though she never knew its thoughts, right now she could nearly *feel* it gloating.

Sirens sounded in the distance, setting the dogs outside to baying even louder. "Oh, God, Mama, you didn't call that good-for-nothing sheriff?" Ellie and her family were mountain folk through and through. Any Law was suspect.

At that, her mother dropped the poker. "You really *are* Ellie. The demon told me you wasn't coming back this time! Told me you'd never return to us."

No wonder Mama had attacked.

"It's me," Ellie said over her shoulder as she hastened to the window, her boots squishing across the carpet. She pulled aside the cigarette-stained curtains to gaze out into the night.

Down the snowy mountainside, the sheriff's blue lights glared, his car snaking up the winding road. Another cruiser sped behind it.

"I had to call them, Ellie! Had to stop the demon. And then the nine-one-one dispatcher heard the deacons just a-screamin'. . . ."

What should I do . . . what can *I do?* Nineteen was too young to go to jail! Ellie would rather die, had already considered suicide if the exorcism didn't work.

Because these five ministers weren't the demon's first victims.

There'd been at least two other men since the creature had possessed Ellie's body a year ago. Early on, she'd woken to find a middle-aged man in her bed, his skin cooling against hers, his slashed throat gaping like a smile.

None among her extended Peirce family had known what to think. Had a rival clan planted the body? Why single out Ellie? Why had there been blood on her hands?

Her close-lipped cousins had buried the man out behind the barn, telling themselves he must've had it coming.

The family hadn't begun to suspect she was possessed until more recently, when the demon had posed a mutilated coal company rep among Ellie's old stuffed animals, then "blasphemed" for her kinfolk in ways a girl like Ellie "could never imagine."

After that, her mother and Uncle Ephraim had started chaining her at night, like Ellie was one of the hounds outside. Though she hated the chains and could easily have picked the locks, she'd endured them.

But it'd been too late for some.

Hikers had found a gruesome altar in the woods, with human bones littering the site. Mama had whispered to Ephraim, "You reckon it was Ellie?"

Not me! The damned thing inside her was *winning*, taking control more often, and more easily.

Just a matter of time till I'm gone altogether.

As blue lights crawled closer, glaring even in the bright moonlight, Ellie had a mad impulse to clean herself up, waylay the sheriff outside to badger him for a warrant, then *maybe* cop to a crank call.

After all, *she* hadn't done these killings. Or maybe she should run!

But she knew the Law would put dogs on her trail; she'd never make it to the next holler, not in the winter.

And that wouldn't solve the problem of the demon within her—

She heard a thud behind her and spun around. Her mother, usually so resilient, had fallen to her knees, her face crumpling. "It told me it'd do me in, then go after the rest of the family, go after baby Josh."

Joshua, Ellie's adored brother. She pictured him toddling about in his footy pajamas, his chubby cheeks growing pink as he laughed. An aunt was babysitting him in a trailer just down the mountain.

At the thought of harm coming to him, Ellie's tears fell unchecked. "Wh-what should I do?"

Mama's own tears poured. "If the reverend—God rest his soul—and his ministerin' couldn't get that devil of yourn out of you . . . no one can, Ellie. Maybe you ought to let the sheriff take you."

"You want me to go to jail?"

"We done everything we can." Mama rose, warily stepping closer. "Maybe them prison folks or even them psychiatrists can keep it from killin' again."

Prison? Or death? Ellie swallowed, knowing that once she decided how she'd handle this, nothing could sway her. If her mother was stubborn, Ellie was trebly so, as immovable as the mountains all around them.

Sirens echoed as the cruisers prowled up the long drive, then skidded to a stop in front of the trailer.

Ellie swiped at her tears. "I'll do you one better than jail." *I could take the demon with me.* If she ran out the front door with blood on her and a gun in hand . . .

Mama shook her head sternly. "Elizabeth Ann Peirce, don't you even think about it!"

"If this *thing*"—Ellie slashed her nails across her chest—"thinks it'll hurt my kin, then it don't know me very good." Though her own gun and ammo had been taken from her, her father's Remington remained in his closet. The sheriff wouldn't know it was empty.

"You ain't doin' this, Ellie! There might be hope, some kind of new-fangled treatment."

"You want me to go from roamin' these mountains to being locked in a tiny cell?" She didn't remind her mother that she'd probably get the death penalty anyway.

Slaughtering five *deacons* in Appalachia? Ellie was done for.

"I won't let you do this." Mama jutted her chin.

"We both suspected it'd come to this." *The demon's just killin' me slow.* "My mind's made up."

At that, Mama paled even more, knowing it was as good as done.

"And just think—if I kill this demon, I'll go to heaven. Be with Daddy," Ellie said, hoping that was where she'd end up. She held out her arms, and her mother sank against her, sobbing. "Now, stop actin' like you don't know this has to happen, like you haven't known for months."

"Ah, God, honey, I just . . ." More sobs. "Y-you want to say a prayer?"

Ellie stood on her toes and pressed a kiss to her mother's smooth forehead. "No time. What if it comes back?" And already the deputies were surrounding the trailer, their boots crunching in the snow, while the pompous sheriff demanded that Mrs. Peirce open up for them this minute.

He knew better than to storm a household on this mountain.

With a steadying exhalation, Ellie turned toward her mother's bed-room, forcing herself to look at the bodies. These men had had families. How many children were fatherless because of this demon?

Because I've been doggedly clinging to hope?

Ellie passed her own bedroom, shuddering at the sight of the chains at the ends of her bed, coiled like rattlesnakes.

Then she stared bitterly at the Middle State University pennants she'd tacked to her room's vinyl walls just before all this had begun.

How excited she'd been about college! To afford the tuition and dorm, she'd worked at her uncle's outfitter shop each day after school and as a guide during every holiday for years.

Ellie had been in classes just long enough to comprehend with wonder,

Holy shit, I can . . . I can actually do this! Coursework had come surprisingly easy to her.

Then she'd started losing time, waking in strange places. They'd sent her packing back home before the semester was over.

She would've been the first one in the family to get a college degree.

When she reached the back bedroom, she spied her reflection in the mirrored closet door. Blood covered her—her long brown hair was wet with it. Her eyes were as flinty gray and hard as Peirce Mountain.

Her sodden T-shirt read: *EPHRAIM'S OUTFITTERS: rafting, fishing, hunting supplies & guides.*

What would Uncle Eph say about this?

She pictured his weathered face and earnest expression, so like her late father's. *You go on now and take care of your business, Ellie. Ain't nobody gonna do it for you.*

She slid the closet door open, reaching past her father's old work gear—a mining helmet, locksmith tools, a handyman belt. Before he'd died in the mine, her adoring pa had never held fewer than three jobs at a time.

With a knot in her throat, she collected his favorite shotgun: a Remington double-barrel twelve-gauge. It was empty, no slugs to be found; Uncle Eph had long since come round and gathered up all the shells—just in case the demon got any ideas with the scattergun.

The familiar heft of the weapon was reassuring. Soon all this would be over forever. At the thought, she felt a strange sense of *relief.*

When she returned to the living room, Mama rushed forward. "Please, baby, couldn't you just try prison?"

I'm doomed anyway. An injection later, or a bullet now.

Ellie would die on her terms—bleeding out in the snow, atop her beloved mountain.

"No, jail's out of the question. Now you need to think about Josh. About the family." Ellie forced a smile. "I love you, Mama. Tell Josh I loved him, too. You know I'll be lookin' down, watchin' out for everyone."

As her mother began to bawl, muttering jumbled words, Ellie pointed to the back room. "You go on in the back and stay in there! You hear? Don't come out till they make you, no matter what happens. Promise me!" At last, Mama nodded. Ellie gave her a shove, and she dragged her feet away, softly closing her bedroom door behind her.

Before Ellie lost her nerve, she turned to the front door, Remington in hand. She began to reach for her hand-me-down coat, then made a fist instead. *Fool. You won't be cold long.*

On the count of three. Ellie took several deep breaths, her thoughts racing. *I'm just nineteen—too young.*

One.

I got no choice. Soon, nothing'll be left of me.

Two.

Imagine waking up to Mama and Josh, dead, their *eyes glassy and sightless.*

Never! With a shriek, she threw open the door, raising the gun.

"Shooter!" the sheriff yelled. Bullets went flying.

She felt none of them; a towering man had appeared out of thin air, standing between her and the officers.

With a furious growl, he shoved her to the ground, knocking the gun from her hands as he took the bullets in his back. She stared up in disbelief. His irises were . . . red. At least five shots hit him, but his monstrous gaze never wavered from her eyes.

—"Hold your fire!"

—"Where'd he come from?"

—"What the hell's goin' on?"

The man's skin was like perfect marble, stark against the black shirt and trench coat he wore. His hair was pale blond, his features chiseled. And those eyes . . . *otherworldly.*

"Another demon!" She blindly rooted her hand through the snow, automatically reaching for the shotgun, but he stepped on her wrist.

When she gave a cry of pain, he pressed down harder, his lips drawing back to reveal . . . fangs. "You dare risk *my* female?" His voice was deep and accented, his tone filled with scorn. At his words, the baying dogs immediately fell silent.

"Wh-what are you talking about?"

"Your attempted blaze of glory, Elizabeth. And all because of a few murders?" He gave her a look of disgust, as if to say, *Grow up*.

The sheriff ordered, "Put your hands where I can see them!"

Instead, the pale-haired demon hunched down beside her, cupping her nape to snatch her closer. With his other hand, he tossed her gun away.

When another bullet plugged him in the back, he hissed over his shoulder, baring those fangs. "One—*moment*," he snapped.

Ellie sneaked a glance at the cops; they looked too confounded to react.

And behind them, Ephraim and some of her cousins had come running up the mountain, rifles in hand. They'd slowed in shock upon seeing the demon.

The male sneered, "Mortals," then turned back to her. "Listen very carefully, Elizabeth. I am Lothaire the Enemy of Old, and you belong to me. After considering my options, I've decided I will allow you to go to jail this eve."

"Y-you've got the wrong girl! I don't know you—"

Talking over her, he said, "In your human prison, you'll be hidden from my kind, which means you'll be relatively safe while I continue my search. I will return for you in two years. Or so." He gave her a harsh shake. "But if you try to harm yourself—and therefore my female—again, I will punish you beyond imagining. Do you understand me?"

"Your female? I'm not yours!"

"I wouldn't have *you*." He narrowed those red eyes. "The glorious being who lives within you, however . . ."

"I don't understand! What's inside of me?"

He reached his free hand toward her face, his black claws glinting in the moonlight. Ignoring her question, he huskily murmured, "I will have *her*, my queen, forever."

When he brushed a strand of hair from her face, she flinched. "Unhand me, demon!"

He stared down at her even as he addressed another in that deep, hypnotic voice: "Saroya, if you can hear me, sleep until I return for you. When all my plots and all my toiling come to bear."

Saroya? It has a name?

With inhuman speed, he rose, looming above Ellie. More words in another language followed, then he disappeared into thin air.

The shaken deputies closed in on Ellie, their jaws slack. Sweat ran from their foreheads even as their breaths smoked. One cuffed her silently, while the others aimed their pistols in all directions—even up.

Ephraim and her cousins looked stricken; they could do nothing to save her, short of killing four cops in cold blood.

Her stunned mind finally registered that she would be taken alive.

The red-eyed demon had prevented her death. And Ellie burned to kill him for it.

2

Ridgevale Correctional Center for Women, Virginia
PRESENT DAY

Does the condemned have any last words?" the warden intoned.

"No!" Ellie squirmed against her bonds on the gurney, pulling taut the electrodes dotting her chest. With each of her frantic heartbeats, the nearby EKG monitor spiked. The IV tubes snaking from each arm swayed back and forth. "No, I'm ready!"

She might have felt dread that she was about to die, but urgency overwhelmed all other emotions. She'd had death snatched from her grasp once before.

And the demon was stirring inside her.

Fearing "Saroya" would rise and attack everyone around her, Ellie had taken no last meal, had met with no family or chaplain. She'd inventoried her worldly belongings—ChapStick, college textbooks, four dollars in change, and her journals—with a swift efficiency.

Ellie had made peace with her fate long ago, had hungered to die ever since the night of her arrest. She'd written apologies to the victims' families, saving them to be delivered after she was gone.

"Please hurry, sir," she begged the elderly warden.

At that, a hum of murmurs broke out in the next room. The witnesses behind the tinted glass window didn't know what to make of her behavior, didn't know how to process such an unusual murderer.

She was young, had filed no appeals to her sentence, and by all accounts had never displayed violent behavior growing up.

There *had* been run-ins with the law. Some minor—getting caught parking with boys. Some not so minor—poaching on state lands and refusing to testify against family members or cooperate with law enforcement.

But there'd never been a drop of human blood spilled by her hand until a yearlong killing spree.

Saroya had been busier than Ellie had ever dreamed.

"I'm ready."

The warden frowned at her, and the two prison guards flanking him shuffled uncomfortably. Against all their best efforts—and Saroya's—they'd ended up liking Ellie, admiring her quiet determination to educate herself, to earn a degree, though she had no future.

Ellie had always had a good sense of people, and she'd ended up liking the three back. "Thank you for everything."

"Then God be with you, Ellie Peirce." The warden turned toward the adjoining control room. As the guards followed him out, one briefly laid his gloved hand on her shoulder. The other gave her a quick nod, but she could tell he'd be affected by her passing.

The door shut behind them, a deafening final click. *I'm alone now.* She stared after them, comprehending that no one would be getting out of this room alive.

Alone. So scared.

I didn't want *to have to die. . . .*

She gazed at her arms, strapped to the padded supports. Her wrists were taped, her palms up. The two IV lines were a dozen feet long, running from her inner arms to a pair of portholes in the wall behind her, continuing into the control room.

Half an hour ago, a nameless, faceless doctor had started a saline drip back there. At high noon, he would add a trio of chemicals, and moments later, the nightmare would be over forever.

Have to finish this. Almost there.

Funny what one would think about on the verge of death. How many people knew—to the minute—when they'd pass on?

She doubted anyone had ever gone to her own execution with such a feverish drive still spurring her, with a *goal* and an iron will bent on achieving it. Far from muting her determination, jail had only honed it, like adding layer after layer of plating to shore up a mountain train trestle.

I'm about to win. To beat her. Saroya had risen only twice in the last five years, both times in the first few months. Ellie's blackouts had resulted in the permanent disfigurement of two fellow inmates.

All done with her bare hands.

Long dormant, the demon now stirred. Sensing its own doom? *That's right, you're going down, bitch.*

Only two things could save her life at this point.

An unexpected call from the governor.

Or Saroya's powerful red-eyed mate.

Not a day went by that Ellie didn't think of the fiend named Lothaire the Enemy of Old. She'd seen the male appear out of thin air and then vanish, had seen bullets *annoy* him. Members of her family, the sheriff, and those deputies had witnessed these things with her, no matter how many times that up-for-reelection sheriff told her they hadn't. . . .

She craned her head back to look at the clock on the wall behind her. Three minutes till noon.

One hundred and eighty seconds until death slipped down the tubes.

Though driven, Ellie wasn't without regrets. She wished she could have *used* her hard-won psychology degree, had a career, made friends with women who weren't murderers.

She regretted never having a family of her own. Maybe she shouldn't have been so careful not to wind up a teen mother like her mama and grandma.

Hell, maybe Ellie should've given it up to one of those eager boys she'd gone parking with. She probably should've been less rigid and unbending in general.

Unbending. But that was the Peirce in her; Ellie *would* get her way in the end. *Best step aside.*

Another glance at the clock. Two minutes till—

The lights flickered, ratcheting up her anxiety. Another power surge a moment later had the witnesses muttering nervously.

With the third flicker, Ellie froze with dread even as the EKG went crazy. *Nothing can stop this!* Heart rate 150, 170, *190 . . .*

Darkness. The EKG went blank with a last jagged spike.

No windows in the death ward. Pitch blackness. The witnesses were banging on the door, clamoring for an evacuation.

"What's *happening?*" Ellie cried. For some reason, no generator fired up, no backup lights to cast a glow.

Lying in the dark, strapped to a gurney.

In the distance, a scream rang out.

About to hyperventilate, she twisted against her restraints, cursing her bonds. "What's going on out there?"

An agonized yell sounded, but she refused the thought that surfaced. A jarring clap of gunfire fueled her fears. Some man bellowed, "I can't see him! Where the hell did he go—" then came a bloodcurdling scream. Another man begged, "Please! *Nooo!* Ah, God, I have a fami—" Gurgling sounds followed.

Realization took hold.

He had come. Lothaire the Enemy of Old had returned for her.

Just as he'd promised. . . .

3

"That little *súka*," Lothaire sneered as a guard's neck snapped in his fist. Elizabeth was about to be executed—voluntarily—for a trifling number of murders.

In mere moments.

The guard's partner fired wildly in the dark; bullets plugged Lothaire's skin, but he hardly noticed them.

He'd fed yesterday and was strong from it. At least, his body was. His mind, however . . .

With a yell, he lunged forward to slash his claws across the shooter's throat. When blood splattered over his face, Lothaire's fangs sharpened for flesh, his thoughts blanking.

Madness. Licking at my heels.

Even now with so much at stake. Too many victims, too many memories. Forever tolling.

No, focus on the Endgame! Get to her, save your female.

His foes had prevented him from reaching her sooner. *If I'm too late . . .*

He charged forward through lightless corridors, easily seeing in the dark, but the place was a maze of hallways and minuscule rooms.

Blyad'! He couldn't scent her over the odor of ammonia. Another hallway came into view, more labeled chambers: family rooms, visitation rooms, cells.

No time. He'd warned Elizabeth not to hurt his female. Yet she'd opted to have herself condemned, directing her public defender to file no appeals, to broker no pleas.

After living thousands of years, Lothaire was very rarely surprised; her actions had surprised the hell out of him. Running into a hail of bullets was one thing, tirelessly plotting a years-long suicide quite another.

He couldn't decide if she was fatally flawed with willfulness or crazed.

In any case, she was proving to be a thorn in his side, costing him in untold ways. Lothaire was known throughout the Lore for collecting blood debts from immortals in dire straits, bargaining with them to make deals with the devil. Though he was proud of his overflowing ledger of entries, hoarding them, he'd already burned two because of Elizabeth.

He'd forced a beholden oracle to keep tabs on her incarceration. And just minutes earlier, an indebted technopath had accompanied him here to cut all the facility's power, including the backup generators, leaving no lights, no cameras.

Only utter confusion.

And that was the extent of Lothaire's plan today: technopath cuts power while vampire massacres his way to female. Laughably simple for a born strategist.

As if to sacrifice themselves to the plan, two guards intercepted him in the corridor, shining their flashlights into his red eyes. During their stunned silence, Lothaire had time to anticipate their reactions.

The larger one to the right will fire first, three shots before he realizes I've plucked his spine from him. The one to the left will stutter an answer to my question, though he knows he'll die directly after.

"Hands where we can see 'em!"

Lothaire attacked. First shot, second shot, third—

A tortured scream. The big one's spineless body crumpled to the floor. With one hand, Lothaire tossed away the length of bone. With the other, he lifted the remaining guard by the throat. "Which way to the execution chamber?"

Lothaire eased his grip just enough for the man to grit out, "R-right, then . . . then second left. All the way to the end. But p-please—"

Snap. By the time the guard's body collapsed, Lothaire was already at his second left.

He'd put Elizabeth from his mind, assured she'd be *relatively* safe. After all, he didn't care about her mind, only about her body, the temple that housed his Bride.

My mate. The female meant only for him. And what a glorious, bloodthirsty female she was. . . .

Did Saroya sense this execution? Was she desperately struggling to rise, to protect herself?

His black claws dug into his palms till blood flowed. *Focus. Focus!*

As he delved deeper into the building, Lothaire fought to distance his thoughts from his own recent imprisonment. *The reason I'm late for my Bride's execution.*

Weeks ago, when he'd learned of this date, he'd been on the verge of rescuing Saroya. Then he himself had been captured by the Order, a mortal army.

He'd escaped them . . . but in time?

Beams from more flashlights shone ahead. Three guards in riot gear escorted out a handful of civilians.

"Is someone there?" one guard demanded.

Lothaire envisioned cutting a swath of blood and screams through the group. *No, focus!* Though pleasurable, it would be selfish.

To save time, Lothaire traced past them, disappearing and reappearing in an instant.

When he reached the viewing room, he teleported inside. Two young males had just burst through the door of the adjoining execution chamber to guard her, fumbling with Maglites and assault rifles.

Then, for the first time in five years, Lothaire's gaze fell upon Elizabeth. The last time he'd beheld her, she'd lain in the snow, her unusual gray eyes peering up at him with delightful fear.

Now she lay restrained, dressed in a dingy orange uniform. Her long, coffee-colored hair was pulled back severely from her face.

Again, she was terrified, her eyes darting blindly in the dark, but he felt no sympathy, only hatred.

This was all her doing! With Elizabeth's blessing, needles had been sunk into both of her inner arms—

A transparent liquid already flowed down each tube.

His heart felt like it might explode. *Too late?*

With a roar, he traced inside, batting the two males away, launching them headfirst into opposite walls.

"Who's there?" Elizabeth cried when he laid shaking hands on her delicate arms to thread those needles out of her veins. "What's happening? Can't see!"

He leaned down to scent the fluid, nearly sinking to his knees with relief. Saline. No chemical odor, merely salt water.

To be certain, he sliced the line with one claw and dripped the liquid on his tongue.

Safe.

But if he'd been seconds later . . .

As he ripped free the electrodes covering Elizabeth, he grated, "You've been a bad little mortal."

A sucked-in breath. Then she yelled, "Stop this, you bastard! You leave me be!"

Once he'd slashed through her bonds, he clamped his hand around her wrist and yanked her to her feet.

Before Lothaire traced her back to the safety of his home, he promised her, "Now, Elizabeth, you will pay."

When the ground suddenly reappeared beneath her, Ellie pitched forward. She knew that monster had ahold of her, would recognize Lothaire's voice anywhere.

That deep, accented timbre had haunted her dreams.

As nausea washed over her, she realized that she was no longer in the prison. Somehow he'd transported her into a fancy sitting room, some type of mansion.

Just as she regained her balance she felt her body lifted off the ground. "Ah! Stop, *stop*—"

"I warned you, mortal!" the demon bellowed as he hurled her away from him.

With a strangled cry, she landed sideways on a couch halfway across the room.

Get up! Dizziness . . . *Keep him in sight, Ellie!* After a clearing shake of her head, she clambered to her feet. The demon strode back and forth in front of her, vanishing and reappearing as he paced.

He was bigger than she remembered, and this time he looked even more murderous. His fists were clenched, tendons straining in his neck. His irises glowed red, veins of blood forking out over the whites of his eyes.

His face was spattered with blood, his pale hair stained with it. Again he was clad all in black, from his trench coat to his boots. Bullet holes riddled his shirt.

This can't be happening! Stolen from death row at a maximum-security prison? By *him*.

"I promised you punishment!" He swung one long arm out to the side, bashing a marble column.

Chunks of it landed on the plush carpet at her feet, the entire building seeming to rock. His strength was monstrous, just like everything about him.

"You disobey me at your peril."

She should be cowering from him. Instead, she felt a blistering rage boiling up inside of *her*. Ellie had thought she'd finally be free, that she'd at last defeat Saroya. She'd been two minutes away from death, *ready* for it. But this devil had thwarted her yet again.

He'd already taken away her freedom, ensuring she'd spent half a decade in a tiny, rank cell.

Five years despairing.

As she recalled those years, she found herself screaming, "What do you *want* from me? *What?*" Out of the corner of her eye she spied a vase, snatched it up. "Why can't you leave me the hell alone?" She flung the heavy piece—it struck him in the chest and *shattered* from the impact.

As though she'd bashed it against a brick wall.

Even as she stared in disbelief, a heavy candleholder found its way into her grip. *Two minutes. So damned close.* She lobbed it overhand.

He . . . *dematerialized*, and it flew through his hazy form.

She gave a shriek of fury. Another candleholder went flying, a paperweight, a lamp.

He just dodged the missiles.

Can't be happening! She was out of breath, desperate to hurt him, to punish *him*.

Eighteen hundred and twenty days without seasons, without snow or blooms, without friends or family. Her baby brother didn't remember her. While Josh had been steadily growing toward manhood without her in his life, Ellie's existence had been stagnant, punctuated only by bouts of evil.

She no longer felt like a . . . person.

I'm not a person, I'm Virginia DOC Inmate #8793347. I'm Saroya's host.

Because of him.

Ellie's gaze landed on a sword in a display cradle. She leapt for the weapon, yanking it free from its ornamental sheath.

The glimmering metal reflected light into her eyes. In that instant, clarity came.

She knew what she had to do.

Clutching the hilt in both hands, she turned on him. "I'm gonna gut you, demon!"

He drew back his lips so she could see his horrifying canines, then flicked two fingers at her. *Come on, then. . . .*

Her eyes widened and she charged, sword poised to sink into his chest.

At the last moment—she turned it on herself.

"No!" he bellowed. Then somehow he was between her and the sword tip, wedged against her body.

The blade slid into his lower back until it met bone.

She gasped, feeling his muscles tensing against her, sensing his escalating rage. The red of his irises bled over the whites of his eyes completely. He bared those fangs down at her. "This makes twice that you've defied me, *súka*. You've erred for ill."

With a snap of his wrist, he sent her flying to the floor.

Stunned. Flat on her back. Hysterical tears threatening.

She heard him removing the sword from his body, then tossing it away. *Won't cry in front of him. Won't surrender to his bitch.*

For courage, she recalled the years spent staring at cinder-block walls. Counting the blocks, the grout lines, seeing patterns and shapes. She'd called it the Cinder-Block Channel.

All block, all day. No interruptions. Ever.

Gritting her teeth, she twisted to her side, working to rise. Her hair had come loose, spilling over her face. She shoved a lock from her eyes.

"Stay—down," he ordered, towering over her. He was a fiend, an animal, still had blood sprayed on his face. How many had he murdered today?

"Go back to hell, asshole." Then she spat on his boots.

4

Lothaire snatched her upper arms, yanking her against him, ignoring the pain from his new wound. *She tried to end herself again. Almost succeeded . . .*

"Let me go!" She thrashed against his hold.

Elizabeth had nearly robbed him of his coveted Bride, had disobeyed his orders—twice—and had *stabbed* him.

Yet *she* was furious with *him*?

When she continued to flail, his grip tightened until a cry was wrenched from her lips, and she stilled.

Control yourself. He inhaled deeply. *Else forfeit your Bride.* He was far too strong to lose control when she was near. The rage . . . madness . . .

Inhale. Exhale. Saroya was in his keeping, safe for now. Disaster averted.

After long moments, he found his wrath ebbing, the haze dissipating somewhat. He eased his grip but kept her close to him. "Are you done?" he snapped.

Expression mulish, she muttered, "For a spell."

Challenging me still? Lothaire knew he balanced on the very brink of insanity; now he realized this human might already be there.

But in the wake of his anger, the pain of his injuries lessened, drowned out by an excruciating awareness of her. He gazed down into her striking eyes with bemusement.

The feeling was almost . . . hypnotic.

She permeated all his senses. His Bride's body was giving off an unbearable heat as it trembled against him. Her rapid heartbeat was a siren's call to him, flaunting its coursing rush. A vein in her neck pulsed invitingly.

Pain? He felt none.

His gaze fell on the silky spill of her hair flowing loose past her shoulders. Dark brown waves made the color of those eyes stand out: smoky gray, framed with thick black lashes.

She'd grown prettier in the intervening years. Curvier. Her hips rounded enticingly, her high breasts straining against that threadbare top.

He rubbed his tongue over a fang as he recalled the first night he'd seen Saroya. She'd been in the woods at a makeshift altar, covered in blood beneath the light of the full moon.

One look at her, and his heart had awakened from its long slumber. Breath had filled his lungs. His shaft had stiffened with a swift heat, demanding its first release in millennia.

He hardened now, remembering how he'd licked her victim's blood from her sweet skin as he'd stroked himself. She'd stood passive against him—a giving female, the softness to his strength—as he'd shuddered and spilled his seed upon the leaves. . . .

Whatever Elizabeth saw in his expression made her suck in a breath, her cheeks pinkening. "What do you want from me?"

His gaze fell on her neck, his fangs throbbing for that tender flesh. *To touch you. To drink you and make you grow wet from it. . . .*

No, not *her*! Lust rode him hard, but he would never act on it. Though Lothaire killed so readily, though he unfailingly acted without honor, he wouldn't betray his queen.

Especially not with a worthless mortal, a female normally beneath his notice.

He released Elizabeth, shoving her away from him. Lothaire would slake himself with his Bride alone.

When would she rise?

Saroya had explained much of how the possession worked with Elizabeth. Neither female knew what the other was thinking, though Saroya believed the girl could sense her intentions at times—just as Saroya could perceive changes in Elizabeth.

The goddess found it difficult to rise unless Elizabeth was weakened in some manner, physically or emotionally, or when she slept.

The more Saroya herself slept, the more readily she could regain control of the body.

Yet once the girl began shoving her way back to the fore, Saroya would be overwhelmed with dizziness, blurred vision, and a feeling of movement within the body, a shifting inside.

Lothaire had asked her, "Why can't you stay in control?"

With her gray eyes glittering, Saroya had hissed, "The mortal's too strong."

Now, as then, it appalled him that his Bride was subject to the whims of a human—a situation all too similar to his mother's.

Blyad'! If Elizabeth could sense Saroya's intentions at times, then couldn't the goddess sense the presence of her mate?

Until she rose, he'd have to deal with Elizabeth. "Sit," he commanded her.

Chin raised, she remained standing.

His brows drew together. So few ever disobeyed him, especially not on the heels of his rage.

Lothaire had stayed alive this long by using his ability to predict his adversaries' moves. He knew how they would behave, oftentimes before they did. His life was an endless chess match, a calculated march taking him ever closer to his Endgame—of kingdoms seized and retribution delivered.

Yet this female continued to prove *unpredictable*. When she'd turned the blade on herself . . .

"Sit now. Or I'll return with chains for you to sit shackled."

She swallowed but didn't move.

He almost found it a pity that she'd be gone so soon. Breaking her would have been amusing sport. "Very well." He traced to one of his many hideaways, this one a strategic keep in the Ural Mountains, to retrieve a set of manacles.

Though immortals with untold strength and abilities routinely quaked before him, a powerless human who was not even a quarter of a century old was defying him.

Powerless. He thought again how easy it would be for his enemies to kill her. Why couldn't Elizabeth have languished quietly in prison? This rescue couldn't have come at a worse time!

Multiple factions—demonarchies, Horde vampires, Valkyries, Furies, Lykae—hunted him, seeking revenge, or, better yet, his death. As soon as they found out he had a Bride in his possession, they'd target Saroya as well.

Thousands of years spent plotting would soon come to fruition—his Endgame finally achieved—as long as he didn't get distracted in these final weeks.

He considered the Endgame his master because he served it alone, thinking of nothing else. . . .

No, he wouldn't allow Elizabeth to alter his course.

He returned with the manacles. The girl had only gotten a few steps away when she froze at the clinking sound.

❧⊱✦⊰❧

Ellie slowly turned to him, eyes widening at the sight of the chains in his hands.

When he'd disappeared, she'd thought to escape. Now she trudged to the couch and sank down on it, inwardly pleading, *Don't chain me, don't chain me. . . .*

"Do you fear me, human?" He fingered the links.

Of course she did! He had supernatural powers, he'd just killed, and for some reason this maniac had fixated on her.

But Ellie usually had a good sense about people, and she suspected he would respect mettle. So she answered honestly, "Right 'bout now, I'm pretty scared." Her accent had grown more pronounced, a mountain twang that thickened whenever her emotions ran high. "But I reckon I'll work through it."

"And you fear these shackles?" His every movement spelled menace.

This devil's playing with me. "Yessir, I do. But you don't want to be chainin' me."

He raised his brows. "I don't?"

"What if *Saroya* wakes? I'm sure she'd be pissed to find herself all trussed up. And you don't want to ruin your . . . reunion." She could barely say the word. What would they do together?

Surely he'd want to make love to his *queen* at last. Because, for whatever reason, he never had before. Ellie was still a virgin. Which meant that Saroya had never taken a lover when she'd gained control.

After an endless moment, Lothaire let the shackles drop to the floor. The concession didn't feel like a victory to Ellie, more like a baited trap.

But with the immediate threat averted, she dragged her gaze from him to evaluate her surroundings.

The room was multiple times bigger than the entire trailer she'd grown up in. The furniture looked rich but modern, like from one of those design magazines. The curtains were drawn so tight, she couldn't tell if it was day or night. "Where am I?"

He crossed his arms over his broad chest. "New York."

"New York," she repeated dumbly. She'd never been outside of Appalachia but had always wanted to travel. Now everything was too surreal. "Why have you brought me here?"

"Because this place is mystically protected—inescapable and impenetrable."

Mystically? At that moment, she decided she'd better keep her mind open, lest it break from strain.

"You will be kept here for a time, until I cast your soul from your body."

"Wh-what are you talking about?"

"Your body will become Saroya's alone."

He had the power to steal Ellie's body from her? Forever? "I'll kill myself before that happens!" She leapt to her feet, starting for a bronze statue on a pedestal. "You hear me?"

"If you harm yourself in any way, I'll murder your mother and brother."

She stilled, fear shivering through her.

"Perhaps I should end one of them today to demonstrate good faith on my threat," he said, as though remarking on the weather. "Any message you'd like me to deliver?"

Her mind cried, *Oh, God, no!* Yet she forced herself to sneer, "Do it. Don't give a damn. None of those assholes came to my execution today." She'd forbidden it.

Had her family obeyed her other orders?

Lothaire disappeared right before her eyes. From just behind her, he murmured, "You are quite the accomplished bluffer, little human . . ."

She felt his breath on her neck before she whirled around.

". . . but your racing heart gives you away," he finished.

He could disappear and reappear directly into Mama's trailer, murdering them in seconds.

If her family was there.

Expecting Lothaire to want payback for the execution, Ellie had made her mother swear she'd get herself—and the entire family—scarce in the days surrounding it.

Surely there'd be news coverage of Ellie's mysterious disappearance; her mother would be in defense mode, unlikely to return to her home until she'd heard from her escapee daughter.

Ellie was almost certain they were out of Lothaire's reach, but could she bet her family's lives on it?

No.

Then he's won. All her brazen anger petered out, and she sank back down onto the couch. She'd always believed she'd win the battle against Saroya because she'd thought it would boil down to a test of wills.

But this man . . . this animal . . .

As her gaze flitted over the bullet holes in his chest that he seemed not to notice, then up to meet his chilling red eyes, she comprehended, *I can't beat him.*

5

Lothaire could see the defeat in her bearing.

At last the mortal had accepted her situation, accepted that he had all the leverage he needed to force her cooperation. Now he merely had to await Saroya. "Allow her to rise, Elizabeth."

"She's not trying to anymore. I can't prod her to it."

"But she was trying before? To escape the execution." When she didn't deny it, Lothaire imagined Saroya trapped, clawing to rise, to defend herself. . . .

Gods, he hated this girl—and he couldn't kill her! He paced once more, grappling to control his rage while ignoring his weariness and the twinges from his rapidly healing wounds.

When was the last time he'd really slept? Days ago? Weeks since he'd rested for more than an hour at a time?

Need to sleep, to dream. The memories come in dreams. He needed to begin his work, his seven little tasks—

"If you can cast out my soul," Elizabeth said, "then why do you need her to rise? And why'd you put me on ice for five years?"

He slowed, gazing past her. "I didn't possess the means then."

"But you do now?"

Not *yet*. After years of deceiving, slaying, and manipulating, Lothaire had seized the *Ring of Sums*, a talisman of great power—a wish giver. Only to have it stolen from him during his recent capture.

Mortals from the Order had attacked with their charge throwers, draining his strength, forcing him to kneel . . . the blood blinding his eyes and pooling around his knees.

He'd never forget the deafening scrape of the ring across the floor as their leader, a soldier named Declan Chase, had snared it.

"Do you have the means now?" the girl asked again.

Somewhere in the tangle of his mind Lothaire knew the ring's location. He just had to access that information. "I've budgeted anywhere from one night to a month until your end." Time enough to wade through the millions and millions of stolen memories.

Like his father before him, Lothaire was a *cosaş*, a memory harvester. A blessing for some vampires, a curse for one of the Fallen.

Damn his uncle for tempting him with the power all those centuries ago. . . .

"You must drink to the quick to be strong enough to destroy my brother," Fyodor had told him when they'd been reunited once more.

"My eyes are red, are they not?" Lothaire had said. "I've been a scourge upon humans."

"Or you can drink *immortals* to the quick and steal their strength, even their powers. Join with me, Lothaire."

"Ivana warned against this."

Fyodor had smiled thinly. "Your fair mother probably assumed you would have long since slain Stefanovich by now. . . ."

Impatient for power, Lothaire had begun targeting immortals. Yet their souls were much more decayed than humans'. And they had exponentially more memories. Ruinous to a *cosaş*.

His uncle had promised and delivered strength beyond measure, but had downplayed the side effect.

Insanity. Memories forever tolled. Lothaire balanced on the edge of a razor.

Though Fyodor, also a *cosaș,* had lost his mind long before his death last year, Lothaire had somehow pulled back, limiting his kills and memory harvests, scrabbling his way back to reason. *All to serve my Endgame. . . .*

He peered over at the mortal sitting on the couch. How long had he been pacing, his thoughts drifting? Her expression had turned from defeated to devious as she eyed the fireplace tools.

In another situation, he might have admired her tenacity. Now he snapped, "You must want them dead."

She jerked her gaze straight ahead.

With a scowl, he continued pacing, pondering his reaction to her earlier. He couldn't remember his body responding that wildly during his one night with Saroya.

For years, he'd remained apart from her easily, once he'd taken his initial release with her in the woods.

Now lust seethed inside him. *Ignore it, Saroya will rise soon enough.* And when she did, he'd touch her, taste her. Explore her new curves.

"Whoa! Your eyes are getting even . . . weirder."

Behold madness in a vampire. Everyone in the Lore knew Lothaire was on the brink; no one knew how close he was.

Most of the time, he had difficulty discerning his victims' memories from his own. When he slept, he uncontrollably traced to strange locales, as if sleepwalking. With increasing frequency, he'd been overwhelmed by rages.

One beckoned even now. "I want Saroya to rise," he told the human.

"Can't you take *her* from *me* instead? Maybe put her in the body of a red-eyed female demon—"

"She's no more a demon than I am! Saroya the Soul Reaper is the goddess of death and blood, the Vampire Horde's ancient deity."

"V-vampires?" Elizabeth whispered as she unsteadily stood. "Are you . . . you're not a *vampire?*"

He bared his fangs.

"You . . . you drink from people? Bite them?"

He enunciated, "Delightedly." Though not without express purpose, not any longer. His last prey had been calculated—Declan Chase, his jailer. The man would know where the Ring of Sums had been taken. Lothaire needed only to sleep to experience Chase's memories in dreams. . . .

Elizabeth put her hands to her knees, panting her breaths. "No sun. That's why the curtains are drawn so tight. A *vampire*. Sweet Jesus preserve me." Blood began trickling from the needle puncture on one inner arm.

His gaze locked on it, hunger racking him. He'd been injured repeatedly. Surely that was the only reason why he wanted so badly to sample her.

Not because the scent of her blood was exquisite . . . making his cock swell in his pants and his fangs sharpen. He ran his tongue over one, savoring the spike of his own blood.

Elizabeth cried, "Look at you!"

He hadn't allowed himself a taste of her before. Her blood would serve no purpose, might put him over the edge. But gods, its call was irresistible.

"You're not gonna bite me! Come near me with those fangs of yourn, and I'm gonna knock 'em out—"

He was behind her in an instant, one arm looped around her waist. With his free hand, he fisted the length of her shining hair and yanked her head to the side. Her pulse fluttered before his eyes.

How many times had he hungered for flesh but denied himself?

Yet never had his fangs throbbed like this, dripping to penetrate her. . . .

"Don't touch me!" She thrashed, digging her nails into his arm, but he enjoyed his enemies' struggles. Always had.

He raked a fang down the golden skin of her neck, cutting a shallow length, blood gently pooling.

Voice gone hoarse, he said, "I'll like it more if you fight. You'll like it more if you don't."

Scores of women—and men—had enjoyed his bloodtaking. It made *them* hunger, made them cling to him as if they wanted to sacrifice themselves on his fangs.

Mortals seemed particularly susceptible. Many came in his arms.

Would Elizabeth? The idea made him harden even more. He dipped his head, mouth closing over the fine wound. When his tongue touched a drop of blood, his body jerked as if lightning-struck.

A searing current seemed to electrify every vein in his body. . . .

Delectable.

"Wh-what are you doing to me?"

He licked the seam again and again, wanting to roar when she began trembling, her resistance easing.

She leaned into him, her back pressed against his aching shaft. When he snatched her tighter still and ground it against her, she moaned.

Yes, mortals liked his bloodtaking, but she was *shaking* with need.

"Oh! Ohhhh, no. . . . Oh, please!" Her voice was throaty, her breaths shallow.

Yet just when he'd widened his jaw to pierce her neck for more, she began fighting again. "No, not now!"

Lothaire tore his mouth away, saw her face go even paler.

She swayed on her feet. "Not *now.* . . ."

Saroya was rising! "Don't fight her, girl!" he commanded, yanking Elizabeth upright.

"No, no, no—" Her lids slid shut.

He caught her against him, turning her in his arms. "Saroya, *return to me.*"

After a long moment, her eyes opened, narrowed; then her palm shot up to crack across his cheek. "How dare you leave me to rot in prison, you filth! I'll play with your spleen before the night is through."

"Saroya," he grated, barely keeping his rage in check. Inhale, exhale. "Ah, my flower. I've missed you too."

6

When Saroya drew back her hand to strike Lothaire's smirking face again, his expression turned deadly. "Once was forgiven, goddess, but twice would prove unwise."

Her hand faltered. Lothaire was a notorious killer, and as long as she was trapped in this mortal shell, Saroya was vulnerable.

Though her spirit would continue on after this human's death, just as it always did, *this* was the body she wanted. Saroya was determined to keep it alive and unharmed. To do so, she needed this vampire's assistance.

Galling.

"Release me, Lothaire."

Without a word, he did. She took a step back, surveying him for the first time in years.

Of course he'd changed little, frozen for all time into this immortal form. He was at least six and a half feet tall, lean but muscled. His features were flawless, gold stubble covering his wide, masculine jaw and strong cleft chin. His pale collar-length hair was thick and straight—now stained with blood. "You killed? Without waiting for me?"

"To effect your escape from prison, yes."

Finally out of that hellhole!

She scanned her surroundings, finding them scarcely better. The area was decorated with a subtle flair, rich colors and fabrics of obvious expense, but it was uncluttered—aside from a pile of smashed marble and various shattered vases.

Saroya preferred flashy ornamentation, the elegance of a tomb filled with sacrifices to her, piled high with flesh trophies and bones.

Shimmering black silk against blood-spattered granite.

"Where have you taken me?" she asked in a pained tone.

"New York," he answered. "To one of our homes."

"I assume we have many."

"We own mansions, villas, châteaus. Any dwelling you desire will be yours."

As if she needed him to tell her that. She glanced down at her arm, at a drying track of red. "Did you *bite* me?" Narrowing her eyes, she added, "And do not think of lying to me."

A muscle ticked in his jaw. "You know I can't lie, Saroya." Natural-born vampires were physically incapable of it. Whenever a lie arose, a vampire would feel the *rána*, the burn, a scalding sensation in his throat.

"Did you dare pierce my skin?"

"There is little daring to it. But in this case, I only grazed your neck."

She reached up and brushed the nick with her fingertips. For some reason, her body seemed awkward, her breasts heavy. "Taking straight from the flesh, *cosaş*? Twenty thousand years of my memories will undoubtedly send you over the edge," she said. "You must have been very desirous of blood to have stolen hers."

Was there a subtle flush on his face? "I wager you have to be at the forefront of consciousness in order for me to harvest your memories. As for Elizabeth's—I believe I can handle twenty-four human years."

"How long did you leave me in that prison, Lothaire?"

"A mere half decade."

"What was more important than I?"

He shrugged. "Finding a way to circumvent your curse."

"I assume that you've found such a means. Else I'd still be locked up."

"I freed you because the body was about to be executed. By mortals."

Too shaming to be borne! "I'd sensed a threat, but an execution? For such a paltry number of deaths?"

Some of the tension left his broad shoulders. "My exact thoughts."

"So we're no closer?" At least now that she was free, she'd be able to kill once more. In the past, she'd reaped souls from her kills, each victim providing her strength. She'd been a true vampire. Now she stole lives solely for pleasure.

"After years of searching, I unearthed the Ring of Sums."

"Sums?" Her eyes widened. "Clever Lothaire." For him to have thought of this possibility! That talisman was steeped in power.

"It will allow me to extinguish Elizabeth's soul and make your body undying. You're to become a vampire like me."

Female vampires could only be born—never made. Though vampiric blood could potentially transform human males into vampires, a mortal female like Elizabeth would never survive the turning.

Even a former deity like Saroya didn't know why.

But the ring would overcome that. *What else might the ring do . . . ?*

She almost felt like smiling—which she never did. Then her satisfaction dimmed. "I understood the ring to be lost centuries ago. Along with its owner." A sorceress named La Dorada, a particularly treacherous adversary of Saroya's, had guarded the ring.

No matter how zealously Saroya had sought Dorada's death, her assassins could never deliver it. "You stole the ring from the Gilded One?"

He inclined his head regally.

Her lips parted. "I knew you were ambitious, but this is scarcely believable! Even gods tread carefully with Dorada. Especially the evil ones." *I've never been more defenseless against her. . . .*

"I faced the sorceress and her lackeys seven days ago, yet here I stand."

He'd survived a confrontation? "She will target your Bride to punish you! Unless you killed her?" *Am I free from the prophecy at last?*

"Not yet."

"If you left her alive, then she will be coming for us."

"Yes," he said casually.

"We must use this ring to return my godhood, Lothaire! And quickly."

"Even the Ring of Sums has limitations. If the ring could make one a god, then Dorada would have commanded it to do so. I believe we are bound to the realm of the immortals."

"In any case, give the ring to me."

"Three weeks ago, I was trapped by foes, an organization called the Order. They imprisoned me and confiscated it."

She was tempted to disbelieve such a story—few in the Lore were as formidable as Lothaire—but he couldn't speak untruths. "Why would they target you?"

"To examine me, determine my weaknesses, then execute me. Many other warriors from the Lore were captured as well."

"These foes must be exceptionally cunning to have trapped you."

"Their weapons are advanced. But I will steal the ring back. I depart tomorrow night, once you are settled. And once we have . . . caught up," he added.

"You must destroy Dorada, Lothaire. You *must*."

He narrowed his eyes. "I intend to, as soon as I reclaim the ring. Consider the sorceress as good as dead."

Reassured somewhat, she asked, "How long will it take to retrieve it?"

"A night? A month? I can't say for certain," he said. "I drank the blood of my former jailer. He knows how to find the ring, and I can tap his memories through my dreams. Have already seen some."

Saroya wasn't a patient god. "This body ages with each day."

Lothaire prowled around her, shamelessly raking his gaze over her form. "It is *much* changed."

"Mirror!" she ordered imperiously.

With a bored lift of his brow, he pointed behind her, to one hanging on a paneled wall.

Saroya crossed to the glass and gazed into it, cringing at her prison garb.

The scratch on her neck drew her attention. Would that scar? Would it heal before she was made into a vampire? Once this body became immortal, it would be frozen forever—its appearance fixed.

Lothaire traced to stand behind her. "You've suffered no ill from your time in prison, have only grown more beautiful."

She scrutinized her figure. Had Elizabeth lost weight? Saroya had resigned herself to her new short frame—mere inches over five feet—but she couldn't accept this leanness. "The body's too slim."

She recalled one of the few times she'd risen in that fetid jail. She'd read Elizabeth's journal, noting that the mortal "worked out" every day in her cell. Unfortunately, it showed.

How Saroya missed her own features! Her eyes had once been large and feline yellow, slit down the center with a thin black iris. Her lips had been bloodred, her skin pale like the moon. She'd been almost six feet tall and voluptuous to an obscene degree.

Whenever she'd descended from her godplane to earth, men had been awestruck just to behold her. Once she beckoned for them, they'd offered themselves to her insidious brand of death. . . .

She ran her hands over this new lean figure, groping for softness. *How much flesh can the body gain before Lothaire finds the ring?*

At least Elizabeth's bust had grown to a decent size. When Saroya cupped herself with relief, Lothaire's eyes grew hooded.

Saroya abruptly dropped her hands. In a brisk tone, she said, "This face is the most lovely of my temples'."

Though this present guise couldn't compare to hers when she'd been a cat-eyed enchantress, Saroya had enjoyed some success luring victims. Males wanted to protect the vulnerable-looking girl and pluck her innocence. Instead, Saroya had plucked their hearts, eyes, and testes.

Unlike her twin sister, Lamia, a goddess of life and fertility, Saroya was a virgin deity and forever would be, defending her chastity to the death. . . .

To others' deaths.

Yet Lothaire believed she was a sexual creature, believed she'd never taken a lover into Elizabeth's body out of faithfulness to him. . . .

"Indeed lovely." His voice had grown huskier. "Who came before this human?"

"I possessed a middle-aged professor of Americana. I had much to learn from him, kept him alive for most of the nineties. After him came a shovel-toothed hunchback of a woman. I leapt off a building to be rid of her." She frowned. "That transfer hadn't proved as instantaneous as I'd hoped."

"How are these temples chosen for you?"

"It could be based on a bloodline. Only the one who cursed me can say." *Lamia, damn you to the Ether!* "All I know is that I will do anything to remain in Elizabeth—and you would do well to help me. I promise you, the next form for your Bride cannot possibly be better, *if* you could even find me. I might possess a male, or a baby, or an octogenarian. Not a young and fair innocent."

Yet another reason this body was a seamless fit. Elizabeth was a virgin, much to Lothaire's fascination.

He reached for her waist, turning her to face him. She stiffened but allowed it. "I'm quite content with your host as well. How long can you hold her off?"

"She'll rise this very night. She is exceedingly strong-willed. Lothaire, I want her gone."

He brushed a lock of hair from her forehead, his red eyes following the movement of his hand. "And you shall have everything you wish once I reclaim the ring. For now, I will make her fear ever to rise again."

"You think you can make one like her go dormant? How? When you can't harm the body to torture her into submission?"

His lips drew back from his fangs, not a smile. "Let me worry about our pathetic little mortal."

"Such vitriol." One thing she'd learned about Lothaire? He despised humans even more than she did.

"Elizabeth just attempted to destroy herself, thinking that would kill my Bride. Yet I can't punish her for her transgression!" he grated. "Be assured that the next time she rises *will be her last*."

Saroya had never met a man so certain of himself. But then he was powerful, brilliant, calculating, and, above all things, perfectly fashioned.

Lothaire was as compelling as a virility god.

The night of their first meeting, she'd allowed him to lick her prey's blood from her skin as he'd stroked his own organ to release. Though she'd been repelled by his animalistic needs, even she had been reluctantly entranced by the sight. And she was above such urges.

Saroya despised all things sexual. Blood and death were all she revered—certainly not an act designed to *create life*.

In fact, she loathed males—those reckless carriers of seed—entirely.

Now this one was cupping her nape, his gaze locked on her lips, no doubt intent on claiming her. How to put him off once more? "As I told you years ago, Lothaire, I won't yield this body until it's fully mine to give you."

He straightened, meeting her eyes. "And as I told you, Saroya, I can't take you until you're immortal, else risk killing you with my strength. But there are other ways to pleasure each other."

Disgusting primate.

"Despite ample opportunity, I haven't been with another since my blooding."

Yes, he *would* have ample opportunity. "I suppose females throw themselves at you wherever you go."

"To a tedious degree." He studied her expression. "Jealous to think of me with another?"

"Not at all." She no more cared whom he mated with than she would about an ant on the sidewalk.

His grip on her neck tightened, a clear threat. "I'm not a selfless male—when I give, I expect to get. Today I gave you freedom."

Though it appalled her, she knew she'd have to manipulate him. "Vampire, I reek of prison, poverty, and fear. Look at my appearance, my atrocious garments. I want to feel beautiful, to be desirable. I need clothes, jewels, cosmetics. My hair must be shorn, my skin bathed."

She thought he might press the issue. Instead, he released her, offering his hand. "Then welcome to New York." He drew back a curtain, revealing a balcony that overlooked a green park and a vast city. He ushered her forward into the sunlight as he drew back into the shadows. "Whatever you need, we'll find it here."

Did he expect her to be impressed by this view? She was confused. *Impressive* would be this vast city enslaved to her will. . . .

7

His penthouse had been turned into a female's sartorial dream.

Blue velvet draped the dining room table, dotted with gemstones the size of his Bride's fist. Racks of costly garments lined the walls in the living area. Designer shoes littered the floor. Cosmetics were laid out in the dressing room.

And in the kitchen, a chef prepared a meal fit for a queen.

After Lothaire had cleaned himself, he'd made a few select calls. Within the hour, his home had been filled with the city's most exclusive stylists, beauticians, and shopkeepers, all peddling their wares and services.

At least, the most exclusive *mortal* proprietors.

Normally he would have purchased through Lore vendors, but gossip about the Enemy of Old's new woman would be impossible to suppress unless he killed all the witnesses.

Which he was hesitant to do; he enjoyed their luxurious wares himself. Even if he wasn't yet a king, he would dress as one. . . .

So humans it would be. He adjusted the sunglasses he was forced to wear in front of them.

For the last several hours, Saroya had been closeted in her suite of rooms with aestheticians and a "wax specialist"—whatever that was— spending the afternoon doing gods-only-knew-what in the bathroom.

To pass the time, he was tempted to tackle a new mechanical puzzle he'd acquired—a polyhedral assembly, solvable in sixty-five moves—but his concentration suffered on most days as it was.

And now the sound of his Bride's voice teased him. Her scent kept his body strung tight. As ever, madness threatened.

Lothaire knew one thing that would relax him. He traced into the closet of his suite, opening a safe within. There lay his most treasured possession: a weighty account ledger.

He didn't use it to track monetary expenditures and incomes. Instead, he recorded blood debts, chronicling all the immortals who had sworn to do whatever he demanded of them.

Like a miser palming his gold, Lothaire would review his debtors, reverently brushing his fingers over the ledger pages—

He froze, sensing something that couldn't be right. A presence from long, long ago. He shoved the book back into the safe, slamming it shut, then traced to the shadow's edge of the balcony.

The setting sun was veiled by misty clouds, but he still had to shade his sensitive eyes as he gazed out over the city.

Was he being stalked?

How to anticipate a threat when he could scarcely untangle reality from reverie? Waiting . . . watching . . .

Once night fell, the presence disappeared. Or had he imagined it?

Unsettled, he returned to the living room. Saroya emerged shortly after. At the sight of her, he shrugged off his disquiet.

The wait had been worth it.

A floor-length gown of black silk molded over her every curve. The front was a deep V cutting down all the way to her waist. Thin leather ties crisscrossed over her chest, holding the material in place over her full breasts.

Want to see them. For the first time. Lothaire had never gazed upon her naked form.

His eyes were riveted to her movements in that ingenious garment—one created to make males fantasize about slowly unlacing those ties to free her bound flesh.

She sauntered across the room, her stilettos giving her the illusion of height. Her damp hair smelled of scented shampoo and hung heavily down her back.

Her makeup had been applied liberally. Bold blush strokes over her cheeks and heavy foundation nearly blunted the nuances of her finely boned features. Her eyes were made up with sweeping shades of brown, black, and silver. Her lipstick was scarlet.

She had lips like a sexpot, a pouting bow.

And her wicked nails looked as if blood dripped from each fingertip. *Very nice touch, Saroya.*

Overall, the effect was flagrantly sexual.

By all the gods, she was a lovely piece, and soon he'd claim her. At the thought, his shaft swelled. He shifted uncomfortably, adjusting the long jacket that disguised his reaction to her. The growing pressure . . .

Lothaire had been thirty-three when he'd last had a woman beneath him, the night before his heart had stopped its beating and he'd frozen into his immortal form. Until that age, he'd enjoyed females from all factions in the Lore, had taken a new one every night.

Now he was to suffer the urges and drives of his youth all over again?

Between his dwindling sanity and this inconvenient erection, he found it impossible to concentrate on his Endgame.

He began to pace, having to remind himself not to teleport in front of the mortals.

I can't lose focus. At long last, he was on the cusp of seizing the Horde throne. He'd completed the most challenging task—slaying Stefanovich—ages ago.

Though not before the old king had lashed out against his bastard with incomprehensible malice. *The earth grinding over me . . .*

No, focus on the Endgame! On the ring. It would enable Lothaire to destroy Elizabeth and transform Saroya into a vampire—a vital measure of protection for his Bride, and the key to securing the Horde throne for him.

And the ring would give him the power to find and annihilate the Daci. To locate Serghei at last.

One ring equaled Lothaire's eternal mate, two kingdoms, and the vengeance he'd hungered for since his mother's murder. . . .

Saroya began to finalize her purchases, her demeanor bored. She pointed out every rack of clothing, ordering, "Put them in my wardrobe." Her bedroom, the one adjoining his own, had an oversize closet; he doubted everything would fit into even that cavernous space.

With an aggrieved air, she perused the jeweler's offerings. "I will take all the baubles."

Eight figures' worth of *baubles*. Lothaire sighed. *Welcome to matrimony.*

All eyes fell on him. With a negligent wave of his hand, he approved the expenditures. If possible, the humans groveled even more, which increased his irritation.

When Saroya returned to her suite and settled into a chair to have her hair trimmed, he followed her.

"Am I to have no privacy?" she asked.

"No," he said simply. No longer. He owned the body as much as she did. He'd be there for any alterations. "And after this, I want to see you in the garments I've bought for you." He leaned down to say at her ear, "See you in the lingerie." His gaze dipped, greedily taking in the swells of her breasts.

One tug of a leather tie . . . golden flesh spilling out.

"Of course, lover," she said, too smoothly.

He pinched her chin, turning her to face him. "Saroya, I don't buy you these things for your benefit." Never would he give a gift with no thought of a return on his investment. "I buy them for *both of us* to enjoy. Just as we will this new body."

She subtly arched her back. "A body like this is made for sex, is it not?"

He ground his teeth before saying, "I can only guess, as I've never *seen* it."

"Soon, Enemy of Old. I promise."

Lothaire debated whether to believe her. Saroya's mythology was sparse at best, and contradictory. Some said she'd been as frigid with—and deadly to—males as her twin Lamia was sexual with them. Others said Saroya had participated in depraved orgies in her temples.

Seeing her like this—in fuck-me makeup and clothing—had him betting on the latter.

But no matter what her proclivities were, he knew the great Saroya wouldn't happily bed a mate like him, a male who would demand obedience in all ways.

And he would never rape a female. So it would take all his considerable experience to bring her to heel—

"Shear it. To my chin," she commanded the stylist.

"Ah-ah," Lothaire grated. "Keep it long." He'd never seen hair so lovely, curling locks the color of mink.

Now she wanted to cut it all off? After he'd imagined threading his fingers through it infinite times?

After he'd fantasized about gripping it in his fists—as he eased his shaft into and out of her mouth . . . ?

Saroya bristled. "I want it short."

He snapped his fingers, and the stylist scurried out of the room, closing the door behind her. "I prefer it long."

"It's *my* hair."

He gave her a snide look of amusement. "That body is as much mine as it is yours."

Her eyes flashed. "I inhabit it."

"And I stole it from prison. I'll be the one feeding it, safeguarding it. The body would be dead if not for me. Therefore, I *own* it."

"You forget I'm a goddess," she hissed. "Your goddess."

And a bitch as well. But then, weren't all goddesses afflicted with bitchery?

Though he knew he couldn't expect anything different from Saroya, he could begin putting her in line. "*You* forget that you have no power. So for now, *I* am your god. Stop pushing me, Saroya." He held her gaze. "You won't like it when I push back."

8

Saroya parted her lips to curse Lothaire to the surface of the sun, but her vision wavered. She raised her freshly manicured hand to her forehead.

She could feel Elizabeth already trying to rise—as if the girl was ramming herself against whatever internal wall separated them.

A reminder of how much Saroya needed this fiend. For now.

Control your righteous anger, tell him what he wants to hear. "Lothaire, I was a deity of the first Ether. I'm unused to relinquishing control. And now I've been too long downtrodden and trapped. I'm sure someone as great as you can scarcely imagine how low I've been brought, but *try*."

Immediately, she sensed a change in him. Her words had affected him.

"I do understand, goddess." Now he tenderly curled his forefinger under her chin. "But in this matter I will not bend."

He can't lie. Which meant he truly wouldn't relent. "Then I will leave all this"—she waved at the heavy mass of hair—"for your pleasure."

His eyes darkened with need. "And what else would you do for my pleasure?"

Nothing. Never again. That night she'd let him kiss her, she'd barely concealed how revolting she'd found that rutting side of him.

If he hadn't been in such a fervor from his blooding, surely he would have detected her reaction?

She knew he wouldn't be as motivated to secure the Ring of Sums for her if he discovered how sexually repellent his Bride found him. How could she disguise it if he slaked himself on her now?

Stifling a shudder, she purred, "Soon you'll see. But for now, let me acquiesce to your wish about my hair." Before she stood and turned on her heel to call the human back in, she saw his eyes narrow with suspicion.

When the stylist began trimming scant inches off her long mane, Lothaire took a seat nearby, as if to guard every lock.

Watching this process seemed to be both relaxing and exciting for him. As the brush glided through her hair, his lids went heavy, even as he leaned forward, inching toward the edge of his chair.

He clearly needed her for far more than his throne.

How could she put him off for possibly a month? Perhaps by diverting his attention toward another?

Finding a bedmate for him wouldn't be difficult. Even she could admit how handsome he appeared in his tailored garments.

His longish blond hair was cleaned of blood and styled with a seemingly careless air—into a perfectly decadent result. He wore sunglasses to hide his eyes and a long coat to cover his physical reaction to her. Both made him look even more the rogue. Especially with that dark gold stubble on his jaw—he'd been frozen forever with it, could shave his face, but it would soon return to the same rakish length.

The women and men here coveted him so intensely she could *feel* their desire.

He should bed one or all of them. *I'll see to it.*

Once the stylist finished, Saroya gazed into the mirror, disdaining the outcome, but what could she expect, considering Lothaire's constraints?

The soft, flowing curls made her look younger, more innocent. *Less powerful.* Though she detested sex, she made a point of looking sexually receptive—an illusion of desirability, like that used by a Venus flytrap.

Saroya enjoyed luring her victims with promises of fulfilling their wildest dreams—only to deliver their worst nightmares. She delighted in imagining each one's last pitiful thought: *I believed she wanted me.*

His voice a rasp, Lothaire said, "I am pleased."

Saroya informed him, "Then, by all means, the mortal may live."

The woman thought she was jesting and giggled, but fell silent at Saroya's impassive expression.

Then Lothaire began hastening the humans out of the apartment—before Saroya could secure a bedmate for him. He no doubt believed that with his Bride's objections out of the way, they could begin *pleasuring each other in other ways.*

When they were alone, he traced back to her, reaching for her—

As if on cue, her stomach growled.

He dropped his hand. "You haven't eaten all day?"

Another rumble.

He exhaled, seeming begrudgingly amused, as if he found a human trait in her *quaint.* "I've had a meal prepared for you."

"Eat mortal food?" At the thought, she grew queasy. "I refuse."

"You can't *refuse.*"

"I will eat as soon as *you* do." The vampire could eat just as easily as a mortal could drink blood, but he'd be likewise unwilling.

"Saroya, you know that won't happen."

"I will feed when I can drink blood once more. I miss it feverishly."

"You can't stomach it now?"

She shook her head. "I tried it with Elizabeth. At the first sign of nausea, I receded into the background, overjoyed at the thought of her waking to vomit buckets of blood." The little things in life . . .

"And after I force her to go dormant, what then? You'll have to nourish this human body until I can turn you into a vampire."

Repeating his words, she said, "In this, I will not bend. Let Elizabeth feed it."

"You *want* her to rise on occasion?"

Otherwise Saroya would be expected to eat food—and appease his lusts. "Can you keep her prisoner here when I recede? Do you have a guard to protect the body from Dorada while you search for the ring?"

His brow was furrowed, his complicated mind already working through the details. Lothaire might have the urges of a primate, but his mind impressed her. "This apartment is protected from intrusion and escape. It's hidden from any being in the Lore."

"How?"

"I know some of the old ways," he said. "I've used a Druid spell to create an invisible boundary around the apartment."

Even Dorada couldn't cross that boundary. "So where is the lock?" Somewhere in this dwelling he'd inscribed, etched, or painted symbols—a code of sorts. It might be prudent to know where—as well as the reverse code to unlock it.

"Within my room." Anticipating her question, he said, "The combination is updated throughout the day, just in case a talented soothsayer set out to scry your existence."

She'd let this lie for now. "Excellent, vampire." She was assured by the precautions Lothaire had taken and convinced of his dedication to keeping her safe, to returning her to her former glory.

After all, he was bound to her forever.

Yes, she was confident. Enough that she refused to wallow in this weak mortal shell any longer than necessary. "Then you can deal with Elizabeth. And perhaps make her add flesh? Lothaire, if I could trust you to see this done, I could sleep until my turning, building my strength." She'd need it to overpower Elizabeth at will.

"Sleep the entire time?" He was incredulous. "I told you it might take a month! I should go without my female for that time?"

Rutting animal! "A month feels like seconds to me, hardly a replenishing rest. And you've gone this long. Besides, you shouldn't have time for a female because you should be working ceaselessly to find that ring!"

She could see him wrestling for control of his temper. "Circumstances are different now. My needs are strong, and my mind seizes on them. I can't afford to lose my concentration."

"Very well. I'll attempt to rise tomorrow night," she lied.

"Don't *attempt*, goddess." He caught her wrist, forcing her palm to his pulsing erection. "I'm a blooded male. I will have another relieve me of this ache. You or a stranger. Decide."

Saroya yanked back her hand, parting her lips to tell him to have at a stranger. But then she realized that securing a bedmate could take time away from his search, and his dalliances with another would limit the time he personally remained with this body.

Which wouldn't do. Not with Dorada in the picture.

An idea arose. Why not let *Elizabeth* endure his primitive lusts? "You may sate yourself on Elizabeth." At least, up to a point. Saroya didn't want her favorite temple defiled by Lothaire's offspring.

"Sate myself with a *human*," he bit out with disgust. "With *that* human?"

"I give you leave to use her at will. Just save the claiming for me—and don't mar her skin further with your bites!"

"You ask much of me, female."

Time to stroke his ego. "This is but temporary, my king. I only want to be yours in all ways, to rule the Horde by your side. You are a great and powerful male. You deserve a queen to match you, Lothaire." She forced herself to smooth her hand down his chest. "Imagine an eternity of blood-letting together, hunting together, conquering together. . . ."

She knew he'd too long dreamed of these things to go unmoved.

Lothaire's need to rule over his brethren wasn't merely obsessive—it was pathological. Which fit into her plans. For the rest of time, she would strive for godhood, but for the present, she would accept ruling a kingdom of creatures who lived in the manner she had set forth. . . .

Feeding on others, claiming the night as her own dominion.

Of course, ultimately *she* would be the supreme ruler of these creatures, and Lothaire would be her fawning consort. "As your queen, I will lay your crown upon your fair head and rejoice as all night beings tremble before you."

His brows drew together, his yearning for this nigh palpable.

"Soon, my king," she murmured, just before another wave of dizziness washed over her. She moved to the edge of the bed, sinking down.

He shook his head hard, commanding her, "Fight her *now*. Remain with me."

"The girl's coming." Saroya irritably kicked off her stilettos. "There's nothing I can do, Lothaire. Just *use* her!"

"*Blyad*'! You don't know what you're saying. You rise tomorrow night, goddess, or suffer my wrath!"

Her lids fluttered closed and blackness took her.

9

Ellie shot awake with a frantic inhalation.

Each time she rose was like fighting her way along a black, soundless tunnel only to break through with a rush of momentum.

Now she jerked her head around, finding herself in a dim room atop the softest sheets she'd ever imagined.

Not in prison— Memories of the afternoon returned like a crashing wave.

Lothaire's hot mouth against her neck. His fangs raking over her skin for blood. His tongue snaking to the drops.

She shivered. He'd *tasted* her blood. *Oh, my Lord, vampires exist.*

A demon possession hadn't been such a jump for a girl from Appalachia, home of serpent handlers, speaking in tongues, and the fabled Mothman.

But the idea of a blood-drinking vampire had sent her entire world askew.

And if that was true, then she had no reason not to believe Saroya was a deity.

Ellie threw her arm over her face, groaning in misery, "Oh, God."

"I am not the god you're referring to," Lothaire intoned from a murky corner. "Although to you, I might as well be."

She shot upright in the bed, squinting into the dark. His red eyes glowed from the shadows like embers.

"You!" Her nightmare continued. Fitting, since it was now night outside. The curtains were drawn back and a chill breeze blew between opened French doors. A skyline sparkled in the distance.

Another day of lost time. But she supposed all time was borrowed now.

Then she assessed her body. No blood?

She was dressed in a nearly indecent silk gown, with bracelets and rings adorning her. Long red nails tipped her fingers. No skin embedded beneath them? Saroya always left her with horrific scenes. So where were the corpses? "Did Saroya . . . did she kill while I was unconscious?"

"No."

Ellie exhaled with relief.

"My Bride was too fatigued, so we called it an early night." Since Ellie had seen him last, he'd washed himself clean of blood and changed to a black button-down and dark slacks. "But there's always tomorrow."

"If your aim is to make me miserable, just consider this mission accomplished." She always woke from her blackouts exhausted and famished. Even if she wasn't covered with blood, she felt grimy and used-up. "So what'd I miss?" She slapped her palm to her forehead. "Oh, yeah, last I remember, you're a vampire."

"I am." He was regarding her differently. But why?

How could she study a person when she was offstage for half of their interactions? She couldn't get a handle on his mood either. He didn't seem furious or crazy any longer—just held himself with utter stillness.

Like a predator.

She swallowed. "Did you drink more of my blood while I was out?"

In a snide tone, he said, "Somehow I restrained myself."

Relief made her brave, and she snapped, "Be sarcastic all you want to, mister, but you were tonguing my vein like a son of a bitch before I kicked toes-up."

"And you were loving it. Moaning and rubbing against me."

She gazed away in embarrassment. Because what he said was true. The pleasure she'd felt had been bewildering. . . .

"You truly remember nothing of the rest of the afternoon?"

She shook her head curtly.

"How maddening, to have no control over your body. If you hate this so much, then why rise at all?"

"Because this is *my* body." She thumped her nearly bared chest, and the bangles at her wrists clanged. "Mine!"

"Incorrect. I've staked my claim on it. And soon you'll relinquish it to another female."

He was going to cast out her soul! Ellie recalled how defeated she'd felt when he'd threatened her mother and brother—until she'd realized she still had one play left.

If she could get to a phone, she could make sure her family was hidden. Then there'd be no leverage for the vampire. Ellie could take herself out—and Saroya with her.

This raccoon ain't treed just yet. . . .

"If you were ready to die over this, then why did you not recede and allow her to rule you?" he asked. "You would have simply slept inside your physical form, with no more pain, no fear. There would have been no need for me to rid it of your soul."

"I was ready to die to take out a murderer who kills good men. Not to give her a free by-your-leave." She added the last absently, feeling as if something wasn't *right* about her body.

"Don't continue to fight me, Elizabeth. Anyone who crosses swords with me loses. It's merely fact."

"Huh?" Something was definitely amiss *downstairs*.

With increasing irritation, he said, "Crossing swords. You losing . . ."

"Yeah, well, maybe that's because you've never met anyone like me. I'm more stubborn than anyone you've ever encountered."

"A ridiculous statement, from an ignorant girl. I'm thousands of years old. I've encountered millions."

"*Thousands?* That's ancient!" she cried. "So bloodsuckers are immortal?"

"I'll give you a moment to wrap your puny mind around that."

"Mighty considerate of you. But no matter. I'm still more mule-headed than anyone. I can out-stubborn a mountain. It's just my nature." Dang it, why did she feel so weird between her legs?

Lothaire opened his mouth to say something, but she cut him off. "I have to use the restroom."

He exhaled in irritation and pointed toward a hall. "Through there."

Ellie rose from the bed, wincing at her pedicured but sore feet. A pair of stilettos lay at angles on the floor.

Heels, Saroya? That's just cruel. Growing up, Ellie had gone barefoot a good seven months out of every year. In prison, they'd given her flip-flops.

Shoes were foreign, heels torturous.

Down a lengthy hallway, she spied the bathroom. The inside was spacious. A marble floor gleamed, counters to match. Plush towels too pretty to use hung from a heated rack.

When she turned to examine herself in the wall-to-wall mirror, she gasped at her reflection.

The black gown she wore was the finest silk, but it dipped down until her navel was visible. Her breasts were all but spilling out; the thin fabric clearly outlined what little of them was covered.

Being exposed like this might have embarrassed her, but prison—and communal showering—had drilled out any inkling of modesty she'd once possessed.

She had a stylish new haircut and a manicure and pedicure, but layers of makeup covered her face.

Her lips were bright red, her eyes done up with flashy shadow. She looked like a porn-star version of herself.

Makeup also concealed the scratch the vampire had given her. She scrutinized her neck and chest for more bites, but found none. So he'd told the truth.

Considering the way he'd licked that stream of blood earlier, she'd thought for sure he'd bite Saroya and finish the job. So why had he *refrained*?

Had Saroya given Lothaire her virginity instead? For all that Saroya had loved to murder males, she'd never enjoyed one!

Ellie pulled up the gown's hem, and nearly screamed. Saroya had waxed her—completely.

"What the *fuck*?" Bald as a cue ball. "Who *does* this?" Her face heated.

The bareness was so blatantly *sexual*. Surely Lothaire had deflowered her today.

She sat on the toilet, matter-of-factly feeling herself, gently probing inside. No soreness. Her virginity was intact.

So there'd been no sex and no biting? Did vampires even *have* sex? She recalled when he'd licked her blood. Her eyes went wide. "Oh!" He'd had an erection, had ground it against her back.

Perhaps psycho Saroya had denied him. If she was indeed a goddess, then maybe she thought sex beneath her.

So why the waxing?

Ellie emptied her bladder, washed her hands, then headed back to the millennia-old immortal waiting for her.

The bedroom was now lit. Recessed fixtures cast a muted glow.

Once her eyes adjusted, his face drew her attention, and she did a stutter step. The first night she'd seen him, she'd been too petrified to register much about his looks, other than: *red-eyed demon!*

Then earlier today, he'd been covered in blood. Now?

Dear God, he's . . . fine. All chiseled features and tousled blond hair. Even those creepy eyes couldn't detract from the rest of his face, just made him look like some kind of fallen angel.

Once she could pry her gaze from him, she noted other details—like the size of the room. "If only it wasn't so cramped," she mumbled, gawking at the height of the ceiling.

Decorated in shades of cream, the room was so spacious it was divided into study, sitting, and sleeping areas. The furniture was so ritzy, she feared to touch it.

Yet the king-size mattresses lay straight on the floor. "You got something against bed frames?"

"Vampires like to sleep as close to the ground as possible."

"But we're not on the ground floor."

"Twenty-five stories from it. I also enjoy having the penthouse."

She'd never been above three stories before! She spied an enormous park just beyond the balcony. "That's . . . Central Park?"

"What of it?"

She ran outside. *Look at the pretty lights. Better than on TV—*

When she reached the balcony railing, she was shot backward as though she'd run into an invisible wall. Just as she was about to land on her ass, Lothaire gripped her sides, holding her upright.

He drew her to her feet but remained close behind her. At her ear, he said, "Mystically protected, remember." He grasped her wrist, forcing her to touch the invisible border.

Her lips parted when she felt energy pressing back against her hand.

"You can't leave these premises in any way unless escorted by me." He released her but didn't move away.

"One jail to another."

"Precisely," he murmured, laying his palms over her hips.

She froze, not knowing what to do. They probably appeared to all the world like lovers taking in the skyline, instead of a vampire and his captive. Her skin prickled with awareness of him.

At length, he turned her to face him.

Would pay to know what he's thinking. "How do you move so fast?"

"I don't move fast. You, mortal, move slowly." Had his gaze dipped to the revealing V of her dress?

"And how do you vanish and appear?"

"It's called *tracing*—it's how vampires travel." He frowned at her, dropping his hands. "It's been a while since I've spoken to someone who knows so little about our world. Unbelievably, it's even less than you know about your own."

He started back to the bedroom, snapping over his shoulder, *"Come."*

She found her heels digging into the spot. The only thing that held a candle to her stubbornness was her inability to take orders. "You truly think you own me?"

He faced her with a bland look. "Yes."

Hate him! "So earlier, when you were fixin' to inform me how things were gonna be, you were basically gonna tell me that I'll be a slave up to the day you end me!"

"In so many words." He began circling her, an eerie prowling that spooked the hell out of her.

So she jutted her chin. "And where exactly will you be sendin' my soul?"

"Sending it? Hmm. Even I don't know where souls go after this existence." Circling, circling. "My only concern is that yours is gone from your body."

"If I don't take myself out before then."

"You won't. I'll use your weakness—your love for your family—to keep you from harming yourself."

"Are you really the kind of man who would kill a defenseless woman and a young boy?" she demanded, though everything about this male screamed that he was.

Holding her gaze, he answered, "I'll do it without hesitation to get what I want. I'll do it with delight if you continue to defy me."

He's an animal . . . so best treat him like one, Ellie. Show no fear.

"Beg me for their lives now, Elizabeth. Plead for them."

With more bravado than she'd ever feigned, she said, "You'd hate me worse than you already do. So I'll do you one better. I'll bargain with you."

"Bargain?" he repeated, seeming intrigued. Then his expression grew shuttered. "Only those with power can bargain. You have none."

"That's where you're wrong. I've prevented Saroya from rising a time or two in the past. I'll steel myself against her even more. I won't sleep or eat. I will think of nothing but how to bury her so deep inside, she won't ever see the light of day." Ellie thought he'd be furious at that.

Instead, he again looked interested. "I enjoy a good bargain. Yet I also enjoy making my enemies beg."

"You need me alive, but you need more than that. You'll be needing my cooperation. So what had you planned for me to do after I got through pleading?"

"I'd planned for you to dine."

She narrowed her eyes up at him. "I sure am hungry, Lothaire. Could eat a horse right now. See how easy we can be together?"

He pinched her chin, hard. "Careful, little pet. If you play with me, you won't like it when I join the game." He tilted his head at her. "And for this *easiness*, what do you want in return?"

"Don't let Saroya kill."

After a considering moment, he said, "Until you're gone? Agreed. And you'll obey my commands without question, or your next infraction equals your family's end. Try to prevent Saroya from rising or harm yourself in any way and you might as well peel their heads from their necks with your own hands. Do you understand me, Elizabeth?"

"I-I understand." Then she added, "I understand that my entire family is safe from you and anyone who works with you, so long as I'm cooperating."

He quirked a brow as if amazed by her temerity. She suspected she was a novelty to him.

So what would happen when the novelty wore off?

"I wondered if you were crazy. Have now decided you must be." He turned and strode toward another room. "Follow me."

Having had a victory of sorts, she trailed after him. At every turn, she was confronted with more examples of his wealth, luxuries like she'd never imagined—art, oriental rugs, newfangled electronics. But not a single phone or computer.

This place was a paradise compared to jail. The air was drier here, not laden with humidity. While her ward had been ripe with the odor of urine and mace, everything here smelled *new*.

The apartment had two wings with sprawling terraces between them. One terrace even had a pool.

A paradise compared to *anywhere*. "How many rooms are in this place?"

"More than a dozen throughout the three floors."

"You live alone?"

"As of today, I live with Saroya and one temporary prisoner."

Then a thought struck her. "Are we fixin' to eat *together*?"

"Don't want to see me drink my dinner?"

She'd never been squeamish around blood, had hunted deer with her uncle all her life, eventually guiding her own hunting trips for his business. Then Saroya's crimes had hardened Ellie further.

Not to mention when the bitch had drunk buckets of blood. . . .

But Ellie hadn't negotiated that *Lothaire* couldn't kill. Nor that he couldn't drink from *her*. "The blood in itself isn't an issue. I'm more concerned with where you get it."

"From a pitcher in the refrigerator usually. For tonight, you'll eat alone. I'm here only to ensure you put on weight. Fill out your curves more. Saroya finds you lacking."

There wasn't a damn thing wrong with her curves! "Then maybe you two ought to go kidnap a plumper girl, a ready-made one who already meets your requirements."

He appeared beside her in an instant, his hand closing over one of her elbows. "*You* are mine. Your body is mine by right. I do own you. The sooner you accept this, the better off you'll be."

She tried to free herself, but his grip was like a vise. "You're the one who's crazy!"

"Shall I return with your mother's head? Perhaps I'll place it as the table's centerpiece."

"I'm still cooperating!" He was the scariest person she'd ever encountered! No one in the backcountry mountains or even on death row could compare.

His smirk deepened. "And who owns you?"

Say the words! Force yourself to say them! "You—do."

He released her. "Good girl."

10

"S it." Lothaire pointed to the dining room. Atop the extended table were silver-covered dishes and two place settings—with enough utensils to confound the girl.

Elizabeth glanced around. "Who cooked this?"

"A chef came earlier," Lothaire said evenly, surprised by his lingering lucidity. Before Elizabeth had woken, he'd watched the even rise and fall of her chest, his lids growing heavy.

"How'd the cook get past the force field?" she asked. "I thought it was impenetrable."

"It is." In theory, the boundary could *never* be breached, protecting her against the legions of immortals who would give anything to kill or capture her—just to punish or coerce Lothaire.

If they could even find this place.

But Lothaire wouldn't take any chances. In his long life, he'd found that whenever one described something in the Lore as *always* or *never* happening, fate *usually* proved him wrong. "I can open it at will, of course."

When she chose the seat to the right of the end, he snapped, "Ah-ah. Not that one. You do *not* sit there." He'd had no control over Stefanovich's mortal whore all those years ago, but now, in his own home, he would make the rules for this human.

"Okay, okay." She moved the place setting one spot, then sat.

"Proceed."

With a glare, she unfolded her napkin and placed it on her lap, then spooned portions onto her plate. As she began her meal, taking dainty bites of various dishes, he noted that her table manners weren't as crude as he'd expected.

She chose that moment to lift a forkful of foie gras, letting it plop back to its plate. "What is this?"

"It's not the provincial fare you're accustomed to, but you'll make do."

"I'm full."

Her meal was barely touched. "Eat. More."

When she began nibbling the garnish, he said, "That's parsley."

"Only thing I recognize."

"Eat more of *everything else.*"

After a pause that would have gotten others gutted, she cut into a succulent lobster tail, took a hesitant bite, then furtively spat it into her napkin.

Two things struck him. She'd never had lobster; the foolish chit didn't like lobster. Even he remembered the taste of it.

The salmon fared no better. Soon there'd be more food in her napkin than in her stomach.

"The meal smells delicious, or at least it would to a human," he said. "Especially one who could *eat a horse.* Do you challenge me yet again?"

"I was born and raised on a *mountain.* Then I went to prison. I've never eaten food like this. Fancy *sea*food like this. If you wanted me to eat fish, it should've come out of a Long John Silver's bag."

Ah, just so. "Then eat the bread."

She began buttering a flaky roll. "Saroya really wants me to put on weight?" When he nodded, she said, "And you're on board?"

He thought her lovely now, nearly irresistible, but he had no marked preference. More flesh meant more of what he already liked. And Saroya would be the one inhabiting the body for eternity. "If my Bride wants it, then I'm in accord."

"Alrighty, but don't say I didn't warn you, 'cause too much bread and my ass'll get huge." She took a bite.

"Noted."

"You talk funny. Is your accent European?"

He rolled his eyes. "It's *Russian*—"

"Wait! You said *bride*?" Elizabeth sputtered. "You *married* her?"

⬥

The vampire exhaled impatiently, sitting at the head of the table. "Marriage is unnecessary to my kind. Our bond is much stronger."

"Than what?"

"A Bride is a vampire's mate, the female meant only for him. Saroya is mine."

Ellie processed this information—*keep an open mind*—then asked, "How do you know she is?"

He tilted his head in that appraising way, as if considering the pros and cons of answering her. "She blooded me." At her questioning look, he said, "Each adult male vampire walks as the living dead until he finds his mate and she bloods him, brings him back to life. Saroya made my heart beat again, made my lungs take breath." In a husky tone, he added, "Among other things."

"How do you know it's not me who's . . . *blooded* you?"

A muscle ticked in his jaw. "Because fate would not slight me so unspeakably. I'd seek a noon-day sun if I were paired with one such as you."

"Such as me," she repeated blandly. She'd been mocked too often over her lifetime to take offense. Her skin was as thick as armor.

"Yes, you. An ignorant, mortal Kmart checkout girl." He took the sharpest knife from his place setting, absently turning it between his left thumb and forefinger.

"Kmart? I should've been so lucky. Those jobs were hard to come by. I worked at my uncle's outfitter shop."

"Then you're even worse. You're an outfitter checkout girl with *aspirations* for Kmart."

"Still better than a demon."

"Saroya's *not* a demon," he grated. "I wouldn't have one of them either."

"Oh, that's right, she's a *goddess*. And you're a vampire. I suppose pookas are real, too. And shapeshifters?" Then her eyes widened. "Is Mothman real?"

In the Virginias, everyone had heard of that demonic winged being, with its red orbs for eyes. There continued to be sketchy sightings of it flying in the gloom and coal dust.

The sheriff who'd taken Ellie down had joked to others that there *might* have been a Mothman sighting the night of her arrest, an amusing encounter atop isolated Peirce Mountain.

"Everything you've ever dreamed is real," Lothaire said. "Every creature thought to be myth. We call our world the Lore. And for the record, Mothman's a fuckwit."

Her lips parted at that. "How come your kind don't come out to humans?"

"We are punished when we needlessly reveal ourselves as immortals."

"So all these 'myths' are out secretly combing the streets?"

"And running governments, starring in films, infiltrating human monarchies. Your species is notoriously dim and unobservant compared to Loreans, so we roam freely over the earth, gods walking among your kind."

A horrific thought struck her. "If you drank my blood, will that make me a vampire too?" *Say no, say no, say no.*

He exhaled. "If only it were so simple."

"Oh, thank God!"

The vampire didn't like that at all. Tension thrummed off him. He pressed the tip of the knife he held against the pad of his right thumb, twirling until blood began to drip.

Silence reigned. "Lothaire?"

He didn't answer. *Drip, drip* . . .

She fidgeted with her napkin. The unfamiliar quiet ratcheted up her nervousness.

Prison had been a continual assault on the ears. During the day, inmates banged on the bars, guards stomping up and down steel steps. It sounded like a messy utensil drawer opened and slammed shut repeatedly.

At night, eerie moans of both pleasure and pain echoed down the ward. Screams rang out. The serial killer across the corridor from her had loved to hiss at her in the dark. . . .

Finally Lothaire grated, "I've had mortals *beg* me to change them. Most humans would give anything to become immortal. It's considered a priceless gift."

She gazed anywhere but at his new injury. "I would never want that."

"Never to sicken, never to grow old?"

Ellie had an innate talent for empathy, for putting herself in others' shoes. Now she imagined what it'd be like to live for thousands of years, as Lothaire apparently had.

How could he savor each day of his life when the supply of them was unlimited? How could he ever experience wonder or excitement? "All I can think is that it'd be wearying."

Had a shadow passed over his expression?

"So if I'm not already changed into a vampire," Ellie said, "and it's not so simple to do, how will you and Saroya get together?"

"I seek a ring. It has the power to transform her into a vampire."

"Made a vampire? In *my* body? If she's a goddess, why's she been digging into *me* like a tick?"

He merely stared at her with those creepy eyes, twirling that knife as his blood began to pool on the surface of the table.

Though he terrified her, Ellie pressed on. "Why would she be inside of *me*, the checkout girl? Why should I believe she's . . . divine?"

"Understand me, girl. I don't lie. Ever. She was cursed to a human form."

"Who cursed her? Why put her in *me*?"

Seeing he had no intention of answering her, she said, "Look, you guys are getting my body out of this deal. I'm getting nothing. You said you liked a good bargain? You should recognize that this isn't exactly a fair exchange. Would it kill you to tell me *why* she needs my body?"

His eyes got a faraway look and deepened in color, telling her his mind was drifting. *Dissociation?*

She'd seen the same look earlier today as he'd paced. It occurred to her then that this vampire was not just evil.

The Enemy of Old might be clinically insane.

❦

"Another goddess cursed her to a mortal's form," Lothaire finally said, struggling to rein back the madness. *Focus.* "I do not know why *you* were chosen."

"Which goddess?"

Saroya had a twin, Lamia. Each sister derived her strength from life— Lamia from creating it and safeguarding it, Saroya from harvesting it and consuming souls.

When Saroya had made a bid for more power, killing indiscriminately and upsetting the balance, Lamia had joined forces with other gods and cursed Saroya to experience death over and over as a human. "The curse of mortality," he muttered. "Could there be anything worse?" He glanced down, surprised to find himself boring a knife tip into his own thumb.

"Lothaire, *why* was she cursed?" Elizabeth continued heedlessly.

He licked his dripping new wound. "Because she is just like me." A being insatiable for power. "She saw a play for more, and she took it."

"I don't understand."

"*Do pizdy.* Don't fucking care." He was getting sick of others acting as if he'd just uttered nonsense. He killed most who cast him that sharp questioning look.

But he couldn't harm the human before him, the female with her steady gray eyes taking his measure. He stared into them for long moments, surprised to find himself feeling more grounded.

"How could a girl from the backwoods ever get caught up in something so . . . unlikely?"

Without breaking eye contact, he leaned back in his chair. "I asked myself that continually from the time I first saw you. After all, in the beginning, I had no idea you were anything more than a mere human, had no idea how *I* could possibly be connected to you."

Why was he conversing so readily with her? Perhaps because he knew she would take his secrets to the grave? And soon?

For whatever reason, the words seemed pulled from him.

"Imagine my abject disappointment in you, female. Lothaire the Enemy of Old—the most feared vampire alive, the son of one king and grandson of another—paired with a mortal? Much less a mortal of no distinction. I'm given to understand that your people are worse than peasants."

Instead of indignation, curiosity lit her face. "Wait. I came first? You didn't find me because of her? Hey, are you saying you're a prince?"

"Yes, *peasants*," he repeated slowly. "The lowliest of the low among humans." Then he enunciated, "Exceedingly backward and vulgar *hillbillies*."

"Been called worse, mister." At his raised brows, she exhaled impatiently. "Bootlegger, moonshiner, Elly May Clampett, mountain mama, redneck, backwoods Bessie, hick, trailer trash, yokel, and, more recently, death-row con."

"No references to mining? I'm disappointed."

Sadness flashed in her expressive eyes. "My father died in a mine collapse. Ever since then, none of my kin will work underground."

"Naturally the big bad coal company was at fault?"

"I'm sure there are nice, safe coal companies out there; Va-Co isn't one of them. Mining's over for us."

"And so you remain appallingly poor."

"S'pose so. The bottom line is that insults only hurt when they come from someone I respect."

"Then no one's taught you to respect your betters?"

"You think you're better than me because you're a *prince*?" Had she sounded disbelieving?

"I'm a displaced *king* of two vampire factions. Now I work to reclaim my thrones." *Why am I telling her this?* He didn't give a damn if she respected him. "As for the other, I think I'm better than you because you are demonstrably my inferior in every way. Intelligence, wealth, looks, bloodline, should I continue?"

She waved that away. "How'd you find me? You're obviously rich—oh, and *royalty*—why would you be in one of the poorest areas in America?"

He parted his lips to tell her to shut hers, but she dutifully took another bite of salmon, actually swallowing it. "My Bride's arrival had been foretold. An oracle predicted where and when she would be. But not *what*." The same oracle who assisted him now, a fey he called Hag.

He glanced at Elizabeth's plate. She took another bite.

"I found you when you were fourteen, but you didn't trigger my blooding." He'd assumed that she was too young. "I decided then that I'd never return, would walk as the dead before being forever tied to such a base creature as you." No matter that she'd promised to be physically lovely.

"Then why did you return?"

"Pure curiosity." It might have been pure, but it had *plagued* him, and he'd returned to her thrice more.

When she was fifteen, a budding woman, he'd found her swimming one night with a boy, eagerly exploring kissing with him. At seventeen, she'd been on the verge of stunning, with her sun-kissed skin, wide clear eyes, and striking features, yet still too lowly to tempt him.

Until a year later . . . "Just when I vowed to spurn you forever, I found you in the woods at a makeshift altar, surrounded by bodies."

Elizabeth's expression grew stark. "Not *me*. It was Saroya."

"Yes, Saroya," he breathed. Covered in gore from head to toe, bold and lethal, she'd blooded him at once.

Now he stared past Elizabeth, relishing the memory of that night. . . .

Between unpracticed breaths, he demanded, "Who are you?" He knew that the mortal's consciousness had disappeared, sensed the absence of Elizabeth.

Before him was another entity.

"I am Saroya, vampire." Her very accent had changed. "Your goddess, trapped in mortality."

All vampires knew that Saroya had been tricked from her lofty plane, cursed by her sister to live within random humans, one after another, repeatedly experiencing her own death through them.

If Lothaire had felt any doubt about her identity, she'd erased it by speaking to him in Russian, her accent regal. There was no way for an ignorant eighteen-year-old peasant to know his tongue.

And besides, Lothaire deserved *a goddess. He knew fate wouldn't have paired him with lowly Elizabeth Peirce!*

For millennia he'd sought to rule the Vampire Horde. How could they deny his claim with Saroya, the protectress of vampires, as his queen?

"Have I blooded you?" she asked with silky menace.

"Yes. I'm Lothaire, your male—"

"I have no male and accept no master," she snapped. "I am a goddess!"

"That's a shame," he replied smoothly, ignoring his new heartbeats and the unbearable stiffening of his shaft, denying the frenzy to claim her, to sink his fangs deep into her flesh. "Because had you been mine, I would have found a way to extinguish that human's soul, then make your body immortal."

"Lothaire?" She narrowed her eyes. "An ancient one with great power, descended from two royal lines. Even I have heard of you."

"And soon I intend to seize my kingdoms. I will have my immortal queen by my side."

She stepped closer. "You could make me undying in this body?"

"In time, I would find a way. Nothing could stop me."

"Yet you would desire to mate with me now? To complete the blooding."

Each vampire had to experience his first release while touching his Bride's body. Most vampires simply mated their females, but Lothaire knew he couldn't. Tracing within inches of her, he cupped her nape with a shaking hand. *"The only thing greater than my need is my strength. Your mortal form is too fragile for me to claim. But I must finish this."*

"Then I will not yield this body until you destroy Elizabeth's soul and make me whole. For now, you may take your physical release in some way. . . ."

"Lothaire?" Elizabeth interrupted his thoughts.

Reminded of that interlude with Saroya, he cast the girl a look of renewed hatred. That night he and the goddess had talked till dawn, discussing their aims. Again and again, he'd discovered how well she fit him.

Saroya was his match in all ways—*a queen even Ivana would bow down to.*

Blyad'! How could his Bride expect him to use Elizabeth? Maybe Saroya didn't see the dichotomy between the two females, but it was plain to Lothaire.

It would be like taking an entirely different woman.

Once Saroya understood their circumstances better, she would not be so keen for Lothaire to enjoy another. He imagined how he'd feel if the situation were reversed.

Homicidal.

Though he'd scorned Elizabeth in her teens, even he had been misguidedly protective of her. When he'd seen her kissing that male, Lothaire had tossed his truck into a valley. The male had run out of the water to investigate, so Lothaire had dropped him down as well. . . .

Maybe Saroya feels no jealousy because she feels nothing for you, a part of his mind whispered.

Yes, Lothaire prided himself on predicting others' actions; did he truly anticipate Saroya rising for him tomorrow night?

Though he could hardly believe it, the goddess remained unconvinced of *his* charms. An absurdity, he knew, but who could fathom the minds of females?

Lothaire resolved to spoil her further and demonstrate to her his prowess in bed—to ensure she needed him for other things.

He exhaled. It'd been so long since he'd had sex that he might not have *retained* any prowess. He smirked, thinking, *Maybe I should* practice *on Elizabeth.*

A sudden jolt of lust took him like a punch, wiping away his smirk. He sliced his gaze to her. Studying gray eyes met his.

The idea was sound.

Or maybe I'm grasping at straws, rationalizing why I want to touch a human.

No, his Bride's shared body was confusing his suffering mind. That was the only reason he'd desire her.

Unless I'm more like my father than I care to admit?

11

I have work to do," the vampire said as he traced Ellie back to her bedroom, leaving her wobbling on her feet. Would she ever get used to teleporting? "You'll stay in here until I return for you."

"Work? Getting back your thrones?"

"Do you always ask so many questions?"

"Do you always answer so few of them?" she countered, earning another scowl. "Just tell me this. If Saroya is so all-fired important to you, then why'd you leave her in prison?"

"I was assured you'd be physically safe there."

"And mentally?"

"I couldn't care less. I'm only concerned with your body."

Typical male. "What did I need to be protected from?"

"I'm the Enemy of Old. There are many who would harm Saroya to strike back at me."

"Harm her. In *my* body."

He grasped her jaw, his skin surprisingly warm. "As I've told you—you're protected here, girl. The only one you need fear is me."

Which meant this was the last place she needed to be. Ellie could pick a lock, but what about busting out of an invisible jail? If there were mystical locks, were there mystical picks? "What about my belongings? Tooth-brush, underwear, et cetera?"

"Anything you need is in the bathroom. Any clothing"—he opened a door in the hallway—"is in here." He'd revealed a closet as big as her old trailer.

Her thoughts blanked when she entered. Dresses, coats, purses, slacks—everywhere. There must be several dozen pairs of shoes, even more sweaters and blouses.

Eyes wide, she spun in place. "These are the finest clothes I've ever seen!"

Lothaire leaned his shoulder against the doorway. "They would be. Ap-palachian couture is reputedly lacking."

She knew he was pointedly insulting her but chose to act as if he were jesting. She'd fought toe-to-toe with him and lost. Now she'd try another tack.

Mama had always said, "You get more with honey than you do with vinegar. And when you run out of both, you reach for the buckshot."

Ellie had concluded she might've reached for the buckshot pretty early.

Now she said, "*Appalachian* and *couture*? Put a quarter in the oxymoron jar." She meandered toward the back, browsing rack after rack.

At home, she'd had few clothes—a couple pairs of worn jeans, some cutoffs for summer, a few T-shirts, guide gear. Then in prison, four alter-nating uniforms.

This selection was overwhelming. "Did you get all this for Saroya?"

He seemed more relaxed than he'd been in the dining room, maybe gazing at her with a bit less hostility. "I did."

Ellie tried to imagine the reaction of a goddess. "She must've gone nuts."

"She desired every last garment and bauble," he said, his Russian ac-cent thick.

"And you just bought all of it for her?" Ellie snapped her fingers. "Just like that?"

"Of course. She's my woman."

"She must love you very much."

He said nothing, just crossed his muscular arms over his chest.

"Does she?"

"I've told you, she's my fated Bride."

If he'd been telling the truth about never telling lies—which might be a lie?—then Ellie might view his answer as a deflection. "Do you love Saroya?"

"When mortals ask me incessant questions, I customarily snatch out their tongues and watch them bleed to death."

Instead of being horrified, she thought, *Definite deflection! Trouble in paradise?*

Making her tone casual, she said, "Good to know about the tongues." Her red-tipped fingers trailed lovingly over the buttery leather of a coat. "Can I try this on?"

When he shrugged, she slipped into the coat, eyes going heavy-lidded as she hugged it close to her. "Lothaire, I couldn't have even *imagined* things like this."

"Again, I will accept only the best."

Like a goddess for a Bride, instead of a mortal? A deity, instead of a peasant girl he'd found so lacking that he'd watched her for years, disappointed by fate's choice for him?

And all the while she'd never known that a vampire had kept her in his sights.

Seeming to make a decision, he strode to a polished dresser against the back wall. After pulling open a shallow drawer, he returned to his spot in the doorway without a word.

"What's in there?" Jewels. Huge. Shiny. "Oh—my—God." She gasped. "Can't catch my breath."

At once he traced beside her, grasping her upper arm, this time more gently.

"Obliged, Lothaire. The glittering about blinded me." And she couldn't help but think that just one of those stones would probably float her entire family for years. *Might keep the coal company off their asses. . . .*

"You react like this, even though you'll never own any of it?"

In a defensive tone, she said, "They're still pretty. I'm still happy to have *seen* them." She pulled against his hold, but he turned her to him.

She stared up at him, wondering what it would be like to have a man buy her things like this. *To have him want me so badly, he'd kill for me.*

His brows drew together. She noticed they were darker than his hair, bold slashes across a chiseled face with skin as smooth and pale as marble.

As if unable to help himself, he threaded his fingers through her hair.

Normally, she loved to be petted like this, could be made docile as a kitten. But now a murderer was touching her. He let the strands sift through his splayed fingers, his gaze following the movement.

Stroking, stroking . . .

Surprisingly, some of her tension began to ease—

He dropped his hand. "I'll leave you alone in your suite for some time. You will be *alone*," he grated in an insistent tone. As if she were arguing that point with him.

He turned toward a side doorway to a chamber connected to hers. *His?* Well, how cozy.

"There is no escape, no telephone. Consider this room your new cell."

She followed him. "Wait, what am I supposed to do?"

"Go to bed at dawn. Accustom your body to sleeping during the day."

"And tomorrow? What then? You said I might have a month left to live. What do you expect me to do for that time?"

"Put on weight." He slammed the door in her face.

Ellie glared at the panels of the solid door, her fists balling. "You asshole!" She yanked on the door handle. Locked!

She swept her gaze around the room. *My new cell?* No matter how open and airy it was, she remained trapped. She hated being confined!

Hurrying through the French doors to her balcony, she sucked in deep breaths of night air.

New York City lay before her, all bright lights and energy. How badly she wished to be down there! She imagined all the places to explore, all the new and interesting people she could meet.

But she'd never get the chance. Because there were mystical barriers. And goddesses and arrogant blood-drinkers.

She strode back inside, snatched up her dresser stool, and chucked it at the boundary. The stool bounced directly back inside, bounding toward her. She started laughing hysterically until it connected with her shin. That was going to leave a mark.

Ha-ha, Saroya. Black-and-blue's your color. She was just about to run her face into the doorknob when she remembered she wasn't to harm herself, else risk her family.

So she marched into the bathroom. Seeing herself in all this makeup with the Elvira-in-heat dress was like looking *at* Saroya. For the first time, Ellie was seeing what the goddess would prefer to look like.

She turned on the hot water to wash her face. "I hate you more than hell, Saroya."

A psychologist could have a field day with this. Staring into the mirror with hate? Daily affirmations turned to daily accusations?

Damn it, I should be dead *right now!* But the bitch had thwarted her yet again. "You may have won this battle, Saroya, but I'll win the war. I'll destroy you, somehow." Even as she said these bold words, Ellie wrestled with regret over her plight.

Part of her still wished for another chance, for the possibility to live. Why did *she* have to make this sacrifice? Why had it fallen to her?

But she'd long resigned herself to her fate.

Gathering water in her hands, she said, "Your big finish is rolling in like a thunderstorm. No stopping it." She scrubbed her face harder than she ever had, ridding herself of Saroya's war paint.

Another gander into the mirror. *I'm back,* she thought, even though the goddess's presence lurked within, eating away at her like a cancer.

After drying her tender skin, Ellie returned to the closet. Combing through the choices, she threw on a pair of jeans and a simple navy blouse. Feeling more like *Ellie*, she left her feet bare.

Unable to stop herself, she sneaked another peek at those jewels. She recalled the way Lothaire had shown them to her. Without a word, without bragging.

Why had he cared if Ellie saw them? Had he anticipated her floored reaction? Figured she'd go crazy like Saroya?

Then she frowned. Lothaire had never said anything to indicate that he and Saroya liked each other, much less loved each other. He'd talked only of fate and *bloodings*.

Questions about him surfaced endlessly. Did he love the goddess? Why hadn't he bedded his *Bride*? Were all vampires as ruthless as he was?

She wished she could analyze Lothaire at her leisure, maybe use her degree to benefit her.

One of the reasons she'd studied psychology was that she'd always found it easy to empathize with others. A handy tool for a counselor.

But psychology was the science of *human* behavior. He was *inhuman*. . . .

She would just have to work harder to discover what made Lothaire tick, using any means necessary.

When she exited the closet, she remembered that earlier they'd *walked* out of the main doorway from her suite. They'd *traced* back inside. Unlike the door adjoining Lothaire's room, it would be unlocked.

Wouldn't even have to pick it.

Maybe when he left, she'd investigate this place. Did she dare disobey him? He'd probably never even know she'd sneaked out.

With that aim in mind, she knelt at the doorway crack to his bedroom, listening for him.

She heard the rustle of sheets, a stifled curse. He'd gone *to bed*? After telling her he had work to do? And wasn't this kind of his workday?

Again she thought, *Typical male.*

Wait. Had he just . . . groaned?

I'm never going to sleep with this erection.

Though Lothaire was exhausted, it throbbed for relief, impossible to ignore. He couldn't turn on his front without grinding his shaft into the mattress, couldn't turn on his back without his hands descending to masturbate his length.

But he'd be damned if he spilled alone when he was in possession of his Bride.

His eyes narrowed when the mortal knelt at their shared doorway. *Finished shrieking and throwing things, Elizabeth?* He could hear her light breaths panting at the crack under the door.

She spied on *him*? Lothaire was a master at spying, enjoyed few things more.

Over his long lifetime, he'd watched countless beings having sex, was an unabashed voyeur. And he'd noted that every time a couple neared release, they reached a point of no return when all sense and inhibitions were lost, a point past which nothing could pull them apart.

Lothaire himself had never been unaware of what he was doing, nor unable to stop himself.

Now he feared that if he neared climax tonight, he'd cross a line, tossing Elizabeth into his bed. He'd strip her naked and bury his cock and fangs so deep in her, he wouldn't know where she ended and he began. . . .

No. I will not *lower myself to a mortal.*

Lothaire could wait for Saroya to rise tomorrow night. He *would* wait, he swore to himself, even as his mind whispered, *She's not going to.*

But how to sleep? He switched on the metronome beside his bed. *Tick . . . tick . . . tick . . .* Soothing, but not nearly enough to combat the persistent ache in his balls.

Maybe he should drug himself as his former jailer customarily did— Declan Chase, an Irish soldier of the Order, known as the Blademan.

Lothaire sat up, clasping his forehead. Had his escape from the Order's island prison been only yesterday? It felt like weeks had passed.

Less than twenty-four hours ago, Chase had been mortally wounded. Lothaire had given the Blademan his blood in exchange for Lothaire's own freedom—anything to reach Saroya before the execution.

Yet another bargain. Attempt to turn Chase into a vampire; save Saroya.

Centuries had passed since Lothaire had last made a vampire. *Perhaps I'm a sire once more?* But the blood was no guarantee. Did Chase even live yet?

My enemy. And potentially my spawn. He frowned, unsure how he felt about that. Especially since Chase had tortured Lothaire during his imprisonment.

Though the Blademan had himself been brutally tortured as a lad—and therefore knew what the hell he was about—Lothaire had merely laughed at the pain. Even when his skin was burned to ash.

Chase hadn't understood; no misery could compare to hiding in the snow while listening as one's mother was savagely raped and burned alive. No cruelty could compare to what Stefanovich had done to Lothaire years later.

The earth grinding over me, roots threading my body.

Block that memory out! Or stare down into the abyss. . . .

No matter what happened between Lothaire and Chase, they were connected now, had exchanged blood between them. Which meant that Lothaire could reach into Chase's mind with his own, could investigate his memories.

Perhaps I don't need to sleep. He only had to get close enough to Chase.

The Blademan's woman was a Valkyrie. She would have taken him back to Val Hall, the Louisiana estate where her coven resided—with its never-ending fog, lightning flashes, and ungodly Valkyrie shrieks.

A place Lothaire knew well. He was one of only a handful of vampires who'd seen the inside and still lived.

He could go there now, seeking Chase.

Yet if Lothaire had these plans, then others might as well. Immortals from all over the Lore would want a piece of Declan Chase, the bogeyman who'd crept through the night, abducting scores of them and their loved ones for ghastly experiments.

But I get him first.

Especially since Lothaire would get *to* him first. . . .

12

"Are you an extra sentry, then?" Lothaire asked Thaddeus Brayden, one of his fellow prison escapees. The young man had been pacing outside the Valkyries' antebellum mansion, marching in and out of the fog banks stirring from the nearby bayou.

Thaddeus twisted around, his fierce expression relaxing instantly—far from Lothaire's customary reception. "Guess I am, Mr. Lothaire! We're kind of under siege," he said with a marked Texas drawl. He wore faded jeans, a T-shirt, and cowboy boots, looking ridiculously human.

Though Thaddeus was new to the Lore, having only discovered he wasn't mortal a month ago, the boy could be useful tonight.

"How'd you get through Val Hall's boundary?" He gazed past Lothaire. "When no one else can?"

Lothaire smirked over his shoulder at the immortal lynch mob congregating at the front gates, kept from their vengeance by a Wiccan's enclosure spell. It was similar—but inferior—to his own druidic barrier. *Easy for me to breach.*

As predicted, all those Loreans wanted revenge on Chase. What they didn't realize was that the Blademan had been only the muscle behind the Order, had been brainwashed from the time he was a lad by the true leader—Commander Webb.

Webb, the mortal who'd taken Lothaire's ring off the prison island, had a secret hideout.

Chase would know where it was.

Lothaire wished all the best to the bloodthirsty mob, but knew they'd never get past the boundary—much less the Valkyries' second line of defense. The wraiths.

Garbed in tattered red robes, those ghostly echoes of deceased female warriors swarmed the mansion in a whirlwind, a skeletal face peeking out occasionally.

The Valkyries had hired the Ancient Scourge—with their supposedly impenetrable guard—to protect the manor after a recent vampire incursion.

Hadn't Lothaire been a part of that? *Ah, yes. That was I.*

"I've told you, Thaddeus, I have powers that others cannot begin to fathom. And you can too, *paren'*. Merely drink from choice prey."

Thaddeus laughed, though Lothaire was in earnest. Ages ago, he'd consumed a sorcerer who knew how to neutralize Wiccan spells. Lothaire still remembered the taste of his blood, still remembered the unlikely ally who'd helped him seize it. . . .

Thaddeus rushed forward, hand outstretched. "In any case, it's good to see you."

Lothaire gave his hand a withering glare until the boy dropped it with a grin. No matter how unpleasant he was to the young immortal, Thaddeus still thought the best of him.

In their first encounter, Lothaire had been starving from his captivity and singled Thaddeus out to drink. *Young, not so many memories, preferred.* The boy lived only because he was part vampire.

"I guess you're here to check on Chase, huh? I could ask the Valks if they'll let you past the wraiths, but"—he shuffled his snakeskin boots, discomfited—"they don't seem to care for you much."

"I do not *ask* for anything—I *take* it. If I wanted in badly enough, even the wraiths couldn't stop me." *Had I packed appropriately . . .*

But he didn't need to be inside, just nearby Chase.

Thaddeus raised his brows at that but knew better than to disbelieve. Lothaire's feats on the island had mind-boggled the lad. "Chase is hanging in there—barely—but still unconscious."

The man had been gutted with a sword. "To be expected, Thaddeus."

"My friends call me Thad."

The Enemy of Old conversing with a teenage football-playing Eagle Scout named *Thad*? A vampire/phantom halfling named Thaddeus was more palatable.

In any case . . . "We are not friends," Lothaire said, then frowned. The words had made his throat burn, almost as if they were a lie.

How could that be? Thaddeus was everything he wasn't: a good and decent virgin devoted to his loved ones and friends. Other than the fact that he and Thaddeus were both considered remarkably attractive—Lothaire much more so, of course—they couldn't be more dissimilar.

"I gotta tell you, Regin's still really pee-ohed at you for screwing all of us over." He kicked a stone in the path.

Regin the Radiant was a warmongering Valkyrie. Along with Lothaire, Thaddeus, and eventually Chase himself, she'd been part of a group of six allying solely to escape the island, a not-so-merry band. Lothaire had saved their lives in exchange for vows from Chase.

If the Blademan lives, he'll go into my account book.

The six had been on the run together for a week, had fought mutual enemies side by side. Until Lothaire had cut a deal with their adversaries—whom he'd ultimately dicked over as well.

"I saw a play open and took it." In a thoughtful tone, Lothaire said, "And yet, Regin forgave Chase for all *his* sins against her?"

Before Chase had remembered that he'd loved her in a past life, the Blademan had followed Webb's orders and tortured Regin, had looked her in the eyes and released an excruciating pain poison into the Valkyrie's body.

Later he'd been wracked with guilt.

"Regin knew DC wasn't evil, not deep down," Thaddeus said. "She's *certain* you are."

Sanctimonious Valkyrie. Regin had probably killed thousands of Loreans over her long life. Yet she was admired for it. Lothaire? Reviled.

"I hope your blood does the trick for DC," Thaddeus said. "If you saved his life, then they'd have to forgive you, right?"

"You are so naïve, it physically aggrieves me." Besides, not every man survived the transformation.

Thaddeus nodded gravely. "Been hearing a lot about you, Mr. Lothaire. None of it good. I take up for you all the time, but it seems like half of these Lore folks have this really bad impression of you."

"For accuracy's sake, I'd put that percentage closer to ninety. And their impressions are accurate." Lothaire had happily wronged most of them in reprehensible ways. "Taking up for me only makes you appear pitiably uninformed or willfully obtuse . . ." He trailed off, his attention already wandering toward the house. *Keen to get back to my Bride.*

The thought brought him up short. Why did Lothaire feel so connected to her now? Years before, he'd easily parted from her. Now, spending mere moments without her was affecting him. *Blyad'!*

"Regin also said your red eyes mean you're going crazy."

"Surely she phrased it more colorfully than that?" Regin was a loudmouthed attention whore who thought herself amusing.

Thaddeus ran his hand over the back of his neck. "She said, 'Look at me, I'm Lothaire, I am the walrus, koo-koo-ka-choo.' Or something like that. She told me you were gonna be even loopier than Nïx. Is that true?"

Nïx the Ever-Knowing, the Valkyrie oracle. His nemesis for millennia, she'd thwarted more vampire schemes than all the other factions' soothsayers combined.

"Crazier than Nïx? Impossible." She was much worse off than Lothaire. He wondered if she'd foreseen Saroya. The only good thing about Nïx? She was so maddened that she often forgot her visions.

But what if she had remembered? What if Nïx conspired against him even now? *White queen moving against black king on the chessboard . . .*

Thaddeus muttered, "Your eyes are changing by the second. Worse than I've ever seen them."

Uneasy leaving my Bride alone. Mercenaries and assassins from all factions hunted him constantly. Whenever powerful Loreans owed him blood debts, they usually opted to send their best warriors for Lothaire's head. "Occupational hazard. But the benefits are fantastic."

"What was that, Mr. Lothaire?"

Yet now they would target Lothaire's Bride. He reminded himself that technically Saroya couldn't be killed.

But I want her in Elizabeth's comely form. Thinking about her gray eyes, sexpot lips, and fantasy-worthy figure, he again determined it *crucial* to secure her body for Saroya.

Not to mention her delectable blood. *She tastes of wine and honey*—just as his father had said. Lothaire's fangs sharpened even now.

"What about wine and honey?" Thaddeus asked. "You're not making sense."

I spoke aloud? As if to dislodge the memories, Lothaire shook his head hard, inadvertently stepping back into the line of the wraiths.

"Watch out!" Thaddeus cried.

Before Lothaire could trace out of their path, they'd clawed at his face, leaving bloody furrows.

"Are you all right, Mr. Lothaire?"

Pain. Grasp at a thread of lucidity. *Show no weakness, demonstrate no madness.*

When blood dripped to his lip, he darted his tongue for a taste. He detected a top note of Elizabeth's blood mixed into his own, and it calmed him.

The wraiths slowed, and their leader gazed at him with a spectral face.

"I alone know how to destroy you," Lothaire grated. "Touch me again, Scourge, and I will demonstrate."

She shrieked; Lothaire smirked. "I knew you when you were pretty."

Her face flashed to her former visage, that of a beautiful Macedonian warrioress.

In a contemplative tone, Lothaire asked, "Didn't I *do* you when you were pretty?"

Another furious shriek, then she was swept away in the tide of their tempest.

Lothaire shrugged. "Guess I did." Onward to Chase.

Thaddeus persistently followed. "What do you want with DC?"

"I'm going to reach inside his mind and read his thoughts."

"How?"

Imploring the sky for patience, Lothaire bit out, "I drank blood from him, and then I later gifted him with my own. We've a bridge between us forever."

"So that's what you meant when you warned Regin about unbreakable ties."

Partially.

Thaddeus planted himself in front of Lothaire. "Why should I let you mind-meld or whatever with DC?"

Lothaire gave a bitter laugh. "What can you do to stop me? Now step aside." He almost added, "Or I'll kill your beloved adoptive mother and grandmother for your insolence," but the *rána* arose in his throat.

Which meant that would be a lie. *Why would I not murder two insignificant humans?* Why would he feel even a scrap of allegiance to Thaddeus?

Because there was one instance with the boy that affected me. A demonstration of loyalty . . .

Thaddeus put his shoulders back. "I could raise the alarm."

And I could snatch your throat out before you took a breath to yell. But because of their past interactions, Lothaire would spare him this eve. "I plan to use Chase's memories to find Commander Webb—the one who ordered our abductions and those tedious experiments. The one who could still hurt *your* family."

The one who holds the key to my entire future, in the shape of a ring.

The young man's fangs lengthened. "I want to hunt him too."

"Why would you possibly think I need help carrying out a blood vendetta?"

Don't I? Lothaire had yet to complete his age-old ones. He recalled

Olya, that human female in Helvita, recalled how badly he'd wanted to murder her. She'd been drained by Stefanovich long before Lothaire could get to her.

He remembered the mortals brutalizing his mother. *"Avenge me!"* she'd screamed.

Only now was Lothaire on the cusp of retribution. *To find Serghei at last . . .*

"Don't care if you need it, Mr. Lothaire. I'm hankering for vengeance too. Besides, we are friends. And friends watch each other's backs. Just like you and me did on the island."

In the heat of the escape, Lothaire might have saved the boy a few times, without receiving anything in return from Thaddeus, but only because it served Lothaire's own ends.

He'd also endangered Thaddeus's life repeatedly.

Lothaire cut off further arguments with a curt: "We'll discuss this later." To make the statement true, Lothaire envisioned the extent of their "discussion."

Thaddeus would ask, "Can I go with you?"

Lothaire would reply, "No. Now, fuck off."

"I'm gonna hold you to that, Mr. Lothaire. Now what exactly are you looking for with your mind-meld thing?"

Below the window of Chase's room and out of the way of the wraiths, Lothaire answered, "He must have visited Webb's hideout. If I can access that memory, I can trace directly to it, as if I'd been there myself."

"Then access it, and let's go kick ass!"

"Step one is you shutting up."

Thaddeus nodded eagerly. "Right on."

Lothaire steadied his breathing, calming his heart as he listened for Chase's own heartbeat. Once it began to grow loud in his ears, like a repetitive quake, Lothaire briefly closed his eyes—but he still could see. Straight into Chase's afflicted mind.

Lothaire found . . . blackness there. Blankness.

No thoughts, no dreams. *Is he in the grip of death?*

Gods, to have his own mind at rest like this? Might be worth dying. He delved deeper, but all was quiet.

There'd be no thoughts of Webb anytime soon, and Lothaire couldn't scratch at all the scars in Chase's mind to search for a specific memory. He might as well try to navigate his own. At least he knew where the black holes were, the quicksand traps and points of no return.

He released his hold on Chase, exhaling with frustration. Nothing to show for his trespass, no new information.

His claws bit into his palms. *Chto za huy! Must have that ring!* Kept from him though it was *his.*

Thaddeus asked, "Did you find Webb? Anything to help our mission?"

"*Our* mission? I didn't see anything to help *my* aims! You say nothing of this—of anything concerning me—to anyone."

"Why should I keep secrets from my other friends? Do you mean any of them harm?"

Lothaire didn't have *time* to do any of them ill. "I don't. Not *yet,*" he added to prevent the *rána.*

After a hesitation, Thaddeus said, "Okay, I'll keep it close to the vest. But I need to know how I can get in touch with you. What's your number?"

Lothaire stared at him. "Number? Why do you want this?"

Thaddeus rolled his eyes. "One more time. Because—we're—*friends.* I plan to help you with Webb, and give you some backup against Dorada. They said she'll be coming for you."

She is. When last Lothaire had seen her—mummified, hideous to gaze upon—she'd been shrieking, "*RIIIIINNNNNGGGGG,*" as she hunted him through the Order's prison, her Wendigo lackeys prowling beside her.

He'd had quite a surprise waiting for them all. . . .

"Lothaire? Hellooo."

"*What?*"

"I said, I want to meet the missus."

Lothaire tensed, slowly craning his head around at the boy. "Missus?"

"They say you've got your Bride now."

"*They* meaning *Nïx.*" Lothaire bared his fangs, felt them drip on his tongue. Yes, he'd toyed with his enemies, threatening their families, mocking their frenzied reactions while he was ever cold and calculating.

No longer.

Unaware of Lothaire's rising impulse to do murder, Thaddeus continued, "There are a lot of folks around here talking about the bounty on your lady—"

Before Thaddeus could blink, Lothaire had his hand around the boy's throat, squeezing. . . . "What's the bounty? Who posted it?"

Foolish, Lothaire! Why hadn't he acted uncaring? Why reveal his crazed possessiveness of Saroya?

How smug I was in the past, confident I'd never care about anything enough to reveal a weakness.

Thaddeus bit out, "I don't know what it is . . . but they said it's priceless. Don't know who . . . posted it."

Priceless? "Someone set hunters on our trail? Then he's sent me meals to torment. *If* my deadly Bride doesn't get to them first." Lothaire released Thaddeus with a shove that sent him sprawling to the ground.

Between wheezes, the boy said, "I knew you had a lady, then! You made some comments. . . . That's why you would've done anything to get off the island." He was delighted by this, scrambling to his feet and dusting himself off as if nothing had happened. "That's the reason you screwed us all over. I knew you weren't as bad as Regin and Nïx and Cara and Emma and—"

"Enough!" The soldiers of the Vertas army—the supposed white hats in the Lore—acted holier-than-thou. Yet they would punish a female who'd never harmed any of them?

Hypocrites in league.

Have to turn her into an immortal as soon as possible. Saroya had to be able to defend herself, to trace in escape if necessary.

"Well, then, *what* is she?" the boy pressed. "Not a vampire, 'cause Regin told me there were no female ones left. Maybe she's a demoness or a witch?"

Can't think . . . can't think. Why this interest from Thaddeus? "Did they plant you here, to get information from me?"

"No, of course not!"

Even if Lothaire kept Saroya behind a boundary, nothing in the Lore was foolproof. Panic tightened his chest.

Return. Never leave her unguarded again. To Thaddeus he grated, "You forget you ever knew me, boy." Then he disappeared.

13

When Lothaire returned to the apartment, he found Elizabeth just setting out from her room.

Against his orders.

She'd removed all that makeup; though Lothaire was loath to admit it, he found it an improvement. She'd also changed into jeans that lovingly outlined her pert ass—a fact that offset the worst of his anger.

Going exploring, are we? When he imagined her little mortal brain struggling to process her new environment, he decided to shadow her, making himself invisible so he could study her reactions.

When she entered the first unlit bedroom and the lights came on automatically, she spun in a circle, demanding, "Who's there?" Then she stepped out of the room. The lights clicked off. "Oh."

In the living room, she pressed a button for the TV. When it rose from a console, she went wide-eyed.

The theater room elicited an exclamation: "Hoo!" Which he supposed was Hillbilly for "Excellent."

In the kitchen, she peeked into the refrigerator, grimacing at his pitchers of blood. As Lothaire dimly wondered what the mortal chef had thought of his stores earlier today, she sniffed one, then quickly returned it.

She investigated the cabinets, finding them all empty. After examining the appliances, she sang, *"Meet George Jetson."*

Whatever that meant.

In fact, her exploration consisted mostly of button pushing and jumping back in fear.

She might as well have been in a foreign land. She seemed alternately suspicious and dazzled.

But in the main foyer, she gazed up at the crystal chandelier for long moments, tilting her head in different directions, following the complex design with her gaze.

Lothaire could see the prisms of light reflected in her wide gray eyes. She had . . . *intelligent* eyes. Perhaps more was there than he'd allowed himself to see.

He stared at the delicate shape of her face in profile. From this angle, he could see her lips were a touch fuller in the middle, giving them that bow shape.

She was so fragile. Touching her would be like handling gossamer. Claiming her would be impossible. She had to be stronger.

The idea of himself in a blood rage, desperate to spend deep inside her . . .

He ran his hand over his face. If he took her in that state, he could rend her in two, could pulverize her bones.

She rubbed her nape under that fall of lustrous hair, then self-consciously tucked a lock behind her ear. Did the mortal actually sense him watching her?

Some humans possessed a kind of sixth sense. Few of them ever seemed to trust it.

A vampire is eyeing you like prey. Can you feel it, Elizabeth?

She narrowed her gaze, peering around her.

Can you feel me . . . ?

After a moment, her suspicious mien turned determined. With a purposeful stride, she returned to that first bedroom. Inside, she worked the bedside table away from the wall, then dropped to her knees.

What is she doing? he wondered vaguely, his gaze locked on her rounded ass and taut thighs—until he heard the wallpaper ripping. He traced to mere inches from her to get a look at what she was up to.

She'd been digging for a phone jack. Without a phone? Why?

She would search in vain. There were none in the apartment. All had been removed and plastered over.

By the third bedroom, she must have concluded the same, because she sat back on her heels and blew her hair out of eyes. "Sumbitch."

Now she'll put her head in her hands and cry while I look on impassively.

Instead, she slapped one thigh, then rose, marching to the kitchen. Retrieving a butter knife and a chopping blade, she returned to the television console, maneuvering the weighty piece away from the wall.

Then she went back on her knees, her new tools at the ready.

He lifted his brows as bits of hardware began to fly out from behind the console. Small screws, a cable jack plate, sections of wire . . .

The cable box disappeared from its shelf, yanked back by the peculiar mortal.

Again, he traced closer to see her. He found her lying on her front, fiddling with the box.

"Come on, come on." She bit her bottom lip. "Message button."

She endeavored to send a signal through the cable! No, Lothaire wasn't very often surprised; she continued to take him aback.

Elizabeth had proved . . . trickier than he'd assumed. And the flare of surprise wasn't *un*enjoyable.

Just when he was about to stop her, she muttered, "No, no. Damn you, Motorola!" She sat up, leaning against the wall, knees to her chest.

Her eyes started to water. *Now she'll cry while I gloat about predicting this very thing.*

Yet as suddenly as her sadness had appeared, it vanished. She slammed the bottom of her fist against the floor, then began setting everything to rights, at least superficially, hiding the bits she'd removed.

Another determined look lit her face, and she returned to her room. What would she do next?

For some reason, I can hardly wait to know.

She began eyeing the lock on their adjoining door.

No. No way . . .

❖

Though dawn neared, Ellie still didn't hear Lothaire inside his room. And she wanted in.

She tested the lever-style door handle. The lock was a standard pin and tumbler, wouldn't be too hard to pick.

But what if he returned? She recalled how he'd tossed her across the room that afternoon as his eyes glowed red like flames.

He might have a phone in there. *Decided.*

She rushed to the bathroom for supplies. In a grooming kit, she found tweezers. She pulled them wide like a wishbone, then bent one end against the counter into a ninety-degree angle. Perfect for a tension wrench. An opened hairpin would act as a rake.

Back at the door handle, she inserted her jimmied tension wrench into the lock plug. With her other hand, she eased the hairpin in beside it to rake the pin stacks.

Adjust tension. Rake. Adjust tension. . . .

Click. "Candy. Baby."

She cracked open the door, stowing her tools in her jeans pockets.

Lothaire's room was a twin to hers in size and configuration, but the colors in this one were more masculine, with rich earth-toned wallpaper and carpets. Special lights accented paintings on the walls. The pictures looked classy, like they were one of a kind.

Heavy drapes covered his balcony's French doors. His bed was unmade, his sheets twisted. Was that a metronome sitting on his nightstand?

Across the room, an antique-looking desk was covered with complicated 3-D puzzles. Several were complete, but a few appeared ongoing.

She lifted one that consisted of metal rings and wires. It wasn't a brainteaser—it was a brain paralyzer. Another one was mechanized. Shining silver blocks and triangles made up a third.

Beside them, a book lay open to a chapter titled: "Mechanical Puzzles, the Goldberg Principle." Geometric theory applied to puzzle making? Had Lothaire *created* some of these puzzles?

Moving on, she gazed to the left of the desk. Strewn over the floor were wadded-up letters in a language—and alphabet—she couldn't read.

Ever fearful of his return, she swiftly investigated his bathroom. Surprisingly, it looked like a normal male's: shaving cream, razor, soap, a toothbrush. *Gotta keep those fangs white.*

The cabinet contained no medicines. She supposed vampires didn't have ailments.

His closet was filled with expensive clothing—scores of long, lean slacks, tailored button-downs, and jackets, all in variations of black. Polished boots filled the shoe racks.

The vampire loves him some clothes. She leaned in to smell one of his coats, taking in his masculine scent—smooth, woodsy, with the faintest bite of *evergreen?*

Just as mesmerizing as his looks. When she found her lids growing heavy, she gave herself an inward shake, then dragged herself away from the coat.

In an accessories drawer, he'd precisely organized sunglasses, watches, cuff links, and engraved money clips. Toward the back of the closet, she saw a number of swords laid out on a felt-lined shelf. The bottom of each sword hilt was an inch or so away from another one's tip.

In fact, she'd bet they were *exactly* one inch apart, as if he'd taken a ruler to them.

These weapons didn't appear to be decorative like the one she'd almost stabbed herself with this afternoon—*open mind*—but more like useful accessories. A timely reminder that he was a warrior, a deadly male.

What am I doing in here? Curiosity killed the Ellie.

And for all her searching, she'd garnered little insight to help her against Lothaire—and no new hope of escape.

Now that the rush of breaking in had dwindled, she exhaled with fatigue, picturing her new bed. Though she worried about Saroya rising, nothing could keep her from it. Ellie hadn't slept last night before her execution.

Execution. Memories from the morning surfaced, but she ruthlessly tamped them down. She imagined a rubber band snapping her wrist every time she recalled that injection bench, the clock ticking, the screams. . . . *Snap!*

Think forward, never dwell.

Somehow, before Lothaire got that ring, Ellie would figure out a way to communicate with her family. Once she was assured that they were good and vanished, she'd finally get to do what needed to be done. *Take care of your business, Ellie.*

She and Saroya would be no more. *I can still die—just might be a few days off schedule.*

Whipped with exhaustion, Ellie turned back toward her room. Had any day ever been so grueling—

"What in the hell are you doing in here?"

14

The girl's eyes went wide as she pivoted to face Lothaire, her hair a dark wave swinging over one shoulder.

"You picked the lock to my room? Invading my privacy?" he thundered, furious at the intrusion, furious at his reactions to her.

When the mortal had breathed in his scent, going heavy-lidded . . . he'd barely choked back a groan as he shot hard as stone.

Now he traced in front of her, cupping her throat. She recoiled with fear, her heart beating a staccato rhythm he could *feel.* "I've told you I won't harm this body! Yet you flinch from me?"

In a strangled voice, she cried, "Are you *kidding?*"

"Calm your goddamned heart!" he bellowed, his instinct to protect her—to comfort her—nearly overriding his need to punish her. Which infuriated him even more!

He knew he should just return her to her room, then sleep—and not only to dream memories. He was strung out, his madness creeping closer at every moment.

But his ire demanded appeasement. "You flinch like a coward. Are you one? Am I to add *cowardly* to all the adjectives I use to describe you?"

"Fuck you, vampire!" She knocked his arm away—he let her. "I'm no

coward. I've got flint in my veins. Don't mistake my reflexes for fear."
Her fists balled, her fear ebbing. "And you don't get to play the privacy
card! Not while your homeless tramp has set up her cardboard house
inside me."

He reacted better to her anger, his vision clearing. Gods, the rumors
were true. He *was* connected to his Bride's moods, responding to them.
And Elizabeth was a fragment of Saroya, like a placeholder for his female.

Between gritted teeth, he commanded, *"Calm yourself, Elizabeth."* He
knew one thing that would calm them both. Release. With one bite, she'd
be begging for him to ease her.

He wondered if the other rumors about Brides were true. *Will she pleasure me more deeply than I'd ever imagined?*

Wait for your true one! Saroya will be worth it.

Elizabeth stared at his eyes. "Look at me, Lothaire. I'm calming down,
okay?"

"Then answer the question. Why are you in my room?"

"I was curious about you."

"Curious to find a way to thwart my plans? And what did you discover
about me that you didn't know?"

"A few things."

What? What? Anticipation teased him—because he had no clue what
she'd say. He sat at his desk, impatiently waving a hand at her. "Thrall me."

She took a deep breath, then said, "You're an insomniac. You speak
and write at least two languages, but you have difficulty centering your
thoughts enough to write anything at length. You're obsessive-compulsive
with your possessions, which leads me to think that very little of your life
outside of these walls is how you want it to be. You had no friends growing up and that hasn't changed since. You're narcissistic—but I knew that
upon first looking at you."

He tilted his head, grudgingly impressed, though his tone was anything
but. "First of all, I'm not narcissistic." When she opened her lips to argue,
he said, "I *know* Narkissos of Thespiae—while we might share traits, *I*
came first, so he's Lothairistic, not the other way around. Furthermore,

I speak and write *eight* languages. As for my obsession with order, that's obvious from my closet. Insomniac is easy enough to guess. The sheets are twisted."

"And the metronome. You use it to relax you."

Observant human. "My supposed friendless state?" She had him dead to rights there, other than his young halfling admirer.

Then Lothaire frowned. No, he'd once had a boon companion. *Until I was betrayed.*

"I knew by the puzzles," Elizabeth said. "They're a solitary recreation. A couple look very old, so I'd guess you've been interested in them for some time, probably since you were a boy."

Again, how unexpected. She was actually *entertaining* him.

"Look, Lothaire, this won't happen again. I'll just go back to my room—"

"Sit." He pointed to a settee beside his desk. After a hesitation, she perched on the very edge of the cushion, with her back ramrod straight.

"Relax, mortal."

"How can I when I have no idea what you're going to do?" Her gaze flitted over the side of his face.

He reached up, daubing at the slashes he'd forgotten. *Fucking wraith.* "I'm going to attempt to wind down from this day and night."

Still Elizabeth held herself stiffly, though she was exhausted. Smudges colored the skin under her eyes.

"How did you learn to pick locks?"

"On the weekends, my father worked as a handyman who did lock-smithing on the side."

"Before he died in the mine? All that work and you were still mired in poverty?"

She lifted her chin, her eyes flashing.

So proud. So little reason to be. "Did you enjoy searching my home?"

"How long were you watching me?" she demanded.

"How long do you think?"

"Do you ever answer a question straightforward-like?"

He made a habit of oblique replies. His inability to lie had made him skilled at misdirection. He didn't often get called on it, though. "And you? You're nearly as bad as I am."

"Fine. Yes, I enjoyed snooping around your apartment. I got to see things I never had before. I'll probably dream of that chandelier tonight." She bit her bottom lip. "Right after I get done dreaming of those jewels."

He'd surprised himself by showing them to Elizabeth, by wanting to see her reaction. Or perhaps he'd merely wanted *any* reaction whatsoever, any response to his gift.

Saroya's had been . . . lacking.

"You truly think that's what you'll dream of?" he asked. "It's more likely that you'll relive the events of the past twenty-four hours." He didn't think she'd fully comprehended all that had happened to her. Her mind had been too busy futilely planning an escape—or suicide.

But once she truly accepted that she was doomed . . . ? Everything she'd endured would catch up with her.

All miseries catch up eventually.

Would *he* experience Elizabeth's near death in dreams? He'd taken enough of her blood earlier.

"I'm not allowing myself to reflect about today," she said.

"Simple as that—your mind does as your will commands? Mind over mind?"

She shrugged. "Something like that, yes."

He leaned forward in his seat. "So tonight, *I* have learned that you are unjustifiably proud. You believe yourself strong of will and keen of mind—"

"I'm not *un*keen or weak-willed."

"—and you like to analyze things. I wonder what you would make of this?" He traced to his safe, retrieving his weighty ledger book.

Never had he shown another person his accountings. But Elizabeth would soon be dead, and now he was curious to see what she'd say.

He sat at his desk once more, opening the tome. "Come. View my ledger."

She hesitantly rose, then stood beside him. "I've never seen an account book like this."

It contained only two columns: *Indebted* and *Targeted*. "And you've reviewed so many from your trailer in Appalachia?"

"Funny thing about Appalachia jokes—unlike *all other jokes*, they just never get old."

He raised a brow. "It's an accounting of blood debts from Loreans."

"There are so many entries."

He inclined his head. Everything to serve his Endgame. "This represents thousands of years of . . . accounting." Again and again, he'd used his ability to predict others' moves, ensuring he was always in the right place at the right time to exact blood vows.

If Nïx was the queen of foresight, then Lothaire was the king of *insight*.

White queen versus black king. He recalled his last encounter with the soothsayer, on that prison island. He'd told her, "Until our next match." But she'd answered, "There won't *be* a next match, vampire."

What did she mean?

"Explain to me how it works," Elizabeth said, drawing him from his thoughts.

"If an immortal is in dire straits, I'll agree to help him, but only for a price. Then I'll make him vow to do anything I want. The saying *make a deal with the devil* comes from me." If he sounded proud, well . . .

I am.

"So that's why you seemed interested when I offered a bargain."

"Just so." Again he was finding it easy to speak with her, as if the words were pulled from him, as if he'd waited all his life to reveal these things.

I must have needed a confidante, one who could never tell my secrets. Most legendary men do.

"But you do *help* others?"

"So perhaps I'm not completely evil?" He gave a humorless laugh. "Most of the time I'm the one who manipulates creatures into desperate positions. For instance, I'll fatally wound a loved one, then offer to save her."

"Those targeted names are in for one hell of a surprise, huh?"

Elizabeth was cleverer than he'd initially deemed her. "Precisely."

He dragged his gaze from the pages to her face, inspecting it as he might a painting he'd found superficially appealing only to discover layers, nuances.

He shook his head hard. No, if Saroya were at the fore, he'd be feeling this desire, this fascination even, for *her* alone.

"What do you usually demand of them?"

"I don't often collect on these." His debtors always assumed he'd demand their firstborn. *Like I'm fucking Rumpelstiltskin?* What would Lothaire do with countless squalling babes? Raise them in a kennel? "But when I make my move to take my thrones, their accounts will come due."

And the world will quake.

His lips curled as he reviewed some of the newest entries: two royal members of the Lykae Clan MacRieve; the sea god Nereus; Loa the voodoo priestess; Gamboa the demonic drug lord; Rydstrom Woede, king of the rage demons.

"All that work to get those thrones?"

"Yes. Anything for them." He'd fought side by side with a Valkyrie he hated when all he'd wanted to do was exact revenge on her. He'd aligned with various demonarchies, convincing some that he was the devil incarnate, dedicated to leading them back to hell.

He'd sworn fealty to a vampire king—one who'd sat upon Lothaire's own throne.

"If your kingdoms are so important, then why'd you lose them in the first place?"

"I couldn't expect you to understand the political machinations of vampires."

She tilted her head at him. "None of your debtors ever welsh?"

"Vows to the Lore are unbreakable."

"Then I'm surprised they don't just try to kill you."

"Oh, they do, constantly," he said. "And now they'll be coming after you, thinking to trade you for their debt or to cash in on a bounty. Then, of course, there are the retribution seekers, bent on avenging whatever murders I've committed." He leveled his gaze on her. "I've committed many."

She didn't look away. In fact, he got the uncanny impression that *she* was studying *him*.

The insect wants to understand the magnifying glass.

"Is that why you're called the Enemy of Old?"

"Partly. Also because I show up like a plague every couple of centuries, killing masses of beings before disappearing." Sometimes disappearing involuntarily.

"There's an actual bounty on my head?"

When Lothaire found out who'd posted it, blood would run. "My Bride would already be target number one in the Lore. Now thousands will fight for the reward—and they'll believe that *you* are mine. They'll be using oracles to track your movements. So if somehow you were able to escape this boundary, you'd be abducted in seconds. They would do terrible things to you."

She raised her brows. "I can only imagine how bad something would have to be for you to call it terrible. But if they're offering death, don't forget that I *want* to die."

"Some foes would take your life. Most would *keep* you. An anatomically incorrect sea god would love nothing more than to *plumb your depths* and steal your virginity. My vampire enemies would keep you alive for food, piercing you nightly for decades. Demons would consign you to their notorious harems, where you'd be whored out for all the many creatures who'd pay handsomely for a chance to humiliate Lothaire's Bride. You'd learn to polish demon horns in the most degrading ways."

She swallowed. "Harems and whoring and horns, then?"

"Suddenly the fate I have planned for you doesn't seem so egregious?"

She returned to the settee, sitting less stiffly than before. "Just to be clear. My fate, as you intend it, goes like this: In one to thirty days, you'll send my soul packing—to wherever souls go—and my family will never be harmed by you."

"Approximately," he replied, using one of his favorite go-to words. The girl would assume he addressed the number of days. Actually, he spoke of the "soul packing" portion. Her soul would be extinguished—

"By approximately, do you mean the one to thirty, or the rest of it?"

Little witch. "The question you should've asked is why the days are so variable."

"Lothaire. Why are the days so variable?"

"I've told you I need a special ring to make Saroya a vampire. The same ring will free your soul from your body." *Not a lie.* "It might take me weeks to locate it."

"I see. Not that I'm complaining, but if you're supposed to be searching for something, then why were you trying to sleep tonight? Isn't this pretty much your nine-to-five? Shouldn't you be out tracing the pavement even now?"

She made him sound *lazy.*

No one worked harder than he did on his seven little tasks: *find the ring, dispose of the human's soul, turn Saroya into a vampire, kill La Dorada, claim the Horde crown, find Serghei to burn him alive, conquer the Daci.*

He took no pleasure from life, enjoyed no amusements. Everything served his Endgame.

Wearied just to think of all that work, he leaned back in his chair. And again, he got the feeling that she was studying him. "Sleep and work are one and the same now."

"I don't understand."

"When I drink blood straight from the vein, I can harvest my victim's memories. I see his recollections in my dreams, reliving them when I sleep. I feel the bite of cold on his skin, the pain of his injuries, even his death at my hands. Recently, I drank from a man who knows where the ring is. Now I have only to get at that memory, but it's easier said than done. I have to wade through a lot of them."

She ran her fingertips over the graze on her neck. "Will you dream *mine*?"

"Likely. Cannot *wait* for fond remembrances of squirrel stew around the trailer hearth."

She parted her lips, no doubt to deliver a cutting retort, then stifled it. "How do you know what's a regular dream and what's from someone else's life?"

"I don't dream anything but memories, and only theirs."

"No wonder you're crazy. But I affect your sanity, don't I?"

"Saroya affects my sanity. You're merely a placeholder."

"So if the ring equals my death, then every time you sleep means I'm closer to dying?"

"Not to put too fine a point on it, but yes."

Finally she gazed away, saying quietly, "Would you give me advance notice?"

"No. No more than you would those deer you hunted."

"They were animals!"

"Are you much more?" he asked in a thoughtful tone. "And what would you do with your advance notice?"

"I'd want to write to my family."

"Ah, Ellie Ann's last letters. How touching. But there's no room in the Lore for sentimentality." When he folded his arms over his chest, she seemed to be making a mental note of it.

He'd actually felt a jot sentimental earlier when he'd realized that Chase might die—and with him, Lothaire's sole hope of a vampire line. *Am I to leave nothing of myself behind?*

Long ago, Lothaire had created vampires on occasion, but they always predeceased him. He'd lost his taste for it.

Everyone died before him. *And now am I to be maudlin, feeling my age?*

Elizabeth asked, "Have you ever done *anything* for another without expecting something in return?"

"I'll cast my mind back. Further ... further ... Ah, yes. During the

Iron Age, I came upon a dying mortal warrior on a battlefield. He wanted me to get a message to his wife and children. I was in a whimsical mood. 'Give her the message yourself,' I told him, and turned him into a vampire. When he reunited with her, she ran to him, tears of joy streaming down her face, their children trailing her. As their offspring rejoiced, he swung her up in his arms, squeezing her to his chest. Such a poignant moment, such emotion—until she popped like a grape."

Elizabeth was aghast.

"Vampires and humans do not mix. You're too frail. If I lost control and laid hands on your body . . . *pop*."

She fell silent.

Why would I kill to know what she's thinking right now?

Probably because I enjoy killing.

In a clear bid to change the subject, she asked, "Do your targets always fall into your clutches?"

"Ninety-six-point-four percent of the time, yes."

She pursed her lips. "How . . . boring."

"What did you say?"

"Where's the fun in that? Where's the surprise?"

"Life isn't fun."

"Not for most, I suppose." She leaned back on the settee, tucking her legs under her. "But if I was rich like you, I'd have fun."

"If you weren't woefully poor, you'd know that money doesn't buy happiness."

"Spoken like a man who's always had cash."

"What would you do if you were me? To have fun?"

"I'd spend money on my family. And I'd travel." She gazed at the ceiling, as if imagining all the places she would go. "I'd see all the Greats: the Great Wall of China, the Great Pyramids, the Great Barrier Reef. Hell, I'd visit the coast for the first time ever."

She'd never been outside of Appalachia, had never seen an ocean, a beach. He could scarcely imagine that. She had no idea what sea air smelled like, no idea what waves lapping at her feet felt like. How would she react?

Probably not as he would expect her to. "I've seen the world, Elizabeth, several times over. It's overrated. I've no family I'll acknowledge."

"So now you read your book for enjoyment?" She skimmed the design of the settee's fabric, red nails trailing lightly. "What's the last entry in your ledger?"

"It will be a mortal named Declan Chase. If he lives. He's the one who possesses memories of the ring."

"*If* he lives. Did you hurt him?" she asked. Had she stifled a yawn?

"Not I. A demon gutted him with a sword yesterday. But I gave him my blood to make him immortal."

"Isn't that a really big deal? Since mortals *beg* you to do it and all. I believe you said it was priceless?" She rested her head on the arm of the settee.

"I wanted a tie with him very much. Though I acted as if put out to tender my blood."

Lothaire recalled the subterfuge, a simple but elegant plot, and then the culmination—Chase unconscious, his mouth pried open as he was forced to accept a vampire's blood.

Even though the Blademan would consider it a defilement, a poison in his veins. . . .

"Now I can locate him anywhere in the world, at any time," Lothaire continued. "Can read his mind if he's nearby. Yes, mortal, under the right circumstances I can read minds. Yet another way that I'm superior to you."

She'll gasp with astonishment, raising her hand to her temple, fearing that I'm reading her mind right now. . . .

Silence. He glanced over at her; his hands clenched into shaking fists.

Elizabeth was sound asleep.

He'd finally opened up and actually talked with someone—had shown her his fucking book—and she'd fallen asleep? Had he *bored* her?

Súka! He was tempted to trace her into the middle of a ghoul cage fight, see if that would wake her up!

He loomed over her, staring down, confounded by this mortal's behavior.

And why he could never predict it.

Over the pounding of his heart, he heard Elizabeth's even breaths. In sleep, she looked soft, even younger. So beautiful, but profoundly lacking in potential.

She seemed intelligent enough—*except when challenging me*—yet other than her looks, there was nothing noteworthy about her, no accomplishments she could boast of.

She'd been athletically inclined with all her wilderness expeditions and such, but she wasn't a distinguished athlete. She played no instrument, and she spoke only one language—poorly.

If not for Saroya, Elizabeth would have lived a wasted existence, just like her loathsome mother. Thrift-store clothes and cheap perfume in a dingy, leaking trailer.

At least now Elizabeth served a higher purpose.

As her breaths deepened, her lips parted and her heartbeat grew lulling. Like a metronome . . . like the waves she'd never see.

So young, this mortal. Gazing at her now, he could almost forget how much he detested humans.

Almost.

His thoughts were interrupted by his sudden yawn. Watching her sleep had calmed him. His Bride—or at least her body—*could* soothe him. *A tool I can use?*

After unfastening his sword, he kicked off his boots, drew off his shirt. *Now I sleep.* Now the memories would come.

As he traced to his bed, he thought, *Your days are numbered, young Elizabeth.*

15

Ellie woke to a groan. A *male's* groan.

She cracked open her eyes, found herself curled up on the couch in the vampire's bedroom. She groggily reached over and turned on a nearby lamp, lighting the area enough for her to see Lothaire.

He lay asleep in his bed.

She rose and crossed to him, curious to see if she'd find him so handsome now that she was rested—and not acutely traumatized.

At his bedside, Ellie exhaled in resignation. How could he be so damaged mentally—and morally—and yet so stunning on the outside?

Clad only in dark jeans that hung low on his hips, he reclined on his front, the side of his head resting on his forearm. His longish blond hair was tousled, those unnerving eyes concealed.

His face was hauntingly flawless, with his proud, patrician nose and broad cheekbones. Even the stubble covering his bold jawline was enticing to her. Her fingers itched to trace his lips, to determine if they were as firm as they looked. She'd never really noticed men's lips before, but his were sexy.

Now that his wounds had healed, the smooth skin of his back seemed to demand her touch. Those brawny shoulders . . .

He groaned again, his brows drawing together sharply. *Dreaming?*

If he truly experienced the memories of all his victims—thousands of years' worth—how could he *not* be going insane?

Surely he wouldn't be dreaming of that ring already. Maybe he was seeing *her* memories?

She'd never done anything she'd be too ashamed of him discovering, but she didn't want him to *feel* exactly how much she loved her family—or to know how dire their straits currently were.

The last time she'd spoken with her mother, there'd been mutterings about the Peirce men returning to the mines. Mama had said, "Over my dead body, Ellie," then had grown embarrassed by her comment to her death-row daughter. . . .

When Lothaire turned on his back, Ellie's mouth went dry. His torso was hard as stone, with cut abs and pecs. Darker blond hair, almost golden in color, dashed the center of his chest, and a fine line of gold trailed down to his navel and lower.

Her starving senses drank him in, almost blunting her hatred for him. Dear God, the vampire was so . . . *beautiful.*

Masculine perfection. Especially with his eyes closed. *I could look at him all day.*

No! *Rubber band snap.* He was a *murderer* who wanted to do her in. He was partly responsible for her imprisonment.

She'd best not have any confusing attraction to him. In fact, she briefly considered opening the curtains to the morning sun, but decided against it. He was too fast, would just trace from the light.

Instead, Ellie dragged herself away, planning to shower, get dressed, and mentally prepare for her next go-round with him.

Inside her room, she locked the adjoining door between their suites from her side—as if that'd do anything to keep him out. Then she drew back the curtains to her balcony. Her lips parted.

Late afternoon? Exhausted or not, she couldn't believe she'd slept so long. In prison, she'd awakened at 6 a.m. on the dot for her entire sentence.

She headed for her bathroom, finding lavish toiletries inside. The promise of a shower with piping-hot water—and no guard's eyes on her—called to her.

Once the steaming water cascaded over her, she sighed with contentment, leisurely scrubbing her body with a scented soap.

Yet soon her sweeping hands slowed, bathing turned to stroking. It'd been so long since she'd been able to touch herself like this—fully naked and unobserved—that she'd forgotten what she felt like.

She blocked images of Lothaire's chiseled torso from her mind, telling herself she was just getting reacquainted with her body.

When she cupped one breast, a shaky breath escaped her. Damn, but she missed being caressed, missed masculine sounds of appreciation as she'd touched in turn.

Ellie had enjoyed men, had been an incurable flirt all her life. She'd fogged up so many truck cab windows that she'd gotten a reputation.

That was Ellie, the easy virgin—who was up for naughty talk, petting, *grinding*. As long as her jeans stayed zipped.

But then she'd been sent away, banished from flirting and laughing and touching.

In prison, she'd longed to feel the roughness of boys' hands on her breasts, to hear their desperate moans in her ear. *"Let me have you, Ellie. . . . I'll only put the tip in, I swear."*

She rested her forearm on the marble shower wall as her free hand descended down her belly and lower. Since she was now bare between her legs, Ellie perceived every different sensation—water drops running along her flesh, the rasp of one of her long nails. . . .

She was slick inside, so tempted to do more than explore. She bit her lip and glanced around, half-afraid Lothaire would trace into the room and catch her.

What would he do?

When he'd snatched her against his body yesterday, she'd felt the unyielding power of his muscles, had felt his impossibly large erection.

Her sex clenched at the memory of that hardness.

A spray of water misted over the graze on her neck, making her shiver. The vampire had sampled her there, had seemed to relish her taste, groaning as he took.

For some reason, the idea of that was so . . . erotic to her—as if he'd wanted her so much, he had to take a part of her into himself.

Her breath shuddered out.

What would've happened if Saroya hadn't risen? Would the vampire have cupped Ellie's breasts? She remembered how they'd ached. At that moment, she couldn't have stopped him, had been in a sensual stupor from his mouth.

Would he have trailed his kisses lower . . . and lower? She pictured those firm lips closing around one of her nipples, his blond brows drawn with pleasure as his pale hands kneaded—

No! What was *wrong* with her? She detested the vampire, yet she was fantasizing about him? She dropped her hands at once, turning off the water. Leaning back against the wall, she caught her breath, getting control of her need.

Vampires were always portrayed as hypnotically attractive in the movies. Surely he had some kind of uncanny sway over her—some supernatural quality about him.

Although the more likely explanation was that she was simply hard-up after her long prison stay.

After drying off, she padded to the closet, staggered anew at all the selections. She could spend hours mixing and matching. She'd never followed fashion in women's magazines because she'd known she would never possess enough choices to create outfits, to have a "personal style."

In fact, she'd vaguely resented the women who had the resources—and the time—to spend on fashion.

Still don't have the time. Reminding herself that she had only a month at the most, she quickly chose a pair of beige slacks and a blue sweater with a low cowl neck. The outfit looked silly without shoes, so she slipped on a pair of tobacco-colored pumps.

Would the vampire be up yet? Would they have another conversation—or confrontation? She wondered if the fluttery feeling in her belly was hunger. Or nerves.

She quickly braided the crown of her hair, leaving the rest to curl past her shoulders. After debating makeup, she opted for a light sheen of lip gloss—

A thunderous bellow sounded from his room. Followed by another, and another. Louder, louder . . .

Then quiet.

16

When Lothaire awakened, he lay in a bank of snow. Though it was surely still day in New York, the moon's yellow light streamed down over him.

Sleep-tracing. Again. *Where the hell am I now?* Was it to happen every time he slept?

He darted his gaze around, recognizing his whereabouts—because it was a property he returned to often, one he now owned.

The field where his mother had died.

How distinctly he recalled Ivana's death and the night that followed. On a still eve just like this one, he'd finally been able to rise from his snowy cocoon. . . .

The sun had barely set when he began clawing himself out of the snow. The humans had long since gone, but Lothaire had been forced to wait in agony for twilight.

At last he broke through the outer layer of ice and ran in search of his mother . . . hoping against hope. Then he spied all that was left of the proud Ivana—black ash against glaringly white snow.

With a choked yell, he reached for her remains, but a slight breeze soughed, scattering her ashes across the field.

"No, no, Mother!" Crying, frantic to touch even a fragment of her, he lunged for them—

And he traced *instead, brushing his fingertips over disintegrating ash.*

The first time he'd ever been able to teleport. Shock welled. Hours earlier, that skill would have prevented Ivana's sacrifice.

He sank to his knees, filled with a bitter hatred for himself. I failed her. *Tears fell—until he perceived a presence.*

The Daci, all around him, cloaked in mist.

His mother had told him that her family might come for him once the humans were gone. Indeed, they had.

"Lothaire," they whispered like the wind.

He shot to his feet, jerking around in circles. "Show yourselves!" He turned the hatred he'd felt for himself outward. He heard his mother's voice in his mind: "Rely on cold reason." *But he couldn't.*

Fury burned inside him just as the sun had burned her.

"You filthy cowards! Where were you last night? Where is Serghei?" he screamed till spittle sprayed from his lips, freezing there. "Let me see your faces!"

"Lothaire . . ."

He traced forward, flying into the mist with his fangs bared. Couldn't see them. Eyes wide, he realized they were *the mist—and within it, so was he. "You let her burn!" he yelled, throat gone raw. "Fight me!"*

From all around, he heard their broken murmurs: ". . . her curse . . ." ". . . he traces within the mist . . ." ". . . Horde blood . . ." ". . . lacking . . ." ". . . rage . . ."

"Yes, I've Horde blood! The better to destroy you with—"

They merely traced away, dissipating.

The night was still, utter silence. Utter aloneness. . . .

Over the centuries, Lothaire had returned here time and again, desperately seeking his mother's people, seeking Serghei.

But never had he sleep-traced this kind of distance. The snow bit into his bare feet, a chill breeze leaching the warmth from his uncovered torso.

Despise this place. Lothaire could still remember the smell of Ivana's flesh burning on that freezing dawn.

Because her father, Serghei, the king of the Daci, had forsaken her.

The grandfather Lothaire had never—in his endless life—been able to find.

When young, Lothaire hadn't comprehended the pain his mother had felt. Since then he'd known torture many times, had felt his own skin seared away in the sun.

Now he understood what Serghei had subjected Ivana to. *I can still feel her brittle ashes against my fingertips. . . .*

At the memory, rage seethed inside Lothaire, as fresh as that eve. Shouldn't it have dimmed?

He felt crazed, wanting to rip apart an enemy until steaming blood sprayed like rain and painted the snow. *"Face me, Serghei!"* he bellowed. *"You fucking coward!"*

For an instant, he thought he sensed their presence. Or was it only a lingering remnant from his dream? "Face me!" No one met him; no one answered his challenge. "Goddamn you all, *fight* me!"

This might be the moment when I topple off the razor's edge, irretrievably mad.

Another bellow erupted from his chest. *Crave blood, carnage . . . bones shattering . . .*

The rush when flesh gave way to his fangs.

Atop a razor, staring down at the abyss. And the abyss stares back.

Just when he realized he was about to lose this battle, he pictured his Bride's skin yielding, giving up that crimson wine of hers. *Sink your fangs into her, plunge them deep. . . .*

His eyes widened. *She's alone.* Unguarded.

In less than an instant, he'd returned to the apartment. Needing to protect her. Needing *her.* He would bury his face in her hair and inhale her intoxicating scent, could imagine it so clearly.

He found Elizabeth standing out on her balcony under the cover of sun.

Not her, not *her.* Saroya only. He grated, "Let Saroya rise."

She turned. "You're back— Oh, my God, your eyes."

"Let her rise!" *Abyss.*

"She's not trying to."

He threw back his head and yelled.

"Lothaire?" He heard the mortal swallow in fear, and yet she eased closer to him, hands out in front of her. "Wh-what's happened to you? Is that *snow* on your jeans?"

He narrowed his gaze on her, willing her, *Yes, come to me.* She took a step closer to the shadows, then another. Her hands trembled. *Want them on me. Come and touch me, female.*

Touch me, and I might last another night.

The vampire's eyes were more frightening than Ellie had ever seen them. They were filled with both rage—and *anguish.* Red forked out over the whites, giving him an even more sinister look.

Yet they were spellbinding to her.

His bared chest heaved with breaths, his hands clenched into fists, the promise of violence in every rippling muscle and whipcord tendon. His fangs glinted as if razor-sharp.

And still she found herself crossing to him, wanting to smooth his windblown hair off his brow, needing to feel his flawless skin.

When she joined him in the room, something began happening that Ellie didn't understand. He positioned himself closer to her, *closer,* with a silky, predatory grace.

It dawned on her; he didn't want to frighten away his prey. She shivered, commanding herself not to bolt.

Because she sensed that might . . . *excite* him.

Soon they were so close she had to crane her head up to meet his gaze. Her lips parted at the blatant need she saw there.

But what *does he need? What does he want?*

Why did she feel like she'd die if she didn't know what his pale skin felt like?

"Elizabeth," he bit out, his voice raw, his expression crazed.

Maybe she could touch him, could satisfy her curiosity, and he wouldn't even remember. "Can I . . . can I touch you?"

He shuddered, then hissed, "*Yes*. Touch. Me."

To test the waters, she brushed a straight length of hair from his face. When he merely moved closer to her, she tentatively laid her palms on his chest, against his freezing skin. Where had he traced to? What snowy land?

He flinched, even as his muscles leapt to her touch. "Elizabeth," he rasped brokenly, "you *scald* me." She was about to drop her hands when he ordered, *"More."*

"O-okay." She fanned her fingers over his chest, inching her hands out until they lay over his rigid pecs, his flat nipples.

She didn't understand this man, this evil vampire with his anguished eyes. He still hadn't placed his hands on her. Because he feared to? "If I lose control . . ." he'd warned her.

But she sensed that she calmed him, that she affected him physically—and mentally.

Sure enough, his agitation began to ease, his lids going heavy.

Ellie was just as affected. She grew enthralled with the ridges flexing beneath her fingertips, begging to be explored.

When she sifted her nails through the golden hair on his chest, his hooded eyes closed.

"Is this better?" Her voice was embarrassingly throaty. But she'd been aching for contact for half a decade—how could she *not* appreciate a man like him?

All tousled hair and bulging muscles.

Seeming to wake, he gave her a hate-filled look. He swiped her hands away with a muttered curse, then strode toward the kitchen.

Since he didn't trace, she figured he wanted her to follow him.

She stared with reluctant awe at the sculpted planes of his back, the way they tapered down to those narrow hips. . . .

Even his walk is sexy. Lothaire walked like she imagined a powerful king would.

In the kitchen, he opened the refrigerator, leaning on the door as he withdrew a pitcher of blood. It looked like a cream pourer in his big hands.

He turned up the carafe, gulping its contents while Ellie sank into a chair, staring in fascination.

She saw him glance at her out of the corner of his eye, knew he noted her breaths shallowing, her cheeks flushing.

Now that she'd touched him, she was even more attracted to him. Flying-into-a-lightbulb attracted.

Maybe he was a tad less intimidating without his fancy tailored clothing and expensive boots? And his chugging out of a pitcher at the fridge was so normal, so *masculine*, she couldn't help but respond.

Even when a line of blood ran from the corner of his lips.

Vampire. Blood. Still, she couldn't look away. *How can this sight be wetting my whistle?*

When he finished, he ran his forearm over his mouth, over the stubble on his chin. "Look your fill? *Grope* your fill? Don't worry, I'm accustomed to women of all species lusting after me."

She felt a flush of embarrassment, but curbed it. Ellie had an expiration date on her life that was closing in fast; she couldn't waste a minute being embarrassed over *anything*.

And she resolved not to beat herself up because she was attracted to a deadly, vampiric maniac that she yearned to kill.

Ellie tilted her head in a considering manner, saying honestly, "Well, at least you're pretty on the outside." At his expression, she said, "Oh, come on. In all of your endless life, no one's ever insinuated that you're *ugly on the inside?*"

***

Those weaker than Lothaire didn't make a habit of insulting him. Of course, she *wanted* to die. "You won't provoke me into killing you," he said, adding, "this evening. But court my wrath, and I'll punish you in other ways."

His wrath was at the ready, his mood foul. Though he'd slept for hours, the only memories he'd dreamed—or experienced firsthand—were his own, something that hadn't happened in ages.

Which meant he'd reaped no new information about the ring's whereabouts.

If he couldn't access Declan Chase's memories, he'd be forced to set off searching for the ring all over again.

When he'd first taken his uncle's advice and drunk "live" immortal blood from the flesh, Lothaire had accepted the risk: madness.

But he'd convinced himself that his mind was too strong to be overly afflicted. Perhaps he'd grow more fiendish, his conscience further eroded.

He'd never expected the sleep-tracing and the rages, the times when he couldn't hear an enemy sneaking up on him because of the thundering of his heart.

He'd never expected to lose his strategic abilities. In the past, he'd easily contrived multiperson, decades-long plots, foreseeing each player's move as if they were chessboard pawns.

Now mere puzzle solutions eluded him. He could rarely sleep. When he did, he couldn't filter through his dreams to get to the information he needed.

Also strange? He hadn't experienced Elizabeth's memories at all. She was his latest take, so why hadn't he seen hers?

The only good that had come from his rest was that his injuries had healed completely. At his age, he could go weeks between feedings, but regeneration had left him starved.

He poured more of the cool blood into a glass—*glug, glug*. He would leisurely drink it in front of the mortal, just to fuck with her.

But she didn't comment on his breakfast, only said, "I didn't find anything in here that I'd care to eat."

"Don't worry, I'll feed my new pet."

"Pet?" Her eyes glittered. "I never knew I could hate someone as deeply as I do you."

"I often help others discover the outer limits of their hatred. It's a talent of mine." Musing on his own perplexing situation, he said, "It must confuse you to desire a male you despise."

"No, I figured out what's happening."

"I'm unwillingly intrigued. Tell me what your little mortal brain *fie-gered* out," he said, imitating her drawl.

She narrowed her eyes. "I've always liked men. Before prison I had boyfriends enough, went parking every weekend."

Jealousy flared inside him, though he'd be damned if he knew why. *Elizabeth* wasn't his.

As if remembering a former *boyfriend*, she gazed past Lothaire. Her eyes gone languid, she twirled a lock of hair, running it over her plump bottom lip.

That hair. Those lips—

"Miss me some parking," she absently murmured, a blush spreading along her high cheekbones. "Hot, hectic . . . *parking*." Just when he was about to smash something, she met his gaze. "In the last five years, I've seen a total of *nine* men. Think about that for a second. Then you'll understand how even *you* can look good."

"Even I?" His tone was scoffing. "My natural attributes would have nothing to do with that?" He gestured at himself, indicating his faultless physique.

He'd grown to be perfectly wrought.

Exactly as promised.

But, by all the gods, what will it take to keep my own promises?

"Lothaire, just because I'm sexually desperate doesn't make you a peach."

Sexually desperate? His mind flashed to that time he'd seen her in the water eagerly kissing that boy, her fingers biting into his shoulders as her mouth had moved on his. The male's expression had been one of wonderment before his eyes had slid closed, lust overwhelming him. . . .

Red covered Lothaire's vision. Elizabeth had writhed against the boy, as if unable to get close enough to him—

Lothaire hurled his glass across the kitchen, blood and shards exploding against the wall. He traced before her, clutching her upper arms to yank her out of her seat.

Her heartbeat raced, her eyes widening with delightful fear. . . .

17

Ellie's hands flew to the vampire's chest as his mouth descended to her neck. "What is *wrong* with you?"

"This body belongs to me now! It will never be touched by another." Against her skin, he grated, "Damn you, allow Saroya to rise!" His lips parted, and his tongue flicked out.

"Oh! I-I can't—she's not even trying." *Is he gonna drink from me again?*

His skin was warmer than it'd been earlier, growing hotter and hotter beneath her fingers.

Another wicked lick on her neck sent shivers coursing through her. Ellie's nipples tightened into sensitive points, her breasts swelling.

"You're in need of my touch. Fade back and make her come to me," he commanded, his voice gravelly. "I'll pleasure this body, and then you'll be relieved of this ache when you wake."

"I don't know how to fade back," she cried, her accent growing thicker. He was kissing her neck so greedily, not biting, but still with an urgent hunger. "Oh, God, I can't think when *you're doin' that*." Had she moaned the last?

She must have, because he broke away from her, gazing down to gauge her reaction. She was panting, eyes focused on his sexy mouth, those lips.

He unfastened the button on her slacks. "You hate me . . ."

She gulped with fear. And anticipation.

". . . but you'll still let me do whatever I want to you." He pinched her zipper, rasping words in Russian to her as he slowly began to tug it down.

"I-I hate you more than anything! But that—that mouth of yourn feels so *good*. You probably got some kind of unnatural vampire control over me." Something had to explain this animal craving she felt for him.

When he spread her slacks open and fingered the lace on her silk panties with a groan, Ellie bit her bottom lip, struggling to keep her eyes open. Would his fingers continue to dip down, discovering her wetness . . . ?

How much more could he control? Her life, her future, and now her desires? She was suffering from temporary insanity, understandable considering everything she'd been through.

Everything *he* had put her through.

At the thought, she hated him all over again. Ellie gave a hard shake of her head, then met his fiery eyes. "No, I *won't* let you do whatever you want." She grabbed his wrist, pulling his ever-descending hand from her panties. "Because I do not want *you,* will *never* want you."

A muscle ticked in his jaw.

She didn't know if he was going to kiss her more—or kill her.

He turned and punched the kitchen wall, sending up a plume of plaster. "As if I want you—I detest you so much it burns! And I can't kill you!"

"Yet."

He swung his gaze on her. "Not yet. But soon." He vanished, reappearing seconds later, completely dressed.

His broad chest was still heaving under a dark gray sweater of some fine material, probably cashmere or something expensive. Whatever it was fitted over his muscles like a second skin. His black slacks were obviously tailored for him. He wore a sword belt and sword.

Staggeringly handsome.

"We're going for a jaunt."

A chance to escape? "Where?"

"To see a hag."

Lothaire traced Elizabeth inside a seaside shack at the edge of a solitary beach on the Outer Banks.

He needed an emergency meeting with his oracle, a fey female known as the Hag in the Basement.

"Where are we?" Elizabeth whispered. "You said your enemies would find me outside of the apartment!"

"Not here. Her protections are identical to mine." Elizabeth would be safe enough. Besides, he had no choice but to consult with Hag—his mind was growing more disordered.

Dangerously so.

Moments ago, he'd decided to yank Elizabeth's pants to her ankles, then bend her over the table to fuck her right there. He'd briefly thought that a *brilliant* idea.

Making her moan my name before I allow her to come, plunging into her tight heat, feeling her grow slick around me . . .

No, no! Focus! Aside from the fact that he awaited Saroya's rising this very night, he could kill Elizabeth. If he lost control, pounding into her with all his strength . . .

His nostrils flared and his fists clenched. Bloodlust warred with sexual need. He'd already come close to piercing her this morning.

Hag could help him find focus, could help him sort through his memories—so he could get rid of Elizabeth as soon as possible.

The oracle was the one person he even marginally trusted with his Endgame. She'd foreseen his Bride and had told him how to find her. She'd made sure Elizabeth's body was safeguarded during her imprisonment.

For years, Hag had guarded his secrets. . . .

Her home's shutters were closed against the last of the day's sun. The oracle had been expecting him.

As Elizabeth surveyed the open living and cooking areas, Lothaire tried to see this place through her eyes.

Bat wings and skeins of herbs hung from the ceiling to dry. Animal carcasses lay on a butcher block in various states of slaughter.

Hag's bubbling concoctions brewed on a modern gas stove, while lengthy work benches held an assortment of flasks on burners.

Her collection of demon skulls decorated a top shelf—they looked human except for the protruding horns and fangs. Ghoul heads lined another shelf, their putrid green faces frozen in horror. Preserved centaur phalli filled jars.

"Hag," he called. The oracle was actually a young-looking fey who'd been transformed into a powerless crone for a few centuries before recently returning to her true form—that of a comely, pointed-eared brunette.

Balery was her real name, but he liked Hag better. Lothaire wanted to remind the fey of her be-croned past as often as possible.

Because he was the one who'd saved her from it. *Another name in my book.*

Hag emerged from a back room. "Lothaire, I can't say this is a surprise." She wiped her blood-soaked hands on a stained apron.

Though she wore modern clothes under the apron—a short skirt, boots, a T-shirt—she had a decidedly *un*modern black pouch of seer bones affixed to her belt.

Aside from her talents as an oracle—which had weakened from involuntary disuse—Hag was also a concoctioness, specializing in poisons and potions.

Elizabeth gaped at the fey's bloody hands, sidling closer to *him* as if for protection. The vampire who intended to destroy her very soul.

He heard her whispering to herself, *"Open mind, open mind,"* and thought she had her finger curled through one of his belt loops.

"Staying close to the *bloodsucker* now?" Elizabeth's fear was so mortal, so *unqueenly*. Another example of how inferior she was to courageous Saroya.

Elizabeth's attempted blaze of glory five years ago? Her joining him in the shadows earlier? Mere feeblemindedness, Lothaire decided.

"At present, I'm figuring you're the lesser of two evils."

He gave a mirthless laugh. "You couldn't be more mistaken."

"She's the *hag*?" Elizabeth murmured. "She doesn't look like one. Does she turn into one at night or something?"

Hag sighed at her ignorance. In a disdainful tone, she said, "And you brought *human* company."

"My enemies already know she's in my keeping."

"Within mere hours?"

"Nïx." He didn't need to say more.

"We should update our encryption keys every hour."

He nodded.

The fey circled Elizabeth, her pointed ears twitching. "She's even prettier than in my visions."

"Did you expect anything less from *my* Bride?"

"Visions?" Elizabeth's timid stance disappeared, and she pushed away from him to glare at Hag. "You're the one who told this freak how to find me?"

Hag ignored her as she might a yapping dog. "Her body will breed well, even after you turn her," she remarked to Lothaire.

He'd been so preoccupied with the *act* of breeding that he'd never thought about the result.

What would his offspring be like, when gotten upon this body? Though vampires reproduced sparingly, he pictured numerous towheaded children with determined gray eyes. "I'll require many heirs."

Comprehension—and horror—dawned in Elizabeth's expression.

How bizarre to realize that one's body would go on, Lothaire mused, would produce young for others.

"*My* children." Elizabeth balled her fists. "Raised by you and your disgusting bitch." If she struck him as she so longed to do, she'd break the bones in her hand.

When Hag gave an assessing squeeze of Elizabeth's hip, the girl whirled around, swinging one of those fists. He traced between them, catching it with his palm. "Never touch this fey. *Never*. Her skin is poisonous."

Hag was a *Venefican*, a poisoned lady. As a girl, she'd been fed small amounts of poison until her skin had grown permanently lethal. She'd also been trained as a courtesan—put those traits together, and she was a perfect weapon.

"And before you get any suicidal ideas," Lothaire told Elizabeth, "know that she'll heal you before you could die. But you'd experience agony as never before."

Elizabeth yanked her hand away from him, chin raised.

"She's a feral little human, isn't she?" Hag said.

"Elizabeth has not yet comprehended her place in the grand scheme of things." He gave the girl a measured shove toward the kitchen counter. "Sit down, shut up, and touch nothing."

She hesitated before sitting on a barstool, still bristling.

"What brings you here today?" Hag asked.

"I've come for a potion. I need to clear my mind to get to my memories." *My Endgame is so close.* Then he'd have everything he'd always wanted. *Then I'll finally understand the incomprehensible. . . .*

"I need to focus." On something *other* than Elizabeth's allure.

Hag slanted doe-brown eyes at him. "Do you wish to discuss business in front of her?"

He shrugged. "She'll be gone soon. But she does need to eat until then."

Hag told her, "Go into the back room and look for a green chest decorated with leafy vines. Open the top and tell it whatever you wish to eat. Do *not* open the black chest decorated with spiderwebs."

When Elizabeth merely narrowed her eyes, Lothaire said, "Do as she commands. You should follow her orders just as you will mine."

Elizabeth rose with a huff, then sauntered into the back room. He heard a creaking hinge, then her enunciating, "Fun-yuns."

A second later in that country drawl: "Get the hell out!"

Over his shoulder, he ordered, "Eat something *nourishing*."

After a rebellious pause, she said, "Blo-berry waff-els. May-pole see-rup." Then she cried, "Hoo!" *Excellent.*

She returned with a laden plate and silverware, sitting at the nearby dining table. Now that she'd regained her equilibrium, she acted unconcerned by all this, but he knew the wheels were turning, could see that calculating glint to her eyes.

Yet I can't predict what she'll do.

She cautiously took a bite of her breakfast, murmuring, "Oh, my God, that's good."

Another bite, and another. She relished her meal in an almost sensual way. He wondered if she'd be like that in bed, savoring the taste of his skin. *As I'd savor hers.*

Hag was telling him something and he wanted to concentrate, but he kept hearing Elizabeth's fork on that plate, her little noises of enjoyment. He found himself rapt as she twirled a bite of waffle in syrup.

"Are you enjoying your *vittles?*" he grated to her.

"Prison grub tastes like trench foot. So, yeah, you could say I'm liking this." With a smug air, she added, "Plus, I'm enjoying the fact that I can do something you can't."

"Can't I?" He traced to the seat beside her.

With a challenging lift of her brow, Elizabeth held up a forkful of waffle. "Wanna bite?"

"You have *no* idea."

"Of *waffle.* Oh, but you're a *bloodsucker.*" She gave an exaggerated frown.

He found it imperative to wipe that look off the mortal's face. Though he knew Hag was gazing at him in bafflement, he didn't give a damn. He grasped Elizabeth's wrist and took the bite.

At once, his taste buds screamed *wrong!* He hadn't masticated in ages and was clumsy with it, but eventually he could swallow the food.

Elizabeth cast him a surprised half-grin. "You've got syrup on your lip. Here." She licked her thumb and reached forward to smooth the syrup away.

The air between them was electric as he debated tapping her wrist for a drink to wash it all down—

Hag cleared her throat. "The *ring*, Lothaire?"

Reluctantly, he rose. "You still haven't seen it in visions?"

She made room for him to sit at the counter, stowing a pile of what looked like bird skulls. "I've had no more luck than you. It's hidden, with some *very* strong magics. Every time I try to uncover its location, I weaken my ability."

I can feel *the mortal's gaze still on me.* Which meant he was having difficulty keeping his eyes off her. He shoved his fingers through his hair. "Can you aid my concentration?"

"Possibly. But we have other concerns as well. La Dorada."

The Sorceri Queen of Evil. A few weeks ago, he'd located her slumbering in a hidden Amazonian tomb. She'd been half-dead, mummified for centuries in a sarcophagus, with the Ring of Sums on her thumb.

Though she'd had protection spells attached to her, including one guaranteed to wake her, Lothaire had ripped off her crusty thumb and stolen the ring.

And possibly he'd flooded her tomb with a tidal wave.

Perhaps I oughtn't to have brazenly stolen her most beloved possession off her body, waking her and potentially heralding the apocalypse?

I might've left her thumb. . . .

"I've seen Dorada in visions, have sensed her," Hag continued. "The Queen of Evil will stop at nothing to punish you."

A "Queen" was a sorceress who wielded more control over something than any other sorceress. When Dorada was fully regenerated, she could control evil beings—including Lothaire.

But he hadn't been concerned about her power, figuring that with the ring he could defeat her easily enough. Yet just when he'd been about to slip it on his finger, he'd been captured by Declan Chase.

"I'll deal with her once I've found the ring," Lothaire said. "We've got some time. Just seven days ago, I managed to cast her into a fiery chasm." When all hell had broken loose—or rather, when all the immortal prisoners had broken loose from the Order's holding cells—her zombie Wendigos had attacked him as a pack.

He'd defeated all of them, a particularly noteworthy feat considering he'd been starving, recovering from torture, mystically weakened, and unable to trace. Then he'd turned his hate-filled gaze to Dorada. . . .

Hag fiddled with a smoking flask. "The sorceress is already coming for you."

"Risen so quickly, has she?" After dispatching the Wendigos, he'd leapt over a crevasse to reach Dorada, casting her down. But she'd caught his leg. As they'd dangled, he'd done what anyone would in his situation—booted her in the face until her skull caved in and an eye popped out.

In the end, she'd plummeted into an abyss hundreds of feet deep.

"Yes, Dorada is rebounding from the injuries you inflicted—and from her mummified state. Lothaire, if you barely prevailed against her last time, and she is regenerating now . . . ? Her control over all evil creatures will be absolute in a matter of weeks, maybe even days."

Then she could command him to greet a noonday sun in an equatorial desert, which would kill even him.

Elizabeth coughed, hiding a grin behind her fist.

"Why are you amused?" he demanded.

"Sounds to me like you almost got your ass spanked by a chick. I don't know who this Dorada is, but I'm wishing her all the luck in the world."

Hag gasped. Lothaire slammed his fist onto the stool beside him, smashing it, splinters flying.

As he and Hag watched in astonishment, the mortal calmly picked them off her plate and out of her hair, then ate another bite of waffle.

18

Several realities had become apparent to Ellie as the immortals had talked in front of her like she was an oblivious toddler in a high chair.

One: Lothaire was having difficulty finding the ring that equaled Ellie's death.

Two: His concentration suffered when he went round the bend.

Three: Ellie needed to make him go round the bend as often as possible.

Four: She risked dying with every attempt. And that was okay. *Win-win.*

Yet now his forbidding expression was doing a number on her courage. To bolster it again, she reminded herself that she was already as good as dead.

Ellie had once read an article about wartime post-traumatic stress disorder. She remembered one particular army officer would tell new frontline soldiers, "You died the day you signed on for this war. You're *already* dead. So why not be brave now?"

I died the day Saroya landed in me. So why not take Lothaire's sanity down with me?

His voice vibrating with rage, the vampire said, "I'd been tortured and deprived of blood for weeks before I faced Dorada."

Ellie gave him a look as if she was mildly embarrassed for him. "But wasn't *she* still a mummy or something? Regenerating and all? Sounds like you're the flyweight to her heavy."

Out of the corner of her eye, she saw Hag's jaw drop.

Lothaire traced in front of her, clenching his fists so hard blood began to drip from them. "The sorceress had a dozen Wendigo guards that I defeated."

"I don't know what a Wendigo is. Could be a Lore bunny. But it sounds like *you* consider that feat a big deal."

Hag intervened. "Wendigos are ravenous zombies, contagious even to immortals, lightning fast, with claws and fangs as long as blades. In the past, *one* has been enough to decimate an entire species of immortals. Much less a dozen."

In a chipper tone, Ellie asked her, "You're sweet on Lothaire, ain't you?"

Now Hag strode toward her with undisguised malice.

In a disbelieving tone, Lothaire grated, "Your *insolence*—"

"I'm just funning with you two chuckleheads. But in all seriousness, Lothaire, you should defeat Dorada before you worry about the ring."

Hag said, "If you won't shut your mouth, I'll seal your lips for you."

Elizabeth shrugged. "Guess you don't want my advice."

"He told you to *shut up*."

But Lothaire raised his hand. "Occasionally my new pet does tricks." To Elizabeth, he said, "Speak."

"If Dorada can control all evil creatures, then you better get while the gettin's good with that one." She held his gaze. "I'm keenly aware that there's no fighting someone when they have complete power over you."

"If I find the ring I seek, then I could defeat her with it."

"You told me it might take a month to find it?"

"Unlikely. Yet possible."

"Dorada will be at full strength in a fraction of that time. You should always attack the time-sensitive task first."

"A reasonable deduction, but you don't have all the variables. The ring's location might change. If I don't reach it, I could lose it forever."

"And that would be a *shame?*"

Just when Ellie decided she'd pushed too far—and met her goals—he told her, "I will talk with Hag privately now."

"Where exactly do you want me to go, Lothaire?"

"You wanted to see the ocean?" he said in a cryptic tone. "It's just outside. Go. Behold."

Excitement trilled through her. "Truly?"

"We're in the Outer Banks."

Ellie leapt to her feet, racing to the front door.

⬥⬥⬥

Lothaire murmured, "In five, four, three . . ."

"What are you talking about?" Hag asked.

"The mortal's about to run face-first into the—"

"*Ahhh!*"

"—boundary." He smirked.

"You don't usually torment your prey, Lothaire."

"Yes, I do," he corrected. "And besides, my prey doesn't usually *start* it."

"Is her mind faulty? Mortal minds break so readily."

"She wants to provoke me, to goad my madness, so I'll attack and kill her."

"She's taking advantage of your greatest weakness so soon? Then she's surprisingly clever, is she not?" Hag added an envelope of green crystals to a flask, and it briefly fizzled. "Are you certain she's not your Bride?"

"Careful, Hag," he warned her, seething that she would even consider Elizabeth for him. "Your past employers might have forgiven your impudence; I will not."

"I never predicted your female would be Saroya."

"In so many words, you did. 'A great and fearless queen beloved by vampires, who will secure your throne for you,'" he said. "*Ellie Ann*, late of Appalachia, just isn't going to inspire Hordely, vampirely love."

Elizabeth was not a royal, not a noble, not a vampire. Not even one among the lowest of the Loreans.

Saroya was a deity.

Hag's lips thinned. *Still unconvinced?* How could she be? *Of course* Lothaire's Bride was a goddess.

He intended to start a dynasty with her that would last for eternity. The mother of that dynasty could *not* be an ignorant mortal peasant.

"Do you remember when I first found Elizabeth?" he asked. "How I came back and told you there'd been an error? I railed and denied your vision, until I found Saroya and everything made sense. It was like an epiphany. And you do recall that I was never blooded until I saw Saroya."

"I could roll now. Find out for certain."

"You might as well roll to find out if the sky is blue. To waste your power on that, when you can barely eke out enough to aid me as it is? Among other things, you were supposed to have located the Valkyrie queen. But to no avail."

When she opened her mouth again, Lothaire cut her off. "Goddess of blood trumps mortal trailer trash. Period. To even entertain the alternative is ridiculous." He leveled his gaze on her. "I will never—and can never—forsake Saroya. Raise this subject again in any fashion, and I'll slit your throat to your spine. Understood?"

She muttered, "Understood."

At least one female knew when to back down before him. Not that Hag was cowardly, but above all things, the fey female excelled in picking her battles. "Now, in regard to Dorada. I don't want to use the ring to defeat her."

He'd planned to use it no more than three times. Though the Ring of Sums was simple to utilize, it was one of the trickiest talismans in the Lore. The ring could make almost any wish come true, but the more one used it, the more it chose to *misinterpret* the wishes.

In the past, he'd heard of two different possessors. One man's first wish was for a fortune in gold. Chests of it had appeared outside his front door.

Another man's *fourth* wish was for the same. Gold had fallen from the sky, burying his family.

And the ring allowed no wish to be reversed.

Lothaire could either put Dorada on hold and risk the ring's misinterpretation later, or face her now and risk that the ring would be moved from Webb's compound.

The logical move would indeed be to seek out the sorceress. "Find her for me," Lothaire said, "and I'll face her."

Hag nodded. "I'll be on the lookout as much as my visions will allow."

"And what of my confusion, my lack of focus?"

"Your Bride can calm your mind as well as anything I can concoct for you."

"What should I do? Bring Saroya with me as I fight to reclaim my ring?" *She won't rise anyway,* his mind whispered.

No, tonight she would. She must. Would it be enough to soothe his mind?

In any case, he would still seek a potion. "I can't expose her to the Lore. My enemies would annihilate her."

"Then return to her proximity as much as possible. Talk to her. *Touch* her."

"It's inconvenient. Just brew something for me."

"There's a remedy, but I'll need five ash vines to make it. The vines aren't usually found on this plane. I'll have to roll to locate some."

"Do it."

She pulled that wad of black cloth from her belt, unfolding it onto the counter, loosing dozens of small bones of various shapes. She scooped them up and rolled them like dice, then studied their placement, focusing her foresight. "There's a pack of wolverine shifters in the forests of Moldova. They use the vines to heal their mortal slaves after vigorous sex."

"How do I find the pack's den?"

She hesitantly rolled her bones again. "It's somewhere within a day's travel of Riora's temple."

Riora the goddess of impossibility. "I know the location." There'd be roughly six hours left before dawn in Moldova. He would trace outward from the temple, mile by mile, while checking back for Saroya's rising every hour. "I go directly. I want the potion base ready for my return."

"There will be dozens of males," Hag said. "Can't you use a blood debt for an extra sword or two? Only a madman would storm a shifter den alone."

He raised a brow. *And your point is?*

19

The shore.

Ellie was staring at it, her hands and cheek pressed against the invisible boundary.

She was so close she could smell the salt air, could hear the waves, but she could touch nothing.

The boundary extended only to Hag's covered porch, as Lothaire had obviously known. Ellie's forehead still throbbed.

The scene before her was so different from her beloved mountains, the view here open and startlingly endless—

Her shoulders tensed when Lothaire traced beside her. She dropped her hands, furious with herself that he'd caught her staring longingly at the ocean. "You let me get this close but won't let me touch the sand, the water?"

"It's just like with the jewels." His words dripped with amusement. "You'll be happy simply to have *seen* this."

She quietly said, "I hate you more than hell."

"I know. Comfort yourself with the knowledge that you'll only have to deal with me for mere days more. With Hag's new potion, I could dream of the ring tonight. Why, you could be dead tomorrow!"

"I plan to come back and haunt you."

"Then you'd have to get in line. For now, I'll return here in a few hours or never."

"I know what I'm hoping for."

After he disappeared with a muttered oath, Ellie turned over idea after idea for escape. But she just didn't *know* enough about this world to navigate her current situation.

She remained at that boundary until daylight vanished over the ocean in a riot of purples and oranges. Sights like this could make a girl want to *not* already be dead.

With a heavy heart, she went inside, taking a stool at Hag's counter.

The fey was working on some potion, looking frazzled. Perspiration beaded above her top lip, loose curls dangling over her flushed face. Even the tips of her pointed ears were pinkened. And still Hag was gorgeous with her soulful brown eyes and dainty features.

Two out of two of the immortals Ellie had met were supernaturally beautiful. Which begged the question—how had this one earned her name?

Hag collected what appeared to be hardened blue eggs, then began to grind them with a pestle and mortar. When her apron gaped, Ellie froze. The fey had a cell phone clipped to her belt.

She decided to win Hag over, perhaps talking her into one phone call. With that thought in mind, Ellie returned to the chest-o-meals and ordered, "Two Coca-Colas on ice."

Two glasses of iced Coke appeared. For someone who loved food as much as Ellie, this chest was like the holy ark.

Ellie carried the drinks back to the counter, setting one in front of the oracle. "You don't look like a hag to me."

"And I'd so hoped not to disappoint you."

"So what's your real name?"

Silence.

Ellie's gaze fell on an old book lying near the pestle. "Is that a spell book?" She picked it up, running her fingers over the cover. "Never felt such soft leather."

"Made from a human devoted to skin care."

Ellie dropped it with a shudder. "Can you really see into the future?"

"Yes."

"Can I open a window?"

"No."

"Your ears are pointy."

"And your eyes work."

"I could do that grinding for you," Ellie offered. "Why don't you put me to work?"

"I believe Lothaire's orders were to sit down, shut up, and touch nothing. I suggest you obey them, Elizabeth."

Her condescending attitude rankled. "I'm not a child."

"To us, you might as well be."

"What if I knocked you out and stole your phone?"

The fey rolled her eyes. "Try it, mortal."

Planning to. "Count yourself warned, Hag."

"Even if you could somehow wrangle it from me, I have it code-locked."

Dang it, back to sympathy. In a more conciliatory tone, she said, "You can call me Ellie, if you want to."

"I don't want to." Hag ran the back of a blue-stained hand over a glossy brown curl. "Look. If this is the part where you try to befriend me in order to get me to help you, save your breath. I serve Lothaire's interests only."

"And Saroya's? You don't care that a psycho killer's about to be loosed into the world?"

"If that is Lothaire's wish, then it's mine as well."

"You fear him that much?"

"I owe Lothaire my life. Regardless, you'd be crazy *not* to fear the Enemy of Old."

"Are you two involved?"

"Of course not. He has a Bride he remains faithful to."

"But Saroya and Lothaire aren't intimate." *At least, I don't think they are. . . .*

"I'm not discussing this with you—"

Lothaire appeared in the room, making Ellie jump in her seat. Since she'd seen him last, he'd donned a long trench coat, tailor-fitted over his wide shoulders. He was out of breath, with streaks of dirt along one cheek and mud splashed up his legs. "Has Saroya attempted to rise?"

"She's not in right now," Ellie said tartly. "Can I take a message?"

"You vowed to me that you'd allow her to rise!"

"Saroya's not even trying." *Where's the fire, vampire?* He'd been away from the goddess for years. Now he just *had* to see her?

"What did you say?"

"Not—a—twitch."

Lothaire launched his fist into the wall, then disappeared.

Hag sighed over the hole, then got back to work.

"Is he always so . . . intense?" Even when Ellie and Lothaire had shared a somewhat normal conversation last night, he'd been thrumming with *something*.

"You are stupid to taunt him. If he loses control, you will die—badly."

Note to self: find out her definition of badly. "What would it take to get you to help me? All I need is one call."

"Nothing you have. Now, shut up."

Two minutes later: "You got a bathroom?"

"Thinking to escape?"

"Thinking to pee, actually."

Hag waved her toward a side hallway. "Do not open the windows or shutters anywhere in this house."

"Fine." In the bathroom, Ellie closed the door behind her, pacing. "What am I going to do?" she murmured. "What to do . . . what to do . . . ?"

"Come with me," a whispering voice answered.

A voice. From the freaking mirror!

Ellie flattened herself against the door. "Wh-who are you?" *Open mind!*

"The cavalry, here to save you." A woman's hand appeared directly beside Ellie's stunned reflection—it looked as if it came from *inside* the mirror.

Cavalry? Her heart leapt. But then she remembered what Lothaire's enemies would do to her. *Harems, whoring, and horns.*

Ellie whirled around and flung open the door, racing back into the kitchen. "Hag!" she cried. "There's—there's something *in the mirror*, something that wants me to go with it."

Hag dropped the leaves she'd been sorting. "Mirror?" She collected a machete from a hook on the wall. "*Mariketa the Awaited.* She must have searched every mirror in the world for your reflection."

"Who's Mariketa?"

"She is the leader of the House of Witches, a notorious band of mercenaries." Weapon in hand, Hag started for the bathroom.

This isn't gonna end well for Mariketa. Ellie cautiously followed Hag. "Witch mercenaries? You have got to be kidding me!"

"They've deciphered our boundary encryption. Or at least part of it." At the door, Hag said, "Go inside and tell her that you want to go with her."

"Uh, all right." Ellie entered, then faced the mirror. "Hey, are you there, cavalry?"

The voice answered, "Don't have all day, Bride of Lothaire. Got nickel beer and disco bowling tonight." Mariketa sounded so human, so normal, that Ellie had misgivings. Especially when Hag crept to the side of the mirror and raised the machete.

Mariketa continued, "I can't breach the plane of the glass, 'cause of the old-skool boundary spell. But you can reach into the mirror and grab my hand. Hup-two, and I'll do the rest."

Hag waved her on, so Ellie said, "Yeah, okay, here I come."

The fey eased her hand inside the mirror, as though dipping it into a pool of water.

Mariketa said, "Gotcha."

Hag replied, "No, I've got *you.*"

Her machete struck through the glass. A shriek erupted. *"Ahhh! You BITCH!"*

In a spray of blood, the fey leapt back; Ellie gaped. Hag was holding the witch's severed hand.

As some kind of beast roared from within the mirror, energy began building in the air, making the fine hair on Ellie's arms stand up.

Using the blood, Hag frantically drew weird symbols onto the glass, finishing just as a flash of what looked like lightning torpedoed toward them.

"Hold . . . hold steady," Hag muttered. The bolt ricocheted off the plane of glass and back into that darkness. Another scream sounded—"*You'll pay for this, fey!*"—then silence.

The glass was solid once more, the symbols seeming to seep into the mirror before disappearing.

Hag sagged back against the wall. "They knew enough of our key to find you. Dark gods, that was close."

"You saved me, thank you."

Her face paled. "It was *too* close. I should have changed the encryption an hour ago. You weren't invisible to enemies. Lothaire will kill me for this."

"No harm, no foul? I don't have a scratch on me."

"You do not know Lothaire." Hag's expression was stricken.

"What if I didn't tell him?"

"And what would you want in return?"

Ellie's gaze dipped to her phone. "You know what I want."

"I vowed to the Lore never to betray Lothaire. Even if I wanted to let you call, it's impossible to break an oath to the Lore."

"Then what *can* you give me?"

Hag's eyes darted. "I don't know . . . I can't think."

"Better hurry. He could return soon. Hey, maybe you could answer twenty questions for me."

In a rapid patter, Hag said, "I'd have to reserve the right not to answer certain questions if said answers might adversely affect Lothaire's interests. A clever person could glean much solely from the questions I refused."

Like how I just gleaned that it was even possible *for Lothaire's interests to be adversely affected? And that you think I'm clever?* "Then promise me information about this world, about immortals in general."

"Help me clean up, and I'll make it worth your while."

"Um, yeah, I'm gonna need you to vow that to the Lore."

Hag squinted at Ellie. "I have a very portentous feeling about you. But I want to live. So, I vow to the Lore to give you information about our world."

"All right. Tell me what you want me to do. . . ."

Hag gave her a powder to pour over the sink and along the machete to make the blood disappear while she disintegrated the witch's hand in another vat.

When everything was set to rights, Hag said, "It doesn't matter how clean we've made it—you're going to give us away. He'll see right through you."

Ellie returned to her stool. "Look, it's just like when the Law comes around asking about a still or a lab. Even if I'm caught with a jar of shine in my hand, I'll deny it. I turn into a brick wall. I'm not the weak link here—"

"I smell witch blood," Lothaire intoned from behind them.

The fey whirled around a little quickly, but Ellie was an expert at this. "Yeah, I cannot believe you freaks ship shit like that through the USPS." She drummed her nails on the counter. "I plan to report you when I escape."

"Uh-huh." Lothaire narrowed his eyes at Hag. "What potion called for witch's blood?"

"I strengthened the boundary spell against them specifically after you told me of the bounty. The House will stop at nothing to capture Elizabeth."

He scrutinized Hag's face, clearly suspicious. "Such foresight."

"I *am* an oracle."

Good one.

"How goes your search, Lothaire?" Hag asked.

"I get closer." He turned that penetrating gaze to Ellie. "Saroya?"

"Not a peep."

"If I find out you have held her back . . ."

"Dang it, I'm not!"

Lothaire evinced the most terrifying look that Ellie had ever seen on a man. It gave her chills, made her want to dive for cover. Then he disappeared.

Ellie was about to exhale a pent-up breath when she remembered an old cops' trick. "Straight face, Hag. He's coming right back."

20

They're up to something.

Lothaire returned to Hag's home seconds later to catch them sharing a confidence, a look of relief. . . .

He'd made himself invisible, but he merely found the fey stirring her pot while Elizabeth continued to drum her nails on the counter.

With narrowed eyes, Lothaire returned to his task. *Yes, up to something.* But he didn't have the time—or the clarity—to delve.

Over the last few hours, he'd covered miles, racing outward from Riora's empty temple through an ancient forest.

Since he could only trace to places he'd previously been or places he could see, he had difficulty covering large amounts of ground. It was almost as easy to run, following the trails animals made as they fled his presence. *Even other predators fear me. . . .*

Though this task could help him complete his Endgame, he found his thoughts drifting to Elizabeth yet again, this time to the look of longing on her face as she'd stared at the sea.

His satisfaction over that had proved curiously *less* than he'd expected.

Why couldn't he stop thinking about her? Or how she'd melted for him earlier at the apartment?

Because even I look like an option.

He'd never had trouble with females before. Now two had come into his life, as if solely to plague him.

One didn't seem to desire him; the other did, but only because she'd been deprived of *any* male. *That mouth of yourn feels so good. . . .*

What would he do if Saroya still hadn't risen by tonight? Betray his Bride?

Lothaire's need to be faithful wasn't for sentimental reasons, but for logical ones. He'd studied the truly great kings and queens in the Lore, and historically, royal couples who amassed power together did not sleep with others.

The males didn't take concubines. The females didn't secretly slip into others' beds.

The pair presented a united front to the world, with no cracks in their foundation for enemies to worm their way into. Each demonstrated utter loyalty—only to the other.

Lothaire couldn't argue with facts.

He'd expected this unity with Saroya, had planned for it. But *technically*, Elizabeth and Saroya were one and the same. If his Bride didn't see the difference, then perhaps he shouldn't scruple over it. He could enjoy Elizabeth and still be faithful—

He tensed, catching the shifter pack's scent. He tracked it to a den entrance, then plunged inside.

Into the earth. *Stay focused.* Five ash vines. In. Out.

He followed a tunnel to a vaultlike cavern—their central gathering place, with offshoot passageways in all directions. Around a fire, bedding covered the ground, and stone benches lined the walls.

Roots dangled from the ceiling like grasping fingers. *The earth grinding over me . . .*

Block out that memory. Or stare into the abyss. Block it out. Focus!

He scented mortals somewhere deeper in the cavern. *Their slaves.*

The shifters began to emerge from other tunnels. Dozens surrounded him, all in their human forms, but tensed with aggression.

The largest one, the alpha, said, "A vampire dares to enter our territory, trespassing near our women?"

"There is little daring to it." Only a madman would enter a shifters' den? Lothaire was beset with boredom. How many packs had he faced and slaughtered? Incalculable. "I seek ash vines. Give them to me, and I'll spare you all."

"Who the hell are you?" the alpha demanded.

"I'm the Enemy of Old."

Alpha's eyes went wide. "You killed my father and three older brothers."

Lothaire drawled, "*Never* heard that before." Apparently, he'd killed so many family members that he must have significantly affected the Lore's population. *Doing my part for the environment.*

A burly no-necked male said, "The leech targeted an alpha's line? Now he's going to die."

Broken record.

"Let's leave him be," a more cowardly—or wise—shifter advised. Others murmured in agreement.

"Are you all crazy?" Alpha glowered. "There's thirty of us. One of him."

Out of the corner of his mouth, the coward insisted, "But . . . but it's the Enemy of Old." Then to Lothaire, he said, "We're out of the vines, and our supplier won't have them for weeks. I vow it to the Lore."

"Shut the fuck up!" Alpha ordered.

No vines. Lothaire should trace away, not risking his bloodlust, ensuring he didn't drink any of these animals in the heat of the fight—

"Look at that," No-neck said, "he's going to trace away, run back to his king. Oh, wait—your king got killed, just last spring. Assassinated in his own castle."

The king Lothaire had served. The king he'd failed.

The death I both mourned—and celebrated.

A quiet rage simmered inside Lothaire. His mind grew tunnel-visioned. Everything around him slowed until even their racing heartbeats sounded ponderous, like clocks ticking in oil.

The alpha will slash with the claws of his dominant left hand. I'll slice off his arm

with my right, use my left to sever his jugular. Coward will hesitantly attack from be-
hind. A kick backward will connect with his chest and crush his rib cage. No-neck will
snatch up a stone bench, swinging while I punch through his chest and remove his heart.

The rest will react uncontrollably, shifting and attacking as a pack.

"You've erred for ill." Lothaire bared his fangs. "Now you all get
to die."

21

"S o what's my reward for saving your fey ass?" Ellie asked when Hag returned to the kitchen.

Shortly after Lothaire's last suspicious pop-in, Hag had excused herself, saying she needed to check on something. Now that she'd returned, she stared at Ellie with a strange intensity.

"Go to that bookshelf." Hag pointed out a rickety set of shelves. "Look for a very old tome entitled *The Living Book of Lore*. It's a self-updating encyclopedia of our world."

"Encyclopedia?" Score! Ellie found it, cracking open the musty pages. The words were handwritten in an old-style script, but legible.

"If Lothaire returns and finds you with it, I'll deny pointing it out to you."

"Ten-four." Moments later, Ellie reclined with the book on a deck lounge chair under the nearly full moon.

At once, she searched for a "goddess of blood" or "Saroya" or "soul reaper," but came up empty. Discouraged, she turned to the *Vampires* entry. Now there was information for the taking! She began reading intently about the vampire factions.

Lothaire had sneered to her, "I couldn't expect you to understand the political machinations of vampires."

Therefore it was *imperative* for Ellie to understand them.

The *Forbearers* were a relatively new army of turned humans led by a natural-born vampire named Kristoff the Gravewalker. They'd vowed not to drink blood straight from the flesh—to forbear. Their eyes were clear, their minds strong. Kristoff ruled them from his castle on Mt. Oblak.

The *Daci* were supposedly another faction, thought to be the first vampires. They were rumored to exist in an underground kingdom—with a fabled black castle that no one in the Lore could find. Nor could any prove their existence.

The *Horde* was the main vampire kingdom, populated mostly by the Fallen—red-eyed vampires like Lothaire who'd killed as they'd drunk their prey. They were led by Tymur the Allegiant, so called because he served whatever king sat upon the throne.

Even if his previous master had been slain by his new one.

Since King Demestriu's death the year before, Tymur and other loyalist vampires had held Castle Helvita, the royal seat, as they waited for the next heir to come forward. They would only accept a legitimate royal heir who held sacred the Thirst—the need for vampires to drink from the flesh.

Lothaire certainly had no problem drinking from others. So was he *illegitimate*?

From what she could gather, he was probably interested in either the Horde or the Dacian throne—or both. But how could he be sure the Daci even existed? Her eyes widened. Was *he* a real-live Dacian?

Ellie memorized all she could, repeating facts in her head.

Forbearers. Kristoff. Oblak. Forbear from the flesh. Clear eyes.

Horde. Tymur. Helvita. Comprised of the Fallen, red-eyed killers.

Daci. Fable? Castle in Dacia. The first vampires. Eyes unknown.

Next, Ellie perused all the vampires' species-wide traits. Natural-born vampires did in fact get sick if they lied. *I'll be analyzing Lothaire's deflection techniques.* They could trace over the entire world, but couldn't teleport out of certain mystical traps, chains, or even from the grip of a stronger opponent.

Male vampires usually froze into their immortality in their late twenties or early thirties, becoming the walking dead—until each male found his Bride and she *blooded* him.

Which meant that Lothaire had gone thousands of years without sex. Thousands.

Concentrate, Ellie!

After studying every word on the subject of vampires, she turned her search to another entry. Hadn't Lothaire said that Hag was a fey?

The Fey of Grimm Dominion were masters in the art of poisons. *Check.* They had their own mystical realm called Draiksulia. *Yet Hag settled in North Carolina?* They usually warred with vampires and various demon monarchies, or demonarchies.

So why was Hag working for Lothaire?

Next Ellie flipped around, reading about nymphs, ghouls, and Cerunnos—massive snakelike creatures that could talk. She swallowed at the hideous illustration of a Wendigo, feeling a grudging respect toward Lothaire for defeating so many.

Within the Lore, there were power factions, such as the Valkyries, Lykae, and the House of Witches. Sure enough, Wiccans were mystical mercenaries who sold their spells to the highest bidder. Apparently, their leader's hand would grow back.

Vampires weren't the only species with regenerative powers.

Hag and Lothaire had also talked about La Dorada, a sorceress Queen of Evil, so Ellie thumbed past *Sand Devils, Sasquatch, Shifters* . . .

Sorceri. Most of the sorcerers had the ability to control matter or living entities in varying ways. A sorceress was known as a Queen if her particular power was stronger than any other sorcerer's.

So Dorada truly could control evil.

Unable to help herself, Ellie looked for *Aliens.* Instead she found *Accession*—a mystical phenomenon that occurred every five hundred years, compelling factions to war while bringing together mates.

The Accession acted as population control for the undying. And one was under way right now. . . .

When the sky began to lighten, she glanced up with dismay. The sun would rise soon, and she hadn't even scratched the surface—

Suddenly the book was slammed shut, wrenched from her hands. "What do we have here?"

Lothaire. Standing before her. Covered in blood and bits of . . . skin. His eyes blazed as he clenched the book.

Shit.

When he traced inside, she quickly followed.

Lothaire waved the book in Hag's face. "Why did she have this?"

Ellie quickly said, "I saw it and snagged it. I just wanted to learn about this new world."

In a seething tone, he said, "You won't be in it long enough to bother."

"She's impossible to contain, Lothaire," Hag said, calmly stirring a brew on the stove. "As you know, she's cunning. Tell me, did you find the vines?"

He shook his head. As if he could feel Ellie studying him, he whirled around on her. *"What?"*

"You're covered with . . . skin and gristle."

He glanced down at himself. "So?"

She tsked. "Sandbox fight, Lothaire? Did you play dirty with the other little vampires?"

"Poshyol ty. Fuck. Off. Has Saroya tried to rise?"

"She's down deep, all but hibernating. Not even a shiver. Which means she won't be coming round anytime soon."

At that, fury fired in his eyes. He seized Ellie's upper arm, tracing her back to his apartment bedroom—with the book still in hand.

When he released her, she cringed at her sleeve. "You got skin on me!"

As Lothaire began to pace, she snatched one of the crumpled letters from the floor to wipe the gore off. Though tempted to run and take a shower, she had to at least try to get the book away from him.

"I wasn't done reading that."

He frowned at the book as if he hadn't remembered that he held it.

"You *should* let me read it, Lothaire. I was actually more impressed with you once I saw an illustration of a Wendigo. Almost like you'd bagged a thirty-point buck."

He swung his gaze on her, his expression saying, *Who* are *you?* Then, with a scowl, he traced to his safe, locking the book inside.

When he returned, she said, "You can't be *this* pissed off just because I read some musty old book—or because you had to play dirty with other little vampires."

"They were *shifters!*"

"I didn't get to read about shifters yet, so I can't appreciate the tussle you must have had. But I'm sure *you* consider it a big feat."

He traced before her, looking positively insane. He clasped her throat, putting just enough pressure to tell her he was to be taken seriously.

She acted unconcerned. "Or maybe you're pissed because Saroya didn't rise." Considering the heated encounter between Ellie and him earlier, she'd figured he wanted to get busy with Saroya, but then rejected the idea. Surely, he wouldn't be *this* hard-up hours later.

Again, he'd gone *half a decade* without a glimpse of his mate.

"Lothaire, why were you so positive that Saroya would rise? She usually *doesn't*. Especially if there's no one to kill or maim."

He released her with a muttered oath and shrugged out of his soiled trench coat.

"Is there something dire you have to discuss with the goddess? A murder to plan or some evil to check off a punch list . . . ?" Ellie trailed off, words failing her, and sank down on the couch.

Because she could now see his blatant erection straining against his pants.

So there's the fire, vampire.

When she finally stopped gawking at the sheer size of it, she dragged her eyes upward. His shoulders were tense. Blond brows drew tight over hungry red eyes.

The vampire did need to get busy! And Saroya was nowhere to be found.

This all came down to lust? Not murders or plots?

Lust was within the realm of her knowledge.

She had experience enough with it from all her truck-cab *flirtations*. And when growing up, she'd learned much by simply keeping her ears open. She'd been raised in Appalachia, for God's sake.

Not to mention that the women in her family had made sure Ellie knew how to handle the opposite sex, because in times past, everything depended on men.

She remembered her granny telling her, "Men are like coal boilers, Ellie. If you find a man you reckon to keep, you got to feed his belly every day, make him burn for you, then release some steam purty regular, or you ain't ever gonna get him to work."

Hell, Saroya could take a lesson from Granny Peirce!

Ellie watched Lothaire pacing so aggressively, imagining the pain he had to be feeling down there. And in his mouth, too. He kept running his tongue over his fangs.

His fangs are sharp, yet my skin isn't marked anew; his shaft is raring to go while my body's untouched.

Saroya, that silly bitch—who'd had time yesterday to amass a new wardrobe, wax her privates, and get her nails done—had consigned her vampire to this condition?

Then left him in another woman's company . . . a woman who looked exactly like her?

If she's stupid enough to leave him unsatisfied, Ellie half-jokingly thought, *then maybe I ought to feed his belly and release his steam. Turn him to my side.*

She stilled.

What if she . . . did?

Could she win him over? Tempt him until he preferred her over Saroya?

Her eyes went wide. If there was a way to get rid of Ellie, maybe the reverse was true? Then she could coax Lothaire to cast out Saroya!

I could get my body back. My life back!

The vampire paced, reaching one end of the spacious room a split second before the next. His movements were as dizzying as her thoughts; for the first time in years, she realized, *Maybe I . . . maybe I* don't *have to die.*

Ellie could bed Lothaire if she had to. She could close her eyes and pretend he wasn't evil and that she didn't hate him to the core of her being. Surely.

You didn't seem to mind when he was licking all over your neck, Ellie.

At the memory, her nipples tightened again, but she forced herself to ignore her reaction.

Could she let him have her? Risking bodily harm? *Pop . . .*

What choice did she have? If all it took was a ring to be rid of Ellie, sooner or later Lothaire was going to find it.

Then Saroya would win.

Never.

I'm gonna seduce Lothaire. Make myself irreplaceable to him. But she knew that would take more than merely seducing his body.

If I were an ancient immortal, what would I want?

Energy, surprise, excitement.

Ellie could keep him on his toes, keep him guessing. She'd win over this vampire's *mind* as well.

Then they'd boot Saroya's ass to the curb, and Ellie would own her jewels!

I don't *have to die. My future is in my hands once more.* She would use everything in her arsenal, all the lessons she'd ever learned, drawing on all her truck-cab follies, her vices and victories.

She'd pit her country wisdom against his worldly—and otherworldly—knowledge.

My fate boils down to making a vampire want me more than he does a goddess.

Lothaire paced, raging inside. Dawn had come and gone, the night over.

And Saroya was dormant. Which meant she had no desire to see him.

Even after he'd explained to her that his lusts couldn't be quelled. Even when the burgeoning pressure within him had turned to pain.

That bitch! I'd been right about her, I predicted this. Saroya would wait as much as a month to rise? While he was out battling for them?

Where was the loyalty, the *unity* between them?

His suffering mind could hardly process this situation. He should have forced her into his bed yesterday—instead of buying her goddamned clothes!

With a bellow, he swung a fist, crushing an antique whiskey service.

Never had he wanted a woman who didn't desire him back.

"Lothaire?" Elizabeth murmured. "I need to tell you something."

"Then *say* it!"

"It's embarrassing. I'm not going to shout it across the room." She twisted her hair up, leisurely tying it into a knot.

She played with those silky strands as if she knew just how it affected him. Eyes riveted, he imagined she'd bared her neck for him.

Bared it in invitation. His shaft throbbed harder. "Tell me."

She crooked her finger. "Kindly come?"

He rubbed his tongue over a fang, then traced to stand just in front of her. "*What?*"

She stood, going up on her toes. When she laid her delicate hands on his chest, he nearly shuddered.

At his ear, she breathed, "Lothaire, I can tell you're stiff as timber."

That was . . . *unexpected.* Another near shudder. "You think I didn't notice?"

"Just wanted to let you know that others could too."

"Look at it, Elizabeth." He pinched her chin and pulled her head down. "Would I ever be so deluded as to think *that* could go unnoticed?"

She kept staring down at his shaft even after he released her. His own head fell back.

Can feel her pretty gaze on it.

He envisioned pressing her to her knees, then feeding his cock between her lips. He'd command her to suck it until there was nothing left of him. . . .

She murmured, "Maybe you want to come back in here afterward."

"After what?"

"After you go take care of that."

"You assume *I* need to tend to myself." After the first stroke, he'd be right back with her, roughly groping, desperate to spend with her. Or rather, with Saroya.

My Bride. Who won't deign to see me. Then fuck her. He would use this mortal for his own pleasure. And if the fancy struck him, he'd make her luscious little body come, climaxing so hard that the goddess would still be feeling it when she did make an appearance.

"*You* are going to tend to me, girl."

Elizabeth displayed no fear, no surprise, just took his measure with studying gray eyes.

"You're not going to fight me?"

"No. All I ask is that you shower off the blood first."

"What's your plan?" With a sneer, he said, "Perhaps you'll try to make me want you more than I do Saroya?"

Elizabeth raised her brows.

"I've predicted every move on your chessboard, every play you could possibly make. This is the only move open to you."

"Maybe that's exactly what I plan."

Another sneer. "Then I'll give you a chance to demonstrate how badly you want to sway me. When I return from my shower, be wearing the red silk gown and go to your knees before me."

Just as he was tracing away, he heard her murmur, "I'll make sure you'll be . . . pleased."

22

Ellie masked her shock until he'd traced away.

The vampire meant to just use her in the most cursory way imaginable?

Wrong, on so many levels. First, she'd never gone down on a man before. She'd limited her encounters to third base, a *soft* third—grinding fully clothed to climax. No muss, no fuss, no pregnancy. Ideal for her.

And second, she needed Lothaire to desire her so much that he would choose her above a *deity*.

There'd be no seducing his body *and* his mind if she was just a vampire receptacle.

Ellie had suspected he would crave wonder, surprise, excitement. Now it struck her that the surest way to surprise him would be to disobey his orders.

As she hurried to her own shower, she debated her options.

On the one hand, Ellie needed to obey him so as not to risk her family. If she were gambling with only her own life, then this would be a no-brainer.

On the other, if her plan succeeded, she could win the jackpot—her body back from Saroya and maybe a chance to escape Lothaire, preferably with a pocketful of jewels to improve her family's financial situation.

After a quick shower, she threw on a robe and sat at her dresser. Since he seemed to be partial to her hair, she pinned it up loosely—just to let it down in front of him. Then she used some of Saroya's makeup. Mascara, lipgloss, a little eyeliner.

But when it came to dressing, Ellie wasn't so sure. She stared with dismay at the red teddy in her lingerie drawer.

She wasn't embarrassed to wear it—no remaining modesty and all—but she didn't want her encounter with Lothaire to go as he seemed to plan it: her in a teddy giving him a mouth hug, then him leaving without a word.

In the end, she donned sexy undergarments, but chose to wear another pair of jeans and a tank top, a red one in compromise. She even pulled on stiletto boots.

When she'd finished dressing, she checked herself out in the mirror. Her jeans and her top were both skintight, her high-heeled boots sexy. But even she could see the outfit needed something. . . .

With a swallow, she yanked off her top, removed her bra, then pulled the top back on. *That'll do it.*

She imagined seeing herself from his eyes. *What would I look like to a millennia-old vampire?* The jeans accentuated the curves of her hips and ass. Her breasts jutted against the thin material of her top. He'd probably want to touch her there.

Just thinking about his hands on her made her nipples hard. *Not gonna beat myself up for desiring a bastard like him.* She was anticipating this because she was emotionally stunted—and sexually desperate—from prison.

The outfit was sexy, but not as much as the gown he'd wanted her in. *I'm gambling with chips I can't afford to lose.* She exhaled, about to change—

Lothaire appeared in her room, his hair still damp, clad in another expensive outfit. She briefly wondered why he'd redressed but figured he would want to intimidate her—or leave directly after his blowjob.

Showtime, Ellie.

He looked lustful, his body tense. "I gave you an order." He traced to stand just before her, gripping her elbow. "You defy me, when I'm already on the verge of rage? I could kill you so easily."

"But you won't."

"I might. Though I won't *intend* to. In case you haven't noticed, I'm quite mad."

In a deadpan tone, she said, "I think you're just misunderstood."

Double take from the vampire.

"Besides, Lothaire, could *your* chess game recover from a move like that? You're not so far gone that you'd risk losing everything."

He cast her an appraising glance; she made a mental note—*learn how to play chess.*

"You understood what would happen if you disobeyed me."

She forced herself to give him her brightest smile, as if she were delighted with him. "Oh, I didn't reckon you *really* wanted me to wear that."

He raised his brows. *Didn't I?*

Drawing on every ounce of courage she possessed, she said, "Definitely not the first time we're to be . . . intimate."

"And why not?"

"You'd want me to feel comfortable. I'm more comfortable in jeans."

His grip tightened. "Do you truly believe I give a fuck about your comfort?"

Courage, Ellie! "I told you I would please you, didn't I?"

Dropping her arm, he strode through the connecting doorway to that settee in his room, with no doubt she'd follow. He reclined against the back of it, his long legs stretched in front of him.

He clasped his hands behind his head, saying in a snide tone, "I'm ready to be *pleased*. And, of course, to be seduced away from Saroya's clutches." He sounded like he was just stifling cruel laughter. "Proceed."

"You think you know my plan—and you don't believe I have a shot in hell."

"None whatsoever."

"But you're still going to let me try?"

"I welcome your most inspired endeavor. Though I hardly think it's fair—since you wouldn't have been able to practice your seduction skills in prison. Or perhaps you *had* been able. Who knows what goes on behind bars?"

His expression was so mocking, stinging her deeply, like a *wound*. "This is funny to you?"

"Uproarious."

"And what will Saroya think about what we do?"

"I'll be sure to recount all your clumsy attempts to supplant her—so she and I can laugh about them together."

Ellie narrowed her eyes. Yes, his mocking stung, but he hadn't cowed her; he'd just waved a red flag in front of a bull. *He's never had a country girl.*

An earthy, dirty-mouthed girl—whose very life was on the line.

She could throw him for a loop. She recalled overhearing boys talking about her in high school: "You ever been parking with Ellie Peirce? It's life-changing." She decided then that she knew just enough about males to be dangerous. He'd underestimated her at *his* peril.

Reminded that *everyone* had always underestimated her, she put her shoulders back and strode over to join him, noticing his gaze was locked on her braless breasts. His bulging erection almost made her falter, but when she reached him, she straddled his lap, resting above him on her knees.

"I want to call the shots tonight, Lothaire."

"You?"

"Yeah, I'll do all the work. You just sit back and relax after your busy day doing evil. Will you keep your hands to yourself?"

"Unlikely."

"You said you might hurt me if you touched me."

"Which is why I demanded head, Elizabeth."

"Surely you're not scared of the mortal virgin driving the truck? Of course, I do have *some* experience that you might like."

He pinched her chin again. "Ah, I'm to enjoy your *parking* skills."

She flung her head back out of his grip, but still smiled at him. "When the only tool you own is a hammer . . ."

"Every problem begins to resemble a nail."

Of course he would be familiar with her favorite saying.

He absently licked a fang. "I can't wait to see exactly how you'll . . . drive."

Then I'm gonna give you a ride you'll never forget.

23

She mulishly defies me while giving me a mind-scrambling smile.

What was she *thinking*? The idea that Lothaire would choose this ill-bred peasant over the goddess of vampires? Laughable.

But, oh, he looked forward to Elizabeth's inexperienced campaign to sway him. "Do show me how you're superior to a deity. Or are you losing your nerve?"

He'd quickly get bored with her game, and then he'd rip off that top and fondle those big, pert breasts of hers for the first time. *I'll tongue those nipples straining against the material.*

"Maybe that's not the only reason I want to be with you," she said.

"Explain."

"I'm going to die soon. Maybe I don't want to die a virgin."

"But I won't fuck you. That I save for my Bride alone."

She nibbled her pouty bottom lip. "Then I want to be with you because I've gone ages without a man's touch."

Her nipples were so hard he could almost believe she truly desired his hands on her. "I'm not a man."

"No. You're not. But you'll do." She reached up and unpinned her silky mane, letting it cascade over her shoulders. Curls bounced over her breasts, tickling the peaks, her tantalizing scent washing over him—

Wait. I'll do?

Then she reached forward to undo the middle button of his shirt, spreading the opening as wide as it would go, baring the center of his torso.

With another smile, she eased in and pressed her mouth to his skin. His muscles tensed beneath her lips.

She gave a lick. He hissed out a curse. Another button opened, another accompanying kiss. Again and again she did this with the lightest kisses. Sweet but sexy.

By the time she'd drawn his shirt off his chest, she'd kissed from his collarbone to his navel and started upward again.

When she reached one nipple, she hovered just over it, letting him feel her warm breath before she grazed her lips over it. At the contact, his shaft pulsed in his pants.

As he gazed down at her, she flicked his nipple with her tongue, making his body go rigid. Then she sucked it.

Just as he was about to groan, she . . . bit it. His hips shot up uncontrollably.

"You like that?" she asked.

"I'll do the same to you, girl. See if you like it."

She gave his other nipple a lick, murmuring against it, "Promise?"

"Playing with me? I'll pierce you, drink from you. Take off your shirt and watch me."

She rose up and collected the hem of her shirt, lifting it slowly, baring inch after inch of her trim torso . . . then the beginning swell of her breasts.

Higher, higher, about to reveal her nipples—

She let the material drop. "I'm driving. Not ready to put the top down yet."

He grabbed a length of her hair, wrapping it around his fist. "Understand me, Elizabeth," he began, about to tell her that he was done playing her game. But the *rána* came over him. *Can't lie.*

Apparently he . . . *wasn't* done playing her game?

Might I even like *it?*

Not with her! He tugged sharply on her hair.

Instead of crying out with fear, she said, "Looks like you're going to drive, then. It's a shame you won't be seeing the one thing I'm really, *really* good at."

Damn her. Again she'd spurred his curiosity. He recalled the pleasure he'd felt merely from watching her dismantle his cable box. He certainly hadn't expected her actions then; what other surprises did she have in store for him? "Hmm. *How* good?"

"I'm probably better at it than you are at killing."

"You've got five minutes to impress me," he said. "And know this, my killing skills are exceedingly well-honed. You had better have me yelling to the rafters."

"Hell, Lothaire, I can do that in four. Now, if you're done chattin' me up, I'd love to show you my tits."

He stifled a shocked cough. *Mask your surprise. Show no reaction.* Eyes narrowed, he released her so she could remove her top.

When she was bare to him, he hissed between his teeth.

The mortal's breasts were . . . divine. High and full, with smooth, golden skin. Her rosy nipples were upturned.

As he stared transfixed, she lowered herself atop his shaft, wrenching a groan from him and a cry from her. "Damn, vampire, you came loaded for bear!"

"What does *that* mean?"

"Hunters in bear country have to go out armed to the teeth, even if they're hunting small game. So what I'm saying is you're hung, and very, very hard."

"I'm superlative in every way."

"Uh-huh." She laid her hand flat on his chest, then leaned forward to press her breasts against him. With her hand fitted between their bodies, she stroked his nipple—and her own—as she tenderly kissed his cheek, then the corner of his lips, giving a little lick there. "I like the way you taste, Lothaire."

When she was lustful like this, her accent grew thicker, the cadence more *pleasing*.

For some reason, he found it . . . sexy as hell.

"You taste all *superlative*."

Was she making fun of him? Another stroke of his nipple. He couldn't think.

And then she really began to talk. After sucking on his earlobe, she whispered to him how she felt—*wet and aching*—how he felt against her—*hot, rigid like steel.* How she imagined licking him from his knees to his neck and feasting in between. "Would you feed me my fill, vampire . . . ?"

Yes. Yes I would. All the while he struggled to resist the heat bearing down on him.

And Lothaire realized he might like her games indeed.

What had started as an exercise, a means of self-preservation for Ellie, soon burned out of control.

Just the way he was *gazing* at her aroused her like nothing in memory. He stared at her as if he wanted to *devour* her.

Would he really bite her breasts? At the idea, her nipples puckered even more, as if taunting him to do it.

His flawless skin called to her lips; the unyielding planes of his body made her breath shallow. And every intake of air brought his delicious scent into her—woodsy, masculine with a bite. "I love your scent too."

"I know. I saw your reaction when you smelled my coat."

She was too turned on to be embarrassed, her attention spellbound by the muscles of his torso, by the promise of that incredible strength in every sculpted inch of him. "Your muscles are hard, vampire. They feel so good."

"My cock's hard too," he rasped. When his shaft surged beneath her, her sex throbbed in readiness for it. "Does that feel good, pet?"

His rough accent, his challenging tone . . . desire as she'd never known flooded her. "Just when I think it can't get any harder, it does."

She gazed at his lips while licking her own. She needed to kiss him. But would his fangs cut her?

Soon she'd be uncaring. . . .

Ellie was losing control. When she got turned on enough, her mind seemed to go blank until all she cared about was reaching her orgasm. There'd never been any communion with her partner, no meeting of their eyes and minds.

Just her working to get off.

She'd never set out to rock a boy's world or anything like that. It was only a fortunate coincidence that the guy beneath her always got off, too.

And now the seam of her jeans and the top of Lothaire's shaft had aligned against her aching clitoris. She was about to start moving on him, and then it'd be all over. She'd find a rhythm that would bring her to her end.

"I can feel your heat," he grated. "Want these pants off you."

Take away that perfection? She pressed her forefinger over his lips, giving him an indulgent smile. "Just let me do what I'm needin' to."

24

Lothaire put his hand over her throat, pushing her back. "You *are* mad, then?"

Again, he saw no fear in Elizabeth's eyes. They were heavy-lidded, a deep, lambent gray.

"You flirt with my rage, as if trying to bring it forth?"

"That's not what I'm trying to bring forth just now. Busy on something else." She used both hands to draw her silky hair up, piling it atop her head. The sublime scent of her hair washed over him as her breasts swayed. His thoughts grew indistinct.

No! He was angered over something, needed to discipline her. "You've had your five minutes. Now it's time . . ." His words trailed off.

Because she'd begun to *move.*

Gods almighty. His head dropped forward, his gaze riveted as she languidly rocked her hips up and back over his lap, sensually rubbing her sex along his swollen shaft.

After another undulation, she moaned, drawing his gaze up.

His vampiric instincts fired, noting the changes in his prey. She panted her breaths as her pupils dilated; blood tinged her high cheekbones, spreading down her neck to her breasts, stiffening her nipples even more.

Yes, he'd seen lovers reach a point of no return when all inhibitions were lost, when nothing could pull them apart. Elizabeth was there.

For once, he thought he might like to experience that point himself.

"Lothaire, you're looking at my nipples . . . still wantin' to bite me?" She lowered her hands, released dark waves of her hair, then clutched his shoulders.

"Lean forward, pet. I'll only use my tongue on them."

She shivered. "That's what you want?"

"Yes."

She leaned *back.*

Though her boldness attracted him like a font of fresh blood, his anger couldn't be denied. "*You* want me to suck them."

"Aching for you to."

"Then obey me now, Elizabeth!"

Eyes closed, head falling back, she whispered, *"No."*

He was the master, she was his belonging. She would *mind him.* Just as Lothaire reached to grab her by her breasts and drag one to his mouth . . . he caught the scent of her arousal.

Like breathing a drug he knew he'd never get enough of. He groaned, "You're wet for me."

She wrapped her hands around his nape, holding on to him as she used his lap. "Sopping. Surprised you can't feel it through my jeans."

The idea of her so aroused that she soaked her panties and jeans . . .

A predator's impulses racked him, drives to master her, to *take* from her—his release, her blood. He imagined pinning his woman beneath him, her thighs forced wide to accept his cock . . . or his mouth on her.

My fangs on her lush female flesh.

"Don't anger me, Elizabeth. My control slips."

She grasped one of his hands, bringing his forefinger to her lips. When she sucked it into her mouth, wetting it liberally, his cock jerked in answer.

Then she placed his slick finger against one of her nipples. Eyes rapt, he slowly circled the tip. "Can feel it throbbing."

With a cry, she spread her knees wider to get lower. The more he circled, the harder she rode him.

He was going to spend like this if he didn't stop her soon. *Slumming with a mortal?* But, gods, it felt so good. He couldn't prevent himself from bucking beneath her.

She moaned with delight, finally drawing his hands to her breasts. When he felt her nipples strain against his palms, he almost lost his seed.

"Eager little Elizabeth." He used her breasts to press her down while grinding his cock up against her. "Is this what you like?"

"Right . . . *there.*"

"You're going to come?" If he was, then she would too.

"I'm so close." She bit that bottom lip as he yearned to do. Then her gaze settled on his own lips. "Vampire, I'll come from ridin' you . . . come hard till I scream, if I can kiss your mouth. You want me to?"

"You like to talk dirty, show me what else you can do with your tongue."

She hitched in a breath. Just as he perceived another flood of desire, she brushed her lips against his.

Hers were soft, giving. When she darted her tongue into his mouth, he met it, twining his with hers, swirling over and over.

Seeming to melt for him, she wrapped her slim arms around his neck as if she'd never let go, as if she couldn't get close enough. . . .

When she began sweetly sucking on his tongue, his eyes rolled back in his head.

Elizabeth!

How could this feel so good to him? The tales about a vampire's Bride were true? Infinitely more pleasure with his Bride. Too much pleasure.

No, she was a mortal, not his woman. *Confusing her with my Bride.* Even as he told himself this, his fangs readied for her. *Take from her . . .*

Against her mouth, he groaned, *"Bite you."* She didn't pull back; had she nodded?

Didn't matter. He sank one fang into her bottom lip, as if into a plum.

Blood spilled onto his tongue; his body jolted. *"Uhn!"* Her essence raced through his veins, like a fever spreading over him.

Frenzy took hold, lust mounting. Drop after drop wetted their tongues while she bore her sex down on his cock.

Nothing could feel this good.

He licked, he sucked. His vision wavered. *Want to consume her, take her into me.*

Too much. *She's too fragile.*

Too mortal.

Somehow he broke away from her to catch his breath and gauge her reaction, knowing she'd be disgusted by the blood.

He wanted to see that disgust, to remind himself that the human girl would never understand how he lived.

Her lids were heavy, but her gray eyes were fierce on his mouth. As if she hadn't noticed the blood trickling from her own, her hands shot out, her fingers tunneling into his hair. She grabbed two fistfuls and yanked him back into the kiss, licking his bloody tongue.

Fuck! Hot little piece!

With shaking hands, he cupped the back of her head and clenched her ass, drawing her to him, shoving her breasts against his chest. As she rode him, her nipples rubbed up and down over his sweat-slicked skin.

Make me come like this. Don't care. He grew light-headed. His cock was engorged with seed, the crown thick with it. *Just don't stop.*

Between kisses, he rasped, "You'll come, I scent you're close. . . ." He knew if he cupped her right now, her jeans would wet his palm. He wanted to slip his fingers inside her, to lick her honey from them.

She pulled harder on his hair, writhing on him faster. Faster. *Faster.*

Her blood in his veins. Scorching friction over his cock. "Ahhh! Whatever you do . . . do not stop this . . ." Tongues tangling. Pressure building—

His body stiffened, back bowing. The pleasure made him break the kiss to throw back his head and roar, *"Fuck! Elizavetta!"*

For a moment, his mind rolled over, grew blissfully blank. All he could perceive was her heart racing.

Then he heard his own savage groan: "Woman, you're making me . . . *come!*" Seed shot from his cock, the ejaculation so strong he bellowed curses in Russian. He yelled uncontrollably with each jet, louder and louder.

Her undulations grew frantic. As she bathed semen all over his shaft, he thought, *Follow me, Elizavetta, follow me down.*

"Lothaire!" Ellie screamed. "Oh, God, I'm coming, *coming*—" Her lids slid shut. Her orgasm overwhelmed her.

Wave after wave of searing, slick rapture.

But the intensity continued to build, almost frightening her. Her eyes flashed open. "L-Lothaire?" she whispered as her sex helplessly continued to spasm, empty. "It won't end!"

His fiery gaze was locked on hers. He spoke foreign words to her that she didn't understand, but they throbbed with ferocity, with *hunger.*

Those eyes . . . lost in them.

Finally, her release subsided. With a whimper, Ellie collapsed over him, burying her face against his neck.

I'm out of my depth.

She'd never known anything like this. There were orgasms, and then there was *coming!*

Wrapping his arm around her neck, he yanked her beside him, dragging her close until her breasts pressed hard against his side. She had no other place to put her hand but on his heaving chest, above his thundering heart.

Emotionally stunted, sexually desperate, she repeated to herself. That was the only reason she'd just screamed in abandon with the male who was bent on killing her.

The vampire who'd bitten her lip for blood.

After a hesitation, he rested his chin on her head. Just when she thought they were acting like normal lovers, he grabbed her wrist and shoved her hand into the wet heat of his pants. "Eager little Elizabeth. Feel what you made me do."

Without thought, she closed her fingers around his damp shaft, still semihard. When it pulsed in reaction, she sighed softly. The first one she'd ever held.

She longed to see it, to kiss it. Never had she been interested in giving head, as he'd called it. But now she licked her top lip, imagining it was the swollen crown. . . .

"If I wasn't so spent, I'd make you clean me up." He sounded angry, but then he leaned down to brush his lips over her ear. "With your tongue."

She shivered at his husky tone. As she pondered whether he was serious, and what her own reaction might be, he said, "The blood kiss didn't bother you."

"I was kind of in the moment. I pleased you, didn't I?" She gave him a squeeze, earning a growl. "Made you yell to the rafters?"

He suddenly went tense, clutching her wrist hard. "All your effort was in vain, little pet." He yanked her hand away. "Your pathetic attempt to garner my affections failed. You can't compare to Saroya."

Without another word, he disappeared.

25

Wallowing in a human, just like my father.

Appalled with himself, Lothaire traced into his bathroom, stripping for another shower. As the water sluiced over him, he pressed his palms against the wall, grappling for calm.

In the throes, he'd wanted to *consume* Elizabeth, so frenzied he'd reverted to his native tongue.

He'd never lost control like that, couldn't remember ever coming so hard—as if he'd been dismantled like a puzzle, then slowly pieced back together.

And he hadn't even claimed her.

He would never forget the look in her eyes when she'd grabbed his hair, yanking him close for more of that blood-drenched kiss.

I'll never forget coming like a fountain as my Bride orgasmed over me.

No, no . . . she wasn't his Bride. Being near Saroya before had primed him; Elizabeth had merely been in the right place at the right time.

If Saroya had bothered to rise, *she* would have wrung that staggering ejaculation from him. Saroya would be the one intriguing the living hell out of him right now.

Of course.

Still, he kept replaying what had just occurred with the mortal, finding himself aroused all over again. Just moments after that kind of release?

He scowled down at his rampant cock. *This will not do.*

He'd ridiculed Elizabeth's intentions, expecting to be amused by her inexperience. At the very least, he'd expected her to feign desire. Instead, she'd been desperate to come, working his seed from him without using her mouth or hands.

By *riding* him. Wantonly. Which made him imagine her naked, riding other things. *My thigh, my mouth . . .*

Elizabeth had said she'd had boyfriends enough. How many had she practiced on to be able to move like that?

How many had been just like him, lost in her, powerless to do anything but spill beneath her? Lothaire's fangs sharpened with aggression at the thought of her with another.

At least none of her "boyfriends" had taken her virginity. He wondered why she hadn't squandered it. Lothaire hadn't been there to interrupt every swimming session with young males, and obviously she enjoyed her sexuality.

As did I.

He smirked. *Elizabeth's maidenhead belongs to me alone.*

His smirk faded. He would never know *her* like that. He could only claim Saroya.

Never to experience Elizabeth's unbridled passion? Never to inch his cock into her dripping sex?

So he'd be no different from all her other conquests.

His fist shot out, connecting with the wall. Marble crumbled; his erection waned.

He wanted to kill anyone she'd been with. To annihilate them all. Horde vampires were notorious for seizing on sudden ideas, acting on stray impulses. Just as his mind was about to seize on murder and his seven little tasks became eight, he heard her marching into his bathroom.

Curiosity ruled him once more. What would she do?

He turned to lean his arm against the glass, resting his forehead on it. "Back for more, pet?" he said casually, though he felt anything but. She'd marched in with her breasts still bared, her shoulders back. His fists clenched, his cock distending once more.

She looked impetuous, her eyes defiant. She flipped that mane of hair over her shoulders, which almost earned her a position in his shower.

"I'm here to remind you of something."

Of what, of what? Pleasure rippled through him, almost like amusement. But his tone was bored. "Hmm. Remind me?" Why was his voice hoarse?

Ah, from my shocked yells to the rafters.

She snatched up his discarded pants from the floor. "When you do recount my *clumsy attempts* to Saroya, be sure to mention the part where I rode you like a lazy horse and made you cream-jeans faster than a fifteen-year-old schoolboy squeezin' a tit for the first time." She flung his pants into the shower. "You might wanna get these cleaned." She turned on her heel and sauntered out of the room.

He stared after her. Cream-jeans? Lazy horse?

Unbidden, his lips curled into a grin.

◃━◆━▹

After washing off and changing into the most modest of the sleepwear choices—a long, white silk nightgown—Ellie crossed to her bed.

When she eased into it, she sighed at the softness that greeted her.

Never knew sheets could feel like this. Here she lay, clad in silk, nestled in the finest linens she'd ever imagined, basking in the sizable bed—even though it lay on the floor.

She was being kept in a paradise of a prison, by a red-eyed jailer who doubled as a walking sexual fantasy.

A jailer who'd awakened something in her tonight, something Ellie instinctively feared she wouldn't experience with others.

Just as she began fretting, wondering how she was going to live without the ecstasy she'd discovered with Lothaire, she remembered she likely wasn't going to live at all.

Rubber-band snap. Snap. SNAP!

Finally, she calmed, her whirring mind slowing. Just as she was dozing off, a dizzying sense of vertigo hit her; when she opened her eyes, she was standing in his room. *Traced me again?*

"Entertain me," he commanded, taking a seat at his desk. He was shirtless, barefooted. His damp hair hung carelessly over his forehead. So gorgeous, *too* gorgeous.

"Entertain." She rubbed her eyes. "That wasn't part of the job description."

"I believe the job description was for you to do whatever I command. Besides, you're clearly dressing for the job you want and not the job you have, and my Bride will entertain me after we spend."

"Dance, monkey, dance. That it? Lothaire, I'm exhausted."

"*Do pizdy.* Don't fucking care. Sit. Speak with me."

She hesitated to return to *that* settee, but eventually sank down with a huff.

"I find I have questions about you. Amazing, considering it's . . . you. But I can't control my curiosity."

"What do you want to know?"

"Why are you still a virgin?"

She didn't want to tell him the real reason, that she'd feared getting pregnant with some high school boy, feared having to abandon her long-held dreams—of a fulfilling career, a doting husband, and lastly, when she was ready for them, kids.

So instead, she said, "I guess Saroya somehow resisted your charms all those times you went off killing together."

"I've never gone off killing with her."

"She just went out by herself and murdered? Why?"

He shrugged. "She used to take sustenance from the act. Now I guess it's habit."

"That doesn't make sense."

"Suppose you no longer needed to eat to live, but you *could* eat. Wouldn't you miss the taste of food, the ritual of meals?"

He had a point. Ellie *loved* to eat.

"You didn't answer my question," he said. "Did no prison guard try to deflower you?"

"Most of them were decent."

"But not all? Did any of them . . . touch you?" His expression darkened, his fangs seeming to grow.

He's going round the bend again. And when his eyes grew vacant, her senses went on red alert.

"Slow your fucking heart!"

She cried, "Maybe I could slow my fucking heart if you'd stop fucking yelling at me!"

"I hold your fate in my hands, yet you show me disrespect at every turn."

"You haven't *earned* my respect."

"It could be today that I dream of the ring. Then you'll be gone forever."

She crossed her arms over her chest. "You love holding that sword over my neck. Are you trying to make me go crazy like you? Make me check out mentally before I do physically?"

"Is it a possibility?" he asked in all seriousness. At least he'd calmed down a fraction.

"How much more do you think I can take?"

"You'll take whatever I give you—"

"And I'll like it?" She rolled her eyes. "Do you torture everyone like this?"

He grew still as a statue, his voice dripping with menace as he said, "You don't know the meaning of torture."

"You do? Have you only dished it out or been on the receiving end?"

"Both."

She wished she wasn't curious about him. But . . . "*How* were you tortured?"

"Take the worst agony you can possibly imagine, multiply it by a thousand, then suffer that every second for six hundred years. And that was merely one among many times."

"Six centuries?" *He's exaggerating. He* has *to be.* "Is that why you're crazy?"

"Partly. Also because of the memories."

"Did you see mine when you slept last?"

"So far, no recollections of coal dust, leaking roofs, or the pungent aroma of myriad *critters* sizzling in old cooking lard."

He made it sound so awful—but what she wouldn't give to be back there right now! "You watched me more than you'd let on."

"I had to learn about you, investigating your belongings, spying on your shuddersome family."

She gasped. "You were in my home?"

"*I* have a home. *You* lived in a conveyance."

"It's bought and paid for. No one can ever make us leave." Unlike the land it was parked on.

The Va-Co representative Saroya had killed had been sniffing around Peirce Mountain for a reason. Deep down, it was laden with coal. Va-Co had begun putting pressure on the family to sell. When that hadn't worked, they'd gone after the mortgage bank.

Though Ruth and Ephraim and the rest of the family had been cobbling together payments, it was only a matter of time before they defaulted on their loan.

"You are so proud," Lothaire murmured, his tone perplexed. "And I cannot comprehend why."

She choked back a retort. *Cool it, Ellie. Get information.* "Tell me what Saroya's like."

"Vicious, contemptuous, fearless. She's a queen whom other queens would bow down to."

Ellie quirked a brow. "A vicious female who doesn't mind you spending so much time alone with the beautiful Hag?"

"The fey and I are *not* involved."

"Saroya's agreeable to having all those heirs you want?"

"She will give me as many as I desire," he said coolly.

Deflection? "Don't you want to get started on little vampire princes?"

"I can't claim her until she's in an undying body, else harm her with my strength. Remember? *Pop*."

"So that's the delay." Or was there more? Saroya could still *satisfy* the vampire. Perhaps the goddess didn't enjoy sexual situations? "I have a hard time imagining that kind of strength."

"There are four things that make a vampire more powerful than his brethren. Bloodlust, a beating heart, Dacian blood, and age. I'm a vampire gone red-eyed with bloodlust, a Dacian with a beating heart. I've lived for millennia, growing stronger over the endless days of my life."

Great. She'd been nabbed by the Hulk of vampires. Then she glanced up. "You're a real Dacian?"

"Ah, that's right—you've been reading after school. My mother was Ivana Daciano, heir to their throne. I am Lothaire Daciano, now the rightful heir."

"But they're thought not to exist."

"Of course they exist. Immortals can be just as bad as humans, thinking that if they can't *see* something, it must not be."

"Your interest lies in the Horde *and* the Dacian thrones?" When he inclined his head, she said, "If you're so powerful, your subjects must be hankering for you to be their king."

He made a scoffing sound. "I intend to subjugate one kingdom and lay waste to the other."

"And then what?"

His blond brows knit. "What do you mean?"

"Laying waste, subjugation? There's got to be a *reason* for doing these things."

"Pure gratification."

"How long will *that* last? A hundred years? A thousand? Surely you have an ultimate goal?"

He rose, abruptly enraged, all towering intimidation. "I have an *Endgame*!"

Round the bend. He muttered to himself in Russian, then jerked his head sharply in that way insane people did—as if he'd just seen or experienced something no one else had.

"This 'endgame' is your *end goal*?" she asked. "Okay, then what is it?"

His gaze drifted as he paced. "Seven little tasks."

"Tell me."

Sounding as if he recited a list, he said, "Find ring. Dispose of Elizabeth's soul. Turn Saroya. Kill Dorada. Take over Horde. Find and kill Serghei. Conquer Daci."

Dispose of my soul. How easily he said that! And who was Serghei? "Vampire, I hate to tell you this, but those tasks are *not* an end goal."

He swung around to face her. "Hold your tongue, little mortal! Or I'll have it from you."

She fell silent, on edge as he paced/traced.

Long moments later, he snapped, "What the hell were you talking about?"

"An ultimate goal should be the result, not the process of reaching it."

"Perhaps I take pleasure in the process itself."

Ellie said, "Then the ultimate goal is pleasure. The tasks are still the process."

"My ultimate goal is service to a blood vendetta. I work for that alone, have for millennia."

In a small voice, she pointed out, "Still a process."

"*Ahhh!*" he roared, punching the wall yet again. "Shut the fuck up!"

In as casual a tone as she could fake, she said, "Most people have goals of a fulfilling family life and a rewarding career, with happiness and pleasure resulting."

"And what do you know of happiness?" He calmed, seeming intensely interested in this subject.

"I experienced it for most of my life. And I appreciate it all the more after my recent miseries."

"How could you have been *happy* in that trailer, forced to hunt for food, having so few possessions?"

She blinked. He wasn't insulting her? Lothaire was genuinely curious about this. "I cherished the good times spent with those I love, and I quickly worked past the bad times. What's done is done. I never dwell on the past."

"That's simplistic."

"It's not a complicated thing," she countered.

"It's an abstract one."

"And yet it can be learned. You can teach yourself to be happy. You said your killing skills were well-honed. What if you put all that effort into finding happiness?"

"Then I wouldn't have survived all these years."

"Maybe you can find it sharing interests with Saroya."

"Leave her out of this."

"She's kind of instrumental. What does she enjoy doing?"

He narrowed his eyes. "Saroya hunts, just as you used to do."

"She does *not* hunt like I did." The idea made *her* want to punch a wall! "Did you see me leaving deer carcasses all over the mountain to rot? For no reason? There is *no* comparison. I would never be wasteful and disrespectful of life like that."

"Touchy subject? Have I found a chink in your armor?"

"Any comparison to her riles me up. We are *nothing* alike."

"True, you are—"

"Oh, just save it," she interrupted. "I already know I'm her inferior in every way, blah, blah, blah."

He quirked a brow, then continued, "As for sharing interests, Saroya and I will rule together, protecting and educating our offspring."

My offspring! "I can only imagine what a goddess of death would teach her kids."

"You won't sow dissension. Your ploy is transparent."

"It's only a ploy if I'm being dishonest. Otherwise, it's an observation. And I truly do wonder about Saroya's parenting skills, not to mention *yours.*"

He frowned, his demeanor turning contemplative.

"Lothaire, have you never thought what it'd be like to be a father?"

"It would be a risk—although few would dare harm Saroya's offspring. Certainly no vampire enemies of mine would. . . ." He crossed to the balcony and gazed out. As a breeze sifted through his hair, his shoulders tensed. "A mist rises," he said in an odd tone.

She was getting nowhere with him. "Am I done entertaining you, vampire? I'm tired. This inferior mortal needs to rest."

He turned back to her. "You'll sleep in here." At her disbelieving look, he said, "I don't exaggerate the threat to you. I'd hoped to have separate rooms—not because I wished to afford you privacy, but because I didn't want to look at you. Unfortunately, we do not have that luxury."

"Fine." She rose, retrieved a pillow and a blanket from her room, then returned to the settee.

"Do not touch me when I sleep," Lothaire said. "Do not get near me." When he held her gaze, she suddenly recalled the haunting bellows echoing from his room the last time he'd slept. "No matter what occurs."

26

here am I now? Lothaire woke in the snow once more, this time during the day. The filtered sunlight on his bare chest was like a leather strop slowly rubbing it raw.

Shading his eyes, he peered around, his heart beginning to thunder in his ears. *Ah, gods, no . . .*

He knelt in the middle of a forest. All around him stood trees that wept blood. Morning sun streamed between the gnarled trunks, over the seeping bark.

Again, he'd returned to a place from his past—the Bloodroot Forest flanking Castle Helvita.

I grew up within those walls. Later I knew torture in these woods.

The constant grinding pressure of dirt over him, as if the earth had fed on him, digesting him like a meal . . .

He hadn't returned here since King Demestriu had died. Now, with no king in residence, loyalist vampires held the seat, waiting for an heir with two qualifications: he had to hold the Thirst sacred, and he had to be a legitimate royal.

Led by a soldier called Tymur the Allegiant, they'd rejected all contenders.

Tymur would assassinate Lothaire on sight.

Why did I return to this place of treachery? Why was his subconscious focusing on this memory of his torture—

Cold metal kissed his neck. A real sword? An imagined threat?

He eased his head around to find two daytime sentries, a behorned demon and a Cerunno. They would've been ordered to take him prisoner, to be questioned.

The demon could teleport a retreat; the Cerunno's speed was legendary. Yet they remained.

Then they have no idea who I am.

The demon said, "Who dares to trespass on these hallowed grounds?"

Lothaire bared his fangs. *I will trace with a speed even they can't follow, appearing behind the demon, whispering my name in his ear. He'll quake with fear before I wrench his head from his neck. The Cerunno will flee—until I fling the demon's sword, catching the creature in the spine. . . .*

"The Enemy of Old," Lothaire whispered in the demon's ear before gripping his horns and twisting. The head came loose in a rush of frayed tendons and crackling vertebrae. "And there's little daring to it." He gazed impassively at the sentry's collapsed body.

I was mistaken. There'd been no quake of fear; instead, the male had pissed himself upon hearing Lothaire's name.

The second guard had already begun its slithering retreat, racing across the snow, around the trees. Lothaire snatched up the demon's sword and flung it at the Cerunno, hitting it in the back, crippling it.

Thoughts already on other things, Lothaire traced to the being, stepping over its twitching serpentine tail to retrieve the sword.

As he cleaved off the Cerunno's head with one swing, Lothaire realized his damaged mind was trying to tell him something by sending him here. Yet he'd likely be dead before he could interpret it.

He'd traced directly to his enemies without a weapon, only to wake disoriented in the sun. *If the demon had merely swung first, I'd be dead.*

At least Lothaire hadn't *relived* the torture he'd experienced here. He would surely fall into the abyss then.

I'd want to be insane.

Memories forever haunting him. But not a single new one of the ring. After several hours of sleep, he'd garnered no new leads.

With both opponents eliminated, Lothaire tried not to notice that the tree trunks seemed to yawn closer to the corpses.

The trees in this forest needed neither sun nor rain to live—like most everything else in this vampiric realm, they fed on blood.

He blocked out the groan of a ravening trunk, the whistled hiss of a limb. . . .

With a shudder, Lothaire traced back to the apartment. Though he still needed to sleep, to dream, he was concerned about the risk. Would he have to procure bindings that prevented tracing? Chain himself to his bed each time he slept?

Back in the dimly lit room, Elizabeth was sleeping peacefully. She was warm, soft-looking, so far removed from the violence he'd just meted.

As he stared at her, the skirmish began to blend into his memories, congealing with nearly a million nights' worth of them—each one filled with torture, war, or death. *Blood up to my ankles, and endless screams in my ears.*

Yes, Elizabeth was far removed, must always be so. . . .

He dragged his gaze away from her, frowning down at a dripping sword he hadn't remembered holding.

Losing my mind. With a practiced move, he flicked the blade and blood went flying.

Unsettled, he tossed the weapon away, then sat in his desk chair, lowering his head into his hands.

Madness crept ever closer, the abyss awaiting. *What am I going to do?* For the first time in ages, he didn't know. To be so close to his Endgame and cede control now?

Never!

He raised his gaze, narrowing it on his most complicated puzzle. *Mind over mind?*

A chill in the room.

Ellie had awakened, wondering if a window had been left open.

But the cold had come from Lothaire as he'd reappeared from some mysterious trip, with snow still caked around the legs of his pants and a bloody sword clutched in his fist.

She'd kept her lids cracked, her breathing deep and even, watching him as he'd stared at her with an unreadable expression. Finally, he'd sunk down into his desk chair.

Then he'd given one of those puzzles a challenging look, as if he *would* defeat it or die trying.

Now she watched as he seemed to be making progress, placing a block here, turning the structure to insert a triangle.

She was enthralled as his pale fingers worked. Though tipped with black claws, they were long and elegant. Like she imagined a surgeon's would be.

Yet Lothaire used his hands not to save, but to destroy.

When those fingers abruptly ceased their work, tension radiated from him, escalating like a ticking bomb about to explode. His eyes fired red—

With a bellow, he flung the puzzle across the room, so hard that pieces skidded along the floor and embedded into the far wall.

God, he's so strong. She held her breath. *Apparently, one of the strongest.*

But this wasn't enough destruction for the vampire. While she stared in astonishment, he crushed furniture, tossed lamps. He ran his forearm across his desk and swept all the puzzles to the floor.

He stilled, his brows drawing together. Regret? He clearly couldn't stand seeing his beloved puzzles in disarray. Heaving his breaths, his eyes glowing in the dark, he dropped to his knees.

Maybe I should help him, to sway his affections. "What's the matter, Lothaire?" she asked, gathering her courage to join him on the floor.

"So simple before," he said absently, studying a block from all angles. "Child's play."

She knelt in front of him. "It's okay. Shh, vampire," she murmured as she began gathering similar pieces in like piles, then placing them on the desk.

He lifted his head to face her fully. His eyes were definitely out of focus. He seemed . . . vulnerable. Even with his fangs and black claws, his fiery irises. Even though he'd surely just ended a life minutes ago.

"We will never live near the blood forest. The trees cry blood, drinking deep. Never near them again." His words were the ramblings of a madman, his accent as marked as she'd ever heard it.

Though she wanted to demand what that meant, she said, "Of course not. Why were you in the . . . forest?"

"I trace when I sleep. Trace to enemies. How long will fate let me get away with that? How many times can I have a sword at my neck—before one cleaves true?"

"Can't you prevent the tracing?"

"With chains. Hate being chained. Caught fast in anything."

"I do too."

"When I was a boy, I was caught in a net." He gazed past her. "Couldn't trace from it. The metal was cold and heavy on my skin. They dropped down to collect my head and fangs."

"Who?"

"Look at the lordling leech in rags," he sneered, imitating another's accent. "He must be hungry." A long exhalation. "I was spared. But to what end . . . ?"

Without warning, he laid aside his puzzle and drew her into his arms, tracing them to the bed. He sat up against the wall, curling her in his lap, gazing down at her. "When I take the castle, I'll chop them all down."

"Um, every last tree?"

That seemed to mollify him some. "Yes, beauty, I knew you'd agree," he answered, brushing a lock of hair from her forehead.

The room darkened even more as rain began to fall outside, seeming to cocoon them from the world. Would he even remember this conversation? Maybe she could delve for information. "Lothaire, tell me of your blood vendetta. How do your seven tasks fit in?"

"I'll avenge my mother's death." He raised his gaze, seeming to stare at something Ellie couldn't see. "She died for me; didn't have to. Serghei could have saved her."

"And Serghei is . . . ?"

"Her father. The one who allowed her to be raped by dozens, then burned to death."

Ellie just kept her jaw from dropping.

In a distant tone, Lothaire murmured, "No boy should hear those things. The Daci forsook her, returning when she was no more than scattered ash. But I will make them pay."

He'd been *nearby* when his mother had been raped and murdered? Why had Ivana's father done nothing to save his daughter, to spare his grandson?

Doesn't matter, Ellie. Lothaire's past doesn't concern you. No matter how tragic.

"How does the ring come into play?" Ellie knew that Lothaire planned to use it to turn Saroya into a vampire—*and get rid of me*—but how did that serve his blood vendetta? Shouldn't acquiring his female have been on a different task list? "What does the ring do?"

"Almost anything one wishes. For a time," he added cryptically. "It's a powerful talisman, yet deceptively simple to use. Just twist it on one's finger and make a wish. But not too many."

"What does that mean?"

He didn't answer, just stroked her hair.

Realizing she wasn't going to get more from him on this subject, she said, "I know you'll find it soon."

He grinned down at her, revealing even, white teeth, his fangs not so intimidating in this twilight. Lothaire Daciano was *stunning* when he smiled. "I will. And then you'll be my queen forever."

"Yes, forever, Lothaire."

He curled his finger under her chin, instead of pinching it. "You want to be with me."

This unexpected tenderness, coupled with his vulnerability, was making her chest ache.

"Waited an eternity for you." He ran his knuckles along her cheekbone, his expression one of longing. And she had the strangest urge to cry. "I didn't know what you would look like. Imagined for centuries, searching faces."

"Are you happy with how I look?"

Another roguish smile made her heart clench. "I could stare at Saroya for hours."

A compliment, Ellie supposed. She tilted her head at him. Lothaire appeared younger when he grinned. "How old were you when you turned immortal?"

"I was thirty-three when my heart stopped beating." He sighed. "Last time I took a maid."

As she'd thought. Thousands of years without a woman. "Are you truly evil, Lothaire?"

"Yes," he answered without hesitation.

"Do you really mean to do me harm?"

"When I find the ring, yes. To you, I'm nothing more than death," he said, even as he gave her cheek another tender stroke.

"Will it hurt when you cast out my soul?"

"The ring might bring you pain. I don't know."

Disturbingly vague. "You won't show me any mercy?"

"Mercy? My father begged me for it once. After I decapitated him, I fed his remains to the dogs." Lothaire gave her a sinister smile, so different from his heartbreaking grin. This was more a baring of his fangs. "He hated dogs."

"You k-killed your own father?"

He tensed around her. "Perhaps he oughtn't to have buried me alive for six centuries."

"B-buried—"

"Sent to my grave. Before I was dead."

Oh, dear God. Last night, she'd recognized that she was out of her depth with Lothaire. Now she realized she was out of her depth with this entire new world of his. A world filled with hate and torture and murder.

No wonder he wanted Saroya.

And still, she found herself reaching out to smooth her fingertips along his strong jaw. "I'm sorry for what you've suffered—"

He snapped his head around and bit her forefinger.

"Ow." Like some rabid animal!

When blood rose, he clasped her wrist and drew her hand to his mouth, closing his lips over her fingertip. As he began to suck, his lids grew heavy, then closed altogether. Those sculpted muscles relaxed all around her.

And oh, she responded to his obvious pleasure. Watching his lips work made her melt. When his tongue twined around her fingertip, she felt a slow, wet ache build between her legs.

Why hadn't she let him suckle her breasts before? To have his hungry mouth working her stiffened nipples?

Suddenly he released her, his expression intent. "Need you."

She swallowed, wondering what he would do now. "Lothaire?"

"Do you want me to touch you?"

Did she? Would he hurt her? If he could caress her as gently as he'd worked that puzzle . . .

Before he'd thrown it in a rage.

Ellie had planned to seduce him away from Saroya. *Am I gonna give up after one failure?*

He cupped her breast with a hot palm, those elegant fingers tugging at her nipple through the silk. She gasped, her body gone boneless.

"Answer me." He dipped his mouth to her neck, teasing her with small grazes of one fang. "Yes or no, Elizabeth, before I stop pretending your answer matters."

When he began slipping her nightgown up her thighs, she shivered with need, lost. "Yes, yes. . . ."

27

The fog receded. Lothaire wasn't dreaming.

He had one of his hands on a tender breast, his other steadily inching Elizabeth's lingerie up her taut thighs.

How had he gotten into this position? He couldn't remember. Why did he taste her delicious blood? Why couldn't he recall—

Wait. Had she been *questioning* him? As his mind began to clear, he realized the mortal had thought to take advantage of him. "You were digging for information?"

She swallowed.

"You little bitch!" He wanted to punish her—and he couldn't. *Blyad'!* What would it take to secure the ring—and to finally be rid of *her*?

Frustration bubbling up inside him, he rose and brusquely tossed her back onto the bed, making her cry out.

Yet as she scurried to right herself, her nightgown rode up and he caught the fleetest glimpse of her sex.

Bare? At once, he traced to the bed, throwing her back down. "Have you a surprise for me? I'll see it now—part your thighs."

"No!" She yanked down on her nightgown.

He clamped his hands on her knees, spreading them, rucking up the gown.

Face gone red, she fought, but he easily overpowered her, wedging his hips between her thighs. "I did things your way the last time. Now I'll do them my . . ." His words trailed off at his first sight of her female flesh. Glistening lips opened like petals.

A growl escaped him as his hand dipped to her.

He didn't want to want her. But the sight of her aroused sex and its luscious scent made him lust beyond control. When she needed release, he instinctively needed to sate her.

His first feel of her . . . wet, hot to the touch, unimaginably soft. He gave a reverent groan.

"Let me go!" She shoved at him.

To take this prize away from him? "*Mine*, Elizabeth!" He cupped her possessively, giving her a harsh jostle. "This belongs to me. You don't deny me what's mine."

When her nails dug into his arm, he laughed cruelly. "Like the claws of a kitten." Another jostle. "Understand me, woman, I own your body, will enjoy it for the rest of my life. Licking it, fucking it, all at my leisure."

She'd begun trembling with fear, gazing past him with bleak eyes. . . .
Damn her, that won't do.

Yes, he hated her and enjoyed taunting her—especially since she'd questioned him. Yes, he was furious to have no new leads from his earlier slumber, and he wanted to take it out on her.

But now he had an aching cockstand, which meant he craved the uninhibited sexuality she'd shown him. *Want her wetter, want her abandoned.*

With effort, he calmed his tone. "Relax, pet," he forced himself to say. "I won't hurt you tonight." *Hmm, not a lie?*

Still tension thrummed off her.

"You don't trust me?"

She shook her head, her flowing hair stark against the sheets.

"I only want to finger you, just play. Watch me, then." To illustrate, he leisurely rubbed his forefinger over her clitoris. Once, twice . . .

She lessened her grip on his arm. Another light caress and she began to relax.

"That's it, female." When he teased her, she lifted her hips for more. "So responsive." He skimmed his forefinger between her damp, silken lips. "You're quite pretty here, Elizabeth," he said hoarsely. To utter that statement without the *rána*, he had to add, "I find you *exquisite* here."

She swallowed nervously, studying his expression.

"Put your arms over your head. And keep them there."

"Why?"

"Because I'm driving. Do it. Clasp your elbows." When she hesitantly did, he fisted his hands on her nightgown and ripped it clean from her. Leaving her wholly naked.

Gods almighty.

"Lothaire! Your eyes . . ."

Between breaths, he grated, "I've needed to . . . to see you. Like this."

Tiny waist flaring to shapely hips. Generous, mouthwatering breasts. Skin the color of honey.

The lush heat between her legs . . .

Lothaire believed he deserved all good things coming his way, considered them his due; but even he felt giddy with fortune as he beheld her spread before him.

When she started trembling again, he lay on his side next to her, bending his arm and propping his head on his hand. His casual position belied the need exploding inside him as he gave a slow circular stroke of her little clit.

She gasped again. "You make me crazy, vampire."

"Of course I do, Elizabeth." Another stroke.

This male was like sex incarnate.

Compared to Lothaire, the boys Ellie had been with before were ham-handed brutes.

Now she was dealing with a seductive immortal who used his talented fingers—and his cunning mind—to do sinful things with her.

An immortal whose eyes had seemed to catch fire, red deepening across them as he'd gazed at her naked body.

When he drew moisture up to continue those lazy circles, she relaxed her arms over her head and let her knees fall wide.

"Greedy for more?" Grinding his hardness against her hip, he nuzzled her neck, her ear, murmuring words in Russian.

His warm breaths against her made her shiver wildly. "Wh-what did you say?"

"I talked filth in your ear." Voice gone ragged, he said, "I told you that you've got the prettiest little pussy I've ever seen, and then I told you what I'm going to do with it."

She moaned, her nails digging into her elbows. "Lothaire!"

"Be my dear," he rasped with that deep accent, "and finger yourself for me. Show me how you like to come."

His accent . . . the rough edge to his dirty words . . . his wicked voice was like a touch, caressing her all over.

She readily obeyed him, slipping her hand between her legs, stroking her clitoris. Though he hadn't asked her to, her other hand cupped a breast, which seemed to please him.

"You don't penetrate yourself?" His eyes were locked on her fingers.

She could only shake her head.

"You wouldn't know to, would you? Soon I'll teach you how good it feels to have something inside you."

"Lothaire . . ."

"Once your body becomes immortal, I'll feed my length into you, spending deep inside here"—he tapped the pad of his forefinger right at her core. "And in here"—he raised his hand to her mouth, dipping his thumb inside it.

When she dutifully sucked, he hissed, *"Yes.* Ah, sweet Lizvetta, I'll be at this flesh dusk, midnight, and dawn."

Imagining his thumb was another part of his anatomy, Ellie suckled in bliss.

"I feel your little tongue. Are you to make me come just from that?" He drew his hand away, rubbing his wet thumb over one pouting nipple, then the other.

"Lothaire, I'm *close*. . . ."

"Without waiting for me?"

Rising, he unfastened his pants, shoved them off, then went to his knees between her legs.

She stared in awe at his naked body, at his huge penis—the most beautiful one she'd ever imagined. The veined shaft was so rigid, the head broad. Moisture beaded the swollen slit.

When thought returned, she said, "I want to touch it. Learn what you like."

He gave her an unreadable look—*pleased by that?* "You're busy with something else." He gave a pointed look at her fingers, then grasped his erection in one hand, rising above her.

With his arm muscles bulging, he pressed the crown against the center of her chest, hissing an inhalation at the contact.

Slowly he dragged it over one nipple, then the other, making her moan low.

She swallowed when he positioned himself between her breasts, cupping them until they pressed against the sides of his shaft.

With a groan, he thrust, his head falling back, tendons straining in his neck.

"Oh, my God . . ." *I could come just watching him move.* He clamped both of her nipples between a thumb and forefinger, then thrust again.

And again. "About to spill across your neck if I don't stop."

She whimpered, imagining that hot liquid marking her. "Do whatever you want!"

But he'd already begun dragging the head down her torso. In a haze of sensation, Ellie watched the damp crown trailing over her belly. "Lower, vampire. P-press it against me. Let me move against it."

"Do you want us to touch? You want to feel me against those bare lips?" Again his tone was challenging. "Then kiss me. Rise up and kiss me."

Ellie felt like the vampire was testing her, but to determine *what*?

Dragging her fingers away from her sex, Elizabeth put her hands behind her, raising herself on straightened arms. She leaned up to press her mouth to Lothaire's, wantonly meeting his tongue.

Gods, she makes me *crazy.* He drew back. "Harder. Kiss me like you'll die if you don't come soon."

Her eyes were locked on his lips. "I *will*!"

He grasped her shining hair and tugged her upward. "Do it!"

With a throaty cry, she leaned in. When he caught her mouth with his own, she sucked his tongue again, making his head swim.

And then . . . she tentatively licked one of his aching fangs, drawing her own blood for him.

He stilled in shock even while thinking, *Yes, ah, gods, yes! Do it again.* . . .

The little witch licked the other one. Harder.

Sharing another blood kiss with me?

The pleasure jolted straight to his cock, but the idea of her doing this burned into his mind. Too intense, too *much* from her.

Too . . . unforgettable.

He broke away. Furious with her. Thrilled with her. His cock about to explode. "Lie back, then." He scarcely recognized his own voice. "Grab your elbows once more."

When she obeyed, he rewarded her by inching his hips lower, his cock straining toward her wetness.

She wrapped her leg around his waist, spurring him on. *Hot little piece* . . .

Finally, Lothaire rested his shaft against her quivering lips. *Fuck!*

He had to squeeze his cockhead to keep from instantaneously spilling. "So *wet*," he hissed. "Dripping."

With his other hand, he gently pinched her folds against his shaft, as he had with her breasts. Then he rocked over her clitoris.

"*Oh—my—God!*" Her hands flew to his hips.

"Elizabeth, *still*. Don't you dare come yet!"

"Too late!" She shuddered, her long hair tumbling wildly over the sheets. "*Can't stop.*"

He felt her nails bite into his ass as her hips rolled up and down, sliding her sex along his shaft. As soon as he released his grip, he'd spill. *Can't resist this.* . . .

He spread his knees wider, shoving them against the backs of her thighs. When he thrust faster over her, her breasts bounced, her rosy nipples jutting. *Too much* . . .

Gaze locked on her heavy-lidded eyes, he rasped, "You want my seed."

"*Yes!*"

"Then watch me . . . *come*." He released his cock; his back bowed as semen rushed forth. "*Ah! Elizavetta!*" he bellowed, pumping out onto her belly.

As arcs lashed over her again and again, he grew thunderstruck—because she was writhing in another orgasm.

And smiling. Her lips curled with delight.

"*Lizvetta?*"

When he finished spending at last, he collapsed beside her with a groan, his shaft twitching against her thigh.

Too much from her. He needed to get away from her.

And still, he lay on his side with one arm sprawled over her breasts, his leg drawn up over hers, pulling her closer.

Then he frowned. They *fit*.

Like two puzzle pieces.

Ellie's body was humming, her skin tingling as his hoarse exhalations hit her ear.

They lay like that as they both caught their breath. He even brushed his lips against her temple.

Daubing a finger in his seed, she gave him a saucy grin. "Look what I made you do," she said, repeating his words.

Just as Ellie was thinking she'd made progress with him, he drew back, his face a mask of rage. "Question me again like that, and I'll make you beg for your death!" Before he vanished, he grated, "And you still don't compare to Saroya."

She lay stunned, eyes darting, disbelieving what had just happened. But the glaring proof pooled on her belly.

Before, she'd found it erotic to feel him come over her; now she felt sullied by it.

Used. Ellie covered her face with her forearm, her bottom lip trembling. Not only hadn't she been good enough to sway him, he'd mocked her again for trying to seduce him away from Saroya.

Stings so bad. . . .

She never let herself cry, not even in prison. Now she didn't know if she could stave off her tears.

She'd just gotten off—again—with someone who'd threatened her, threatened her *family*, repeatedly. Someone who murdered.

Someone I hate so deeply.

Before she could burst into tears, she felt a stirring in her chest. Saroya. *I wonder what the goddess would think about his spunk all over her?* If she truly did scorn all things sexual . . .

Hell, even if she *didn't.*

For the first time in her life, Ellie would let her rise without a fight. "For the buckets of blood I threw up. Have fun with this, goddess."

28

"*Oh, you little bitch.*" Saroya rose up in bed, staring in horror at her coated belly. So close to taking fruit.

This was why I was compelled to rise. Lothaire's seed felt as if it scalded her skin, like acid upon her.

Life in every cursed drop.

She rushed into the bathroom of her suite, frantically wiping it away, scouring herself with a wet cloth until her skin was abraded.

How Lamia would laugh.

If Saroya had risen when the vampire had asked, was this what he'd planned for her? Degradation? She'd known she wouldn't be able to hide her revulsion!

Once she felt relatively clean of his marking, she assessed herself in the mirror. There were bruises on her upper arms and inner thighs. Was there blood in her mouth? He'd cut her tongue with his fangs!

Brute.

Saroya's first impulse was to recede. But clearly, Lothaire had just been serviced. If he'd remained in the apartment, this would be an ideal time for her to face him. . . .

As she began to ready herself, Saroya longed for the ages when she'd had scores of attendants to bathe, clothe, and adorn her with jewels. Now she must fend for herself.

After applying her own cosmetics, she picked through the paltry number of garments allotted her, choosing a slinky black skirt, stilettos, and a metallic halter.

Satisfied with the results, she strode to his room, finding Lothaire at his desk, staring absently at a puzzle in his hands. Deep in thought? About what had just occurred with Elizabeth?

All around the room was crushed debris. Had he experienced one of the rages he'd spoken of? *This doesn't bode well.* Perhaps that was why he'd used the human—to vent his rancor.

He raised his head, casting her a sneer. Before she'd said a word, the look faded. "Ah, Saroya has deigned to rise for me."

"Why didn't you mistake me for Elizabeth?" She and the mortal weren't merely twins, they shared a body.

Ignoring her question, he asked, "When did you wake?"

"In time to find your . . . *leavings* on my belly. Elizabeth let me rise just to enjoy that."

He gave a half-laugh. "You deserve nothing less. I waited for you last night, but you refused to join me."

"And is that what you had in store for me?"

"Depends on how good you are. I don't come like a fountain for just anyone."

The gall! "Then she must have been quite talented."

"Surprisingly so."

She might have felt vulnerable that Elizabeth had pleasured him so well, but she was Saroya, goddess of blood and divine death. Besides, Lothaire was bound to her.

He could no more forsake her than the sun could keep from dawning.

"Perhaps I would have treated my Bride differently," he said. "In any case, it should have been you bringing me pleasure."

Saroya examined her nails. It would *never* be her. She'd avoided surrendering to a male for twenty millennia.

Only Lothaire would believe he'd be the one to master me. She raised her gaze to him.

The Enemy of Old would do well not to persist in that belief after she was turned. Otherwise, she'd delight in his last pitiful thought: *I believed she wanted me.*

❦

Lothaire had expected *Elizabeth* to come marching into his room, upbraiding him about his exit and stinging comments.

Was I even looking forward to it?

Instead, Saroya faced him once more.

He was still furious with the goddess for not showing—but he was even more so at Elizabeth for being so inconceivably sexy.

The way she'd licked his fangs . . . her throaty moans . . .

Her passion aroused him like nothing else he could remember. Far from being disgusted by his seed marking her, she'd seemed excited by it. "Look what I made you do," she'd teased, nigh beguiling him.

Don't think of her. Your Bride stands before you.

The one who hadn't risen for him. "Tell me why you didn't meet me as promised."

"*Elizabeth* didn't let me rise."

Pretty little liar. Again, where was the loyalty, the trust? "If so, then she'll be punished. Severely. Though I do wonder how she prevented you from it—while she slept."

If Saroya hadn't risen, then perhaps she'd been afraid to. *The goddess of blood afraid to face me?* Impossible.

"Are you any closer to the ring?" She changed the subject, and he let her, deciding to drop this, to get past his resentment.

Ivana had told him that he'd be a good and true mate to his Bride.

No matter why Saroya had denied him, Lothaire would begin afresh with her.

"No, I'm no closer in my search," he said. "But I might see my target's memories the next time I dream. If not, I plan to capture his Valkyrie female to force his cooperation." *If* Declan Chase lived. Lothaire would find out this eve. "As you know, there's no greater leverage than a loved one."

Of course, Lothaire might kill Chase's female the first time she mouthed off to him. Regin the Radiant could try a fey monk's patience.

"Your plans are sound. And Dorada?"

"My oracle searches for her. So far she has not strayed near you."

He noted her evident relief, but didn't remark on it. "Now that I have you here, you can spend the night with me. Sit." He pointed to the settee.

When she crossed the room to follow his order, he traced to his closet to politely don a shirt, as a good male might.

She called out, "How did you know it was I instead of the mortal?"

Lothaire's hands stilled on a button. He'd known because Elizabeth was . . . prettier.

He'd kid himself no longer—the two females were *not* one and the same. The goddess caked her face with makeup, covering those charming freckles on her nose. And she walked stiffly, not with that sensual roll of her hips.

Elizabeth's eyes were brighter. She smiled on occasion.

No, no. Saroya looked and walked differently because she was a *goddess*. She would comport herself as one. Not commonly like Elizabeth.

When he returned, Lothaire answered, "Surely, I would know my own Bride." He sat in the desk chair; Saroya perched on the very end of the settee, as far from him as possible. Even Elizabeth hadn't done that, and she feared him. *No matter.* "Speak with me, Saroya."

"About what?"

"Whatever is on your mind." Earlier, he'd sat with the mortal, matching wits with her. For a time, their bandying had distracted him from other concerns. Could he expect the same from Saroya?

"Very well. I want servants."

"I can trust no one but Hag."

"Then give her to me. Make her my servant."

"I doubt that would work out as you intend. Some immortals do not make good slaves. Alas, she's one among them. Besides, I need her talents as an oracle."

"This disappoints me deeply, Lothaire."

"It is temporary. We make sacrifices now to be rewarded later." Silence followed. "And is there *nothing else* on your mind?" That sounded harsher than he'd meant it to.

"My thoughts are consumed with the ring."

Another bout of silence.

As a male whose existence had almost always been solitary, Lothaire wasn't used to casting about for things to discuss. "What's your favorite memory, Saroya?" As good a question as any, he supposed.

"Why would you ask this?"

"Just humor me."

She gazed at her nails. "Once, for amusement, I chose a pair of my vampire acolytes, a male and his Bride, and threatened the lives of their two offspring. Of course, the parents would do anything to save them. So I made the father vow to the Lore that he would eat his female, bite by bite—starting from the toes." Saroya sighed. "Afterward, he tried everything to get out of his vow, to circumvent it. At the very least to ease her suffering. But his vow compelled him, and her pesky regeneration ensured that this went on for decades. In fact, he was still at it when I was cursed."

Those unbreakable pledges to the Lore . . . Immortals depended on them, even as they dreaded ever being trapped by one.

Saroya shrugged. "I assured my acolytes that I would raise their offspring while they were otherwise occupied. But I fondly recall drinking them to the quick anyway."

Lothaire's shoulders knotted, any relaxation from earlier vanished. *How good a mother would Saroya be . . . ?* "You harm the young? You will no longer."

"You think to order me again, Lothaire? Understand that I'm a goddess—I have no sensibilities about age. My acolytes were merely organisms I used as playthings. Young, old . . . age matters naught."

"If you target the young, then your enemies will target your own."

She blinked. "I have no young."

"But you will. *I* will." Damn Elizabeth for planting doubts.

"If such is your wish, vampire. I will endeavor to be biddable to you. That's what you want, is it not?"

I might want a woman who will take my orders—and then do everything but. He pushed that thought aside. "Say something droll, Saroya," he commanded.

"What?"

"Are you quick of wit, glib of tongue?" As Elizabeth continued to be. *You're the flyweight to her heavy. . . .*

"Lothaire, I enslave others to be those things, so that they may entertain me."

Silence once more.

He kept recalling that night in the woods with Saroya, how well he'd gotten along with her. Or had he simply been staggered by his blooding? "The first night I found you, we talked for hours. Why is this like pulling teeth now?"

"I'm confused, Lothaire. It sounds like you're auditioning me for a role I've already won. One that is mine beyond *any* rectification. Has the mortal somehow sown discord between us?"

He made his expression neutral. *The mortal has.* He'd never thought past the getting of the thrones and the completion of his goals until a human girl had challenged him.

Now he was forced to wonder what eternity would be like with the female before him.

No, no, most immortals had difficulties with their mates in the beginning. Especially if they were from different factions or cultures. Lothaire was to be no different. *At least in this.*

As other Lorean males did every day, Lothaire would win over his female. He could be charming, if he chose to be. He could coax her to respond to him. "If not talk, then what shall we do this eve, flower?"

"Hunt. Kill. Spill the blood of innocents."

Lothaire didn't understand this need of Saroya's to kill. If she wasn't harvesting blood, then what was the point? He understood murdering his enemies and political obstacles. Reveled in it.

But Saroya slaughtered her prey for no reason. And Lothaire had vowed not to let her kill. "No hunting. You're completely hidden from my enemies only here and at my oracle's," he told her honestly, though he could have taken her out, half-tracing with her to keep her invisible to others.

And there was a druidic tattoo she could wear that would render her untrackable. He could acquire the ink from one of his debtors. *But I'll keep that information close for now.*

"Regrettably, Saroya, there's a bounty on your head—"

"A bounty!" she exclaimed. "Return my godhood, and I shall smite all your foes, afflict them with madness and plague until they boil and fester, groveling at your feet for mercy!"

His lips curled. "I do enjoy when you get like this."

"I will make a fearsome queen for you, as soon as you find the ring for us." She studied his face, couldn't mistake his interest—

"Until then, enjoy Elizabeth," she said. "You seem to be rubbing along well with your mortal toy."

"Rubbing along?" When she writhed as he'd ejaculated over her? "Yes, I suppose we do that quite well. It's a good thing you're not jealous—because the two of us were debauched together."

Show displeasure, female. Give enough of a damn that this bothers you.

Instead, she was incredulous. "The *two* of you? You didn't have to force her to slake you?"

Mildly offended, he grated, "Look at me, Saroya. She can barely keep her hands off me."

"But she just went along with it? Even knowing you're pledged to another?"

"How pledged am I when you direct me to use a substitute for you?" Saroya was clearly feeling none of the vampiric bond that he did. Only one way to kindle that. In bed. "Besides, Elizabeth has taken it into her head that she can win me from you."

"That amuses me immensely."

"Does it? I couldn't tell. Why don't you smile, then?" No expression. "Come, you have a pretty smile."

"You mean *Elizabeth* does. Does she grin coyly for you, Lothaire? Are you besotted? Perhaps you *do* prefer her over me?" she scoffed.

Might Elizavetta be mine? Her name yelled to the sky had felt . . . right.

The thought was so abhorrent, he immediately banished it. "I am dangerously close to harming you, goddess."

"Surely the great Lothaire wouldn't be growing foolishly attached."

Was it Elizabeth's abandon that had aroused him so—or merely his Bride's body? Time to find out. "Attachment? As it so happens, I'm keen to sample her replacement."

"The gall! Do you think I won't remember these snide insults?"

"Come to me, and I'll make them all up to you."

"I can read that look in your eyes. Strange. I thought you'd be spent for the night."

"I can go a dozen rounds if I'm inspired. Come to me. *Now.* That was not a request."

Though her eyes slitted, she did rise and trudge to him. He dragged her into his lap, but she remained tense. "Relax, Saroya."

When he'd lain next to Elizabeth with his leg thrown over hers, his arm draping across her soft breasts . . . they *fit.*

This was like shoving two mismatched puzzle pieces together, forcing them. *No, no. Disordered mind.* "I will be easy with you. Do you not desire to kiss me? To know my touch?"

"You will hurt me. Elizabeth isn't aware of your boundless strength, but *I* am."

"I've managed not to injure her. Twice."

"You've used her *twice*? And she never fought you?" Again she was disbelieving.

"Allow me to demonstrate to you why she acquiesces."

"You say you haven't injured her, but I'm in pain right now," Saroya said. "Bruised and battered. Tell me, Lothaire, do you have any wounds, any twinges?"

"Of course not."

"I have them all over my body."

"Then I will be gentler with you, even more careful with my Bride." Cupping her face, he murmured at her ear, "Just relax, Saroya, and I vow to you that I will only bring you pleasure."

She will squeeze her eyes shut, her body stiffening, as if a frost grows over her.

He leaned in to press his lips to hers, once and again, teasing with his tongue. He deepened the kiss, and she responded . . .

Exactly as he'd predicted.

He recoiled. "You've gone cold." Her eyes were squeezed shut, her lips thinned. And worse . . . he'd caught himself imagining it was Elizabeth to stay hard. "You don't want my touch at all."

She opened her eyes. "I would never be able to relax for fear you'd harm me. Lothaire, imagine going into battle in a mortal state. With no regeneration, no power, no speed. Imagine being defenseless. Would you be so keen to rush into the fray—no matter how much you love warring?"

She had a point. *Convince yourself, Lothaire. You can't lie to others, but you can lie to yourself.*

"When I am a vampire, things will be different," she insisted. "For now, I beg your patience. I beg understanding from my male until then."

Yes, when she's a vampire . . .

And still he refused to accept that his Bride was sexually cold? No, Saroya could be *made* to want him. "Does your mortal body feel nothing but pain? You must have needs."

"No. Apparently you've satisfied any of those urges recently."

Blyad'! He'd wasted that pleasure on Elizabeth!

Saroya awkwardly patted his shoulder. "You'll soon find the ring, and then I'll be yours in all ways. For now, use your mortal."

"Not concerned that I might become infatuated with her?" he asked, though he knew the answer. Saroya simply could not comprehend that someone might not desire her above all others. Her arrogance prevented doubts like that.

And he couldn't help feeling as if there was a lesson inherent for him to be learned.

"Not in the least, Lothaire. If you chose her over me, you'd have to renounce all your aspirations to the Horde throne, everything you've worked for all these *thousands* of years. Besides, you are so intelligent, I know that you can see through her manipulations. You would never let us be the pawns of a lowly mortal."

A pawn. He and his mother had been pawns to a mortal before. *"Beseech Olya's forgiveness . . ."*

Never again.

"You've seen Elizabeth's family," Saroya continued. "Those would be your in-laws. She would want to live among them."

He stifled a shudder.

"I barely survived living in that trailer. How well would you fit in there?"

Lothaire would rather die.

"I have an idea, vampire," Saroya suddenly said. "Take me to your oracle."

"Why?" he asked, still kicking himself for sating the human.

"You asked what I'd like to do this eve? I want to pose a question to her about the future."

He exhaled, tracing her to Hag's.

As soon as they appeared in the fey's kitchen, Hag told Saroya. "Oh, it's *you*."

Between gritted teeth, Saroya said, "How did you know it was I? Before I'd even said a word?"

"Because of the makeup," Hag murmured. "The *gobs* and *gobs* of makeup."

Saroya said pleasantly, "You've just ensured your death. Once your usefulness ends, Lothaire will bring me your head. I'll use it as a fly catcher."

The fey's eyes turned forest green with anger. "That is not in *my* future, goddess—"

"This is my Bride, Hag," Lothaire interrupted sharply, baffled by this hostility. "Not *Elizabeth*. Some respect, then."

"Very well." But Hag's eyes still glimmered.

"You've aided Lothaire in seeing his future," Saroya said. "I want a question about my own answered."

"I can only roll so many times in a day." At Lothaire's threatening look, Hag added, "But I will try."

"Ask your bones if the Horde will accept Lothaire as its king if I am by his side."

"It's not that simple—"

"It is. He's part Dacian. They cut away all the extraneous considerations and focus only on their goals. Lothaire's primary goal is to become king of the Horde. I want to know if I'm the key to the Horde throne."

"Do it, Hag."

The fey grudgingly removed her pouch, spreading the cloth. She rolled the bones, read them.

"Well?" Lothaire demanded.

As if the words were pulled from her, Hag said, "The Horde will accept you if Saroya is by your side—and she is a vampire. Tymur the Allegiant and his men will yield Castle Helvita and swear their fealty to you."

Tymur kneeling before me while I decide if I should decapitate him . . . Lothaire's eyes grew hooded.

"There, Lothaire," Saroya said, "as I promised, I shall place that crown on your fair head. You'll be a king, just as Ivana the Bold wanted. And after you rule the Horde, you'll use that army to seize the Dacian throne. It's all so close. We're only waiting on you, my king."

King. His chest ached with want. *Crowned, ruling, power.* He'd build a monument to his mother in Stefanovich's old castle. *If I don't raze it to the ground, stone by bloody stone.*

"Now, Lothaire," Saroya began, "shall we have more goods and services delivered to the apartment? Your queen longs for rubies. And cat's-eye diamonds. Perhaps a Roman collar studded with emeralds . . ."

29

L othaire just . . . left me," Ellie murmured to Hag, her voice sounding as bewildered as she felt.

For the last seven nights, he'd dropped her off at the fey's—like a brat at the sitter's—while he'd been out tirelessly searching for the ring, so determined to replace her forever.

But this sunrise, he hadn't come to pick her up. It was three in the afternoon. Now she knew what it felt like to be the last kid standing at KinderCare.

"What am I supposed to make of that?" Staring at nothing, Ellie swigged her beer.

She and Hag were out on the fey's deck, reclining on sun chaises with snacks, magazines, and a party pail of iced Corona Lights between them.

After the witch-in-the-mirror scare, the oracle had been much nicer to her. Probably because she knew Ellie was about to die and all.

And Ellie had eventually forgiven her for setting Lothaire on her path—after all, Hag had nothing to do with Saroya parking inside Ellie.

"Make nothing of it, Elizabeth," Hag said. "He's merely late. Let's enjoy ourselves until he returns."

Realizing that Saroya probably wouldn't want a suntan, Ellie had gone

St. Tropez, spending the day out here, slathered in coconut oil. Though she'd always tanned easily, lately she'd been prison pale.

Not anymore. *Feel the burn, freak.*

And since Saroya wanted her to put on weight, Ellie had decided to *lose* it. She was presently on a barley-and-hops diet.

"Something happened after Saroya rose that last time," Ellie said. "Ever since then, Lothaire has been acting different with me." As if all the ground she might have conquered with him had been lost.

When Ellie had awakened, Lothaire had gazed at her as if she'd wronged him, as if he *resented* her.

Perhaps Saroya had proved seducible. Maybe she'd schooled Ellie's attempts. *Though I'm still a virgin.* Of course, Lothaire had explained why they couldn't have sex.

"I'd pat your hand with a well-intentioned but awkward gesture if my skin weren't poisonous." Hag was as unused to having a girl friend as Ellie was.

Each night, once the fey's work was done, she and Ellie had downed drinks and chatted.

Saucing it up with a fey oracle. *My new normal.*

They'd talked about potions, hunting, the craziness of the Lore. And of Hag's single status.

Turned out that ages ago, Hag had fallen for a *demon*—strictly off limits for a fey like her. The brawny warrior had doubted his "delicate little fey's" love, especially since she'd been so young. In turn, she'd doubted he could withstand her poisoned skin for long enough to claim her. They'd decided to meet a decade later under the golden apple tree in Draiksulia—if she still felt the same way, and if he could obtain an antidote for her.

Because of Hag's curse, she'd been centuries late for her date. Now she was unable to find the warrior—even her bones couldn't tell her where he'd disappeared to.

Hag's doe-brown eyes sparkled green with emotion whenever she spoke of him. . . .

"Hey, you don't think Lothaire's . . . dead?" Ellie asked, confounded that she almost felt worried about her captor's safety. *Captor and soon-to-be executioner.*

"He *will* come back, Elizabeth."

And how should I feel about that?

"I would know if he were dead," Hag said as she checked her timer.

The fey was working on a potion, an experimental one she hoped would counteract a spell that protected one of Lothaire's enemies—some Valkyrie named Regin the Radiant. Upon discovering that Regin had a protection spell, Lothaire had hissed, *"Nïx, that bitch!"*

Whatever that meant.

"He might have grown distracted and lost his way temporarily," Hag added.

Ellie could believe that. He'd been deteriorating mentally. One sunrise when he'd arrived to collect her, he'd been covered in blood and raving about his enemies: "Following me! Isn't safe for you."

Two nights ago, she'd awakened in her spot on the sofa to find him kneeling beside her, stroking her hair.

He'd murmured, "Harder and harder to tell when I'm awake . . . can't live like this much longer."

Sometimes he spoke to her in Russian, as if he fully expected her to answer in the same.

She'd never questioned him again other than to occasionally ask, "Am I going to die tonight?"

"Not yet," he would answer distantly. But last sunset, he hadn't replied, just gazed away.

Ellie opened another beer, plugging the bottle with a lime wedge. "Can you tell me why Saroya isn't even trying to rise? Shouldn't *she* be worried about him right now? Why isn't she hankering to see him? If I was evil and Lothaire had showered me with jewels and clothes, I'd be all over him."

"Would you?" Hag studied her face. "Even after all he's done to you?"

As ever, Ellie replayed the vampire's mocking voice in her head. *"You can't compare to Saroya.*" She'd thought herself immune to insults, but for some reason, his had struck home. *"You are demonstrably my inferior in every way. Intelligence, wealth, looks, bloodline . . ."*

The scorn in his tone, his smirk. She sighed. The *truth* of his words.

Her ego had taken a hit.

But then there'd been those glimpses of a different side of him. The seductive, charming Lothaire whose kisses set her blood afire. The vampire who made her toes curl with his accented, old-fashioned phrasings. *"Be my dear . . ."*

"Are you wondering if I could fall for him?" Ellie asked, trying to imagine what it might be like to be loved by Lothaire. But she knew better than to dream of things that would never be. "Even if by some miracle he felt more for me, I'd never love him. Only a fool would fall in love with her captor." She met Hag's gaze. "I'm no fool. My interest in him is purely life-or-death." She took a long pull from her beer. "On that note, is there *any* chance that I'm his Bride?"

Seeming to choose her words very carefully, Hag said, "Mortal mates are extremely rare for Loreans. I'm thinking now of all the couples brought together this Accession and can't cite a single one with a human in the mix. In any case, Lothaire despises mortals more than anyone I know."

"Why?"

"I won't say, and I don't suggest asking him."

"But it is *possible* that I'm his. Why don't you oracle-up and find out for certain?"

"You know I only have so many rolls a day."

Ellie had asked Hag how bone-rolling worked. She'd answered that it was like scanning text in a book, but if done too often, the words would grow blurry.

"What if I am his?" Ellie insisted. "If you serve Lothaire's interests, then how do you think it'll affect him once he realizes he killed his one and only Bride? You think he'd be pissed?"

Hag's gaze flitted away. "I trust Lothaire's judgment."

"Tell me why you owe him so much."

"Very well." Hag retrieved another beer, easily popping the top with her thumbnail. "Centuries ago, I began working for a powerful sorcerer and his sisters. He didn't like one of my foretellings, so he cursed me to appear as a repulsive crone, captive to his will for as long as he lived—a particularly dire predicament, considering how difficult it was to kill him. He was known as the Deathless One." Her fingers tightened around her bottle. Just when Ellie thought it'd shatter, Hag loosened her hold. "If not for Lothaire, I'd still be trapped in a dank castle basement. He betrayed all his alliances, breaking a covenant to free the sorcerer's assassin."

"Lothaire did all that for you?"

Hag gave a humorless laugh. "No, he had other mysterious reasons. My freedom was merely a happy coincidence, but all the same, he made me vow a debt in advance, which put me in his notorious book—" Her timer went off. "I'll be back after a while. Don't get too burned."

Alone, Ellie picked up her travel magazine once more. She turned the page, perusing an article on Bora-Bora, but not really reading. Instead, she reflected on all the things she'd never get to do.

See her family again. Travel around the world. Make a home of her own. Have kids. Ellie's idea of a white picket fence? Her own cabin on Peirce Mountain.

She'd never get to find that man who would dote on her. She'd always imagined the kind of guy she'd end up with, fantasizing in loving detail what he'd be like.

Basically the opposite of Lothaire in every way.

Reflecting like this could make a girl wish she weren't teetering on the verge of death.

Teetering. Ellie was sick of it. At least on death row she'd been able to count down the days till she was freed at last. The magazine edges crinkled in her grip.

Now she lingered in this wait-and-see hell.

She wanted to scream, wanted to strangle Lothaire, could actually see the appeal of ending a being's life.

How she wished for another chance to "cross swords" with him, especially now that she'd learned to decode the way he talked. She had analyzed his statements over and over, and she felt confident that she'd be able to tell when he was deflecting or misdirecting.

If she asked him, "Do you like blue?" and he did but didn't want to admit it, he'd sneer, "Do I look like the type of man who would like blue?"

He started statements with "Perhaps" or "I'd wager" to avoid lies. Or he'd say something distractingly outrageous.

She called it Lothaire-speak.

Ellie did agree with him about one thing: for even the remotest chance of survival, she still had only that one move open to her.

Seducing him.

Part of her wanted to try it once more. Maybe if she got him to claim her totally, she could drive a wedge between him and Saroya.

Or maybe Ellie should just give him the blowjob he'd wanted. She remembered the wise words of her cousin Sadie, the mountainside's resident slut: "If you want to communicate an idea to a man's brain, you talk to him through his pecker. It's like an ear horn, y'all."

Musing on Lothaire's seduction had absolutely *nothing* to do with the fact that Ellie still craved him like crack.

Sure enough, he *had* awakened something in her.

All week, she'd been horny as hell, aching for his hands on her, replaying what they'd done together. When she slept, she dreamed of suckling him, then taking his thick shaft inside her.

She'd touched herself a couple of times in the shower, but could never relax enough to get off, always afraid Lothaire would suddenly appear to catch her—then mock her so viciously. . . .

She exhaled, turning a page, deciding then and there *not* to put out. *I never had a shot at him anyway.*

Which meant there were *no* moves open. *Already as good as dead, just like the frontline soldiers.*

The idea was liberating in a way. The pressure to sway him had been grueling. Especially since he'd avoided her for days.

She was resolved, steadfast.

So why were the pages blurring from unshed tears?

❖

Hate her. Want her.

For a week, Lothaire had kept his distance from Elizabeth, leaving her with Hag and ignoring her when they were forced to be together.

Never had he needed her more than now.

This entire day, he'd tracked Declan Chase—who'd survived through no help of Lothaire's.

It turned out that the Blademan had been an immortal berserker all along, though Chase hadn't known he was.

Again and again, Lothaire had tried to get close enough to him to tap into his mind, but his mate, Regin, had some kind of spell on her that repelled Lothaire.

The *súka* never left Chase's side.

After a day of spying on the couple—including their enthusiastic bouts of sex—Lothaire returned to his apartment, weary but keyed up, lusting for his own woman. His Bride.

When Saroya had last surfaced, he'd sworn off the mortal. And once he'd purchased everything but the moon for the goddess, she'd agreed to rise in two weeks.

But what to do until then?

The separation from his Bride's body was affecting his own—as well as his sanity. There'd been more sleep-tracing, more rages, and even blackouts while he'd hunted.

Instead of visions concerning the ring, he'd been dreaming of things he'd thought long forgotten, random memories—*his own* random memories.

A fair-haired infant reaching for me.

The Valkyrie Helen big with child, her eyes filled with sorrow as she gazed at her husband.

Nix demanding, "Where is your patience . . . ?"

And more, Lothaire had perceived that mysterious presence again. The Daci. He thought he'd felt them outside the apartment on a couple of occasions. But none faced him.

Had they been following him, or had he only imagined their presence?

So many developments, so many moves. *And I can barely keep my thoughts from Elizabeth, my lust under control.*

Before he picked her up for the remainder of the day, he knew he had to ease some of this pressure. Seven days' worth . . .

Lying back in his bed, he carefully unzipped his pants over his aching erection. As he clasped it in his fist and began to pump, he wondered whether Elizabeth had brought herself to come since their last time together.

While he'd been so busy thinking about his miserable sexual state away from Elizabeth, he hadn't thought about *hers.*

She was a lusty female. The little peasant would probably ease herself.

Inside his home, caressing her virgin sex. That delicate bare flesh growing so slick . . .

The idea sent him into a lather and his fist bobbed. Would she take his suggestion and penetrate herself with a finger? Or two? Or would she wait for him to teach her . . . ?

His fangs dripped in his mouth, razor-sharp for her. He licked one, sucking his own blood, fantasizing that it was hers. His back arched as he groaned in Russian, *"Wait for me, Lizvetta. Wait . . ."*

Semen surged up his rampant cock as he rocked his hips, fucking his fist. . . .

Yet then he slowed. What if she *had* waited on him?

I want her *hands on me. I want* her *to see me come.* Elizabeth had enjoyed watching his seed spill. If he returned to her, he might coax her to wring it from him. With her mouth.

This plan made sense—taking his release with her, using her as a tool. If only to shore up his sanity.

With that aim in mind, he painstakingly worked his shaft back into his pants, donned a trench to disguise it, then traced to Hag's.

The fey glanced up from a boiling pot. *Giving me a look of censure?* "Elizabeth's outside."

He found the mortal lying in the sun while reading a *Travel + Leisure* magazine, a bucket of iced beers by her side.

She wore a bikini. A tiny one. Triangles of cherry-red material strung together.

Her golden skin was sheened with oil. Coconut oil—an exotic, and therefore erotic, scent to him.

His jaw slackened, his cock jerking in readiness. *I hadn't even known this sight would greet me!*

Wanting to view her like this at his leisure, he traced back to the apartment, slipped on sunglasses, then returned.

After telling Hag to go take a walk, he traced a chair to the edge of the shadows, silently removing his coat.

There, he watched, captivated, as the sun soaked into Elizabeth's slick skin, heating it, *marking* it before his eyes. Never had he seen such supple flesh.

Her even teeth gleamed white against her new tan. He spied a subtle hint of auburn in that shining mane of hers. She was from Appalachia— somewhere in her line, she probably had a Scottish ancestor.

Her bikini taunted him, the material clinging to stiffened nipples and the faintest hint of her cleft. He'd bite her under each triangle—

She dog-eared the page she was looking at. There was only one reason to save pages in a travel magazine. When dreaming of a future trip.

One she will never take.

He frowned at his reaction to this, then reminded himself that he didn't suffer regrets about decisions already made. And her sacrifice had been determined for half a decade. All he wanted was the use of her lovely body until then. "Take off your top, pet."

She gasped. "Stop calling me that, asshole."

"But you *are* a pet. I feed you, shelter you, stroke you. And you bring me amusement. Now, do as I say."

"If I'd known I'd be spending the day here, I might have packed a bag."

"So that's why you're ireful today."

"Right, Lothaire. I have *nothing* else to be ireful about."

"Ah, you must have missed me."

"Not as much as you clearly missed me." She lifted her sunglasses, rolling her eyes at his erection.

"I gave you an order."

She ran the end of one string tie against her bottom lip. "You want to see my breasts?" she purred, casting him that blinding smile.

He sat upright in his chair, tensing in anticipation.

"Get Saroya to show you." Smile gone, she reached for her beer, crooking her finger around the bottleneck.

As she swigged, he thought, *Not classy. But oddly . . . arousing.* "You don't even aspire to grace, do you?"

"Nope." She noisily sucked on a wedge of lime.

"You really do not want to do this today, Elizabeth."

"But I have to! You see, I'm running out of days too quickly to put *anything* off."

Refusing to rise to the bait, he agreed, "Yes. You are. Now, about your top. Shut up and take it off."

She laughed, and drank more beer. "Take a long trace off a short bridge, vampire."

"Don't you want to further seduce me from my Bride?"

"No, I've decided that *nothing* is worth whoring for you."

"And what about your alternative reason? Merely wanting to be with a man? To know one's touch?"

"It was good, Lothaire, but it wasn't *that* good."

"You came quickly enough." He rather enjoyed this sparring, because it so rarely happened to him.

"Do you really want to go there? Because, oh great king, you came *in your pants*."

His eyes narrowed. "Isn't that what happened with every other one of your conquests? Just because I'm not poor, imbecilic, and vulgar like them doesn't mean I'm immune to your charms. Now. Take off your top." When she didn't, he snapped, "You disobey me because you assume you'll get no punishment."

"How about we play a game of tit for tat. You answer my questions, and I'll tug this"—she indicated one of the top triangles of her suit—"a little to the right."

30

Elizabeth and her games. Which he might enjoy more than he cared to admit. "Continue."

"Where have you been?" she asked.

"Stalking my enemies, Declan Chase and Regin the Radiant. Chase is the key to finding my ring."

She adjusted the material to the right, just enough to reveal . . . her tan line. Fuck, that was sexy to him. He'd bet her skin would be searing to the touch.

"I thought you only needed to dream his memories."

"The memories prove elusive," he said absently. "But we shared blood between us, so I can read his mind if I can get close enough to him."

Another adjustment. "Who's Nïx? You cursed her the other day."

The bane of my existence. "She's a Valkyrie soothsayer whom I've known for almost all my life. She likes to stick her nose where it doesn't belong." *The white queen, with her godlike precognition.*

"Did you have a relationship with her?"

How to answer that? "We were . . . many things to each other," he said, recalling the first time he'd met her, just one month after his mother's death.

He'd been starving, injured, limping down a secluded mountain pass with no idea where to go. A metal net had descended on him, preventing him from tracing.

"Look at the lordling leech in his rags," a dark-haired Valkyrie had said as she and others of her ilk descended from a rock face. "He looks hungry."

He'd snapped his fangs at them, hissing blood and spittle. While they debated who got to decapitate their prey, another Valkyrie had strolled into their midst.

With her jet-black hair and brilliant golden eyes, she'd been incomprehensibly lovely to him. "Spare this one, sister," she said. "He's special."

"How so, Phenïx?"

"I cannot see," this Phenïx said. "In fact, the only way I can tell that he plays a role in our affairs is by reading *your* future, Helen. You two are connected in some way."

"You speak in riddles as usual." Helen had stabbed her sword into its sheath with an exasperated thrust. "He's a pathetic parasite. I would die of sorrow if I was ever connected to one such as him."

But they had spared him, and the golden-eyed Valkyrie had furtively dropped coins for him as they'd ridden off on their white steeds.

An age had passed before he'd met Nïx again. Both of them had sought to capture a sorcerer whose castle was under siege by an invading army of stone demons, one of the more brutal demonarchies.

Nïx had planned to save the sorcerer's life in order for him to fulfill some undisclosed role in the future; Lothaire wanted to drink his blood and steal his legendary knowledge.

The two of them had decided to work together. They would let the demons defeat the sorcerer's army and break into his mystically protected hold. Then Lothaire and Nïx would swoop in to snare the sorcerer for themselves.

As he and the Valkyrie had lain in wait on an outcropping overlooking the clash, Lothaire had worked on a ring puzzle, listening to the Valkyrie's chatter, surprised that he agreed with everything she said.

She'd praised the sorcerer for taking no wife, spawning no offspring, and developing no friendships. "He has no weaknesses. The stone demon king will have no leverage to force magics from him."

Lothaire preyed on those very vulnerabilities. Which was why he himself garnered no friends. *A choice, not a lack* ...

With a claw-tipped finger, Nïx had pointed out soldiers in action, giving commentary. "Idiot. Larger idiot. One-horned idiot." He'd grunted in agreement. "Oh, watch this! Watch this one," she'd said from time to time, predicting a particularly gruesome slaying on the battlefield.

Soon they'd begun conversing, mainly about how foolish immortals could be, until their talk had turned personal.

"Have you no mate, female?" he'd asked, intrigued with her, though she was his natural enemy.

"I was betrothed to Loki for a time. Which did not proceed smoothly for *obvious* reasons. So for now I am an unrepentant *manizer*." At Lothaire's blank look, she'd said, "That will be amusing in the twenty-first century."

"If you're a soothsayer, tell me my future."

"I cannot. I still see nothing on you. Very few render my foresight completely blank."

In the hour before dawn, Lothaire had said, "I grow weary of waiting, Phenïx. Stay if you like, but I will tarry no more."

Her eyes had gone hazy. "Patience, Lothaire. You *must* learn patience."

He'd drawn himself to his full height, furious that she'd dared to scold him. "The day I take orders from a madwoman who begets lightning will be my last." With a mean laugh, he'd tensed to trace away.

Just as he began to disappear, he'd spied a demon vaulting the overhang, sword at the ready. *Leave the Valkyrie to her fate,* Lothaire had told himself. *She means nothing. She's an enemy!*

Yet he'd hesitated. Perhaps he'd been less jaded then; perhaps he'd had nothing better to do. For whatever reason, he'd returned to her side to slay the male—just as the castle boundaries fell. ...

In the coming years, they'd stalked common foes, growing to trust each other, at least enough to watch each other's backs when on extended hunts. But Lothaire had never learned patience, and his obstinacy put them at odds on occasion. Her lucidity continued to dwindle.

Still, they'd had much in common, and a grudging respect had grown. He remembered once confessing to her, "Phenïx, you are the only one—"

"Lothaire!"

He jerked his head up. *"What?"*

Elizabeth was frowning at him. "You and Nïx?"

He shook himself from his reverie. "We belong to different Lore armies, the Pravus and the Vertas. She is guiding the Vertas, and I side either with the Pravus or with no one—whichever suits my Endgame."

"Why didn't you ever kill her? That's what you do to your enemies, right?"

A difficult question to answer. At length, he said, "Though a foe, Nïx is the only one I know who matches me in age and knowledge." In madness and weariness. "We have a history." And so his life would be altered without her in it. "I decided long ago that I could always kill her, but I could never bring her back."

"I see." When Elizabeth took another drink, condensation from the bottle dripped to her chest, meandering down. As his gaze followed, his mind easily turned from the past to this very enticing present. "I believe I answered your question." He raised his brows at her top.

With a huff, she tugged the material aside more. "Do you think about me when you're away?"

"I think about how you're soon to die. A fine sacrifice for Saroya."

As she pulled over her top, Elizabeth asked, "How much time do I have left?"

"Possibly a week."

She gazed away, taking another swig of beer as she adjusted the material. The next shift would bare one impudent nipple. "At any time, were your thoughts tender toward me?"

He'd mused on destroying Elizabeth's soul, and he might have felt a whisper of *something*. "Do I look like the type of male who would have *tender* thoughts, girl? Now you're being ridiculous."

When her eyes widened slightly, he snapped, "What?"

"Nothing."

"If there's to be no more tat, then let's get to the tit."

"Hmm. Maybe I've changed my mind." She ran that sweating beer bottle down her cleavage. Just where he'd thrust his shaft a week ago. "Don't you wish you could see—and touch?"

"I've spent the last seven days wishing I could touch. Now I plan to." Before she could react, he'd traced to her in the light, grabbing her before he burned, then returned with her to the apartment.

He could smell the sun in her hair, could see new freckles on her nose. Golden skin, wicked tan lines . . . her skin *was* hot.

"Let me go!" She shoved against his chest. "What do you want from me now? Maybe there's a quarter inch of my skin somewhere that you haven't spunked yet. That it?"

"These days away from me have made you bolder. Foolishly so. But I'll bring you to heel."

She thrashed against him. "*I hate you!*"

"Feeling's mutual," he grated with difficulty, the *rána* burning. *Blyad'!* Of course he hated her.

She was a mortal, ignorant even of the danger *he* presented to her. His hand wrapped around her throat. "I could throttle you so easily. Squeeze the life right from you."

"Do it!" she screamed, her eyes fierce. "And stop talkin' about it!"

❖

"You won't incite me to kill you," the vampire said. "So cease trying. If I were going to do it by my own hand, I would have by now."

For the briefest second, Ellie thought she saw him frown, as if he'd just realized that was true.

Can't lie, huh? When he eased his grip on her throat, she stumbled back. "I'm not screamin' at you because I want you to kill me, I'm screamin' because you make me sick! You're supposed to be some kind of Lore brainiac? But you're fixin' to choose Saroya over me? Why are you too stupid to see what's just in front of you?"

"In front of me? You mean the mortal shrieking at me in a thick hillbilly accent? The ignorant human with no accomplishments? Perhaps I'm *smart* enough not to lower myself to a creature like you."

"I'm not ignorant. I have a degree!"

He raised a blond brow. "Assuredly. It says H.S. after it. In any case, there's more to knowledge than a degree. You've never been outside of your own state, never encountered any kinds of people but your own."

"Because I'm *young*! I've been in prison since I was a teenager. You have no idea what I would've done if that bitch of yours hadn't hijacked my body. You can't have it both ways—you can't ridicule my ignorance when you had a hand in shaping it!"

"No idea what you would have done? I'd wager you would have lived in a squalid trailer with wailing brats clinging to your apron while you watched TV all day."

He'd just done Lothaire-speak. "You *don't* think that's what I would've done. You don't believe that at all."

Double take from the vampire. But he recovered, saying in a bland tone, "This grows tedious, Elizabeth. Shut up and undress."

"Get Saroya to do it! Or maybe she finds you as hateful as I do!" A muscle ticked in his jaw, warning her that she'd pushed too far. *Don't care. Already dead.*

"You court my wrath because you've never truly witnessed it. I'll remedy that right now."

He yanked her against his chest. "Let's take a trip."

"You said your enemies would find me!" To be a demon's whore . . . ?

"I'll cloak us. Again, the one you need fear most is *me*." In the space of a breath, he'd traced her into a cave. But he hadn't fully teleported them; they stayed in some kind of hazy twilight.

Still she could scent musty earth and rot, could hear flies buzzing. Once her eyes grew used to the dim light, she saw corpses.

The savagely beheaded bodies of young men. Dozens and dozens of them.

Gore, severed limbs, crushed skulls. *Splatter* on the dank cave walls.

She would've vomited the contents of her stomach, if she'd been of weaker constitution. Or if she hadn't beheld a similar scene in her own home five years ago.

When she could trust her voice, she asked, "You did this?"

"Ah, Elizabeth, now do you see what I'm capable of? Slaughtering an entire pack in their own den *bored* me. My heart never even sped up, my bloodlust never quickened. I yawned loudly when I worked one's head free. The last thing he ever heard was me tsking over my impoliteness. You'd do well to fear my fury, to understand that my very name strikes fear in the hearts of those who know me—*for a reason*."

"I understand that you're scary, sick, and perverse! I understand that the Enemy of Old and Saroya the Soul Reaper are absolutely perfect for each other. Two broken puzzle pieces jammed together."

Again, her words struck a nerve. His hand tightened on her arm, his expression promising pain.

"Is this what your life is like?"

He sneered, "Most nights for millennia."

"Then I feel sorry for you. That's right—Elizabeth, your *pet*, the peasant you scorn, 'the body'—*pities* you." She gazed at his face. "Uh-oh, we've got that muscle tickin' in your jaw. Spells trouble for me! What's the matter? You can't take it when someone tells you like it is? I'm probably the first person to do so in centuries."

Was there a flicker in those red eyes?

"Like it is," he grated. "And how is it that *you* could possibly pity *me*?"

"I'm twenty-four years old. I've spent more than twenty percent of my life on death row. And I've still known more happiness in my short life than you have in your unending one."

31

That Elizabeth would fucking dare! "As usual, you speak about things your mind can't even comprehend!"

"*Me?* I bet you don't even *know* what happiness is!"

Lothaire wanted to snap, "Of course I do!" But he . . . didn't.

He believed he'd known it as a child with his mother, but he couldn't remember those early years vividly, not after eons had come and passed, not after his life had become devoted to revenge.

And he couldn't resurrect whatever he'd felt then, because he hadn't felt anything approaching it since.

He often spied on others, studying their ways. He'd watched two Sorceri sisters snickering over wry jokes. He'd observed Lykae roughhousing, then laughing so hard they'd had to hold their sides. They experienced happiness; Lothaire did not.

He knew he was different from others. And yet, he couldn't ascertain if he was *un*happy—since that would mean he could recognize the opposite.

"Well, do you know what it is?" Elizabeth demanded.

Can't lie. Contentment, happiness, satisfaction—all these things were unfathomable to him.

One of the reasons he fought so hard for his Endgame was that he'd surely be content once all his vows had been fulfilled. Once his toiling had finally ended.

She gasped. "You *don't* know. How ignorant am I? I've sat in my 'squalid trailer,' experiencing something *your mind* can't even comprehend!"

"I might not kill you, but I could hurt you, break your fragile bones!"

"You *would*. You'd hurt the one person who could teach you to be happy!" She grasped her forehead. "Oh, God . . . now?"

Saroya rises? "Elizabeth, you do *not* recede. You finish this with me!"

She narrowed her eyes up at him. "Just keeping the terms of our deal. If Saroya wants her turn, then I'm supposed to get out of the way, right?"

"You little bitch, don't you run from this!" His voice boomed in the cavern.

"Uh-oh, here I go. . . . Whoa, whoa, receding right before your eyes. Red Rover, send Saroya right over. See how happy *the Soul Reaper* can make you!" And then she collapsed.

Lothaire yanked her to him, catching her just as Saroya said, "Where am I? I sensed blood and violence."

He gave a furious yell. Elizabeth had mocked him, gotten the last word, then receded purposely! *Fucking throttle her!*

"Lothaire, what is wrong with you?" Then Saroya scowled, fighting to stand on her own. But he left his hand on her arm, keeping her cloaked. "Why am I dressed thus? Oh, my skin!"

Get control. Before he crushed Saroya in fury. Inhale. Exhale. "The mortal proves . . . vexatious." And confounding. She continued to astonish him at every turn.

"You can't handle a human girl?" Saroya peered around at all the carnage. "But look at this splendid slaughter! Yours?"

Elizabeth had been disgusted. Saroya not only accepted what he was, she exulted over it.

"Are there no more lives to take? All of these are completely spent. Selfish Lothaire." She toed a severed leg. "Why have you brought Elizabeth here? Does this have something to do with the ring?"

"I make progress on that score."

"So you have no ring to give me and no lives for me to take—though I haven't killed in years!" She kicked a decomposing head, then winced in pain at the contact. "Are you always so selfish?"

"Yes," he answered absently. They couldn't remain here any longer. He could only half-trace two people for so long. In an instant, he returned them to his room in New York, releasing her.

"Take me to live bodies, Lothaire! In fact, trace me to Elizabeth's old home. I promised her mother that I'd kill her. I demand to have her in my grasp."

"Demand all you like, it won't happen." After all, he felt gratitude to the peasant woman for bearing Elizabeth. Without that mortal, Lothaire would have no body for his Bride.

"I won't remain at the fore if I'm to be treated thus." Saroya began to sway on her feet.

Now *she* was going to recede? The hell she would! "If you purposely recede, I'll brand this body. Scald your face. Gouge an eye out."

Saroya immediately righted herself. "What do you want?" Lothaire was clearly in a dangerous mood.

"You're going to answer some questions for me."

In an aggrieved tone, she said, "Really, Lothaire. What's brought this on? I'm the one who should be infuriated. Allowing Elizabeth to tan my skin like this?"

He traced from one wall to the other. "I need information."

"Such as?"

"We talked years ago of ruling together," he said. "Do you still want this?"

"Of course. I fear *you* are the one with doubts."

"We spoke of thrones and power and vengeance. But what of us?"

"What do you mean?"

"When my retribution has been meted out and our crowns rest easy upon our heads, what then?"

"Then we conquer *more*," she said. "We could rule the world together, while searching for a way to return my godhood. I have enemies who beg for retribution as well. Or have you forgotten that?"

"Your sister, Lamia."

"Among others." *La Dorada, for one.* "You've got the Queen of Evil vowing reprisal against you—which means against *me*." Saroya debated whether to tell Lothaire of her many crimes against the sorceress, but decided against it. He didn't need to know why she'd dispatched assassins after Dorada for centuries.

He doesn't need to know about the prophecy, that foretelling by a long dead vampire oracle. "If you do not vanquish her, she will kill me, Lothaire. I *feel* this."

"Dorada cannot *find* you. No one in the Lore knows of this apartment. You are hidden if you remain here or at Hag's, and I cloaked the body otherwise. Do you think I would ever allow Dorada to steal my mate—and with her my entire future?"

Saroya calmed somewhat. Though she trusted no one, she did know that Lothaire was one of the most cutthroat warriors in the Lore, and one of the strongest vampires ever to live.

He pinched the bridge of his nose. "And after Dorada's been defeated, how do you envision our lives?"

"We will annihilate any remaining enemies, becoming the most powerful partnership the world has ever known."

Growing increasingly frustrated, he said, "And when our work is done for the night, when dawn comes . . . *what then?*"

She smoothed her hair back. "I don't understand."

"Do you know what happiness is?"

"It's watching the light dim in a good man's eyes. It's having subjects grovel. It's wielding the power over life and death."

"No, Saroya. I can't believe I'm about to say this, but . . . each of those things is a *process*. Not an outcome." He gave a bitter laugh. "You have no more idea of what happiness is than I do."

"You *are* growing besotted with your little mortal concubine. Look at you—it's almost as if you're pining for her. Almost as if *she* were your Bride."

Which Elizabeth likely was. Though Saroya had once believed she herself had triggered Lothaire's blooding, she no longer did.

For him to have feelings for such a loathsome creature? Something larger was at work here.

Still, he'd never believe Elizabeth was his; the very idea would be galling to a male of his rank and standing.

If Lothaire hadn't seen the truth by now, then it was because he didn't *want* to.

Doubts ate at Lothaire's confidence, eroding it.

Even if he could bring himself to believe that Elizabeth was his Bride—and that was a very big if—there was nothing he could do about it.

He'd already set his destiny into motion. He was inextricably bound to his fate—compelled not merely to cast out Elizabeth's soul as the girl thought. . . .

It couldn't be her.

Surely.

Because he'd been so averse to her humanity, Lothaire had never allowed himself even to *consider* that Elizabeth might be his Bride.

Now, apparently, I'm going there.

It was possible that Elizabeth hadn't blooded him in their early encounters because she hadn't been old enough. Females from other species usually didn't trigger a blooding unless they were grown.

At seventeen, Elizabeth hadn't awakened him. When she was eighteen, one glance at Saroya had sparked his heart and body to life.

Was this due to Saroya's arrival? Or Elizabeth's age?

No, no, no. Goddess trumps mortal trailer trash.

Lusty mortal trailer trash—with a predilection for licking his fangs and slowly sucking on his tongue.

Of all the matches made this Accession, of all the tales of woe and bliss between mates, not one had included a human.

Why would I *draw the short straw?* Even Regin the Radiant's "mortal" male had ended up being a Lorean berserker.

Saroya crossed to him now. "Imagine how your family would've reacted to Elizabeth Peirce. Would Ivana have approved of her?"

Ivana would have gone into a frothing rage. Her only offspring shunning a goddess for a lowly "animal"? Where was the logic in that?

Stefanovich would have laughed, sneering, "The Dacian son is no better than a Horde vampire." He would have asked Lothaire if Elizabeth tasted of wine and honey.

And I'd have to say yes.

"You know Elizabeth can't be your Bride," Saroya said placidly. "Aside from the fact that I'm a *goddess*, and therefore an impeccable match for a king like you, consider this: no vampire could terrorize his female as you have her."

Saroya was right. Wouldn't his instincts have prevented him from harming Elizabeth?

Instead, he'd subjected this mortal to death row. He'd belittled her at every opportunity, holding her imminent death over her, taunting her with it.

Mentally tormenting her. *Behold the ocean you'll never touch, the jewels you'll never own. Desire the male who will never want you back and feel the pleasure you'll never experience again. . . .*

Bile rose in Lothaire's throat. *It isn't Elizabeth. It's just* not.

Even his uncle Fyodor hadn't tortured his Bride like this, and she'd been a reviled enemy.

Ivana had told Lothaire, "You'll be a good and true king to your Bride." But he hadn't been to Elizabeth. He'd made the girl's life a living hell.

Not her, not her.

And yet, as his restlessness increased and his doubt weighed on him to a crushing degree, his first impulse was to touch Elizabeth.

Not because she was his Bride, but because she could pleasure him, making him forget his troubles for a time. "Force her to surface," he bit out.

Saroya blinked at him. "Are you dismissing me?"

"Yes."

"Why aren't you even trying to seduce me?"

"You feel no desire for me. You never have. I can wait for the human—who does."

"How do you know it won't be better with me?"

"Because it can't *possibly* be better with anyone." The words said aloud rocked him—the *truth* said aloud.

Am I willing to give up that pleasure? What choice did he have?

"What is so superior with her?" Saroya demanded. "Tell me what Elizabeth does that puts you into such a lather. Do her thighs spread in welcome? Does she moan into your mouth?"

Frustration mounted. He resented this female before him.

"Does she look at you with need?"

"Like she'll *die* if I don't fuck her," he hissed.

"I will practice that expression in the mirror for when *we* make love."

"Cease the deception!" He stabbed his fingers through his hair. "You have no intention of bedding me. The rumors of your virginity are true. You've never known a man."

"But only because I hadn't found my mate."

In an icy tone, he said, "You should be above lying to a mere vampire like me, should you not, goddess?"

Long moments passed. "Yes. You are right." Her guise of mild concern transformed into a gloating one. "Oh, Lothaire, you were too arrogant to believe a female wouldn't want you sexually. But I am *above* base desires."

"You freely admit your treachery? You never intended to share my bed!" *Lying to me, betraying me. Already!*

"You have a goddess for your Bride. I was born differently, made differently. Is sex so important to you? We are talking about conquering kingdoms together! Is bedding me so critical? That is what *concubines* are for."

He could maintain a harem, taking a new female every night. He didn't require a Bride for those needs. *United front, Lothaire?* "I hadn't planned to have any other females. They seed dissension."

"You are the most singular male." Then she narrowed her eyes. "It's not a question of sex. It's a question of *her*." When he said nothing, her lips parted. "You're falling for the mortal! Apprise yourself of this fact: soon you will destroy her very soul."

"You think you have me at your mercy?"

"I *do*."

"I could use the ring to force the Horde to follow me."

"Tricky ring, precarious power. You will need me by your side for as long as you seek to rule them—or you'll be challenged constantly."

He couldn't deny this. Lothaire didn't meet one of the Horde's two sacred requirements. Just as Hag had predicted, his Bride was the key to his throne.

"Without me, Lothaire, you face an eternity of sedition. How will you conquer the Daci with your kingdom mired in rebellion?"

"Then perhaps I'll keep you *and* Elizabeth. You will be my queen, and she will be our dirty little secret. A hidden concubine who comes out only in my bed." *Perfect.*

Just as he deserved a goddess for a queen, he deserved a young, nubile female to appease his lusts.

"You want me to share this body, Lothaire? That will not happen."

"I say it will."

"Do you remember the rest of our conversation that first night in the woods?" Saroya asked, her voice velvety. "I do. Often."

He'd thought of it often as well. . . .

Tracing within inches of her, he cupped her nape with a shaking hand. "The only thing greater than my need is my strength. Your mortal form is too fragile for me to claim. But I must finish this."

"Then I will not yield this body until you destroy Elizabeth's soul and make me whole," Saroya said. "For now, you may take your physical release in some way—after you swear you will do these things you've offered. Vow to your Lore, and make this unbreakable pact with me."

They stared into each other's eyes, and he felt as if time had slowed just so he could appreciate how momentous his next words would be. "I vow to the Lore that I will do everything in my power to extinguish Elizabeth's soul forever, then make this body undying."

She seemed vaguely surprised, then pleased. "Very good, my king. . . ."

Now Saroya said, "You made your vows, Lothaire. You will be *compelled* by them to find the ring in order to make this body immortal—and to rid it of Elizabeth."

He'd been right that night; his words had been momentous. Just not for the reasons he'd assumed. "Release me from this pact."

Her lips curled, almost a smile. "I vow to the Lore that I will *never* release you." She was enjoying this. "These vows are so compelling, are they not? Remember my acolytes? Your fate is sealed, Lothaire."

It is. He knew it. His path was clear.

"Console yourself, vampire. If you remain steadfast, you'll soon have everything you've ever wanted. Everything Ivana wanted for you."

But he might have begun to want *more*.

"Now, Lothaire, shall I summon your—temporary—concubine?"

Eyes narrowed, he grated, "Yes, *flower*. Have her bathed and dressed in red silk in my bed. Oh, and skip the garish makeup."

32

E llie woke to shivers glancing up and down her body.

Lothaire lay beside her in his bed, trailing the backs of his fingers from her navel to the valley between her breasts.

She was dressed in a sexy teddy; he was naked.

"I like you in red," he said, his voice raspy, making her shiver even more. "I've been awaiting you."

"What . . . what are you doing?"

"I've decided to give you a chance to atone for your earlier insolence. With head."

"*My* insolence. Did Saroya just recede on her own?" That would mean . . . "Oh, God, she delivered me like this to your bed? Or did you just get through with her here?"

Ellie didn't feel like they'd been intimate. But how could she tell for certain?

"One or the other, it matters naught."

"You're right—either way, it's *sick*. You and Saroya are sick!" She shoved at his chest but couldn't budge him. "Get away from me!"

He easily captured her wrists in one of his hands, pinning them above her.

When he covered one breast with his free hand, gently kneading, she cried, "Don't touch me! I don't want you!"

He bent down to kiss her, but she craned her head away. He pinched her chin, holding her still . . . she clamped her lips closed against his.

He jerked back. "What is this? Be like you were with me the other times! When you melted for me."

"That was before I fully understood what a nasty piece of work you are."

"Because of a few shifter beheadings? Come on, Lizvetta, it's not as if I went around cock-slapping gnomes."

Her jaw dropped. "You are *amazing*! A deadly, wretched, friendless monster. Pretty on the outside and not much more. God, just find the ring and put me out of my misery!"

"Be like you were with me! That was *not* a request."

"Fuck you, vampire."

"*Soon.*"

"Let go!" When he didn't, she screamed, "*Let go, let go, LET GO!*"

"Dark gods, shut up!" he yelled, but he did release her.

She scurried from the bed. "Why would you be unfaithful to Saroya? The first time we were together was because she was late for a date, the second just happened, but this would be premeditated. Why can't you just wait for your Bride? It isn't *me* you want—you've told me a thousand times how inferior to Saroya I am. I swear I will let her rise."

Ignoring her, he commanded, "Return to this bed *now*."

"Did she recede because she didn't want you?"

He gave a raw laugh. "What female wouldn't want me?" Lothaire-speak?

"Me! You asked me why I was still a virgin? It's because of men like you—the takers. Selfish, stupid men! *I* don't want you!"

"Of course you do, Elizabeth. Just looking at me gets you wet."

"Looking at you reminds me of the kind of man I should be with."

"And what kind of man is that? Drunken, poor, pathetic?"

"No. I've never met him, but I see him plain as day. He has crinkles around his eyes when he smiles and tanned skin from working outdoors. Honest labor has callused his hands. He and I will hunt together, cook and eat big family meals together. He'll marry me and love my family, too." Voice gone soft, she said, "He'll give me a baby boy and a girl."

Lothaire's eyes narrowed. "No. *He* won't. You'll never know another but me. Now, come back to bed and stop behaving as if this is some kind of event. We've pleasured each other before, and all I want from you is to exchange a couple of orgasms."

"I'm not the type of woman who'll let a man treat her like trash, then get him off whenever he likes. You've done nothing to deserve being with me."

"But your honest, tanned, imaginary husband has? Think about him all you like, yet it will be me who wrings screams from you tonight. I can *make* you want this. One bite, and you'll be begging for me to touch you."

"A vampire roofie? Can't get it any other way?"

"Do you want me to work for it, then?" Lothaire's voice grew husky. "I will, Elizabeth. I'm not above seduction to get what I want."

His eyes locked on hers with that predatory glint, and she again felt like his helpless prey, the object of a merciless vampire's lust.

For some reason, the idea of that made her breaths shallow. She felt her skin growing flushed as if to attract him—

One instant she stood beside the bed; the next she was in it, lying back under the firm press of his hand.

Before she could even think about defending herself, he'd worked the silk down off her shoulders to pool at her waist.

Indignation burning inside her, she threw a wild punch, but with that supernatural speed, he easily secured both of her wrists in one hand. "Ah-ah, you'll only hurt yourself. And amuse me. Now, relax."

She tensed even more.

"Sweet Lizvetta, with your hot skin and hot blood." He stretched her arms over her head, pinning her wrists there once more. "Let me see if I can't stoke a fever in you." With his free hand, he rolled one nipple between his thumb and forefinger. "Do you like this?"

"No!" She gasped out the word.

"Liar. And what about this?" He pinched the other one.

Her hips bucked. "No!"

At her ear, he purred, "Be my dear, and tell me you want me."

"I won't do it!"

He bent to one of her breasts. She felt his warm breath fanning over it and barely kept her eyes open.

He'd never suckled her before. He'd wanted to the first night, but she'd denied him. During their second time together, he'd been intent on other things. Now his desire was clear.

"Look at your pretty nipples." His tongue twirled one, making her choke back a cry. "They beg me to taste them, blood stiffening them until they're like little berries. It will be everything I can do not to pierce them." He snared the tip between his teeth . . . and gently tugged.

She heard a whimper, could barely believe that carnal sound had come from her.

His lips curled into a grin before he closed them around the peak to suck. His mouth was searing as his tongue lashed her.

When he drew back to watch her reaction with his wicked red gaze, she was panting, fighting the urge to arch up for more.

"Ah, you like that." As he nibbled and sucked her other breast, his fingers trailed down her body, circling her navel. Against her wet nipple, he rasped, "And you liked when I touched you here, didn't you?" His hand snaked under the teddy.

"No!" she cried as his forefinger glided between her folds.

"You don't want me to continue?" He stopped everything—his suck on her breast, the skillful play of his fingers.

"Lothaire . . ."

"Beg me to. Tell me you need me, that you desire me alone."

She shook her head.

"I feel your trembling, feel you getting slick. Why are you being so stubborn?"

Stubborn? That was the one thing she couldn't seem to be with him!

Because right then, all she wanted was for him to make love to her with his mouth and hands.

"For seven days, Lizvetta, I've thought of this constantly. I know you've needed me as I have you." The underlying vulnerability in his words was almost her undoing.

But then he went back to aggressive Lothaire. "Fuck this. I've got a week's worth of seed for you—and you're already on the verge." He began stroking between her legs again. "You might not beg with words, but your body's pleading."

Wait. A week's worth? Realization surfaced in her desire-saturated mind. Then Saroya truly *hadn't* pleasured him tonight? Sex was obviously important—*critical*—to him, and Saroya wasn't putting out.

Maybe Ellie had been right and Saroya had *never* put out. Perhaps the goddess of blood wasn't a goddess in bed? "Lothaire, tell me that I don't compare to Saroya."

His fingers slowed. "What?"

"You heard me. You'll tell me directly after we come, so I just want to get it out of the way now. Tell me, 'You don't compare to Saroya.' Then I can relax—I'll be all yours."

"I'm busy right now." Another rapturous stroke.

Concentrate, Ellie! "Just tell me those five words, and then I'll do anything you want me to."

"Soon you'll do anything that I want anyway."

He can't say it. Lothaire was beginning to feel something for her. When she'd mentioned another man, the vampire had seemed jealous. Earlier, she'd asked him about tender thoughts toward her, and he'd deflected that question as well.

Which means the game—with my one available move—is still in play.

Seduction.

Perhaps she should give the vampire exactly what he'd wanted. *Ear horn, Sadie?* Well, Ellie had something she desperately needed to communicate to him.

I want to live, to be free of Saroya!

"Lothaire, I think I *do* compare to her in your eyes."

"Think whatever you like." Drawing his hands away from her, he lay back, tense with frustration. But again, he didn't deny it.

I still have a shot with him! "She doesn't desire you like I do, does she?"

His fists clenched, his expression heralding another rage.

"What have I said about watching your tongue?" Lothaire hadn't wanted this mortal to know Saroya didn't desire him, but of course, nothing escaped Elizabeth.

His nerves were frayed, his fury escalating. His cock and balls were so swollen with pent-up need they felt like they'd been battered. Suckling her plump breasts and hard little nipples had only made the pain grow. . . .

She turned to her side, cupping his face with her palms. When he eventually shifted to face her, she said, "Saroya *can't* want you as much as I do, Lothaire. No one can."

So similar to what he'd said about Elizabeth.

In a breathy voice, she murmured, "I've been *aching* for you."

Gods, how he loved hearing that, like a balm on his pride. "Say it again. Tell me how much you ache."

"I'll *show* you." When she leaned in and pressed her lips to his, he worked to control himself—taking her mouth in a slow, languorous kiss, their tongues lazily tangling.

Just as in the past, she *melted* for him. *Yes, Lizvetta! This is what I need from you.*

But why give it to him now? He broke away. "What's brought about this change?"

"Do you care?"

"Normally? *Do pizdy.* Now I'm suspicious."

"I thought you'd just been with Saroya and were trying to get with both of us in one night. I was pissed. And damn it, I was as jealous as the day is long."

Jealous? Finally! And only fitting, since jealousy still seethed inside Lothaire for Elizabeth's *imaginary* man, and he couldn't comprehend why.

She rose up and kissed his ear, nuzzling it with sultry breaths, then she pressed her mouth lower to his collar bone. Another kiss on his chest followed.

An imaginative male could think she was taking those lips all the way down. He turned to his back, his shaft surging in readiness.

"My poor, poor vampire"—she tongued one of his nipples, making him shudder—"all you ever wanted was me in a red teddy, giving you head."

Somehow he tensed even more. Voice gone hoarse, he asked, "Am I to have what I want at last?"

"No." She removed her gown all the way, tossing it aside. "Only the head."

"I suppose I'll have to make do."

Her lips curled. "I'm hungry for you, Lothaire."

"Are you, then?" His tone was dubious.

"When I sucked your thumb, I imagined it was the crown." She continued her trail downward. "I've dreamed of it, too."

So that is what she dreams of? "Your behavior is . . . unexpected."

"Now, I've never done this before, so I won't be quite as expert at it like I was at riding you."

Insolent chit.

She dipped heated licks along his torso, his mortal lapping at him as she might a sweet treat. When she reached his navel, she sifted her nails through the crisp hair descending from it. Already he'd begun rocking his hips, his sac tightening.

"You'll have to be patient with me while I stumble my way through this."

Patient? His shaft hadn't been sucked in eons; Lothaire wouldn't last through her stumbling.

Without warning, he traced to stand at the foot of the bed. "I'd rather teach you how."

33

Teach me? Ellie thought dumbly as she lay back, marveling up at Lothaire. The sight of him standing in all his naked glory was dulling her wits—and setting her body afire.

Her eyes lovingly took in the muscles tapering from his broad chest down to his narrow hips . . . the rigid hollows in the sides of his rock-hard ass . . . his erection jutting proudly.

"Come to me," he ordered her. "Sit on the edge of the bed."

Once she did, he took his shaft in hand, easing it to her mouth. "Lick the tip."

As she stared at it, she felt her face flush. Part of her disbelieved she was about to do this.

Suckling a vampire's member.

She swallowed, then leaned forward to tentatively rub her tongue over it. From just that little contact, he groaned—while she grinned in wonder. His skin was so smooth there, so *sensitive.*

"Again," he bit out. "And look at me."

She gazed up, running her tongue along the slit.

Voice strained, he asked, "Did you taste me?"

"The tiniest hint of salt."

"Precum. This won't last long."

"Don't say that! I'm just getting started."

Yet another double take from the vampire. When he grabbed her hand, fitting her fingers along his shaft, it pulsated in her palm.

As he guided her to stroke, he hissed, "Your hand . . . so soft on me." When the bottom of her fist made contact with his testicles, another breath whistled between his gritted teeth.

"Did I hurt you?"

He found that question amusing. "No, you didn't hurt me. My balls are heavy, laden with seed. They need your touch." He made her cup them with her other hand.

His stance widened to give her more access as she weighed them in her palm, fascinated.

"Now run your tongue around the head."

She was spellbound as another drop of moisture beaded there, but she raised her gaze to his when she daubed the tip with her tongue.

All those chiseled muscles in his torso contracted in a breathtaking display. *From just my tongue?* Exhilaration drummed inside her, wonder. . . .

Arousal.

Which was understandable, considering his addictive scent, his delicious taste, his utterly masculine reactions. "I think I'm gonna like this, Lothaire," she said, just before she twirled her tongue around the bulbous crown.

"Suck it . . . into your mouth."

She nodded, then leisurely brought it between her lips. Another groan broke from his chest. His pleasure made her bold, and she drew him deeper, licking as she sucked.

When his head briefly fell back, Ellie realized that she *loved* this.

With shaking hands, he threaded his fingers through her hair. "How is your first experience?" His accent was thick, his words husky.

She gave a harder suck, then murmured, "I could do this all night." His poor testicles did look like they ached. She dipped down to give each a lick, grinning as his knees nearly buckled.

"Ah, good girl!"

When she took his shaft into her mouth once more, he held her head in place and began to rock his hips. Then, as if with great effort, he removed his hands, making fists by his sides. "Do you know how . . . difficult it is not to . . . fuck your mouth?"

That was what he needed? Then *she* needed to make her hand and mouth feel as if he were doing just that. So she pumped her wet fist on his shaft, as her mouth followed in time.

"Yes, that's it!" A low growl began to rumble from him. He grew even harder in a rush, just as she perceived more of that salty taste.

"Look at me." He cradled her face. Veins in his muscular arms stood in relief. So much strength—but he held her gently.

As she worked his engorged flesh, she met his gaze; red eyes consumed her.

"I'm about . . . to spend, Lizvetta." His voice was ragged. "Be my dear . . . take it from me . . . and I'll reward you, beauty."

"I will." Then she set back in, greedy for his release, wanting to feel it, to taste it.

"About to come . . ." Suddenly, he grew motionless. *"Right upon your talented tongue!"* With a brutal roar, he ejaculated, spurting hard jets against the back of her mouth.

She felt every shudder rippling through his powerful body, felt his shaft pumping between her lips as he bellowed to the ceiling.

Warmth slipped down her throat as he yelled his approval, "Yes, yes, Lizvetta!"

On and on it continued, while his hips jerked helplessly to her mouth.

When he gave a last groan, tugging her off him, she collapsed back on the bed, catching her breath, unable to mask her surprise.

How exciting. How *primal*. She stretched her arms over her head and smiled—

"You liked that?" he sneered. He was *angry* with her? "Unexpected Elizabeth . . ."

Too much. Again the pleasure was unforgettable.

As if Elizabeth was branding his mind with these memories.

Her eager exploration of him . . . the way her pouty lips had sealed around his shaft, her little cheeks hollowing as she'd sucked . . . her smile after she'd wantonly accepted his spend.

She'd told him she would haunt him after she was gone. He narrowed his gaze on her.

She might.

"Did I do something wrong?"

Lothaire pressed one knee to the bed. "Part your thighs."

"Guess not."

When she eased her legs open, he began to harden once more, not even surprising him this time. He was insatiable for her.

Which wouldn't do. *I'll worry about that later.*

He cupped her sex—gods almighty, she *had* liked sucking him and swallowing his seed. She was wet with desire, so ready to be fucked—if not with his cock, then with his fingers.

He sank one inside her, probably the first time she'd ever been touched like this.

She gasped. "Lothaire, that feels so *good*. . . ."

"Do you ache for me here?"

"I-is that my reward? Are you going to have sex with me?"

Her seeming delight at the prospect aggravated him anew. *Too much.* He was roiling inside, and *she* was the cause of it. "No. As a mortal, you're not strong enough to receive me." *Not a match for me at all. Lacking in every way!* "I'm going to use my fingers."

He stirred the one inside her. She was too tight, her maidenhead getting in the way. "This needs to go."

"What . . . what are you talking about? That's starting to hurt, Lothaire."

He was hurting her? He *wanted* to. He was obsessing about her more than his revenge, more than his vows.

Something is wrong with me. I despise her kind! He began forcing a second finger into her. Holding her gaze, he commanded her, "Take it, Elizabeth. Take them deep."

When he'd wedged both inside, spreading them, her tears welled. "You can't."

"I can! Your maidenhead's *mine.*" He drew his fingers out, thrusting them back in.

"Please stop . . ." She scrambled back, but he pinned his free hand over her neck. Her head fell to the side, her eyes squeezed shut.

Elizabeth couldn't be his. *I did not subject my fragile female to death row for half a decade.* Of course it wasn't her. He wouldn't have taken his Bride's virginity with a crude thrust of his fingers. . . .

I wouldn't have vowed to obliterate her soul.

Reassured, he relaxed somewhat, able to rein in his anger. "Don't fret—the pain will be worth it." He found himself smoothing her hair from her face as he let her adjust to the fullness inside. "It still hurts?"

When she nodded up at him with glinting eyes, something twisted in his chest. How could anyone harm her? *So beautiful, so trusting.* "Tender little mortal . . . I'll make it better, then."

"J-just give me a second."

"Shhh, Lizvetta." He removed his fingers, kneeling on the floor at the end of the mattress. "I told you I'd reward you." Lowering his head, he kissed her navel, and lower.

"Wait, you can't do that! Not after you just . . . Oh, stop!" Again she scrambled away, but he clamped her hips, snatching her back.

"What are you doing?" she cried.

"Taking all of what's mine." Hands splayed under her ass, he lifted her like a bowl to his lips, pressing his opened mouth between her legs, slipping his tongue into her folds.

"Lothaire, no— Oh! *Ohhh . . .*"

He tasted the sweet bite of virgin's blood mixed with her own honey; growling low in his throat, he almost spilled on the floor. "Dreamed of tasting you, Lizvetta." He nibbled, he licked, he devoured.

When she began rocking to his tongue, he eased his forefinger back inside her wetness, stirring her. Then he curled it upward until he found that subtly ridged flesh.

Her hidden little spot swelled, waiting to be found by a seeking male. "Have you ever had a man tickle you here?" He gave it a stroke.

"*Lo-THAIRE!*" she screamed, her back bowing.

"You sound surprised," he teased. "I take it you like this? Was it worth a bit of pain in the beginning?" As he rubbed it again, he darted his tongue over her clitoris—

"*Oh, my God,*" she sobbed, clenching the sheets.

"I told you I'd teach you how good it can feel."

"Don't stop . . . don't stop!"

He stilled his finger inside her, chuckling against her flesh.

"You devil!" She twisted her hips, writhing wildly to get his finger back on that spot.

Sexy piece!

"Lothaire, stop teasin' me!"

"Tease?" His cock was throbbing. Already, he felt the beginning tremors. "It's the least I can do since you're about to make me come on my carpet."

Panting, she leaned up on her elbows, her eyes wide. "*Are* you about to—"

Another curl of his finger had her collapsing back with a strangled cry, her knees falling wide.

34

Ellie heard the vampire laughing again, but this time it sounded much more strained.

Through heavy-lidded eyes, she stared down at his pale head bent over her as he swirled his tongue, softly caressing her inside.

"*Uhn,* getting so *wet,*" he growled, relentless.

She was close, and he kept her right on the edge. That frightening intensity she'd felt with him before returned stronger than ever.

Yet then . . . movement flittered within her chest. *No. It can't be.*

Then it happened again.

"Ask me to let you come," Lothaire told her, "and I might—"

"No. . . . No!" Saroya had begun taking over. Twice in one day?

He raised his head. "*No?*"

"She's trying to rise!" Ellie leaned up. "Lothaire, I *want* this. Don't make me go. Please, I have to feel this!"

"You obey me, Lizvetta. You *stay* with me."

She gave a shaky nod. "I-I'll try."

"Look at me." His gaze held hers, the hypnotic red mesmerizing her. Like staring into embers. "This pleasure is for you alone to enjoy. You remain with me for this."

Saroya had already stolen so much from her. Ellie refused to surrender this as well. She resisted her with everything she had.

Waiting . . . fighting . . .

In time, the threat passed. "I think I held her back."

"Good." He ran his face against her thigh, as if he was praising her in some animal kind of way.

Ellie swallowed. "You'll keep going now? With that kiss of yourn?"

With his free hand stroking his shaft and a grin tugging his lips, he bent down to her once more.

As he curled his finger, he took her clitoris between his lips to suckle her. Her eyes went wide, then gradually slid shut.

His kiss grew more forceful. Unrestrained. *Ravenous.* The sensations deepened, stronger and stronger as he snarled against her.

The coil tightened until . . .

She screamed. *"Ahhh, Lothaire! My God!"*

Stunning. Ecstasy. With mind-numbing spasms, her sex gripped his finger again and again.

She sat up with a low moan, clutching his hair, rubbing her flesh against his tongue as he caressed her so deep inside.

<hr />

Wicked, how she moves!

With his fist flying up and down over his cock, Lothaire growled between each hungry lick at her glistening, slippery lips.

Her orgasm drenched his tongue. He licked her harder. *Still not enough, not enough.* The taste of her had to last him for eternity.

She tried to press him away; he wasn't to be denied. Soon, she screamed again.

His female wasn't done yet. When her thighs closed around his head as she bucked . . .

Too much. At once, come exploded from him as he began to ejaculate on the floor.

His seed shot free in waves, pooling beneath him as he licked and licked her orgasms.

When he was spent at last and she'd wriggled from his mouth, he fought to catch his breath. He didn't trust his legs to stand, so he leisurely kissed her thighs before tracing into the bed. There, he lay back, drawing her to him.

She will curl up next to me, all but purring with contentment as she wraps an arm over my chest and smooths her leg up over my own. I'll tuck her close, then she'll fall asleep in my arms. Fitting me—

Elizabeth burst into tears, covering her face with her hands.

"What is *this*?" Aghast, he pried her hands from her face. "Are you still hurting?"

"Nooo," she cried miserably. "I-I just want to go to my room."

His ego was taking hit after hit this night. *My Bride doesn't want me, and when I pleasure my mistress, the female weeps in anguish.*

He'd known he was out of practice, but this was ridiculous. "Then what in the hell are you crying for?"

"You're really g-going to do it. You have every intention of casting my soul out."

"Why are you only now accepting this?"

"Th-this was my consolation prize. You wanted me to have that pleasure as a parting gift. Thanks for playing, Elizabeth? But game over?"

He clasped his forehead. Because she was probably right. And a couple of orgasms couldn't atone for what he was about to do to her.

Nothing could.

Tears streaked down her cheeks. "But we . . . but surely this isn't something that everyone experiences together. You have to feel *something* for me."

In a toneless voice, he said, "Whether I do or don't is immaterial. I use people and I discard them. That's what I've always done."

"Have you ever discarded someone and then regretted it?"

"Never."

"But you will with *me*." She ran her forearm over her eyes. "I could make you happy, Lothaire. You're going to realize what you had too late."

His brows drew together. Hadn't Ivana yelled the same thing to his father?

Lothaire gingerly pressed Elizabeth's head to his chest, rubbing his other palm over her lower back as he enfolded her in his arms. Strangely, she let him, even clutched him closer.

"You kidnapped me. You're g-going to kill me. Why am I letting *you* comfort me?"

He stared over her head. *Because I've made sure you have no one else to turn to.*

"Everything between us is sick . . . twisted. And it doesn't *have* to be."

"Shh, shh." He rocked her in his arms. Never had he comforted another in such a manner. He was awkward with this as well.

"I h-hate you s-so much." She sobbed so hard her body quaked against him, her tears wetting his chest.

"I know."

"When I-I'm gone, will you . . . will you t-tell my children about me? Will you t-take care of them?"

"Just be at ease for now, Elizabeth."

"Why couldn't y-you and Saroya just leave m-me alone? I only ever w-wanted to live."

Why was this making his gut twist? Either he was developing a conscience, or Ellie Ann Peirce was his Bride.

Both scenarios were ruinous to him. Because either one meant that it wouldn't be Elizabeth who died—it would be him.

The only way out of his vows to the Lore would be his own death.

She's not mine, she's not mine. . . .

35

Lothaire's bellows woke Ellie at dawn.

She blinked, surprised to find herself naked—and in his bed with him, cradled in his arms. He was clad only in dark jeans, pressing her against his bared chest.

How had they gotten into this position? She had no memory past crying herself to sleep as he'd softly stroked her.

Sobbing herself to sleep.

Though she'd always prided herself on never crying, she'd undammed an ocean of tears.

But how could she not? Last night, she'd gone from the most sublime pleasure to the rawest pain—both given to her by one male.

Now he was obviously in the grip of nightmares. Was he reliving some hideous memory?

Even after everything he'd done to hurt her—and would do in the future—she felt a pang of sympathy.

Untangling herself from his arms, she raised herself up on her knees to peer down at him. "Lothaire?" she murmured, her throat scratchy.

The muscles in his torso strained until they appeared knotted under sweat-slicked skin. He yelled in Russian, his fingers twisting as if he were in agony.

What do I do? Should I touch him?

Though he yelled out again and again, he was eerily still, as if he *couldn't* move.

"Lothaire, wake up—"

"No!" he roared, his eyes still closed. "Nooo!" He flung out one arm, sending her flying.

Landing with a thud some distance from the bed, she did a mental inventory of her body, surprised nothing was broken. Unsteadily, she made it to her feet.

I can't do anything for him. He doesn't deserve my sympathy anyway!

Shaking off her dizziness, she backed away toward her room, where she threw on a nightgown. On her own bed, she drew her knees to her chest, rocking herself as his yells grew louder.

Rocking, rocking . . . She'd never heard anyone in such pain. *Will I yell in pain when he casts out my soul? Will* he *pity* me?

He'd told her he wouldn't show her mercy—

"Elizavetta?" he yelled dazedly.

She closed her eyes as if to block out the sound. He'd called *for her*? Why her name and not Saroya's? *Because he needs* me. *No, you ignore him, Ellie!*

"*Elizavetta?*"

He sounded so . . . lost. "Dang it," she muttered, rising to return to his room. "Wouldn't let an animal suffer like this—"

She froze at the sight of him. Bloody tracks ran from his closed eyes. *My God, are those . . . tears?*

What kind of misery could bring this callous vampire to tears? Ellie's own eyes welled, and she found herself climbing in bed with him once more.

"Don't hurt, vampire!" She brushed pale hair back from his forehead.

What was wrong with him? What was wrong with *her*? She felt the need to take away his pain, and she didn't understand *why*.

"Lizvetta?" he rasped, beginning to calm somewhat.

She caressed his heartbreakingly beautiful face. "I'm here." More of his tension ebbed.

The vampire might think he could do just fine without her; she wasn't so sure about his prospects. He could scorn her all he liked, but clearly he did *need* her.

And realizing that affected her. As she continued to pet him, she again imagined what it'd be like to be loved by Lothaire.

If he'd ever stop planning to kill her, she might be tempted to find out.

Ellie shook her head hard. *Best not be dreaming of things that will never be.*

Then she frowned down at her hand. He'd begun slowly *disappearing.* "Oh, no, no!" He'd said he could be killed if he traced in his sleep. "Wake up!"

The survivor in Ellie thought, *Send him off, girl.* But some other part of her—one she didn't know too well—made her grab his shoulders and shake.

No response. "Lothaire, don't go!" Ellie knew she should abandon him and save herself.

She shook harder.

Yet instead of bringing Lothaire back to her, all she'd done was ensure she went into the unknown with him. Her last thought: *Dear God, what is his nightmare about . . . ?*

◈━◈━◈

Stay sane, Lothaire commanded himself as earth weighed down on him. *How long since his father had buried him here in his eternal pit?*

How many centuries since he'd been left to rot within a forest of bloodroot trees? His punishment for attempting to assassinate Stefanovich.

The attempt that failed. Because I was betrayed. *By the only friend he'd ever known.*

Chains bound him here in the ground. He was unable to trace from them, too weak to break the links. Unable to die from sunlight or a swift beheading.

He could tell another root had met his skin, had begun probing. Soon it would bur-

row through *him, seeking any regenerating flesh, any drop of blood from the husk of his body.*

Roots threaded all his limbs; worms forever feasted.

He burned to yell in agony and frustration, but he was trapped fast, couldn't move any part of his body. Not even to open his jaw or part whatever was left of his lips.

How long since his father had punished him thus?

One parent had buried him to save his life, the other to torment him—

Movement from above?

He could sense vibrations. Sometimes Stefanovich would slit a mortal's throat over this grave, soaking the dirt with blood—so close Lothaire could smell it, but it never reached him.

Always out of reach. Losing his sanity, surrendering it hour by unending hour. The surface always out of reach—

Did he hear spades rending the earth above?

No, no one is digging. *How many times had he imagined just such a scenario?*

Who would dig for him, who the hell would care enough to? His friends, family? Lothaire had none he could count on.

At every second, his torment reminded him that no one in this entire world gave a damn that he suffered.

Yet then he felt some of the pressure above him ease. Could that be tension on the manacle around his neck?

Like a shot, he was hauled upward, the roots violently ripped out of his body, stripping scabbed flesh from him.

On the surface at last? Too bright, too bright! *After darkness for so long, even the starry black night pained his sight. He tried to hiss, tried to cover his decayed eyes with what was left of his arm.*

"Ah, Lothaire!"

Fyodor? My uncle?

"I have been searching for you."

Saved. My uncle is come to save me. *If Lothaire had possessed any blood to spare, tears would have tracked down his face.* I did have someone out there, someone loyal to me.

"Six centuries I've searched."

Six hundred years! In the ground that long? I never imagined. . . .

"And now, Nephew, I'll free you from your bonds. On two conditions."

Conditions? Lothaire wanted to rasp, "Anything! Will do anything!" but his lips and tongue had been eaten away. He would bargain for damnation—it could not be worse than his current plight.

"Otherwise, I will plant you directly back into the ground, never to return."

Uncle, how can you say that to me? *The betrayal* . . .

"My brother did you ill these centuries, Lothaire. But you should not have faced Stefanovich until you were stronger. I will help you heal from this, will teach you how to become powerful enough to defeat him. All I ask for in return is your fealty—and his head. I am Stefanovich's royal heir. The Horde will accept me because he has no legitimate son. I will find a way to leave you the throne if I die."

He frees me only to hunt his brother, loosing me from my cage like a creature from hell.

Fyodor gave Lothaire blood to heal, pouring it into his crusted mouth, just enough that he could speak once more.

"Do you vow your allegiance to me, your future king, until the day I die?" Fyodor said.

Though Lothaire wanted to howl with fury, to tell his uncle to do his worst, he couldn't. "I-I vow it"—gasping, vomiting dirt and new blood—"t-to the Lore." I will never forget this betrayal, Uncle, never.

"Then welcome back to life, Lothaire, to a new beginning."

Against the blinding white starlight, Lothaire had squinted past Fyodor and seen the one he'd once called friend, secretly watching from the woods. . . .

Shaking off the remnants of the dream, Lothaire clawed at his bare chest, sinking to his knees within the Bloodroot Forest once more. As he bellowed to the night sky, moisture tracked from his eyes.

I can't keep living like this. The abyss stared back. *Finally, I topple over the edge.*

He knelt before the towering tree he'd grown, gazing up in horror at the bark, the weeping blood.

My blood. He fucking *wanted* to plunge into the abyss!

Sanity wrought only pain. He gave a crazed laugh, *relieved* as he felt himself falling . . . falling—

"L-Lothaire," he heard Elizabeth weakly call for him. Was he dreaming her memories?

He scented her fear, shot to his feet.

No, no, she cannot be here. This wasn't real.

"P-please . . ." she cried.

He whirled around but didn't believe his eyes. She was on her hands and knees in a snowdrift, crawling toward him.

Elizabeth *was* here. Her lips were pale, her expression stricken. "T-too cold."

Madness must wait. "Lizvetta!" he yelled, tensing to trace—

Enemies appeared beside her. A sword at her throat stopped him cold. Tymur the Allegiant's sword.

Tymur's gang of demons, Cerunnos, and vampires surrounded them.

To take her from me. All bent on taking her from me.

"Ah, Lothaire, I believe I have something of yours," Tymur said, his scraggly beard dangling all the way to his chest. "If you trace away or resist us, you'll never see her again."

More of Tymur's henchmen closed in on Lothaire. Demons whaled blows to his head and his back, stabbing him with short swords. He could do nothing to protect himself—could do nothing to reach her.

His vision clouded. *Blood all around my feet? Mine?* Black blood, from his black heart. Consciousness wavering, Lothaire fought to keep his gaze trained on Elizabeth.

Tymur shoved her to her knees, twisting a length of her hair around his meaty fist.

Her soft cries. Can't get to her. Her terrified gaze met Lothaire's.

Clarity struck; recognition sang within him, coursed through his every vein.

It was her. His Bride.

Dear gods, it was . . . Elizabeth. *You're going to realize what you had too late.*

Was it too late? His woman, captured by the deadliest beings in the Lore. *I allied with them. Am worse than they are.*

"This is rich." Tymur's eyes reddened with satisfaction. "The scourge of the Lore paired with a mortal? You could have no greater liability. So difficult to keep this species alive."

Around a mouthful of blood, Lothaire choked out, "Harm her and I will visit an unspeakable wrath . . . on your house . . . your descendants. I will live for nothing else!"

How many times had he been in this situation, but reversed? How many times had he placed his sword at the throat of a female, smirking at her male's frenzy to reach her, his animal need to protect her.

But I bargained *with them.*

Elizabeth raised her hands over her ears, muttering, *"Not real, not real."*

"What do you want, Tymur? The bounty?"

"Though it's tempting, I plan on keeping the lovely human. And every night that my men and I drink from her thighs, we'll toast the Enemy of Old, the unwanted bastard who thought to rule us."

"You won't fucking touch her!"

A Cerunno bent down to Elizabeth, its forked tongue flicking along her cheek as its tail coiled around her knees. At that, her gray eyes went chillingly blank. Her lips parted, her arms collapsing limply. She stared at nothing.

"No, Lizvetta!" Panic filled him.

"Oh, dear, her mind's breaking." Tymur clucked his tongue. "It happens with them. A shame. She won't know what she's missing. As for you, I'm going to plant you back in the ground, let your tree feed from your blood some more. I believe it missed you."

Lothaire shuddered, even as sweat broke out over his body.

"How long were you buried last time?" Tymur asked in a contemplative tone. "Or perhaps you can give me your legendary accounting book. The girl in exchange for the book, Lothaire."

My thousands of debts to save her? After all those years of toil?

Part of him burned to yell, "The book is yours, just let me have her back!"

Part of him was still . . . Lothaire. He told himself that he could trace from here, then find Elizabeth in the future, could retrieve her from his enemies.

But by all the gods, I want her now!

"Give me your decision. . . ." Tymur trailed off as a sudden mist blew in. The gang grew uneasy. He ordered, "Check the perimeter—"

Four males appeared—massive, pale-skinned swordsmen, each with his weapon raised.

Lothaire disbelieved his eyes. They'd come from the mist. *Dacians.*

When the demons and Cerunnos launched an attack, the Daci began cutting through them coldly, methodically. Fighting without emotion, only lethal accuracy.

And they were battling their way to Elizabeth.

"Seize the mortal," the largest Dacian ordered. "Return her to the castle."

Neither Lothaire nor those swordsmen would be able to reach her before Tymur traced her away from this place. *Away from me.*

As Lothaire thrashed against his captors, the vampire snatched Elizabeth by the hair once more, hauling her to her feet. She evinced no reaction.

Yet when Tymur tried to trace, nothing happened. Lothaire chanced a glance around. None of the demons or Horde vampires could trace in the mist.

That leader of the Daci neared Tymur, neared *Elizabeth.*

If the Dacian swordsman took her back to his hidden realm, Lothaire might never find her.

Panic redoubled. With all the strength left in his body, he surged against the demon guards' clutches, finally freeing himself.

He slew three foes, four . . . Only the Daci, Tymur, and two other guards remained.

Tymur pivoted to defend against Lothaire, releasing Elizabeth; she sank into the snow, her gaze still vacant.

What if she never recovered? Fury lashed him like a whip. "You've erred for ill, Tymur." Bloodlust boiled forth. *"Now you get to die."* Lunging into a trace, Lothaire plowed into the vampire, heaving him away from Elizabeth.

Bone-crushing impact. Tymur wailed in agony. Lothaire wrested his weapon free.

The vampire stared up at Lothaire, knew death had him; when Lothaire eased his lips back from his fangs and tossed the sword away, Tymur cowered.

"You'd make *my* Bride a blood slave?" Lothaire's voice . . . crazed, unrecognizable. "My female?"

My Elizabeth? Mindless with rage, he slashed his claws over Tymur, punched his fists through the male's mauled torso, collected handfuls of viscera. He bellowed with pleasure when arcs of blood sprayed across the snow.

When at last he wrenched free Tymur's bludgeoned head, Lothaire peered up through the haze.

All enemies had been felled but the cold Daci. They circled Lothaire and Elizabeth, their gazes watchful but inscrutable.

Bloodlust tolled within him, the ravening need for carnage. He locked his gaze on the blood still spurting from Tymur's savaged neck. Licked his lips for that steaming font.

The body flailed in death throes, exciting him. Lothaire groaned, claws sinking into the head he carried.

Would the Daci watch him fall upon his prey in a frenzy? Bloodlust, a fever undeniable—

Elizabeth's heartbeat?

Soothing . . . like waves. Like a beacon. Vision clearing, he saw her delicate form—amid the butchery he'd wrought.

He dropped Tymur's head, crouching in front of her to face off against the Daci.

The leader had eyes the color of glacial ice, and just as merciless. *The color my eyes used to be.*

In Dacian, he said, "So close to losing her forever, *Cousin*." He narrowed his gaze on Elizabeth's blank stare, on her blue-tinged lips. "You might still."

Cousin? With a brutal roar, Lothaire traced Elizabeth away.

36

She heard Hag and Lothaire arguing, their voices indistinct.

But Ellie couldn't respond.

When she'd disappeared with Lothaire, she'd suddenly found herself transported to a freezing land, then abandoned amidst black, leafless trees that seeped blood. *The "blood forest" he'd rambled about?* Off in the distance, she'd spied the most haunting castle she'd ever imagined.

Then horned demons and Cerunnos had surrounded her. It was one thing to read about walking serpents, quite another to be captured by them.

The things she'd seen . . . things that couldn't be right.

And the things she'd heard, the hints about Lothaire's torture.

He'd told her he'd been buried alive for six hundred years. When in the grip of a grueling nightmare, had he unconsciously returned to his . . . grave?

She'd only meant to recede a bit, to let Saroya suffer that horrible scene. But when the goddess didn't rise, Ellie had fallen into this stupor. She remembered little after that, had only remotely perceived yells, swords clanging, Lothaire's unholy roars.

And now Ellie couldn't snap out of it, couldn't speak. He'd sat her upright in a chair, but she couldn't move from it.

"Vampire, I warned you of this!" Hag cried as she tucked blankets around Ellie's shoulders. "Mortals can *break*."

"Then *mend* her!"

"How could I possibly know how to treat a mortal for shock? She's catatonic!"

"I don't give a fuck, you heal her!"

"Why would you take her to Helvita? What did you expect? You're lucky she didn't die from the elements."

"I sleep-traced. Must have grabbed her."

No, I grabbed you. Like an idiot.

"It doesn't matter, Hag!" Every word booming louder, Lothaire snapped, "Now, stop being a silly bitch and *fix her*!"

"I didn't think you cared about her mind, only her body. Correct? Saroya will be unharmed by this, vampire. So you can relax."

Good point. Why did Lothaire care at all?

"Silence! Let me think!" In a vague tone, Lothaire muttered, "I remember someone who went through this. Must recall who. Goddamn it, who was it?"

Both of them began pacing, talking at the same time:

—"He wants me to fix a human being! Should I reach for the whiskey? Or perhaps a Band-Aid?"

—"It was a male. He suffered this very thing! Who the hell was it?"

Then Lothaire said, "I remember!" and disappeared.

Hag sounded like she'd begun rifling through some spell book. "Elizabeth, the vampire will be killing mad over this. As he is unlikely to punish *himself*, you must wake!"

Must I? Ellie didn't think she wanted to live in a world like the Lore. Where a father would bury his son alive for centuries. Where monsters dwelled. *The forked tongue that slithered across my cheek . . .*

At the memory, her thoughts grew quiet once more. For how long she didn't know.

Suddenly Hag snapped, "Who is *he*, Lothaire? Is this some kind of a joke?"

Another male was here?

A deep voice said, "Name's Thaddeus Brayden, ma'am. But you can call me Thad."

Lothaire had snagged the boy straight out of the front yard of Val Hall, saying, "Need your help to fix Lizvetta."

The Valkyries had shrieked, "You can't take him! Leave him be, vampire!"

To which Lothaire had eloquently responded, *"Go fuck yourselves!"*

"Can you please explain what's happening?" Thaddeus asked Hag now. "Mr. Lothaire isn't making a lot of sense. And, uh, whose blood is all over him?"

When the fey glanced at Lothaire, he nodded, trusting the boy. *To an extent.*

Hag said, "This girl is new to the Lore and has just been amidst a Lore swordfight. Lothaire won, but she saw Pravus creatures."

Realization dawned on Thaddeus's face. "Gotcha. That's all it took for me to clock out."

And Thaddeus was a Lorean, even if he hadn't known he was at the time. Elizabeth was a mortal. *She's so weak. Weak!*

What if he never saw her stubborn gaze again? Felt her passion? *You were going to end her anyway,* his mind whispered. *She might be my Bride, but she cannot be my queen.*

Struggling to control his tone, Lothaire said, "Then what did it take for you to clock *in*, Thaddeus?"

"A few weeks, and the care of a nice Valkyrie and a fey."

"Weeks!" To Hag, Lothaire said, "It's back to you, Venefican."

She peered down at her spell book as if willing it for an answer.

"Uh, just a suggestion, Mr. Lothaire," Thaddeus began, "but shouldn't you be, like, holding Lizvetta or something?"

If I took her in my arms, I'd squeeze her so desperately, too hard.

"Wait!" Hag cried. "The ash vines help mortals as well. I could clear her mind with the potion I'd intended for you."

"Excellent idea, Hag. Only one problem—*there were no fucking vines to be found!*"

"There is one other source. I hadn't bothered to mention it because it's so impossible—"

"Tell me!"

"Nereus." She said no more.

The sea god. "He owes me a blood debt." But fearing Lothaire's arrival—*no doubt assuming I'll come for his firstborn*—Nereus had recruited guards to protect his lair, some of the most ruthless immortals ever to live. "Hag, get started on the potion once more."

"But how will you get past his sentries to collect your debt?"

"I likely won't." And with that, Lothaire traced to the edge of a mountainous, perpetually storm-tossed coast to confront a god.

37

Where has Lothaire gone? Ellie wondered.

Was he in danger? She didn't know why she should give a damn. Apart from her catatonia, nothing had changed between them. Right?

That young man bent down in front of Ellie, then gently moved her head until she was facing him. But she still couldn't focus her eyes.

"So you're Lothaire's Bride. I knew he'd let me meet you! No matter what gruff front he put on."

I'm not his Bride, just a peasant pet he uses to get off with until he can kill me. At least, that's what she'd thought just hours ago as she'd cried in his arms.

But considering Lothaire's reaction earlier . . . ?

Now she didn't know.

"Lizvetta, is it?" the newcomer asked with a southern drawl. Not a mountain accent, but definitely from the South.

Hag said, "She prefers to be called Ellie."

"And you? I just can't call someone as pretty as you . . . Hag. Maybe you have a *middle* name?"

Ellie thought he was grinning when he said that.

"Lothaire wouldn't like you calling me—"

"You just let me worry about him."

"Very well. My name's Balery."

She'll tell him but not me?

"Nice to meet you, Balery."

"And what might you be, Thaddeus? You look mortal."

"Thanks. But I'm actually a vampire and phantom halfling."

Hag—Balery—sucked in a breath. Why?

"Yeah, I get that a lot." Again Ellie heard amusement in his tone. "Since I'm wicked powerful and rare and all." Then to Ellie, he said, "My name's Thad. I'm a friend of Mr. Lothaire's. And I'm going to help you through this."

Was this guy for real? His deep voice was filled with kindness, but if he was *friends* with Lothaire and part vampire, wouldn't that make him evil?

"Mr. Lothaire came and got me because I was human a little while ago. Or at least, I thought I was. And I went catatonic when I saw some of the creatures you met up with today. Creepy stuff, huh."

The things I saw . . .

Thad took her hands in his. They were big and rough, warming her own. "But you're safe now. No one will hurt you. We're gonna protect you."

Safe. Protected. How Ellie had longed for someone to tell her exactly that! At any time in the last five years.

But still she couldn't seem to focus her gaze, not even to see what he looked like.

"When I was out of it," he continued, "this really nice Valkyrie named Regin the Radiant and a dark fey called Natalya took me under their wings."

Regin the Radiant, the one Lothaire stalked? Oh, boy.

I hate this world.

"Every day the ladies talked to me, about normal stuff mostly. And after a while, I felt comfortable enough to peek my head up." He gave her hands a light squeeze. "So that's what I'm gonna do with you. Talk. 'Cause I got nowhere else I'd rather be. I'm hiding out from my adoptive mom. She's the greatest, but she thinks I'm in high school—and still human—but I'm done with mortal school. So every day from eight to three, I gotta get lost. I hang with the Valkyries mostly, but not one of them plays football. They just like to get high with the witches, play video games, and shriek at stuff."

This is better than the Book of Lore. . . .

"Hey, if you surface, I'll tell you stories about Mr. Lothaire. About how he saved my life again and again."

Had Hag briefly stopped stirring her potion at that?

"So what should I talk about now?" Thad mused. Ellie heard him snap his fingers as he said, "Oh, I know. . . ."

His voice a soothing balm, he told her about the Valkyries giving off lightning with emotion, lighting up the sky like it was the Fourth of July. He talked about how a fairy-godmother-type Valkyrie named Nïx had set him up with a vampire tutor, one who was teaching him how to trace— and to call for blood delivery. He told Ellie how he and his mom and gram were now living in a grand New Orleans mansion.

And all the while he'd pause to remind her that he'd never let anyone hurt her, that she was safe.

As time passed, Ellie's gaze began to focus on him. She could tell he was tall, muscular, and dark-haired. *Handsome.*

"You're coming back, Ellie." He grinned.

Oh, that smile! With *dimples*. So genuine, so open.

"You've just got to come back a little bit more. Not gonna let anything hurt you."

She tried to speak, to move. Struggling . . .

I can do this. Mind over mind. *Just like kicking Saroya offstage.* Ellie began shoving her way through.

"That's it, sweetheart. Come back to us."

Fight . . . fight . . . deep breath. *"Hi?"*

"Welcome back!"

"Oh, thank gods," Hag said, adding in a murmur, "Now we all get to live."

38

When Ellie got out of the shower, Hag was waiting with a change of clothes. "Thad has refused to leave until Lothaire returns, thinking you might need some 'watching over' until his 'bro' gets back."

"Clearly Thad's never seen you wield a machete." Ellie took the clothes—a T-shirt and a pair of cutoffs that she'd left over here.

"Not that the code would allow him to leave anyway. Without a portal or escort, no one but Lothaire can trace in—or out. I'd planned to hold him here until Lothaire decides what's to be done with him."

"Where did Lothaire take me earlier? What was that horrible place?"

"He accidentally traced you to the Horde capital of Helvita."

"The one I read about. That's where he was tortured?"

Hag didn't confirm or deny. "Now, about this boy. If you tell him anything about your current situation, Lothaire will kill him. One word of it will equal his death decree. You can't ask for his help to escape."

Ellie dragged on the cutoffs. "I won't say anything."

"I saw you look at Thad's cell phone before you excused yourself to shower."

"Yeah, well, I saw you see me looking at his phone."

Hag crossed her arms over her chest. "Is that why you didn't ask him to use it? Because you feared my reprisal?"

"True, I didn't want you to cut off his hand. But I also held back for another reason." At Hag's questioning expression, Ellie said, "I'm Lothaire's Bride, aren't I?"

She abruptly turned to arrange a towel on the rack. "Why do you ask me this again?"

Ellie pulled on her shirt. "There was a moment in the fray when he seemed . . . dumbstruck as he looked at me."

The last twenty-four hours had been a roller coaster for Ellie. Last night, she'd accepted her end. Now, something had changed.

How could Ellie believe Lothaire would condemn her after his obvious worry, his panic?

"It doesn't matter whether you are or not, Elizabeth. He needs Saroya to claim the Horde crown."

"Because he's illegitimate."

Hag hesitantly nodded.

"Why can't he just use the ring to get it? Lothaire told me it could do just about anything."

"You can only use it so many times before your wishes begin to go awry. Besides, without Saroya by his side, there would be countless rebellions."

"I don't understand. Saroya has no powers."

"The Horde will only accept a royal vampire heir, or one married to a royal. . . ."

"Or a former vampire goddess."

"Exactly. And since he plans to use the Horde to take over the Daci, Saroya equals *two* crowns."

Ellie equaled nothing.

Doesn't matter if I'm his Bride. He'd have to want her more than he did those thrones.

When Ellie finished dressing, Hag said, "Again, you can't tell Thad anything that might get in the way of Lothaire's plans."

"I've got it. But hey, you don't tell the kid that I was in prison for murder, okay?"

Hag nodded in agreement, and they returned to the kitchen.

At once, Thad stood up from his seat at the counter. *What a gentleman.*

He was dressed in worn jeans that highlighted his powerful legs and a plain black T-shirt that stretched over his well-developed pecs.

The kid was built like a linebacker.

"You got your color back, Ellie. You'll be right as rain by the time Mr. Lothaire returns."

As Hag continued her work on the new potion base, Ellie took a seat beside him.

"Tell me how you and my bro met," Thad said, his eyes excited.

Up close, she could see they were hazel with vivid blue flecks. "Um, Hag brought us together," Ellie answered vaguely.

He frowned at the word *Hag*.

"I mean, *Balery* used her foresight and all."

"Those oracles"—he smiled over at the fey—"always helping folks out."

Bite your tongue, Ellie. "So you . . . you can't truly be *friends* with Lothaire?"

"I am, ma'am," he replied proudly, his chest bowing. "I'm fairly sure I'm his only friend."

Why did that make her heart clench? She hated Lothaire more than ever after last night. Didn't she?

Surely she did. Yet something else was stirring inside her. Ellie didn't dare name it because that would confirm she was a fool.

I'm nobody's fool, least of all Lothaire's.

He might have changed the way he looked at her, but she was still fresh from sobbing about her upcoming execution. Not to mention this morning's trip— "Wait, did you call me *ma'am*? I'm not much older than you are. You look like you're twenty."

"Just turned seventeen." In a matter-of-fact tone, he said, "Everybody thinks I'm older 'cause I'm so tall and built."

Hag muttered, "That you are." After clearing her throat, she asked,

"How did you meet Lothaire? We find you an unlikely acquaintance for him."

"He and I were both captured by these human soldiers, then imprisoned on this island to be tortured and experimented on and everything."

"Oh, my God, that's awful!" Ellie said, briefly clutching his brawny arm. "Why would they do those things to you?"

"They're called the Order. They consider immortals *miscreats*— miscreations. Abominations and all. They plan to exterminate every last one of us."

"How did you get taken?"

"It's the damnedest thing. I'd just gone to pick up a girl to take to the movies, worried about nothing more than Eagle Scouts, my curfew—and maybe stealing a kiss from my date." He winked at Ellie, and she felt like fanning herself. "Next thing I know, I'm waking up in a holding tank with all these creatures. That's when I flipped out."

"It must have been terrifying."

"Well, it wasn't a June picnic, that's for sure. And the cell! You can't imagine what it's like to be caged for days on end."

Can't I? Your friend put me in the big house for five years.

Rubber band snap. Snap!

"I only got one torture session, not too bad, but Mr. Lothaire? They burned him until his skin charred away and you could see his bones. They starved him. He just laughed, messing with the humans' minds and all."

Ellie could easily imagine him doing that.

"When all the prisoners broke loose, he saved my life, repeatedly. And all the while, he was desperate to get off the island. We figured he had someone to get back to. Didn't know it was you!" Clearly recollecting some memory, Thad said, "Mr. Lothaire sure is wild for you."

Not for me.

"So, what do you do, Ellie?" he asked.

Well, previously, I held a position on death row, but lately I've been a vampire's plaything. Soon I'll be sacrificed so the Soul Reaper and the Enemy of Old can make babies.

"What do I do?" Ellie caught Hag's look of warning. In a feigned bubbly tone, she said, "Hey, you want a drink, Thad? I could use a drink. I've gotta show you this chest. . . ."

⋘❧⋙

Three hours later, Ellie slurred to the chest, "Hos-say Kvervo tee-killer, please."

Somehow she, Thad, and Hag had already finished two buckets of Coronas.

Thad had told her he'd never tasted tequila. Ellie scarcely remembered it. One way to remedy that!

"Lime. Salt. Another bucket of Coronas. And chips, thanks."

When Ellie dragged her score out to the deck, she found Thad buzzedly tightening a shutter hinge with a multipurpose pocket tool. *So* the Eagle Scout.

She and Hag were in bathing suits, and he'd removed his shirt. Though it was a cloudless day, Thad had no problem with the sun, and he had the tan to prove it. "Guess it's my phantom half," he'd explained with a shrug.

Behind his back, Ellie mimicked a kitty-cat clawing him; Hag grinned into her beer.

After popping open a round for the three of them, Ellie sank down on the lounge chair to watch sweat trickle along the rises and falls of Thad's cut torso muscles.

Am I feeling lust for him? Or just appreciating his amazing hotness?

It occurred to her that he was exactly the type of boy she'd always imagined herself with. Good-natured, handsome, considerate.

So why was she so attracted to a deadly, forbidding bloodsucker like Lothaire?

Because of mental trauma and sexual desperation?

Or because of his brilliant mind and seductive touch? *That molten gaze . . .*

Maybe she should test out whether she truly desired Lothaire or if she simply needed a male—any male.

Maybe test this with Thad? Countless Coronas said this was the best—plan—*ever*.

When her timer went off, Hag wobbled to her feet, pointing to the sky. "Potion!" she said, like she might say, "Eureka!" Then she veered off to the kitchen.

Alone with Thad, Ellie said, "Thank you so much for bringing me back this morning." Taking yet another swig of liquid courage, she stood, crossing over to him. "You're my hero."

Still concentrating on his chore, he drawled, "Anytime, darlin'." She'd found out that he was a born-and-bred Texan. *A long, tall, gorgeous drink of Texas . . .*

"You mind if I give you a hug in thanks?" Her voice had gone throaty.

He turned toward her with a frown, scrubbing his palm over his chin.

Before he could say anything, she laced her hands around his neck, her nails sifting through the hair curling at his nape.

God, he smells incredible. The muscles of his chest flexed against her breasts, his damp skin so hot she could feel it through her top. "Or how about a thank-you *kiss*?" She stood on her toes.

He blushed deeply. "Uh. You're Mr. Lothaire's female, which means you're taken. *Really* taken. And as for me, I'm—"

Ellie pressed her lips against his, tightening her embrace while he froze in shock.

But his lips were firm, tasting of lime with a hint of salt. *Nice.* She kissed harder, and his lips finally parted on a breath.

He smells, feels, and tastes wonderful.

So where's the lust?

Dang it! Now she could admit what she'd instinctively known. *Without Lothaire, I'll never feel such passion again.*

She was just about to break away when Hag walked out. "Dark gods! What is this, Elizabeth?" she cried. "You want this boy dead?"

Thad and Ellie both stumbled back mumbling apologies to Hag, to each other.

The fey pointed Ellie toward the bathroom. "Go wash your face now!" To Thad, Hag said, "Sit. You're next."

Inside the bathroom, Hag slammed the door behind Ellie. "Wash! Get his scent off you."

Ellie dutifully scrubbed her face. Okay, maybe the beers were wrong and that hadn't been the best idea. "You're not going to tell Lothaire?"

"This happened on my watch. I left two drunken, postpubescent beings alone. Lothaire can *never* know. Why in the gods' names would you do this?"

"I just . . . I had to know why I feel things so strongly with Lothaire. If it was me being straight out of prison, or if it's *him*."

Hag's disapproving mien softened. "No matter how ill-advised your experiment, I can't fault you for your curiosity." She exhaled. "I can only imagine what you must be feeling. But did you at least make a determination?"

"It's only Lothaire for me. Passion-wise, at least." *Nobody's fool.*

Then Ellie frowned. What if there was actually a *future* with a vampire like him? Somewhere—and somehow—to be found?

To save herself, she'd been seducing his body and his mind, with some success. But she'd left his heart out of it.

What if she set out to win the vampire—because she wanted to try a life with him?

"I'm gonna make Lothaire fall in love with me. I mean *really* in love." *Gonna put his heart in my sights. Trace, vampire, but you can't hide.*

"And what if he still sacrifices you for Saroya, for his crowns?" Hag asked. "All you'll be doing is making it hurt worse for both of you."

Ellie would be guarding her own heart the whole time, determined *not* to fall for Lothaire. And once she made up her mind, she couldn't be moved from her decisions. "Then I've got to make him love me *more* than two vampire kingdoms."

"And precisely how are you going to do that?"

Ellie grinned. "I'll figure it out over more tequila. Now, let me go smooth things over with poor Thad. . . ."

39

O *ne love, one heart . . . let's get together and feel all right. . . ."*

When Lothaire traced back to Hag's, reggae music and laughter sounded from her deck. A bottle popped open, glasses clinking.

Though the potion base bubbled at the ready, the kitchen area was empty. Was Elizabeth outside? Had she regained full consciousness without this concoction?

So much for his imaginings. *Hag completing the potion, me administering it, Elizabeth's stubborn gray gaze coming into focus, her arms wrapping around me in gratitude. . . .*

Ash vines clutched in his shaking fist, Lothaire rendered himself invisible, half-tracing to the opened patio doors to find Elizabeth, Hag, and Thaddeus doing tequila shooters on the deck.

Relief washed over him as he surveyed the scene. Elizabeth was awake, her eyes bright. She wore cutoffs and a bathing suit top; since Thaddeus wasn't ogling her body, Thaddeus got to live.

Elizabeth was safe, the boy was being a gentleman with her, and Lothaire could tell that Hag had changed the boundary code since he'd left. All was well.

Still, he was furious with the three of them. Though Lothaire didn't know for what. He just knew that *his* oracle, *his* woman, *his* . . . friend did not need to be drinking and laughing together without *him* around.

Lothaire's eyes narrowed. This felt vaguely like . . . mutiny, but he couldn't precisely say why.

He listened to them talking between shots. Thaddeus was telling tales about him? "Lothaire's the funniest guy you'll ever meet," he said.

"Yeah, right," Elizabeth scoffed. "I can process that as well I did the Cerunnos."

"I'm serious! In the middle of our escape, all the world was going to hell—fights everywhere, explosions going on left and right with blood-curdling screams. And Lothaire shows up out of nowhere just as calm as he can be. The last we'd seen him, he'd been fighting this huge vampire gang. One of our group asked him how he could possibly have survived that battle. In this deadpan voice, he says three words: 'I'm *that* good.'"

As the females laughed, Lothaire leaned his shoulder against the doorway, still unseen, casting his mind back to that exchange. He remembered it because Thaddeus had shown him loyalty directly after.

The group had been about to take off in a plane with Declan Chase, bound for escape, but they hadn't wanted to include Lothaire. Yet Thaddeus had demanded that he be allowed on.

Lothaire had declined, of course. Then he'd ordered winged demons to crash the plane—to bring Chase to him.

But Lothaire would never forget that Thaddeus had stood up for him—though the boy would have gained nothing from it.

One of the first instances of true loyalty Lothaire had experienced since his mother had died. . . .

"Tell more," Elizabeth cried, swigging a beer chaser. The area around her lounge chair was covered with crushed snack chips, which made his lips curl. "More!"

"One night, we were taking a time-out in this creepy lab," Thaddeus began. "Torture tools were hanging everywhere, but Lothaire was completely unfazed. He just climbed on top of this cage to go to sleep, telling the rest of us, 'To anyone who contemplates even nearing me while I sleep: I will garrote you with your own viscera.' I mean, who says shit like that?"

More laughter.

By that time, I'd drunk Chase's blood, was already keen to get to the man's memories.

The boy pounded a shooter. "And out on the trail, Lothaire told this burly berserker to watch himself, 'else I'll revisit my juvenile skull-fucking phase.' "

Elizabeth snorted beer out of her nose, and Thaddeus threw back his head to laugh. Hag didn't join them; she knew Lothaire had been serious.

Ah, my mischievous youth . . .

"And he's crazy brave," Thaddeus averred, exhibiting that unmistakable case of hero worship.

But Elizabeth is hanging on every word he says about me. A satisfying feeling.

"Now, that I can believe," she said. "I know he killed a pack of Wendigos."

Thaddeus waved that away. "That was early in the fight. After that, he took on an *army* of them, saving all our lives. And all the time he was trying to get back to you."

Elizabeth's smile faded. Lothaire could almost hear her thoughts: *Not trying to get back to* me.

"On the island, I was the one who suspected he had a lady," Thaddeus continued. "When Lothaire got spacey, he'd murmur to me about his young Bride gazing up at him with fear, which, granted, is a little weird to hear—"

"I've returned," Lothaire interrupted. They all jumped, heads whipping in his direction.

He hadn't remembered telling Thaddeus those things. *Young? Fear?* Definitely not describing Saroya.

Have I always known deep down that Elizabeth is mine?

Her smile returned now. "Lothaire, you're safe."

As are you. After last night's tears—and this morning's terror—she was happy to see him unharmed? "Of course." To Thaddeus, he said, "You've made yourself at home."

The boy gazed down at his beer. "Thought I'd hang out, maybe give you a hand guarding your lady."

"Did you revive Elizabeth?"

"Just helped her along some."

Lothaire gave him a curt nod. "A word, Hag." He traced inside, tossing the vines on the counter.

She followed. "You secured them."

Barely. The guards had been as vicious as he'd expected. Somehow he'd breached their defenses to face Nereus. . . .

As the god handed over the vines with relief, he asked Lothaire about his new Bride, the one Loreans everywhere were speculating about. "Is she anyone I know?"

"She's no one," Lothaire answered truthfully.

"I really thought you'd demand my firstborn."

"As if I'd want your fucking guppy," Lothaire drawled, tracing away before Nereus could strike him down.

"The stock is ready," Hag said as she folded the vines into a bubbling pot. "Not that we need it now." Was the fey slurring?

"How did Thaddeus bring her back?"

"He talked to her, telling her she was protected. *Amazing* how well she responded to something so simple. I imagine feeling safe is a novelty for her."

Lothaire ignored her censorious tone, attributing it to the spirits, and focused on the outcome. Elizabeth was well, and Thaddeus had demonstrated loyalty yet again.

Maybe the halfling *could* be an ally of sorts. . . .

Now that Lothaire's worry for Elizabeth had been alleviated, he could finally assess the battle this morning—and its ramifications.

Had that Dacian male truly been his cousin? What other living family did he have on the Dacian side?

Perhaps he *was* getting closer to finding that kingdom, to finding Serghei. He had to be if they'd targeted Lothaire's Bride so aggressively.

Yet another enemy to contend with. After witnessing their skill with swords, Lothaire would not underestimate them.

And now that Tymur the Allegiant had been dispatched, political machinations among the vampires would ramp up once more. The Forbearers would likely make a play for the throne, led by the natural-born Kristoff—for whom Lothaire held a particularly lethal animosity, and who'd rebelled against the Horde in the past.

But Kristoff had forbidden his army to drink blood straight from the flesh—to forbear. Which violated one of the Horde's two sacred tenets: the Thirst.

Aside from Kristoff there was one other contender, unlikely though she might be.

Much to analyze, moves to predict . . .

"I rolled to find Dorada, but she's far removed from us at present," Hag said.

"Very good," he answered absently, only now remembering that he hadn't predicted Tymur's movements, hadn't slain the vampire with his customary detachment. In defending Elizabeth, Lothaire had thrown away his greatest weapon, had relied on searing instinct.

She is mine.

Reading him so well, Hag said, "You know it's *Elizabeth* now, do you not? Perhaps you won't slit my throat to my spine if I speak of this?"

He'd been so arrogant during that conversation with Hag, dismissing the idea of a mortal Bride as absurd. He hadn't even bothered to tell Hag exactly how ensnared he was with Saroya.

"How will you get Elizabeth to forget all you've done to her?" Hag asked. "She won't be able to easily, if at all. Trust me on this."

"Doesn't matter if she's my Bride. I can't keep her. My plans must remain unchanged."

Hag blinked at him. "You don't intend . . . ? Lothaire, if you go through with this, it will destroy you."

"I'll be destroyed if I don't fulfill these vows."

"Your mother wouldn't have wanted this for you."

"You assume I speak of the vows I made to Ivana? Perhaps I foolishly made others—"

Elizabeth sauntered in. Tanned, barefoot, grinning in her short cutoffs. So sexy his thoughts blanked for a long moment.

"Hey, Lothaire. Thad's been telling us all about you. How heroic you are." She sidled up to him with a hip-swinging gait that quickened his pulse. "And you went and got ash vines for me?"

Hag chose that moment to turn her stove to simmer and swerve out of the kitchen onto the deck.

Before he ever decided to reach for Elizabeth, Lothaire found his hands circling her waist. "So certain I did it for you?" he asked, lifting her to the counter.

"Uh-huh. You only needed to keep my body healthy. Not my mind."

He eased his hips between her knees. "Perhaps you shouldn't attribute characteristics to me that aren't there."

"And you should stop with the Lothaire-speak." She raised her hand to his chest, making lazy swirls with her forefinger.

"What are you talking about?"

"You ask questions to get around lying. Or you say things like"—she imitated his accent—"'perhaps you' or 'I'd surmise that you.' Yeah, that's right, vampire, I got your number."

It disconcerted him how quickly she'd learned his tells, but he made his face impassive. "Did you worry for me today? In between tequila shots?"

She sighed. "And you also abruptly change the subject. In any case, I did worry about you, Leo."

"What did you call me?"

"Your initials. Lothaire the Enemy of Old? Sounds like Lothaire the Wizard of Oz. Leo suits you better."

His fingers dug into the counter on either side of her hips. "Enemy of Old is not just a name, it's a designation. It takes bold strokes to survive in the Lore; I've *earned* the right to be called that."

"Well, right now you've earned your nickname, too."

"Why now?"

"I'm buzzed and you're looking gorgeous and kissable. You needed a nickname."

In all his life, no one had ever called him by one. Nor felt the casual ease to do so. "Why this . . . affection? Last night you were crying. Aren't you angry that I took you to Helvita?"

"I grabbed you," she admitted. "You started to disappear, so I tried to shake you awake."

"Concern for me?" His spike of pleasure was overrun by irritation. "And yet I'd ordered you *not* to touch me. Why would you disobey me?"

"You called for me, repeatedly yelling my name."

Then some part of him *had* known Elizabeth was his.

"And you'd told me that you could be killed if you traced in your sleep! After seeing the creatures awaitin' you, I believe it."

His shoulder muscles knotted. "What do you remember?"

"Jumbled bits up to a point, then nothing. Anyhow, I'm past it."

"How could you possibly be?"

"I have something to look forward to." In a solemn tone, she said, "I've decided, Leo, that I'm gonna keep you."

Though everything within him was in turmoil, he calmly said, "Have you, then?"

"Even if you've been the biggest dick imaginable."

He glowered at that. "Insolent chit."

"I'm your Bride, aren't I?"

"The idea of a mortal Bride is ridiculous." *Even if the Bride in question makes me weak from wanting.*

"I'm calling Lothaire-speak! You didn't answer me."

"How many times have I told you that you're beneath me?"

Instead of being insulted, she smiled. "Should I call you hubby? Or vampire groom?"

Just when he was about to give her a set-down, she leaned in to whisper at his ear, "If you sip me, will you get tipsy?"

His body tensed. "One way to find out."

"Then take me back to your bed and do really naughty things to me while you talk filth in my ear."

He just stifled a growl.

On their way out, he quickly stopped at the deck to tell Thaddeus, "Hag will open a temporary portal for you to get home, *paren'*. Leave your phone number with her before you go. And of course, you will not give this location to anyone."

"Sure thing, Mr. Lothaire." But again, the boy refused to meet his eyes.

40

"Something's different about you," the vampire said as soon as they'd appeared in his room.

I figured out some things about myself. "I can't imagine." *And about you.*

He'd begun doing that predatory stalking thing around her. "If only I could lie so easily. I will find out your secret."

Grasping for a change of subject, Ellie asked, "What were you dreaming of when you traced earlier?" then bit her tongue when she saw a glimpse of raw anguish in his eyes.

His expression grew shuttered. "A memory . . . one of my own. Something I do not want to speak of."

She had a pretty good idea of what. "Fair enough."

"You're not going to press?"

"You'll tell me when you're ready," she said.

This *really* seemed to please him. He snatched her close to nuzzle her hair. "You smell like salt, sun, and tequila. Exotic to one like me." He inhaled deeply, as if he wanted to take her scent into him—

Suddenly his body jerked with tension, and he set her away. "Why do I still scent a trace of Thaddeus—even when we're away from him?"

"I'm sure we hugged." But she could feel her cheeks getting flushed. Was her heart speeding up?

"You're . . . *lying*. Why would you lie, unless . . ." His eyes shot flamered.

"No, Lothaire, it isn't like that!"

"Tell me what it was like," he said softly before roaring, *"or I'll do murder!"*

"I-I kissed him."

"Then you've *killed* him."

"Thad didn't kiss me back! He was bewildered, just stood there. Afterward, he was mortified."

"Then I'll punish you more, slattern! I should string you up naked to a pole at the demon crossroads!" With a crazed bellow, he launched one of his fists into the wall, hitting it like a wrecking ball. The room shook. Another punch before he faced her, yelling, "Did you *touch* him?"

"No! In any case, why would you care? You keep telling me that *I* am not your Bride. Saroya is! What is one harmless kiss for a woman you're gonna kill soon?"

"Tell me why you did it! Why in the fuck would you kiss him?"

"My reasons are my own!"

He laid his bleeding hand over her throat. "Tell me or I'll wring your pretty little neck."

Nothing had changed with Lothaire. *Nothing.* "You *can't*." She flailed from his grasp. "So take the needle off that record, vampire!"

"No, but I can kill your family! Shall I make you pick one relative over another to live?"

Oh, God, not them! "Please don't, Lothaire—"

He was already tracing her to the mountain.

"Take me back to the apartment, and I'll tell you . . ." She trailed off when she saw that the place was like a ghost town.

No lights, no voices, no TVs going in any of the trailers on the entire mountain. The Peirce family had gotten themselves *lost.*

"Where the hell are they?" he snapped, tracing her inside her old trailer.

The first time she'd been back since the night of the murders.

Belongings were strewn about. Mama had gotten them out in a hurry, and they'd clearly been gone a while.

Empty. Ellie checked a look of victory.

Lothaire swung his gaze on her, tracing her back outside to gaze down the lightless mountain. "Tell me where they are!"

"Gone." She breathed deeply of the country air, squaring her shoulders. "They're out of your reach forever."

Back here on her mountain, she soaked up strength. This place had seen hundreds of years of struggle and hardship, of blood lost and pain found.

Right now, Ellie believed she'd been *honed* by life here, as if she'd just been waiting to go toe-to-toe with a fiend like Lothaire.

"Hmm." She tapped her lip. "Can't kill them. Can't hurt me. Seems you're holdin' a shit hand of cards, Leo."

The last time they'd been at the doorstep of this trailer, Elizabeth had risked her life to kill Saroya, running into a hail of bullets.

Now, after all he'd done to her, she was taunting him.

Did I truly think her cowardly?

"So what's worse, Lothaire? The fact that I'm an ignorant hillbilly human?" She jabbed his chest with her forefinger. "Or the fact that you were just *bested* by one?"

This boldness in her . . . *delicious.*

No, you're enraged at the slattern!

And enthralled with her. Possessiveness and lust and something else he couldn't define warred inside him.

Then he remembered her kissing that boy years ago. How easily Lothaire could envision *Thaddeus's* look of wonderment!

Jealousy—*seethed.* "Hag would never let you call them."

"Nope."

"It couldn't be Thaddeus." Her family had been gone too long. "Tell me how you warned them!"

"Or—*what?*" She laughed derisively.

"I will find them."

"They are hidden, as only mountain folk can get. Face it, Lothaire, you've lost this match. You play your offense; I play *defense*. I set this plan into motion half a decade ago."

Lothaire traced her back to the apartment. "What are you talking about?"

Chin raised, Elizabeth tried to fling herself away from him. After a moment, he let her.

"I reckoned you'd dole out that punishment you'd promised if I succeeded in killin' your queen. So I made my mother swear to make herself and the entire family scarce for a spell."

To clear off an entire mountain of Peirces?

Like scraping an anthill completely clean. Yet it'd happened.

"You want your reputation as the Enemy of Old to precede you, to make your enemies fear you?" When she jabbed at his chest again, his gut clenched with want. "*My* greatest asset is that I'm forever underestimated—by people like you." She pinned his gaze with her own. "I'm the sucker punch that you never saw coming."

Unexpected Elizabeth, with her fierce gray eyes. Saroya might be vicious and lethal, but Elizabeth was cunning, beguiling.

Quietly running circles around him at every opportunity.

Because wasn't *unexpected* just another way of saying *underestimated*?

Sucker punch? She'd left him reeling.

"So no, Lothaire, there will not be any harm done to my family by you tonight. Or *ever. Are—we—clear?*"

Crystal, he thought as his lips parted. *I know exactly what you are now. I know what you will be.*

It was apparent what he had to do. Even he could recognize that he was experiencing some unknown-before need for this mortal girl, something even more than desire. And it was *despite* the goddess inside her.

"Lothaire, I asked you a question!"

He narrowed his eyes as a dim thought occurred. "If you suspected your family was safe, why did you go along with my plans? Why did you act afraid for them?"

She shrugged, casting him a queenly look that dared him to do something; a growl of lust burst from his chest.

Her peccadillo forgotten—for now—he leaned in to kiss her.

41

Get off me, freak!" Ellie futilely shoved at him. "I'm not kissin' you! You were just about to harm my family!" *And you took me away from my mountain yet again. . . .*

"I wasn't going to harm anyone," the vampire said. "I'd planned to get you outside the trailer and scare you. Then you'd see reason."

He can't lie.

"But it seems I am holding a *shit hand of cards*." He stabbed his fingers through his hair. "You refuse to do as I predict."

"You're one to talk about that." He wasn't homicidal that she'd gotten one over on him—he was *impressed*.

And seeing that look in his eyes affected her. Coupled with the rush she'd just experienced from smelling the crisp air of her home—the woods, the very earth—she could almost feel . . . hope.

He took me away from my home, but maybe one day the male before me will bring me back there.

In a weary tone, he said, "Tell me why you kissed the boy."

"To find out if I desired just about *any* male after my prison stay, or if it was only you—"

"And?"

He's holding his breath. Dear God, she might truly have a shot at Lothaire. "I didn't feel any desire for him, because I was wantin' . . . you."

"Me." Pride fired in the red depths of his eyes. "Good. I don't . . . I didn't *want* to have to behead Thaddeus. Or to string you up at the demon crossroads."

"Really? Oh, Lothaire, this is huge! This is what I'd call a breakthrough moment."

"Shut up."

She grinned.

His gaze dipped to her mouth. "You want a real kiss now? From your own male?"

My own male. She nearly swayed. Lothaire had never treated her like his Bride; now his gaze upon her was heated and *possessive.* "I do, Leo, but I'm gonna want it for a lot longer than a week." *I want to live!*

He cupped her face with pale hands. "I'm keeping you, Lizvetta."

❖⊱⊰❖

"Do you mean"—Elizabeth's eyes started glinting—"I don't have to die?"

What monster could kill such a one as she?

I'd been planning to. No, worse than death. "You'll *never* die! Keeping you forever."

Because she would be . . . his *queen.*

At Helvita, he'd recognized Elizabeth as the Bride fate had chosen for him. Now he gazed upon the cunning queen he'd chosen for himself.

Somehow he would figure out a way around his vows to the goddess. He was Lothaire, after all. He could figure out anything.

"But what about Saroya?"

"I'll take care of her."

"How?"

"The ring's still in play, is it not?" he said. "You will live, and I will take care of Saroya, but in return, you must . . ." He grabbed her shoulders. "I'm ordering you to forget what went on between us before."

"What do you mean?"

"Hag told me you wouldn't be able to get past my treatment of you."

"Ohhh. Like the threats against me and my loved ones? Like the mental anguish and never-ending mockery? Like putting me on death row?"

He scowled. "If you want to live, then all that must be forgotten, just as you've done with your miseries in the past. You told me you've done this before!"

"I have, and I will now. All I ask is that you vow *never* to hurt my family, by your hand or order. Do we have a bargain?"

"Always with the vows," he muttered. "I add my own condition. In the next few weeks, you do not question me about my plans and actions. You trust me to decide what is best for both of us."

She hesitated. "Agreed."

"Then I vow to the Lore never to harm your family by action or order."

"And I vow to let you decide what is best for us. For three weeks."

He narrowed his eyes at her qualifier, but let it slide. "You also told me you could make me happy." He curled his finger under her chin. "You've got your work cut out for you."

"I've heard—probably just a wacky rumor—that sex makes males happy. You wanna seal this deal, Leo?"

He drew her tightly into his arms. "You think I don't want to claim you?"

She tilted her head up at him. "But you believe you'll hurt me."

"When a human male hurts a female during sex, what happens?"

"I guess she might walk funny."

"I can lift a fucking train, Lizvetta. What would happen to you?" For the first time in his long life, he regretted his strength—though he'd paid so dearly for it. Now it was an obstacle.

Not to mention his vampiric instincts. He was no turned mortal; he was of a different species, a *born* vampire with no human impulses to temper his predatory behavior. "Imagine if you tried to wrestle with a butterfly, but knew you couldn't dust its wings. It's equivalent to our situation."

She dragged her forefinger down his chest, saying in a sexy drawl, "What if the butterfly rode you like a lazy horse?"

He stiffened all around her. "Continue."

"Instead of grinding on you like I did when we were on the sofa," Ellie said, "I could *ride* you."

The vampire's interest was definitely piqued. But then he shook his head. "I haven't had sex in millennia. What makes you think I won't lose control?"

"I just know you won't." Ellie had made up her mind that this was going to happen. She believed that she was his Bride—though he hadn't specifically acknowledged the fact yet—which meant she believed he wouldn't hurt her.

Plus, in the back of her mind, she did want to seal this deal. To steal him from Saroya completely. *Just guard your heart, Ellie.* His jealousy earlier had done funny things to her.

"This is your first time, Elizabeth, and far, *far* from your last. I cannot risk your being hurt or frightened."

Her hand slipped down to stroke him through his pants, earning a growl. "You haven't scared me in the times we've been together." Much. "All I've felt is pleasure." After a bit of pain.

"I have been denying my instincts with you."

"What do you mean?"

He scrubbed a hand over his tired face. "Vampires don't fuck like human males. The act for us is all about possession, blood, *dominion*. Those drives will be stronger if I'm inside you. When you become a vampire, I won't have to hold back as much."

"Me? Become a vampire?" *Whoa.* She'd never thought it would happen to her, only to Saroya.

"When I told you I was keeping you forever, *I meant it.*"

She swallowed at the intensity in his words, the flash of fang. Clearly a discussion for another day . . . "I have an idea. Let's take off our clothes and fool around on the settee. If I trip and fall and land smack-dab on your cock, then it won't be your fault."

"Lose your virginity while on top?"

"I've already kind of lost my virginity."

Had his face flushed? "It would be easier for you if I lay upon *your* body—once you are turned."

She'd never seen him so torn. Just when she was about to give up, he exhaled a gust of breath. "Can't fight this." He stripped off her top. "Because now my mind has seized on you landing *smack-dab* on my cock. Can almost feel it already."

With no care for his clothes, he ripped at his belt and pants. When his erection sprang free, he traced her to their customary spot.

While he sat, gloriously naked, on the couch, she stood between his knees, slipping out of her cutoffs. "Are you nervous, Lothaire?"

"It's been a while." He raked his gaze over her. "And I want your first fucking to be . . ."

"Superlative?"

His lips curled into the sexiest grin she'd ever seen on a man, and she briefly forgot how to untie her bathing suit bottom.

She'd suspected Lothaire would crave excitement. Now his eyes were aglow with it, his breaths shallow. One of his legs jogged up and down.

Once she was naked, she crawled over his lap, rising on her spread knees above him.

"I'm going to be inside you," he said, as if he was only now accepting it. His shaft jutted in anticipation, the crown nearly meeting her sex.

"Loaded for bear again?" she teased, making him grin once more.

"I did, in fact, come loaded for bear." He leaned in to ever so gently graze his fangs along her neck. "Only to find a butterfly."

She shivered. He could be so charming, so seductive when he wanted to be.

"I want to kiss you, Lizvetta."

She eagerly leaned forward to press her lips against his.

But he took the lead, turning her back on his arm. With his lips above hers, he forced her to accept the strong thrusts of his tongue, until it felt like . . . sex, like he was screwing her mouth with his tongue.

She gave a yelp against his lips when he delved a finger into her sex from behind, thrusting it in time with his kiss. As he wedged a second finger inside, she thought, *He's preparing me.*

Again and again, he kissed and thrust . . . harder. Rougher.

No, he's warning *me.*

Instead he set her imagination ablaze. She'd seen the way he moved; what else could he do with that sinful body of his? What were these drives that he kept talking about?

She and Lothaire had had some touch-and-go moments together, but ecstasy always followed.

When he released her from his kiss, she was breathless, in a haze of desire. "I'm *ready*, Lothaire."

He'd told her that the phrase *deal with the devil* came from him; Ellie felt like she was on the verge of selling her soul.

"You truly trust me not to hurt you." Lothaire shook his head hard, wondering exactly when he'd agreed to claim her.

Earlier, she'd told him she was like a sucker punch. Now he realized he might not *ever* stop reeling.

But there was no turning back from this. Even a better man than he would do anything to possess this lovely creature—with her honeyed skin and sexy tan lines, with her long locks swaying down to tickle her nipples. Those smoldering gray eyes . . .

Much less a vampire who'd coveted his queen for ages.

"I do trust you, Leo. You're my guy," she murmured, gazing up at him from under her lashes. "You're going to take care of me tonight."

How could her words make his chest feel tight? Make him desperate not to hurt her? "Then I can't touch you." He laced his fingers behind his head. "Not till I know I can get through this."

"You make it sound like an ordeal."

It will be. "Just know that you're on your own."

"Fine. I can do this. How hard can it be?"

"As fucking steel."

She arched a brow. "Then we're a perfect match, 'cause I'm feeling hot as a forge right now." Taking him in hand, she stroked unhurriedly, up and down . . . up . . . down, leaving his control ragged.

Barely recognizing his voice, he said, "Begin this, Lizvetta. Mount me."

She nibbled her lip and nodded, lowering herself over him.

When the tip of his cock met her soft, damp sex, he almost spilled against her opening. "Gods almighty, you're *tight*."

She widened her knees, but was only able to take the head inside. "Lothaire, please . . ."

Don't touch her! If he clamped her hips, he'd wrench her down on his length, tearing her tender flesh. His interlocked fingers tightened until he thought bones would snap. "You're . . . doing . . . fine." He dropped his hands, clenching them by his sides.

Once again, she widened her knees, but she was trapped fast. "I can't get lower. Oh, God, I *need* to get lower."

He bit out, "And just how had you planned to take me?"

She blinked. "I thought I'd just slide down."

"Then I'll need you slick, I'll need you dripping." He drew back to behold her swollen breasts. Right before his eyes, a flush radiated over her supple skin, teasing him with all the places he could pierce her. "Cup your breasts to my mouth."

When she did, he held her gaze as he nuzzled one nipple. Closing his lips over it, he tongued the peak. . . .

"Lothaire!" As he began to suckle, she undulated, working to impale herself.

Agony. He felt like he would explode, seconds away from pumping into her with only the crown inside. With a groan, he pierced her nipple, a tiny prick of his fang, blood streaming to his lapping tongue. Delectable! Would he ever get enough of it?

She screamed. In pain? No, she was arching her back. "Lothaire, suck *harder.*"

He did, until the suction on her nipple was nearly holding her upright.

When he forced himself to stop, she whimpered, hastily cupping her other breast to tempt him again. "Here."

He stole another taste. Against her breast, wetted from his mouth and her blood, he rasped, "Can't take more."

Clutching his shoulders, she muttered, "Neither can I." Still he hadn't penetrated her. "You really are too big."

She started to crawl off him. *To get away from me?* His fangs grew even sharper, his instincts commanding him. . . .

Trace her to the bed, pin her down.

Take her blood, flood her with seed.

He gripped her tiny waist, trapping her, just preventing his claws from digging into her skin. "Ah-ah, Lizvetta."

"We don't fit!"

"We *will.* I won't let you go until I've claimed you." *Forgive me.* His hips bucked, bouncing her on his shaft, sending her up, then sliding back down.

"Lothaire!" Her voice was a mix of pain and desire. "Let me go!"

"No. Because right now, you are not"—another buck of his hips—"yet"—a more forceful thrust—"*mine!*" he growled as he hit the top of her sex.

With a choked cry, she dipped her head forward, her body trembling against his heaving chest.

"Look at me. Did I hurt you?" he asked, ignoring the voices in his head, the ones clamoring, *Pin her, claim her, make her understand who'll mark her.*

Who'll master her.

She bit her lip, her expression grave. "It hurt some, Leo."

No, never hurt you! He shook himself, inwardly chanting, *Endgame. Endgame. Elizabeth as my queen. Can't frighten her.*

She'd never know the battle inside him as she began maneuvering over his shaft. He splayed his fingers across her ass, feeling her flesh move so sensuously as she tested her body, their tight fit.

Fuck, he was throbbing inside her! *No, control yourself!* He gnashed his teeth, sweat dampening his skin.

When she gave a cautious rock of her hips, they met eyes, both wondering how she'd react.

Her lids grew heavy . . . a moan slipped from her lips.

He shuddered in response. It struck him that he was actually watching his woman—*his*—discover this pleasure for the first time. The idea gratified him in ways he couldn't describe.

How long I've waited for this, waited for her.

"Now it just feels better and better." She touched her forehead against his. "Baby, I can feel your heartbeat inside me."

Soon you will in more ways than one. "You can never take this back, Lizvetta. I've claimed you for my own." *But not completely.* He still needed to bite her neck. *Ritual.* The mark was a sign of this claiming, the seal between them.

Sink your fangs into her. Make her writhe on them as well.

Just when his eyes locked onto a pulse point in her neck, she whispered, "I never knew it could be like this. Lothaire, I've never felt closer to another."

He dragged his gaze up to hers. Voice thick, he admitted, "Neither have I."

She smiled. "Good."

Don't hurt her. Only gentleness. *Don't scare her.*

Tonight, Lothaire, you don't get to be a vampire with her.

In Russian, he told her, "Little mortal, you've changed *everything.*"

How can I want you this much? To deny what I am?

Because he was feeling something stronger for her—a bone-deep feeling of possessiveness, of *protectiveness.*

No one would ever harm the female in his arms, not even himself.

42

When Ellie rose up and tentatively slid down the first time, Lothaire's eyes widened, then grew hooded once more.

Was he as shocked as she was by how *right* this felt?

Even his irises appeared sharper, their shape more defined, his gaze lucid as it locked with hers.

Connection . . .

In the past, Ellie had never communed with another, had never looked into a boy's eyes and felt something deeper than the need for release.

Now, with Lothaire . . . she did.

This was more than just sex; this was a bond, like a promise between them.

She thought she'd known what kind of man she wanted. Now she realized she'd always needed this vampire lover with his hungry red eyes and his lifetimes of yearning.

He's yearned all this time for me.

When she slowly began to ride him, she cupped his face, leaning forward to kiss him with all the feelings bubbling up inside of her. He met her mouth with a seeking tongue and unyielding lips.

Guard your heart, Ellie. But his possessive kiss . . . who could guard against that?

Or the sensations cascading over her? Her nipples dragged up and down his muscular chest, his hot hands like brands across her ass.

When she drew back, panting for breath, he rasped, "Look at your expression. You're falling in love with me."

She could scarcely think, but for some reason she didn't want him to have that power over her. "I'm not falling in love with you." *I might be falling in love with you.*

"Of course you are."

Guard your heart! "I-I never said that."

"Ah, but I'm *me.*"

"Lothaire, are you always so danged chatty during sex? I can make tea. . . ."

He gave a pained laugh, then groaned when she twisted her hips.

"Lizvetta!" He pulsed inside her. "More of *that.*"

She was already nearing her peak, but she wanted to see to his pleasure. This wasn't just about her getting off; she needed to satisfy her man. She eased her rhythm.

A mistake.

"Move on me!" He twined her hair around his hand, drawing her back to lick her neck. "Harder, faster."

As if Lothaire would ever allow himself to go unsatisfied.

"I'll have more of you!" He released her hair to palm her breasts. "Given or taken."

She wrapped her arms around his neck, riding him with abandon. Yet as she watched his eyes, their clarity faded.

A growl began emanating from him as his shaft swelled inside her even more. His lips drew back from his fangs. "Need to fuck you hard." He looked wild, his eyes like fire.

Fear coursed through her. "Lothaire—"

He enfolded her in his arms and traced her to the bed—with her trapped beneath him.

When he thrust inside Elizabeth, Lothaire roared to the ceiling from the rightness of it.

He was a born vampire, and she was his fated female—now pinioned to the bed.

Through the haze of inconceivable pleasure, he felt her tense beneath him. *No, she can take me.* He withdrew for another thrust, plunging into her tight sex.

"T-too hard," she whispered.

"*What? I want* it hard! You'll give me what I want."

"Please be gentler with me, Leo." She leaned up to kiss his neck with light grazes of her lips. Like a butterfly's wings.

His mortal. So delicate. How easily he could break her little body.

Endgame! This creature is my queen. *About to hurt her with my cursed strength.*

But how could he keep himself from surging inside her? When each time he did, her channel stroked him—a moist, silken heaven that rubbed over his cockhead like a tongue, then squeezed his aching shaft like a fist. . . .

No one hurts her, including myself.

He gritted his teeth, then rose up on a straightened arm. Caging her in with his motionless body, he glided his thumb over her clitoris. "Work your hips up and down on me." Drawing on his last reserves of control, he kept himself from thrusting, until his muscles began to quake from the effort and sweat trickled down his torso.

Then . . . his Bride began to move beneath him. "Ah, that's it!" He dipped his head to suckle her stiff nipples. "Faster," he growled around a peak, giving it a nip with his fang, spurring her.

"Oh!"

She liked that. *Getting so wet.* The scent of her luscious sex made him snap, "Harder!" *Put me out of my misery.*

Her hands flew to his ass, fingers gripping, using him to pull herself up. Her moans grew louder, more urgent.

"You'll give me this whenever I want it . . . let me do whatever I want to you," he grated. "Because you *are* my Bride, Lizvetta. And I've got many years to make up for."

Between panting breaths, she asked, "I'm really yours?"

"Till the day I die," he said, his voice strained. The burgeoning pressure in his cock lashed him with the need to move his own hips, the vampiric urges he'd denied only growing stronger. Somehow he held himself still.

But he needed to mark her neck. His fangs were dripping for her, as sharp as they'd ever been. "Need to bite you."

"Yes! Do it."

"A true bite. Into your neck."

Without hesitation, she turned her head to the side, offering up that golden skin.

He ached to pierce it. "Try not to hurt you . . ." *Must make the bite clean.* He bared his fangs above her, pressed the tips against her neck.

They sank in deep, as if she'd drawn him into her.

Perfection.

He felt her screaming, "Oh, God, yes!"

Delirious with sensation, he swallowed the hot rush. *Consume her completely.* Her blood flowed true, as if straight to his heart, bonding them.

"Lothaire!" She arched beneath him. "I'm . . . I'm coming!" Her nails scored his skin.

He snarled against her, relishing her marks on him. *Consume her.* When she climaxed, he felt her sex milking his organ, demanding its due.

Take as I give. Take . . .

No. He couldn't take more blood, nor could he plant his seed. *Can't spend inside her.* As he so desperately needed to do.

Somehow he fought the utter bliss of his bite, the rightness he'd never known. Somehow he released her neck.

Her back bowed once more. Her head thrashed. *Coming again?*

"Ah, gods, I feel you!" The pressure throbbing in his cock made him throw back his head and bellow, *"Lizvetta! I claim you—"*

At the last second, he jerked back his hips, just as semen began to pump from him, line after line marking her tender body.

❦

Lothaire collapsed beside her, heart thundering, still languidly thrusting against Ellie's hip.

"You're mine now," he rasped, flicking his tongue against his bite mark.

Dazed. Can't get my bearings. The vampire had her not knowing up from down anymore. And she couldn't be happier.

He rose up on one elbow and brushed her damp hair back from her forehead, leaning down to kiss her at intervals.

When she could manage words again, she asked, "Why did you pull out?"

"I won't let you get pregnant."

She frowned. "You said you wanted heirs."

"We will have no offspring until you're a vampire. Tomorrow Hag will give you a contraception potion to last a month or two."

So high-handed. *Not even asking me?* "Do I get a say?"

"Just an hour ago, you agreed that I would make decisions for us."

Well, there was that. She cast him a smile. "You're right. Bottoms up on potions."

With an enigmatic look, he said, "I will guide you rightly, if you trust me."

She stared into his gaze. *Could* she blindly trust a male like him? She forced herself to nod.

"You will also need a cloaking tattoo. I've much to show you outside these walls, Elizabeth."

"What?" she asked breathlessly, because he'd already begun hardening for another round.

"Nothing less than the entire world, beautiful girl. . . ."

At the end of the night, when she asked him for just one more time, he shook his head. "No matter how badly I want you." He dragged her close, until she lay over his chest.

"I'm fine," she said sleepily. "Your mortal can hang with even big, bad vampires."

He curled his finger under her chin, lifted her face. "Let's talk when you wake." He seemed to be really looking at her.

"Your irises are so sharp right now."

"My mind is easy."

She snuggled closer to him. "That makes me happy, Leo."

"You've pleased me this night." He pressed a kiss to her hair. "Above all things, you've pleased me."

It's him. *Lothaire for me.* Deal with the devil? *If this is wrong, I don't wanna be right.*

As she drifted off to sleep, she *did* feel protected, cared for. "I'm glad you chose me."

"I am as well." Then, in a lulling, loving murmur, he said, "But don't ever betray me, Lizvetta."

Once Elizabeth slept, Lothaire remained awake, wanting to enjoy this rare peace.

Her breaths on my chest. Tension easing from every muscle. Warm relaxation.

His mate. Claimed. She was the most exquisite thing he'd ever possessed.

As he threaded his fingers through her glossy dark hair, his thoughts were shockingly clear. Crystalline. *I will figure out a way around my blood vows.* His situation was merely a puzzle to solve.

And I'm the master of them.

His gaze fell on the diabolically difficult eighteen-piece puzzle among his collection. It would take sixty-five calculated moves to assemble it—without a single misstep.

Easing Elizabeth away with a kiss on her forehead, he traced to his chair.

Sixty-five laughably simple moves later, he held the completed puzzle in his stunned grasp.

Then Lothaire smiled evilly. *I'm back.* . . .

43

I'll never get used to this, Ellie thought as waves lapped at her feet on a secluded beach in France. A balmy breeze danced over her skin, most of which was bared in a string bikini.

For nearly three weeks, Lothaire had taken her to moonlit shores all around the world—after Hag had given her a cool druid-looking tattoo around her ankle.

But that pain had been worth it to see the world. "It's gorgeous here, vampire." *Almost as much as you . . .*

He was barefooted, shirtless, wearing only low-slung jeans. Sea spray had dampened his hair and misted his chest. In the moonlight, his skin sheened, his eyes glowing.

Though he'd seen her thrilled expression with each locale they visited, his watchful gaze was locked on her face.

"Thank you for bringing me here."

A short nod.

After that first night of mind-blowing sex, Ellie had awakened, sore but happy, expecting things to be different between them. Instead, Lothaire had dropped her off at Hag's again, as if nothing had changed.

Well, except for the sizzling, toe-curling kiss he'd given her before he left. And then he'd returned early, asking her, "If you could go anyplace in the world, where would it be?

"Bora-Bo—"

She hadn't even gotten the words out before he'd traced them there. Whenever she was at Hag's, she read travel magazines, and then he'd take her to whatever destination she'd dog-eared.

Apparently Lothaire had been *everywhere*. She had yet to stump him in all of their journeys. He'd shown her all the Greats: the Great Wall of China, the Great Pyramids, the Great Barrier Reef. Plus the Maldives, the forests of Asia, glacial floes, and jungles . . .

Now she peered down at the water around her ankles. "Uh, Lothaire, why is the water glimmering?"

"It's phosphorescence."

At each destination, he would teach her new things about the area. He seemed to know everything, and she sensed he genuinely enjoyed teaching her. "Foss fur what?"

He spelled the word, then explained, "Tiny organisms that give off light when disturbed."

"Really?" She splashed for several moments, fascinated.

"You know, this isn't the last time you'll see it."

As someone who'd had time limits applied to her life span—twice— she found it hard to shake the feeling that death lay in wait. "Before we go, can we walk farther down the beach, maybe collect some shells?" She had a shelf at the apartment designated for nothing but sea shells.

"As you wish."

They walked in silence, lost in their own thoughts.

These weeks hadn't been perfect between them, of course. When they did get to sleep together, he had to chain himself to the bed. As he'd explained, "No more unplanned trips for my Bride."

And there were the matters of a bitch squatting inside Ellie and a ring to be found. Not to mention the constant tension she'd sensed in him, as if he was battling some force within himself.

One night after they'd made love, he'd murmured, "I wish I could tell you the things on my mind." Just the fact that he *wanted* to confide in her meant much. "You could help me see them clearly."

Yet no matter how much she asked, he wouldn't tell her. Maybe he was just growing impatient to turn her into a vampire. Could that explain the strain she'd begun to see on his beautiful face?

She was not so eager to be turned.

The idea of transforming into another *species* was terrifying to her. How could she not mourn all the things she'd be giving up forever? Her mother's fried chicken, waffles, beer.

Sunshine. She'd asked him, "Do you ever wish you could spend a day lazing in the sun?"

"I can't miss what I've never known."

"But I could."

"We'll see about that. . . ."

Most of all, she would miss her loved ones.

He'd told her, "You'll never see them again, Elizabeth. *I* am your family now—you took my name the instant I claimed you. Your loyalty is to me alone."

Even if she believed she could wiggle around that proclamation, there were other worries.

She'd learned that there were virtually no female vampires in the Lore—because they'd all died of some kind of immortal plague, one that only affected them. "What if I catch the plague when you turn me?" she'd asked him.

"That should be the last of your worries. Worry about assassins, wars, torturers. But not a sickness."

"Is your world always so violent?"

He'd admitted, "The Lore is a . . . ruthless place."

To survive in it, Ellie would have to grow more aggressive, callous even. He'd told her that the ones who survived longest were the notorious ones, the immortals with reputations based on some bold coup or brave deed.

In prison, she'd worked so hard to hold on to her humanity. Now she would be expected to throw it away.

Did she want to be with him badly enough? To change herself so drastically?

If she loved him, she might. But she *didn't*. Not at *all*. Mind over mind. *Only a fool would love him. . . .*

Besides, every time she felt like she was in danger of falling for him, they'd have an argument over something.

A few nights ago, when he'd been obsessively poring over his prized account book, she'd cleaned up some debris from his various rages and washed their linens.

He'd been aghast. "You . . . you *cleaned*?"

"Someone had to. I don't like sleeping on dirty sheets."

"Until we can hire servants, we transfer to another room. Another property, even! No Bride of mine *cleans*."

"You keep trying to change me, the way I talk and act. You're gonna alter my very species to fit yours. When will you change something for me?"

"This ancient dog will learn no new tricks. Besides, it's a female's place to adjust to her male."

Ellie had bitten her tongue to keep from screaming at him. At times with him, she bit her tongue so hard it'd bleed.

And they'd quarreled because of his irrational jealousy. One night, he'd taken her to a creek she used to swim in when younger. "Why did you bring me here, Lothaire?"

"You once liked this place."

She'd loved it there. Yet her thrill over the thoughtful gesture had faded directly. "How'd you know that?" The vampire must have seen her here—at *night*. "You *spied* on me?"

"I spy on everyone. Why would you be different? Soon you will go spying with me."

Then realization had dawned. "Oh, my God, you're the one who hurt Davis, the boy I was with. You saw us together, and you threw him down a gully. He broke both of his legs!"

"He *lived*?" Gaze narrowing, Lothaire had murmured, *"Not for much longer."*

Ellie had barely kept him from searching out her old beau with intent to do murder.

Getting him to forgive Thaddeus was just as much of an uphill battle. "Come on, Lothaire," Ellie had said. "He only wants to visit us at Hag's. He can help guard me when you're away."

"Forget it."

"He's your best friend." Not necessarily because Lothaire cared anything about Thaddeus, but because the boy cared more about Lothaire than anyone else in the Lore did.

"How do I know you won't *mortify* him with more of your kisses?"

"Because you know I'm infatuated only with you. Besides, you can trust him. Any other man would have kissed me back." When he remained unmoved, she'd cried, "You're jealous of an eighteen-year-old boy!"

"He's *seventeen*."

Eventually, she'd won Lothaire over. Or so she'd thought. At Hag's, he'd backed the boy into a wall, expression brimming with malice. "Elizabeth Daciano is *my* woman."

Thad had swallowed. "And she sure is a nice one, Mr. Lothaire."

"Keep your mouth to yourself today, boy, or your spine will decorate our mantel. . . ."

But after her fights with Lothaire, whenever he found her pensive, he surprised her with new gifts. He'd brought her jewels from all over the world. Ellie's *own* jewels. She supposed the others were hers, too, but these new ones were special because he'd chosen them specifically for her.

Or he would surprise her with wicked sex. Her sensual vampire had so many tricks up his sleeve, and as he'd grown more comfortable controlling his strength with her, he'd unveiled one after another.

Yet each new move made her wonder how many stunning immortal females he'd practiced it on before her. He'd once told her he'd bedded a new one each night: fey courtesans, nymph barmaids, the occasional demon shepherdess.

But never a *human* of course—

He suddenly took her hand. Hers fit into his as if it w̵̵
for her. She peeked up at him from under her lashes and sig̵

Lothaire was like a pale-haired god beside her.

He paused then, looking as if he'd say something, but he close̵
mouth, walking on.

Would kill to know what you're thinking. . . . Ellie didn't want to break this tenuous truce with him, didn't want to spoil this honeymoon period. But at the earliest opportunity, she needed to know how they were going to evict the goddess.

The night that they'd exchanged their vows, Ellie had been too frazzled by all the developments to realize something critical. When she'd asked him how they would get rid of Saroya, Lothaire had answered, "The ring's still in play, is it not?"

Classic Lothaire-speak.

She'd been just as disingenuous, promising him that she would get past all the things he'd done to her. At the time, she would've said anything. She'd recognized that she had him on the ropes, and damn it, she'd wanted to *live*.

Now, even as she held his hand and leaned into his strong arm, she wondered if she could keep her word.

She did truly *want* to work through her resentment—instead of just lying to him about it and snapping her mental rubber band.

But how could she get past his treatment of her when everything he was doing now only reminded her of it?

His telling her she'd never see her family again brought to mind how he'd threatened them so cruelly. Not to mention the fact that he'd stuck her on death row. She tried to reason that he'd prevented Saroya from killing by locking Ellie away. She told herself that he'd saved lives.

Ellie told herself that a lot.

And though she'd taken Hag's contraception potion, he still pulled out during sex. Not that she wanted to get pregnant right now or anything, but he must be horrified by the idea of a part-human heir.

nywhere but *in* her, he reminded her of all

No one had ever made her feel so lacking.

ged his mind about what she was, accept-

ng forward to the time when she'd be *made*

e in their species and they were still worlds apart. He was ... Ellie. *Does he still consider me just a "backward and vulgar hillbilly"? He'll probably be embarrassed of me around others.*

God, that hurts.

And how could she get comfortable with him, when she sensed how dangerous—and evil—he still was?

She'd been *proud* of him because he hadn't wanted to behead his friend.

Way to set the bar there, Ellie. . . .

He stopped walking, drawing her close. "If you could have any gift, what would it be?" The breeze whipped his hair across his lean cheeks. "No expense is too great."

"Paying off my family's mountain. Maybe having a place near them."

"Elizabeth . . ." he said warningly. In the moonlight, his eyes gleamed like an animal's caught in a headlight.

"Alrighty then, maybe something for Balery? You could cross her out of your book!" Again and again, the fey had helped Ellie try to understand an enigma like Lothaire. The other night, Ellie had admitted that she'd be a goner for him if he could tweak just a few things.

Balery had replied, "You have to understand that he was born and raised in a world outside of the human realm, in a different time. Eons ago, he grew up in that ill-omened castle you saw, under the reign of a vicious despot—who was also his father. Even though Lothaire is one of the most intelligent males I've ever encountered, he has no wisdom about women's feelings. None. Yours will be the first relationship he's had with a lover, the learning curve precariously steep. . . ."

Now Lothaire said, "Hag's debt is not yet satisfied. In any case, I was talking about a gift for *you*." Plainly frustrated, he muttered, "Just forget it. You'll simply have to endure it when I bring you more jewels."

"Exactly how rich are you, Leo?"

He'd grown to like it when she called him that, because the name was theirs alone. Just as she'd grown to love being called Lizvetta in his raspy accent.

"*We* are obscenely rich. Befitting a king and queen. I will always provide for you."

And only *for me.* Maybe she could secretly pawn some of her jewelry in the future, mail some cash to her family.

He tugged on her hand. "The water's warm. Join me for a swim."

Smile, Ellie. "You've got that look on your face. I'm about to get laid, aren't I?"

After making short work of their clothes, he reached for her, palms landing on her ass with a measured slap.

She surprised herself by moaning throatily.

"Indeed," he rasped, kneading her spanked flesh as he lifted her, forcing her legs around his waist. "You are about to *get laid*. . . ."

Some time later, with the waves crashing around them, Ellie screamed with pleasure, crying out his name like a prayer as she clung to his wet shoulders.

Directly after, he gave a brutal yell and jerked his shaft out of her. Heaving his breaths against her ear, he pumped semen between their slippery bodies.

So careful not to get me pregnant. That connection she'd felt the first time they'd had sex was missing now.

When he finally released her, she drew away to wash off his seed, her eyes pricking with tears.

"Lizvetta?" He grazed the backs of his fingers along her cheek. Such strength in him, yet he could caress her so gently. "Look at me." When she did, his gaze seemed to burn with emotion. "Have I hurt you, love?"

How could he make her heart melt so easily? When he looked at her like this, all her defenses crumbled. "No, it's not that."

In a hoarse voice, he told her, "You are mine. Your life is with me. Do not fight this."

The tenderness in his tone made her want to throw her arms around him and admit how much she cared for him.

But she forced herself to tell the truth. "Sometimes I have doubts—"

"Doubts?" Like a shot, he coiled a length of her hair around his fist, his expression altered from longing to menace. "The time for doubts has *ended*. This is a done thing, Bride."

"Lothaire . . ."

"If we were ever parted, I would bring you back to me," he rasped. "There is nowhere on earth that I couldn't find you."

From any other man, these words might be a promise about their future. From Lothaire, they were nothing more than a threat.

Put it with the others.

Snap!

"Nowhere, Elizavetta," he repeated, his eyes aflame. Such a contrast to his earlier heartfelt sentiments.

It was as if two men stood before her, one who needed to love and be loved, and one who only wanted the Bride he believed was his by fate. Neither version knew *how* to love.

"I do understand that, Lothaire."

Over the last couple of weeks, her rubber band had gotten so much play she had to wonder why it hadn't broken yet.

44

*S*he isn't in love with me, Lothaire thought as he dropped Elizabeth off at Hag's.

This perplexed him exceedingly.

He'd pleasured his Bride, spoiled her, protected her. He wanted to give her immortality and make her royalty. He was the most handsome male she'd ever seen.

Yet she continued to hold something of herself back.

It maddened him to no end! Why would she cling to her wretched family? To her old life?

He had no answers—because he'd still dreamed none of his Bride's memories. . . .

In greeting, Hag said, "Thaddeus asked about you earlier." The fey sported streaks of purple paste on her hands and one cheek. "He wants to go on your revenge mission, to watch out for you."

"*Do pizdy*. He'd do well to forget he ever knew me."

Hag didn't disagree. "Have you tried explaining to the boy what you're really like?"

"I *showed* him. I tapped his neck within ten seconds of meeting him, directly after he helped me out of a tight spot."

And from those meager drops of blood, he'd stolen Thaddeus's memories easily enough. Lothaire had already experienced a couple of them, had dreamed of running in the sun, feeling the warmth on his skin.

No wonder his Bride dreaded the loss. "Why does no one believe I'm evil anymore?" he asked her.

"Oh, I do. Honest," Elizabeth said solemnly before turning toward the bathroom. "Gonna wash off the salt water. Don't leave till I get back!"

As he watched her saunter away, he thought, *She doesn't believe I'm evil, not really.*

Yesterday when he returned to Hag's to pick Elizabeth up, she'd been asleep. Carefully he'd lifted her into his arms, and she'd burrowed her face against his chest so trustingly. He'd gazed down at her, troubled, thinking, *She still has no idea what I'm truly capable of, no idea what I've done.*

What I would do to possess her forever.

Now he exhaled a gust of breath, sitting at the dining table. In a low tone, he asked the fey, "Does Elizabeth speak of me?" Hag gave a wary nod. "And? What are her feelings toward me?"

"They vary according to your behavior." She dropped leaves into a pot. "Amazing how that works out."

His gaze narrowed. "Watch yourself, Hag." Again his mood was foul. He'd spent the day uselessly dreaming his own memories once more.

"She hasn't told me that she loves you, if that's what you want to know."

It was. He needed Elizabeth to fall in love with him—because only then would he trust her loyalty to him.

Yet a lesser male might suspect that she still *hated* him for all his sins against her and merely bided her time until she could be free of him.

And free of Saroya.

Hag asked, "Do you not see her thoughts in dreams?"

He pinched the bridge of his nose. "None." Even though he continued to sip from her.

Whenever he slept, Elizabeth was like a quiet blank spot in his mind. And no matter how much he prompted, she'd never told him of her feelings.

Yet nightly, she said or did something to remind him of how much she longed for her family.

Though he felt like a petty, jealous lover, he knew that if she was loyal to them, then she couldn't be fully loyal to him. The situation would be ripe for betrayal, because she would choose their interests over his if a conflict ever arose.

And let's be realistic, when would I not be in conflict with those ill-bred humans?

Severing contact with them was the wisest course. News reports held that Elizabeth had been mortally wounded in a botched prison escape. Her family would believe her dead.

"You're ceding your heart to her," Hag observed.

He gazed in Elizabeth's direction. "She is"—he paused, then admitted—"treasured. If anything should happen to me, you are to protect her. Search for a way to free her."

The fey nodded. "Speaking of something happening to you, Dorada's been *felt* in the South, near the Valkyrie coven in Louisiana."

The sorceress had previously lived in the Amazon; now she was in Louisiana? He'd bet the hideous mummy and her Wendigo lackeys were hiding out in the swamp basin.

"I'll go there this eve." He would trace to a bayou bar called Erol's, one frequented by scores of immortals. Perhaps Dorada had journeyed to that area because of the Lore energy. Or perhaps she'd sensed *he* had been there recently.

"Has Saroya risen?" Hag asked.

"Once. While Elizabeth slept." The girl had never even known.

He'd wasted no time castigating Saroya, taking out his fury at himself on her. "You knew you weren't my fucking Bride!"

"Are you so sure?"

How could he ever have been fooled? "You're not mine. I'd seek a noon-day sun if paired with you." Hadn't he told Elizabeth the same thing? He flinched when he thought of how incredibly much he'd insulted her. "You knew all along that I had no fated tie to you."

"I used your own arrogance as a weapon against you. Such a plentiful arsenal. Besides, deep down you recognized Elizabeth as yours but refused to accept it. Which is understandable in the extreme, Lothaire. Regardless, you'll forsake her for me, because you still want your crowns." She'd gazed down at Elizabeth's body with contempt. "Even though you're obviously mating with her."

"I'll find another way to get my kingdoms."

"If you discover a way for a vampire to break a vow to the Lore, do let me know. . . ."

His vows bound him like shackles, forcing him onto a path from which he could not veer.

They compelled him to search tirelessly. In order to spend time with Elizabeth, he had to resist the compulsion, but could only do so for limited amounts of time.

She returned then, showered, dressed, carrying a loaded breakfast plate. "Will you play nice with all the other little vampires when you're out searching tonight?"

He ignored Hag's inquiring look. He knew the oracle wondered what his Endgame was now.

Lothaire only wished it were as clear as it'd been for the millennia before. "Of course." He stood. "I leave now."

"At least kiss me like you'll miss me, Leo," Elizabeth demanded in a saucy tone that made him want to do nothing more than trace her back to their bed. "Else I won't think you're sweet on me."

The corners of his lips curled. He liked her accent now. Even if he hadn't started to find her mountain drawl sexy, it was an asset for her— people heard her speak and saw her beauty and underestimated her.

Just as he had. *Sucker punch.* But no longer. Each day with her, he was learning what a formidable female she was.

Whenever they traveled, her keen mind soaked up knowledge like a sponge. Teaching her proved rewarding, enjoyable. And experiencing those locales with her cast them in a new light, making them exciting for him once more.

She made him feel young and *alive*.

Elizabeth Daciano was a drug to a male like Lothaire.

So why couldn't he shake the feeling that she was drifting away from him?

He bent down to press his lips to hers, taking her soothing scent within him. "Will you worry for me when I'm gone?"

She shook her head. "But I'll pity anyone who crosses you."

His chest bowed. *Like a drug, Elizavetta . . .*

Reluctantly he traced away. As soon as he appeared in Erol's oyster-shell parking lot, he perceived a heavy presence. Dorada was nearby.

Rain drizzled, thunder rumbling. Music blared from inside the dilapidated shack of a bar. The scents of so many of his enemies muddled together in one place had him wishing he'd brought a mystical bomb. *To eradicate them all so easily . . .*

No. Focus.

He crossed to the black water's edge, spying an old duck blind far out in the middle of a cove. Tracing to the blind, he crouched atop it, listening for Dorada.

Over the strengthening rain, he heard only expected sounds—reptiles gliding through the swamp, a stray Valkyrie shriek. He scented the wet air, perceived a faint trace of Dorada's rotted skin, but couldn't pinpoint its source.

In the past, he would have waited here until dawn, stalking his enemy, envisioning their upcoming battle in gory detail.

Now he was impatient, knowing his thoughts would grow more chaotic every moment he was away from Elizabeth.

Lightning forked out above, momentarily setting the bayou aglow. The reflective eyes of Lore creatures flashed all around the water. None were his prey.

Where are you, Dorada? He didn't have time to pursue her—

His head jerked around as he caught that scent once more. He lunged into a trace, landing at the perimeter of the bayou, spinning in place. The smell seemed to come from all around him.

Then I'll scour every inch of this godsforsaken mire. Half tracing, half sprinting, he began to cover ground, dematerializing through thickets of briars, then charging around trees.

The winds began to howl, sheeting the rain sideways, dispersing the scent. Still he ran, his thoughts growing as tangled as the underbrush. *Find Dorada. Slay her. Then nothing will distract me from the ring.*

He'd considered forgiving the Blademan's debt in exchange for Webb's location. After all, Chase surely hated Webb; the commander had gone behind his back and had Regin "studied."

But Lothaire knew the Blademan would tell him nothing. He despised Lothaire even more than he did the man who'd ordered his female cut open—while she was conscious.

Navigating a dense stand of cypress, Lothaire ducked under a limb, startling a pack of crocodilae shifters and the nymphs who slummed with them.

The beings beheld him, screamed with fear, then scattered in all directions.

He didn't spare them even a hiss. That scent . . . why couldn't he run it to ground . . . ?

No, there'd be no negotiating with the Blademan; tapping into Chase's memories was Lothaire's only hope of reclaiming his ring. Yet instead of dreaming them, he'd continued to experience his own.

His last? Lothaire had relived the night he'd finally captured Stefanovich for Fyodor, ages after Lothaire's torture had ended.

In a mindless rage, Lothaire tortured Stefanovich for hours—days—reveling in his father's pleas for mercy. Once Fyodor gave the order, Lothaire raised his sword for the deathblow, steadying enough to comprehend that the king's heart was beating. "Blyad'! He's been blooded, Uncle."

Fyodor looked aghast. "Then he might have sired a secret heir." He pressed his own sword edge against Stefanovich's throat, beginning to slice it back and forth. "Where is your Bride?"

"Dying," Stefanovich grated with difficulty; he was scarcely alive himself. "Like the others."

Female vampires had been afflicted in number by some kind of plague. King Stef-
anovich considered this such an embarrassing sign of weakness—immortals succumbing
to sickness!—that he'd kept the tragedy secret, disseminating wild rumors. . . .

"*And where is your heir?*" *Lothaire asked, preparing for another round of torture.*

"*Where you'll never find him, bastard.*"

But Lothaire had.

Moving like a shadow, silent as death, he loomed over a cradle. A fair-haired infant
gazed up at him, grasping his finger with a tiny hand. . . .

Why see this scene again? What was his consciousness telling him?

When dawn neared, he eased his unrelenting pace, lurching to a stop.
Sweat poured down his back and face to mingle with the rain.

He cast an accusing look at the lightening sky. Lothaire had uncovered
no signs of Dorada. That heavy presence had faded to nothing.

Yet another wasted night. *Will this be the one when my mind fails me for good?*
He squeezed his head in his hands.

Though he'd given only passing thought to his crowns, his apprehen-
sion for Elizabeth was ceaseless, grinding him down, as the earth had once
done centuries before.

Want her so much! What the hell am I going to do?

Eventually, he would find the ring. Then three scenarios would open
up before him.

He could wish to go back in time, erasing his vows completely. While
there, he'd cast out Saroya, then take time to *court* Elizabeth, treating her
like a queen.

Or he could wish to go back, yet be denied—the vows themselves
might prevent him from using the ring in that fashion. He'd made an oath
to *do everything in his power* to transform Saroya into an immortal and to
extinguish Elizabeth.

Which meant that any attempt to do *otherwise* would be met with op-
position.

If all else failed, he could leave Elizabeth in Hag's care, then burn himself to ash in the sun.

To seek my own death, after surviving so long . . . ?

But attempting suicide would also break his oaths to Saroya. Would it even be possible to withstand the compulsion—and pain—long enough to die for Elizabeth?

All three scenarios would mean he had indeed retrieved the talisman that could destroy his Bride.

The *risk* . . .

He could tell no one about his predicament, could ask for no help, without breaking his pact with the goddess.

He couldn't even warn Elizabeth to leave him. Not that it would matter. The ring would work no matter how near or far she was.

In a deadly maze of his own making, he could determine no escape.

Undone by my own arrogance, by my insatiable need for vengeance. Will my flaws literally be fatal ones?

All those blood vows he'd collected could do nothing to help him shirk his own. His hope—or his Bride's doom—lay with the ring.

Just as he tensed to trace back to Elizabeth for the day, to lose himself in her body and scent, he heard a Valkyrie shriek carry over the dwindling patter of rain.

Could it be Nïx's? As treacherous as she was, she did always seem to understand him. Perhaps she would grant him one boon; he deserved no less from her.

His embattled mind on the verge of breaking, he decided to swallow his pride and call on the one person who might discern his bind.

He traced to Val Hall, standing in the fog, awaiting.

Moments later, Nïx strolled out onto the front porch, proffering a lock of black hair to the circling wraiths.

The hair was their negotiated toll. Lothaire knew that when the Scourge collected enough to make a braid of a certain length, they could bend all Valkyries to their will for a time.

The mighty Valkyries would be enslaved. He could hardly wait.

Nïx sauntered toward him in the drizzle, her demeanor nonchalant. In the past, she'd told him he defied her foresight.

Fitting, since she defied his insight.

But now he was betting on her ability to all but read his mind—basically having the powers of a goddess.

Yet she carried a fucking bat on her shoulder? Her pink T-shirt read: ♪ *Why can't we be friends?* ♪

Subtle, Nïx. Real subtle.

She stopped mere feet before him. They stood wordlessly, appraising each other.

Her long sable hair was damp and wind-tossed, her wide-set golden eyes inscrutable. Her flowing skirt was tattered at the hem.

Just weeks ago, he'd seen her on the prison island; since then, she appeared thinner, fatigued. She'd always been petite, but now she seemed smaller.

Even so, she was blessed in form, as fine physically as she was damaged mentally.

She tilted her head then, as if she could spy inside his own.

He silently urged her to see—to *know*—what he needed so desperately. *Help me from this bind.* With difficulty, he bit out, "Nïx, I must have Elizabeth." He could say no more, could explain nothing. Even that statement tested the boundaries of his vow; simply remaining in Nïx's presence drained his strength.

She smiled, her gaze vacant. "Black king seeks white queen's aid, then?" Lightning flashed above, harshly illuminating her face. Her comely features sharpened, her visage foreboding as she whispered, "Lothaire, you've been mistaken about something. The abyss doesn't *stare* back. It winks."

Then she turned on her heel and left him.

Disbelief. She was past the wraiths before he found his voice. *"You fucking bitch!"* he bellowed, while thinking, *I am lost. . . .*

That day as he slept, with Elizabeth clasped in his arms, Lothaire dreamed of the ring.

45

Chase's memories of the ring's location had been chaotic and confused. Which meant Lothaire had been right at home with them, using them to trace directly to Webb's hideout in the Canadian Rockies.

Never would have guessed Canada.

Earlier, when Lothaire had awakened, he'd acted as if nothing was amiss, dropping Elizabeth at Hag's.

Though once he'd started kissing Elizabeth good-bye, he'd found it hard to stop.

Now he surveyed the front of a nondescript ranch—one surrounded by some of the most high-tech security on earth.

And more, Chase had been familiar with every safeguard, which meant Lothaire was, too. He circumvented them all, easily breaching the structure's defenses.

Making himself incorporeal, Lothaire half-traced down dimly lit halls. Invisible to mortal eyes, he entered Webb's private quarters. The man's safe would be behind a wall within these chambers, the ring inside.

He found Webb seated at his desk, in the middle of a phone call, his shoulder muscles bunched with tension. Lothaire could hear both sides of the conversation.

Webb was speaking with the Blademan, Declan Chase.

Interesting.

"I can't tell you how much it means to me that you called," Webb said.

"I've no wish to resume communication with you," Chase said in his thick Irish accent. "But to repay you for saving my life, I've decided to give you a warning."

"About what?"

"The Enemy of Old drank my blood on the island. He has my memories, which means he'll eventually dream of your ranch's location, your security, everything. He'll be coming for you. And the ring."

Already here. Lothaire just stifled a laugh. *Time is of the essence, Chase.*

"He won't have the combination, and there are countermeasures in place," the commander said. "But I'll move out at once, hiding it from him this very night." A weighty pause. "Unless *you* want to do it. Come back into the fold, Declan. We need your strength. There's still work to be done to stop the tide of immortals from taking over the earth. From enslaving us."

As if we'd want you.

"My connection to the Order is terminated," Chase said. "Just keep the ring out of that vampire's hands. Amazingly, I trust Lothaire with it even less than I do you."

Words hurt, Chase.

"You're truly going to ally with miscreats?" Webb demanded. "Have you forgotten that those abominations tortured and killed your parents? Tortured and nearly killed *you*? I saved you from them!"

"*I* am one of those miscreats, Webb. A born berserker."

Shaking off the Order's brainwashing, are we, Blademan?

Though Webb's face was flushed with rage, his tone remained fatherly, concerned. "Son, your mind's unclear. That female has swayed you."

"I'm not your son," Chase snapped. "And *that female* is going to be my wife. Better Regin sway me than you."

Debatable.

"I reported to the Order that you died on the island," Webb said. "And I'll stick to that, but only if you stand down against our mission."

Chase replied, "You told me I was either on your side or theirs. You were right. Harm any among my allies, and I'll retaliate." Click.

The Blademan rises a notch in my estimation.

As soon as the call ended, Lothaire said, "Ah, was that Chase warning you against me? Shame. If only he'd done so *sooner*."

The commander whirled around, firing a charge thrower at him.

Lothaire laughed as the electrical stream passed through his torso. "Half-tracing, Webb. You can't touch me. But I can touch you." He briefly materialized to knock the gun from Webb's hand, breaking the mortal's arm with a satisfying crack.

Webb yelled with pain, his other hand darting for a button under his desk.

"Ah-ah, don't touch that alarm." Lothaire secured the man's hand in his own fist. Giving the lightest squeeze, he shattered Webb's bones like a crushed walnut.

As the man bit out a scream, Lothaire smiled down, knowing how terrifying he looked—the face of death. "Now you have two choices, human. If you tell me the combination to your safe and reveal what countermeasures are in place, I might spare your life. Or I can torture you for the information, then drink your memories so I can find and punish your family as well. You have one hidden somewhere, don't you?"

"Never. Never will I tell you!"

"Very well. I'll enjoy it more if you struggle. . . ."

Ultimately, he tortured Webb until the man *begged* to divulge all. After a while, Lothaire let him.

"And one last question," Lothaire said, rising above the man's mutilated body. "Who gave the Order my name? Who put me on Chase's capture list?"

Blood bubbled from Webb's lips as he laughed brokenly. "Vampire . . . deep down . . . you *know*."

At that, Lothaire's composure faltered. He'd had a suspicion, of course, but it couldn't be correct. "Not possible."

Between choking coughs, Webb grated, "You *know* . . . who gave you to us."

He had to be lying. Only one way to find out for certain.

Lothaire's gaze dropped to the man's neck. Would this be the victim that sent him into the abyss? Could he stop short of drinking Webb to the quick?

Must risk it. "I'm going to drain you now." Lothaire hauled the man to his feet. "Do resist. It adds something." Then he pierced Webb's jugular, grimacing at the blood.

The commander tasted like sewage compared to Elizabeth. But the impending kill teased Lothaire, beckoned him to suck harder as Webb's flailing body grew lighter and lighter from blood loss.

When the man fell limp, Lothaire dropped him, staggering back. *What's in his blood?*

A narcotic haze shrouded him. Raw, potent. Lothaire was high from it, too high to ponder why. He slid his back down a wall, closing his eyes against the spinning room.

As Webb took his last rattling breath, images began to stream through Lothaire's mind at light speed. He fell into a quasi-sleep, immersed in the man's twisted memories.

What felt like hours passed before Lothaire could seize on the memory he sought. . . .

The commander *hadn't* lied about Lothaire's betrayer.

Bile rose in Lothaire's throat, a spike of pure hatred reviving him. He slitted open his eyes. Everyone he'd ever trusted had died—or betrayed him.

Elizabeth can still do one. Or both.

Forever betrayed. Stefanovich, Serghei, Fyodor, Saroya, even the one being Lothaire had called friend. . . .

But not Elizabeth. Never her.

He lumbered to his feet, kicked Webb's lifeless body—*good riddance, prick*—then started for the safe.

Now to disable all the safeguards. *Press a button there, enter a false code, turn the lever once. Enter the real code.*

Puzzle moves. If Lothaire didn't have so much on the line, he might have enjoyed this.

With a hiss, the safe door opened. There. A black velvet pouch.

He slipped the ring from it. As he donned the plain gold band, he felt an unfathomable power radiating from it.

Wasting not one second, Lothaire twisted the ring, making his wish. *Go back in time to undo my vows to Saroya the Soul Reaper.*

Nothing. Lothaire felt no surge of power as he had in the past with other lesser talismans.

Maybe the ring forbade time-travel. He amended his wish: *Erase my vows to Saroya.*

Again, nothing. Dear gods, the ring had denied him; the vows remained sacrosanct. The pull to destroy his Bride grew overwhelming.

Death was the only move left on the chessboard. Elizabeth's or his own?

He gazed out the study window. The sun was rising, rays of light erupting over distant mountains.

Like clutching fingers. His instinct was to go to ground, to evade their grasp.

Could he sacrifice himself for Elizabeth? Part of him could scarcely believe that Lothaire—the black-hearted Enemy of Old—was even contemplating this! To spare her, would he render himself to ash?

As Ivana had all those years ago to protect him . . .

He told himself he was considering this only because Elizabeth's death would alter him. How could any vampire go on living without his Bride? He tried to convince himself that his heart held no sway in this decision.

But it did. *Little mortal, you've changed everything. . . .*

Before Ivana had gone to meet her death, Lothaire had asked her, "How can you do this?" At last he understood her answer.

Because anything that is worthy in me began with Elizabeth.

He rubbed his hand over his chest, startled by the ache he felt there. *I wish I could have seen her one last time. . . .*

Shoulders back, he traced outside to meet dawn, challenging an enemy he'd eluded all his life.

An enemy he now prayed would defeat him.

46

I t's happening," Ellie admitted to Balery as she sipped a Coke. "I'm falling in love with him."

She and the fey were on the deck watching the sunset as Ellie anxiously
awaited Lothaire. He'd been missing all day.

As he'd set off, Ellie had again told him she wouldn't worry. *So much for
that.*

Earlier Thad had visited. For hours, he and Balery had tried to distract
her, but her sense of dread had grown steadily throughout the day.

At four in the afternoon, she'd demanded that Balery roll her bones.
Whatever the fey had seen had leached her face of color, had wrested one
gasped word: *" . . . burning."*

Yet once she'd collected herself, Balery had pasted on a fake smile and
deemed that roll a "dud." No matter how much Ellie wheedled, she'd refused to offer more on the subject.

Now Balery said, "I could tell, just by the way you look at him. Have
you told him?"

Ellie muttered, "Not yet." Holding on to a thread of her formerly stubborn self, she'd backed herself out of her vows. *Never falling in love with
Lothaire* had turned into *not telling him I love him first. . . .*

"Elizabeth," Balery began in a pained tone, "there's something you need to know about Saroya and—"

Lothaire appeared; Ellie's jaw dropped.

He was burned in deep patches, his muscles bulging, sweat and blood seeping from his charred skin.

Before either Hag or Ellie could manage a word, he'd snatched Ellie's arm, tracing her to their bedroom at the apartment.

"Lothaire, my God! What has happened to you?" *What did Balery witness?*

His irises were a deeper red than Ellie had ever seen them, the color bleeding across the whites of his eyes. "Look what I've retrieved, Lizvetta." He pinched a simple gold band with two white-knuckled fingers, his expression a mix of insanity and agony.

"That's good, right?"

He laughed bitterly. "Good? It's your *doom*."

"What are you talking about?"

"I can't save you. . . . No matter what I try, my vows control me."

Chills skittered up her spine. "I don't understand. Please calm down, Lothaire. Did you drink from someone?"

"Lizvetta, I can't even kill your body first to spare your soul—"

"Kill me? What about my soul? You're talking crazy again!" she cried. "Just use that ring to cast Saroya out of me."

He began to pace the room, never a good sign. "I can't betray her. You don't understand!"

"Then make me understand!"

As if with great difficulty, he grated, "I vowed to the Lore to make Saroya immortal—and to destroy you. You don't merely die. Your soul is *extinguished*. Tried everything to get out of the vow . . . fighting it even now."

He'd known all along that he'd have to do this? Even she understood that vows to the Lore were unbreakable. "Let me run, Lothaire."

More pacing. "You could be on the other side of the earth. Won't make a difference when I'm forced . . . forced to . . . end you."

She couldn't quite get enough air. "Will my soul be extinguished from this body—or from *everything*?"

"Gone! As if you never were!"

Breathe, Ellie, breathe. "This is what you were hinting about! Why didn't you tell me? To prepare me?"

"Couldn't . . . *physically couldn't* set you on a path that might interfere with my vow. Thought I could save you anyway."

Desperation deepened. *And still I'm going to die.* Right back to where she'd started.

No, now it was so much worse. At least before, she hadn't been falling for the vampire. At least before, she would have gone from death row to heaven, or so she'd believed.

Now she was to go from a paradise of pleasure to . . . nothingness.

I'm to be no more? Destroyed by the man I'd started to love?

He shoved his fingers through his sooty hair. "Couldn't even remain in the sun. . . ."

Her lips parted. That was why his skin had burned? Balery had told her that pain was excruciating for a vampire. "You tried to die for me?"

"Of course!" he bellowed, yanking her into his arms. "I would rather die than hurt you!"

She couldn't quite believe that, but knew he couldn't lie.

Today, Lothaire had sought to end his life for her, had defied a survival instinct that had kept him alive for thousands of years. "How are you able to tell me all this now? Because it's as good as done?"

He clutched her shoulders, gazing down at her face. His expression answered her.

"Oh." Tears gathered and fell. Why not cry? She'd never felt more hopeless.

At last she knew what he'd been struggling with. "Will it h-hurt?"

At her words, he roared with anguish, blood tracking from the corner of one eye. *"Lizvetta, don't. . . ."*

"Can you use the ring to bring me back?"

"Can't reverse a wish! But I will find a way to bring you back!"

"Lothaire, I'm"—she gave a sob—"I'm *afraid.*"

Another agonized bellow followed, then he enfolded her against his chest. He was shuddering all around her, fighting that inner battle. "If I can't save you, I will follow you." Clasping her tighter, he rocked her, murmuring unknown words in Russian.

His charred skin and clothes smelled of ash. *He tried to burn for me.*

Would that be the last scent she ever perceived? "Don't follow me, Lothaire. I don't want you to—"

"*RIIIIINNNNNNNGGGGG!*"

Ellie's head whipped up. "What is *that*?"

"*Remove my riiiinnnnngggg!*" sounded a woman's shriek from just off the balcony—twenty-five floors up.

At once, Lothaire pushed Ellie aside to take off the band. "*Dorada.* How the fuck did she find us?"

Some female outside was controlling him? Just as they'd feared!

"*Enemy of Old!*" Dorada's words sounded staticky, as though they'd been passed through a filter. "*Allow me entry. Do not resist me.*"

"I can't fight her," Lothaire snapped under his breath as he crossed to the wall beside the balcony door. Symbols were etched into the plaster. "Get to the front door, Elizabeth! You'll be able to open it soon."

Once Lothaire had unlocked the boundary, Dorada dropped down over the balcony railing, as if she'd just stepped through an invisible entrance. With a wave of her hand, the French doors flew open.

While Ellie gaped, the sorceress floated inside, half a foot off the floor.

Lothaire had revealed some things about Dorada—how she'd been half-mad, grotesquely mummified, shrieking for her ring.

Now the sorceress was regenerating. She still had only one eye, but it was striking—olive green with sweeping lashes. Some strands of her hair were a thick, luxurious black, others lank strings. Half of her face had smooth, tawny skin; the other was crusted with rotting gauze.

A solid-gold breastplate covered her torso, a skirt of golden threads wrapping around her hips—

"*Run, Elizabeth!*"

Ellie snapped her jaw shut, and whirled around, sprinting toward the front door. Down the halls she ran. The front entrance in sight.

She reached it, unlocked the ordinary deadbolt, then threw open the door—

Ellie drew up short with a scream; Lothaire gave an answering bellow from his room.

Wendigos blocked her way.

Their emaciated bodies were hunched and misshapen, their fangs the size of her finger. Pasty skin stretched tight over their skeletal frames, yet seemed to *billow* in places—

Horror struck. They were wearing *others'* skin.

Sleeves, vests, collars . . .

Ellie slapped her hand over her mouth, backing away. *Too much. I can't handle much more of this.*

As they scuttled into the apartment, they licked their lips at her, their red eyes alight.

With hunger.

She fled back to Lothaire, pumping her arms, running as she never had before. They were on her heels, grunting, slavering. Into the bedroom she scrambled.

Eyes wide, Lothaire held out his hand for her, but didn't move, didn't try to protect her. She darted behind him anyway.

"She's controlling me, Elizabeth! Told me not to move. I'm trapped as I stand."

Dorada pulled out Lothaire's desk chair, taking a seat with a casual air. But her movements were sluggish.

"How did you find this place?" he demanded.

The sorceress held the band up to the lamp's light. "An old acquaintance told me." She slipped the ring onto her thumb, then waved for Ellie. "Come, girl."

She shook her head slowly.

"Come, or I'll make your vampire drink you to death."

Lothaire gripped her wrist—until Dorada commanded, "Release her." He did at once.

Seeing how much control the sorceress had over him, Ellie crossed the room to stand before Dorada. *Will she kill me? Turn me into one of those things?*

"Kneel."

With no other choice, Ellie did.

The sorceress scrutinized her with that one eye. "Is that Saroya the Soul Reaper buried deep within this mortal, Lothaire? Was the goddess of vampires the Bride you sought? Perhaps you wanted to make this human host into an immortal with my ring."

He remained silent.

"Do you guard the body so vehemently to preserve Saroya? Or is the girl yours?"

"Did you come here to insult me? You know the answer to that question." *Lothaire-speak?*

Dorada raised her good hand to touch Ellie's forehead, commanding, "Face me, Saroya."

Ellie recoiled, resisting Saroya with all her might.

"No, sorceress!" Lothaire yelled. "Don't do this!"

"I know you can sense me deep down, goddess," Dorada said, ignoring him. *"Now rise!"*

The female's gold plates seemed to vibrate as power infused the room. Ellie could feel Saroya skittering wildly in her chest, but still she fought.

Lothaire too strained against Dorada's control. "This has to do with more than my crimes against you. What do you want from Saroya?"

"Revenge."

Ellie remained silent, grappling to hold the goddess back.

"For what?" Lothaire grated.

"Why do you think I was in that tomb, vampire?" Dorada said. "Because Saroya's assassins hunted me down without cease! In desperation, I turned to the ring, but she was too powerful for it to vanquish. So I wished never to be found by her killers, to be freed of her torments. And the ring made sure I was forever out of her reach—by having my other enemies trap me in that tomb for ages." She stared off with her sole eye for long moments, then turned back to him. "Until you came along, waking me. At once, I sensed Saroya's lack of godhood. I refused to let you use my own ring to empower her in any way."

"This makes no sense, Dorada. Saroya would have no reason to assassinate you. Who were you to a goddess?"

Ellie's vision wavered. She was losing ground, couldn't hold on much longer. . . .

Dorada frowned at Lothaire. "You don't know about the prophecy?"

"What are you talking about?" he bit out. "What prophecy?"

Amusement. "Hmm. Just know that it's about to be fulfilled."

With that, Ellie gave a cry, collapsing as her sight went dark.

Saroya felt herself compelled to rise, blinking open her eyes. She was in Lothaire's room? Hand to her forehead, she rose to her knees . . . and found herself surrounded by Wendigos.

Facing her old nemesis.

The foretelling! Fear surged within her, seeming to swell inside her throat. But Saroya would bluff as if she still had power. "Dorada," she sneered. "It's been ages."

The Gilded One grinned, revealing rotted teeth among gleaming white ones. "You're no longer the cat-eyed goddess," she said, speaking staticky English through some kind of translation spell.

"You're no longer decent to look upon. Fitting that you keep the company of drooling beasts."

"Regeneration." Dorada shrugged. Her customary adornments were nearly blinding, gold plates so heavy they looked like they'd crush her putrefied form. "Your male harmed me quite thoroughly. I wanted revenge on Lothaire. I had no idea I could mete it out to you as well."

This couldn't be happening. *It is foretold . . . It is foretold . . .* Dread inundated Saroya, but she forced herself to give a dismissive wave. "What can you do to me?" *Am I sweating from fright?* "I am a goddess."

"You have no powers. And you're pure evil. Easy for me to control. Shall I do as was divined so long ago?"

Saroya swallowed. "If you attempt this, you will fail. And then I will smite you with a god's wrath."

Dorada smirked, her face drawn into a repellent mask. "I believe I will risk it."

Saroya turned to Lothaire. "Vampire, do something!"

His muscles were knotted, his expression strained, but he remained unmoving. Dorada clearly had him under her thrall.

"Don't take Saroya, sorceress. There must another way to settle this!"

Comprehension hit her. Lothaire was acting as if she were his Bride, because he knew that Dorada would cast her out to punish him.

Sure enough, he'd discovered a way out of his vows. "Dorada, I am not his Bride! If you seek vengeance against Lothaire, then you must kill—"

"Why do you deny me now, Saroya?" Lothaire yelled.

Dorada raised her hand, her splayed fingers directing mystical energy at Saroya. The gold jewelry on her body reverberated, her sole eye glittering. The Wendigos howled as the air grew electric.

"No!" Saroya shrieked. "Do not do this!"

"I never would have harmed you, goddess, never would have targeted you, had you not beset me with your assassins. Fool! You turned me onto this path. *You* fulfilled this prophecy."

"You will pay, Dorada! My sister—"

"Sends her regards." Dorada shut her eye and snatched closed her fist.

Blackness spread before Saroya, the prophecy repeating over and over as her consciousness began to dim.

It is foretold that La Dorada, the Queen of Evil and of Golds, a sorceress of great power, will destroy Saroya the Soul Reaper, Goddess of Divine Death, condemning her to the Ether that spawned her, forever as formless as the chaos whence she sprang. . . .

Foretold. A self-fulfilling prophecy. Dark. Silent. Cold.

Nothingness.

Saroya's last thought: *My actions had a consequence.*

47

Elizabeth collapsed to the ground, her body limp. Hours seemed to tick by as Lothaire—and Dorada—waited for her to wake. *Waiting* . . .

At last, she rose, shooting upright in a rush, anxiously patting her chest. "Saroya's gone?" Elizabeth faced him. "Ah, God, she's gone!"

Lothaire's jaw slackened as he gazed upon her, taking in her radiant skin and vivid eyes. Those lips shaped like a bow . . .

Before, her allure had tantalized him. Freed of Saroya, his female was irresistible.

The being inside Elizabeth must have diluted his need for her. Now it was as if the fierce desire and protectiveness he'd felt for her had been multiplied exponentially.

Then injected straight into his heart.

My Bride. This was what everyone spoke of.

Elizabeth's face . . . as if a stained-glass window had shattered to let pure light shine in; she was ablaze with utter beauty—

"Kill her, Lothaire," Dorada said.

Fighting her control, he made his tone scornful. "Why would I bother? You've taken Saroya from me."

"In case this mortal is your actual Bride."

Before, his *own* vows had chained him—now that he was freed of them, he felt more powerful than he'd ever been. Elizabeth was a beacon focusing everything inside him. "I will never harm her. And you know I can't lie."

"I suspected she was your Bride. Now I *command* you to kill her."

"I don't give a fuck, sorceress." The only thing stronger than Dorada's hold over him? *Elizabeth's hold on me.* "You can't compel me to hurt her. You're not fully healed, and you've just debilitated yourself to kill a goddess. I will fight you till neither of us has any strength left to hurt Elizabeth."

"I will make this simple," Dorada snapped. "You kill her. Or I will force you to kill yourself."

He laughed. "Then make it slow for me, *súka.* I like foreplay."

"Slow, Lothaire? I have all the time in the world to watch you peel your skin from your body."

"No!" Elizabeth rushed to stand protectively in front of him. "Please don't do this, Dorada!"

The sorceress didn't even acknowledge her. "I want you to remove your flesh like a shirt, vampire. I'll make one of my beasts wear it till it rots from his body."

"*You* are the one who dresses them in . . . skin?" Elizabeth swallowed repeatedly, like she'd be sick.

"Start with your neck, Enemy of Old," Dorada said. The Wendigos eased their ghastly bodies to the floor, settling in for a show—and his remains.

He found his own claws slicing his skin at his neck. *Can't stop myself. . . .*

"Wait!" Elizabeth cried. "Why not bargain with us?"

<hr />

"You dare address me?" Dorada swung her creepy one-eyed gaze on Ellie.

"We have something you want," she said, having no idea what she was doing.

Between the Wendigos, this mummy lady, Lothaire's confession, and Saroya's exorcism, her mind was so opened it'd nearly cracked wide.

Still she was trying to hold it together to save her vampire. "Lothaire's accounting book of blood debts. Just stop with the mutilation for a minute, and let me tell you about it."

Dorada waved at Lothaire to stop, then addressed her. "Explain."

"There are thousands of debts. He's worked forever on this. In exchange for lettin' both of us live and troublin' us no more, we'll give you . . . half of the book."

"And who is in debt? Lorean dregs?" Dorada unraveled a length of gauze, peeked at the seeping wound beneath, then sighed. "Weak-willed immortals?"

Ellie shook her head. "We've got kings, queens, gods. Good ones too—the ones you've got no hold over." Making her voice stern, she said, "But you can't be forcin' Lothaire to hand it over just because he's evil and you can control him like a Muppet. This has got to be an even trade."

Dorada blinked her eye. "Why must it be?"

Good question. Think, Ellie, think! "For you to collect on these debts, they have to be willingly, uh, bestowed upon you." That sounded logical. "If you take away his free will and steal the blood vows, they won't be worth the paper they're scribbled on."

To Lothaire, Dorada said, "You may speak. Does this book exist?"

Ellie had expected him to roar over this, refusing to trade his life's work. *Instead, he's gazing at me as if with . . . awe.*

"The book is exactly as my Bride says." Lothaire-speak. The book part was, but the free-will part *wasn't*.

Dorada canted her head, sending glossy waves of hair tumbling over lifeless strings. "I would choose my own debtors, decide the division."

"If you grant me the use of the ring," Lothaire said, "I'll give you the entire thing."

Ellie gasped. "That ring is nothin' but trouble. It's dangerous!"

"You have *no* idea," Dorada muttered. "I bear it, but I use it no more."

"Then there's no reason not to lend it to me, sorceress!"

Ellie shook her head sadly. "No, Lothaire."

His voice rising in volume with each word, Lothaire said to Dorada, "Now that we're in negotiations, and you have the ring—*I'd like to be able to fucking move again!*"

Another wave from Dorada, and he was freed.

He grabbed Ellie's arms. "I must have this power. Lizvetta, you must be made a vampire. And though I'm elated that Saroya is gone, the Horde crown disappeared with her. I'm not going to shelve my ambitions like a goddamned board game."

"Please, we'll figure that out together," Ellie said, but he was unmoved. "What if there are more vows you're hiding that I don't know about?"

"There are none. Trust me on this."

"I've *been* trusting you, and I've almost died twice tonight because of you."

He winced. But still he told Dorada, "Allow me the use of the ring until tomorrow at midnight, and the book is yours."

Dorada briefly closed her eye, going silent. "Bring it to me," she finally told Lothaire. "If it is as your mortal says, then I will bargain with the ring."

On the periphery of the room, the Wendigos chuffed, as if pissed they wouldn't get a kill.

Overriding Ellie's further protests, Lothaire retrieved the book from his safe, displaying it for Dorada. The sorceress's eye lit up. The two of them made their vows.

Lothaire's ledger, freely given, would buy twenty-four hours with the Ring of Sums. After which, she would return for the ring here.

With a pointed expression, Dorada slipped it off and handed it over. "This time I'll keep my thumb, Enemy of Old."

And when Lothaire surrendered his priceless accounting book to Dorada, he did it without a second glance.

Because his gaze was rapt on Ellie.

48

H ow does it feel to be free of Saroya?" Lothaire asked. He'd just gotten through showering off his healing flesh and redressing; the smell of smoke that had lingered on him seemed to particularly bother Elizabeth.

He hadn't relished the reminder of his repeated, crazed suicide attempt either. But now everything was falling into place, the pressure of the last few weeks lifting at last.

"I promised her I'd win the war against her," Elizabeth said. "Still, I can hardly believe she's gone, her *and* Dorada. I can't believe all that is over."

"Because of you." His cunning Bride had yet again surprised him. "You bargained with Dorada, *bullshitted* the Queen of Evil. I couldn't be prouder of you, Lizvetta."

She blushed, self-consciously tucking her hair behind her ear. He could tell she was pleased with—but surprised by—the praise.

Then he frowned. She was acting as if he'd never praised her. He must have. Surely.

But he couldn't quite put his finger on an instance.

As someone who knew the importance of protecting one's ego, he was aghast at himself. *That will be changing. Much will. . . .*

"Lothaire, I don't suppose you had a chance to mark Balery out of the book when you fetched it from the safe?"

"What do you think?" he asked, in all seriousness.

"I think you . . . did."

"Wrong."

Her face fell. "Oh."

"Yet I did manage to cross out a fey oracle named Hag."

"I knew you would!" She gave him that mind-scrambling smile of hers.

"It was meant as a gesture to you. Nothing more."

"Doesn't matter why, just that you did." But then her smile faltered. "Explain to me what happened earlier, with you and my . . . soul."

"Eventually, I will tell you all"—*how I was blinded by prejudice and the thirst for vengeance*—"but we have no time now." He held up his finger, brandishing the ring. "We must complete this one last step for you, and then plan for our future."

Lothaire would have to amend his strategy. With Saroya gone, the Horde would not fall under his thrall—but then, he'd spared a wish when freed of his vows. *Spared Elizabeth. . . .*

Now, plots and schemes began to unfold with a shocking clarity. His tasks, in order of importance: *make Elizabeth undying, devise a way to trick Horde into submission, find and conquer Daci.*

So I can kill Serghei.

He could still have his eternal mate, two thrones, and his revenge. All was yet well. . . .

But when Lothaire took Elizabeth in his arms, he frowned to find her trembling. "You're safe now, love. I restored the boundary. And you'll be tucked away at Hag's when Dorada and her Wendigos return. I intend for you never to see another one of those beasts as long as you live." He curled his finger under her chin. "And, Elizabeth, you're going to live for a very, very long time."

"I don't want this, Lothaire."

Inhaling for patience, he said, "To steal the ring from Dorada, I defeated cults and beasts of legend; to reclaim it once more, I survived the Order's prison, decimating armies. I've sacrificed my book. I did all these things for you! Can't you understand the gift you're about to receive?"

"I have a hard time viewing it as one. You told me I'll never be able to see my family again. I'll never be able to return to my old life. In the sun, hunting, hiking. Eating big family meals with loved ones."

Lothaire was growing angered . . . jealous once more. "You need to forget about those other mortals. They are in your past. *I* am your future."

"You can't just abandon your family!"

"Of course you can. I have."

"Yours are all dead!"

"Are they?" He raised his brows. "Elizabeth, remember what I told you—mortals and vampires don't mix."

"You and I did."

"If you knew how many times I came close to losing control . . . Besides, the gods rain down punishment on immortals who reveal themselves needlessly to humans. I didn't make this law, but even we must abide by it. Now, don't ruin this night for me, Bride."

"Make love to me first, Leo. One last time as a human."

"You'll delay this no longer."

"You're not listenin' to me! Just give me time. I'm not sayin' I won't agree to it, but just give me time to come to terms with this. An hour ago, you were gonna snuff out my soul! It's too much to get my mind around."

Tears slipped down her cheeks, and he didn't like the sight of them at all. They made him feel unsettled—like a failure. *My Bride should never have cause to shed tears.*

He tenderly brushed them away. "You vowed that you would let me make decisions for you for three weeks. My time's not yet up."

"Please. I am *beggin'* you not to do this to me. Let's just *talk* about this."

He paused. But even if he were the type of male who discussed decisions with his female, they didn't have time for it. *She won't be safe—not until she's turned.*

"Lothaire, if you care for me at all, you won't do this."

He clenched her upper arms. "*That* is the absolute worst thing you could have said. It's because I *care* for you that I must do this."

"You can't use that ring on me! You said yourself that you don't know what it will do."

"The first wish is the most accurate. So far, I've been granted none, so I'll start fresh with it."

"Do you understand how *vague* that sounds? This is *my life*! I read in the *Book of Lore* that the catalyst for transformation is *death*."

"We're not doing this in the customary way. Look at me, Elizabeth. Listen to my words: I have no doubt whatsoever that this will work exactly as I plan—or I would not risk you." When she began to shake harder, he said, "Do you think I haven't gone over my wish repeatedly, checking each iteration with Hag's foresight? In things like this, I am *wise*."

"You can't convince me of this!"

"Then you must trust me to know best, Elizabeth. The difficult part was in *getting* the ring, then devising the wish took skill, but the *process* will be effortless. In the blink of an eye, you will become a vampire, as if I'd sired you myself."

"You said people usually get turned because they're about to die. I'm not. I'm healthy. I'm young—"

"My enemies will target you. Even without the blood debts, I will still have foes seeking to harm me through my Bride. You are my most glaring vulnerability."

"Glaring vulnerability," she repeated softly.

Speaking to her as if she were a child, he said, "Think, love—if you could trace, you could have vanished in the face of those Wendigos. How can I bring you into my world if you don't have the strength to defend yourself or the ability to slip away from a threat in an instant?"

"Then I don't want to be in your violent, messed-up world! How about that? I wouldn't have to trace from Wendigos because I wouldn't see them in my apartment!"

He drew back his head. "You wouldn't accept this gift in order to be with me? You're in love with me—you would do anything I ask."

Women in love made sacrifices. That was simply what they did.

He'd watched the world over the span of his life, and for the great majority of it, women had yielded to the men they desired. Surely the last fifty years had been an anomaly. . . .

"You're askin' too much! If you use that ring, I will hate you."

"You'll get over it. Just as you have everything else."

Her brows drew together, her gaze stark. "I won't get past this, Lothaire."

"As Dorada said, I'll risk it."

<hr>

He's really gonna do this! Panicked, Ellie whirled around, bolting from the room once more.

Behind her, she heard Lothaire's irritated sigh. Then he called out, "Prepare, Elizabeth."

As she dashed down the hall, she heard him saying something else, but couldn't make out the words—

Suddenly, a fire raged inside her. Clutching her chest, she slowed—yet she was still speeding through the apartment. She felt fangs growing in her mouth.

No, no, no!

He appeared in front of her, catching her against him. "It's done, Elizabeth. You are like me now. See how easy that was?"

She buried her face in her hands as dizziness hit her. Everything was too loud; her body felt light as air.

The *scents* . . . was that his blood she smelled? Against her ear, his heart sounded like the drum of a watchtower clock.

He peeled her hands away. She noted with horror that her nails were dark—and more like claws.

"No, let me see you, love. Your irises are black—lovely beyond words. But you must calm yourself. Everything's all right now, you're safe with me."

"I-I'm a *vampire?*" *Open mind, open mind.*

While she stood dumbly, he held her hands, pressing one of his fingertips against her claw, seeming delighted with its sharpness.

"And look at your little fangs." His voice went hoarse. "Ah, Lizvetta, I could come just looking at them. You are perfect in every way."

He sounded like a boy with a new toy—while she was raw with loss, sick with confusion.

Emotions erupted within her, impulses she didn't understand. Her thoughts raced. *Hate him! Love him? Need to taste him. Drink me!*

Never had her body felt less like her own. Not even when Saroya had lived inside it.

He could change me back with that ring. If she gave him reason to, if she scared him enough . . .

"Be at ease." He cradled her face. "Now nothing will separate us."

"Hold me?" she murmured.

"Ah, anything!" He drew her tight against him, tucking her head under his chin. "Now I don't have to fear hurting you."

Hate him. . . . Love him. . . . His scent! "Lothaire, I-I *need* you."

"You couldn't make me happier, Elizabeth." Now that she was undying, Lothaire could finally acknowledge what he felt for her, could stop fighting it at last.

When she twined her fingers behind his neck, pressing her breasts against his chest, he rasped, "This is just another sign that your transformation was flawless—vampires are notoriously lusty creatures."

She raised herself on her toes to kiss his chest in the V of his shirt, nuzzling—

Her fangs pierced him.

Pleasure such as he'd never known jolted through his body. *"Uhn! Elizavetta!"* When she moaned and sucked, his mind briefly blanked. . . .

"No!" he roared, prying her bite free. "You drank from the flesh, from *me*." He grabbed her shoulders, still hazy with lust after her bite—even as alarm filled him. "Do you not know how wrong my mind is? How poisoned with memories? And I've no doubt you're a *cosaș* like me!"

"Turn me back!" she screamed, her irises solid black with emotion, blood trailing from the corner of her lips. "Or I'll go insane!"

He shook his head hard. "I'd meant . . . I'd meant to ease you into drinking with a mere drop on your tongue. To teach you to love it. But you tapped the font your first time out."

"So change me back!"

"I'd considered this possibility, had played with the idea of using another wish to make you immune to my blood. After all, you were bound to take it directly from me sooner or later. But then, I'd also wanted both thrones." He exhaled. "I can't believe I'm about to do this." Raising his hand, he twisted the ring on his finger. "Whenever my Bride drinks from me, she will harvest only my memories made from this night forward. None of my victims' memories will ever affect her, nor mine from my past."

Her face fell, and she swayed on her feet.

"Well, Elizabeth, that just cost us a kingdom. And yet . . . the outcome is necessary. We don't usually feed from our own, but now you can drink from me. You will drink *only* from me."

His blood taken from the flesh would make her even stronger. And now they had a bridge between them. Unbreakable ties.

"I could have wished that you took no memories," he continued, "but I want you to know my acts, to see my bravery in battle as I fight for you and our young. I want you to be prideful of your male."

And every day, she would dream of his feelings for her—experiencing how sharp they were, how his obsession only continued to grow.

That bond would make his life easier. He had little knowledge of relationships, of going about a life united with another, of discussing his feelings. Now he would have no need to learn.

She'd simply know his mind as well as he did.

Her lips moved wordlessly.

"I will be everything you need, will nourish you." She'd had a meager sip before; now he intended to feed her thoroughly.

The thought of her taking her fill from his body, her new fangs sinking deeper into his flesh . . .

His cock swelled so swiftly he had to stifle a groan. Perhaps, he could revisit his plots and schemes *after* he'd claimed and fed his vampire Bride.

Her gaze darted as she cast about for another recourse. He would make sure she had none.

Yet then, her tongue daubed at the blood on her lips. The taste made her wild eyes grow hooded, her breaths shallowing. "L-Lothaire?"

He could hear her heart racing, could scent her arousal. But the hunger in her expression nearly felled him.

Everything you need, Elizabeth.

49

Ellie could hear the hypnotic pounding of Lothaire's heart, could perceive it speeding up as he gazed down at her face.

"So beautiful. Elizabeth, you've amply rewarded my long wait." Never releasing her hand, he traced her to his safe, tossing the ring inside. "It's done now." He led her to their bed. "Tonight we start our lives anew."

Already she throbbed all over—her sex dampened in the heat of her panties, her nipples strained against her top, her . . . fangs lanced her tongue.

That brief sample of his blood had tasted like a *homecoming*.

And yet she was so infuriated with him she could choke on it. "I-I didn't want this." These feelings were so intense, too much so. *Frightening*.

"You're angry. But this will pass."

She said nothing, just tried to keep her focus.

"After tonight, I will show you how much pleasure is yours for the taking, and you will forgive me."

She shook her head. "I've ruined your endgame—don't you want to forsake me? Disown me?"

He merely grinned, that sensual curl of his lips. "With you by my side, who knows what I can win? Together we will be invincible. Besides, I've no time for revenge at present. I must teach my Bride to trace, to *feed*. To know her own strength and control it." He drew her close. "But first, I must coax her to admit that I am her male and she loves me, so she'll accept it herself."

The satisfaction she sensed in him was heady. He seemed to be thrumming with it, even as she could tell how much he ached to claim her.

"I never told you that I loved you."

"You must," he said in a patronizing tone. "And now that you're of my kind, you'll feel even more bound to me." He cupped her nape, bringing her close to brush his lips along her neck. When his tongue flicked out, sensation bombarded her until she sagged against him.

"Want you naked, Bride." In the space of one of her gasps, he'd torn off all her clothes, piling them at her feet. "Take off my shirt," he rasped at her ear. "I want to feel those nipples rubbing against my chest."

Oh, God, so did she! With a moan, she reached for his shirt. The material seemed to fall away under her fingers.

"The strength is intoxicating, is it not?"

She'd ripped it to threads? Exactly how strong was she . . . ?

Her thoughts drifted, her gaze locking on his bared chest, on her bite mark. Why had she never fully appreciated the beauty of his flesh, the smooth skin that tempted her to bite once more?

Tempted her to sate this hunger . . .

He made her grasp his leather belt, gazing down into her eyes. "Pull this free if you want more of me."

She couldn't have stopped this even if she'd wanted to. Her body pulsated like a plucked guitar string.

She barely tugged. The leather ripped in two. *"Empty,"* she murmured, yanking at his jeans. *"Hungry."* His clothes were no match for her frantic fingers, and soon he stood naked before her. "Lothaire . . . what's happening to me?"

"I'm going to take care of you. All will be well, if you trust me." He took Elizabeth's small hands, laying them against his chest. Of their own volition, her claws dug into his muscles, securing what she desired, trapping him close.

As if I'd ever leave her side.

"Tonight you'll become acquainted with your body all over again. As will I."

Her appearance had changed, but thankfully not too much. Though she had no tan lines, her skin was fully golden, as it had been when he'd seen her at nineteen. The long mane cascading over her shoulders was even richer in color, silkier. Her irises shimmered from glowing gray to jet black, her fangs sharpening before his eyes.

Seeing these vampiric traits in her made his own long-denied instincts rage to the fore. For weeks, he'd kept himself from pinning her against anything.

No shoving her front against the mattress as he railed into her from behind.

No forcing her knees to her shoulders, driving more of his inches inside her.

Now he maneuvered her back against the wall, his hand caging her throat as he kissed her ear, her cheek, her bottom lip. He licked the blood from it, tasting himself on her. "You're infinitely more powerful now." But compared to his age-old strength, she remained delicate to him.

"Then you won't have to hold back?"

Can't lie. "I'll give you everything I can."

At his words, her gaze locked on his neck, on the vein pulsing there.

"You want more blood?"

She glanced away, but not before her tongue darted to her lip.

"Never be ashamed of your thirst. We hold it sacred. Look at me, and tell me you want more."

She slanted her gaze up at him. "God help me . . . I-I do."

"Right now, my blood flows strong to one place on my body."

Her eyes widened with realization.

Before she could protest, he had them in the bed. "Lie back, then." When she hesitantly did, he rose up on his knees beside her head. Fisting his shaft, he told her, "Sink your beautiful fangs into me here." He could tell she wanted to, knew she could hear his blood coursing there. "Drink, Elizabeth."

She stared at it covetously. "But I'll hurt you."

He cupped the back of her head, pulling her up to him until her lips pressed against it. "Drink."

Take from her. Hadn't he always had that thought during sex? Tonight, he thought, *Give everything to her.* . . .

With a lost moan, she covered his flesh with savoring licks, easing down to nuzzle his sac, then back to his shaft. But she wouldn't bite.

Instead, she whispered his name, smoothing loving kisses along his length, caressing her face against it . . . cherishing him.

He tenderly tucked her hair behind her ear, wanting her to continue doing this forever—even as he was desperate for her to bite.

To tempt her, he ran a claw along the side of his shaft, drawing a line of blood. "Lizvetta, love . . . take!"

<hr />

Ellie's gaze was transfixed by the crimson drops beading the top of Lothaire's erection. A cry escaped her when her fangs dipped, seeming to swell inside her mouth.

"I will be anything you need." Had his accent ever been so thick? "Taste me!" His big hand covered one of her hips, his claws digging into her skin. He was more forceful with her now, more animalistic.

Though his aggression called to her, summoning an answering wildness within her, she shook her head. "Lothaire, I can't hurt you!"

"Do your fangs ache?"

"Oh, God, yes!"

"You need to sink them into flesh. *My* flesh. The pain will only get worse."

Gazing up at him for courage, she parted her lips.

"Yes, Bride, *feed*. . . ."

She darted her tongue to the stream; with the first contact, a delirious moan escaped her.

His blood seared her, seeming to leap to her tongue, bringing that sense of homecoming, of *rightness*.

At once, thirst and arousal suffused her. Unbearable.

He hissed in a breath. "You must bite. . . ."

Before she'd even made a conscious decision, her fangs began sinking into the side of his thick erection.

She pierced his flesh; her eyes rolled back in her head.

"*Gods, yes!*" he roared, his back bowing.

Undeniable. As Lothaire's delicious blood drenched her tongue, his mighty heart thundered in her ears, a drumbeat to his groans of ecstasy. "Suck, Lizvetta, until you can't anymore. I'm strong *for you*."

She did, drawing a rich, sultry rush from him. She felt as if she'd waited her entire life to drink like this. With each swallow, her breasts and sex swelled, her nipples jutting wantonly. She was aflame, her body seeming to throb with each beat of her heart—or of his?

Lothaire's blood was affecting her in ways she couldn't understand. She felt more alive than ever before, but her emotions were out of control.

One moment she thought she'd cry, the next, laugh hysterically. She sucked harder.

"Don't stop, don't release your fangs." Easing onto his back, he rasped, "Must kiss you in turn."

She kept him under her bite as he maneuvered her body to his side. "Scream, Lizvetta, scream for me." When he burrowed his head between her legs, pressing his opened mouth to her, she did scream.

"Ah! Keep *feeding*," he commanded her with a lash of his tongue, "and I'll reward you."

Dimly, she remembered the last time he'd said that. She wanted her reward, wouldn't stop her suck until he pried her away.

He thrashed with pleasure when she kneaded her claws into his torso, drawing with greedy pulls. And then he covered her clitoris with his mouth, suckling her.

Rapture. *Never take this away from me.* She sank her claws into his ass. *Never want this to end.*

When he growled against her flesh, the vibrations pleasured her even more. *About to come.* To orgasm as she never had before.

His blood on her tongue. His flexing muscles snared beneath her claws. His shaft in her ravenous mouth.

She could feel his seed rising, thought she *tasted* it.

And when she perceived a tiny prick of his own fang, her eyes flashed open. She toppled over the edge.

Screaming . . . sucking deep . . . screaming more.

He snarled against her as his semen began to pump over his torso, reaching his chest.

The scent of seed, of sex. Of blood. *Heaven.*

Even after he'd come, he remained hard between her lips.

Between harsh breaths, he grated, "Love, you're going to have to give me this back for your reward." He cupped her face, pressing a thumb against her jaw muscle to make her release him.

She reluctantly did, giving his shaft longing licks as he pulled it from her. *Losing my mind.*

He carelessly wiped away some of his seed marking his chest, then traced between her legs. "Now that we've gotten that first frenzy out of the way . . ." He slipped his finger inside her slick core.

"Lothaire!" He gave her no quarter as he wedged a second finger deep inside. With flicks of his wrist, he wickedly thrust them, faster . . . deeper. The veins in his bulging arm and neck muscles now looked doubly sexy to her. "Is it . . . is it always like this?"

Human orgasm, firecracker. Vampire orgasm, *atomic blast.*

"Once we learn what your body can do? It will only get better. I'm going to make you love this, going to make you thank me for turning you into my kind."

She shook her head hard. "I still haven't accepted this—"

He tickled the top of her channel until she screamed.

"What was that, Bride?"

When he paused, she cried, "That's not fair!"

"Should I be unfair once more, Lizvetta?" Another stroke, another pause.

Staring into his eyes, she again felt like she was making a deal with the devil, her soul given over in the space of a plea. "Please don't stop. . . ."

50

Elizabeth's irises were dark with emotion as he stroked her heat, her breaths shallow between her bloodstained lips. Simply looking at her made that ache return in his chest.

But Lothaire couldn't allow himself to savor that unfamiliar feeling—or the staggering release they'd just shared. He had an agenda. He must convince her that this was the right course.

If his Bride had a fatal flaw, it was her stubbornness. Of course, now he loved that trait in her, found it admirable. Didn't mean that she shouldn't be coaxed from it at times.

He was up to the challenge.

Again he curled his finger inside her. Because his blood coursed within her, that little ridged spot had swelled—so much so that he would be able to feel it against his shaft when he took her, would feel it catch the rim of his engorged crown.

And, gods, how *she* would feel it. . . .

"I will shower you with pleasure, with wealth." He began circling his thumb over her clitoris as he rubbed her inside. "You will never regret this. Tonight, I'm going to make you come a dozen more times, each one stronger than the last."

A flicker of distress passed over her face. He'd heard from turned humans that sex as an immortal was a thousand times more intense. No wonder she feared.

"Shh, shh, love, you can take it now. I'd never do anything to your body that you wouldn't thank me for later."

"Like changing my species."

Unashamed, he said, "Just so." Removing his fingers, he shoved his hands under her ass and lifted her. With one swift thrust, he mounted his female.

Lothaire withdrew and delved his shaft deep, twisting those lean hips to make Ellie feel things she'd never known she could.

"Yes, yes! *Yes?*" She began to orgasm before she'd even comprehended how close she was. "Coming . . . *oh, God!*" She could feel her sex clenching his shaft again and again, while he shuddered and sweated above her, already on the verge himself.

"It won't stop, Lothaire!" His cock was sliding over that spot inside her, making the orgasm go on and on.

He was merciless, kept plunging, plunging, until she was sobbing for mercy—while raising her hips for more.

But he gnashed his teeth, slowing his pace. "Do you accept this?" He threaded his fingers through her hair, gripping it, lifting her face to his. "Accept me?"

She could almost imagine he was saying *forgive* instead of *accept.* "I do! Oh, yes!" She would've told him anything at that moment, anything to keep him moving inside her.

He dipped down to kiss her, licking her lips, her sensitive fangs. As rich blood streamed between their tongues, she shredded the sheets with her new claws.

The first time they'd had sex, she'd begged him to be more gentle. Now she demanded, "Harder!"

"You want it hard?" His tone warned her that she might not.

Yet she found herself scoring his back to spur him. He shuddered, arching into her claws. And for the briefest moment, he cast her a look of . . . wonder?

Then the ruthless Lothaire returned. With a growl, he shoved her hips into the mattress, pounding against her. The sounds of their sex grew deafening—their skin slapping, her continuous moans, his guttural words in Russian.

And always the thundering of their hearts. She was on the verge, about to climax again.

This raw bliss would have killed her as a human.

Between heaving breaths, he rasped, "Tell me that you love me."

She almost screamed that she did. But even in this haze of emotion, she held fast to a whisper of stubbornness. *Won't tell him first. . . .*

And once she began to orgasm, she could do no more than cry out his name.

Just when Ellie feared she couldn't take any more of his thrusts, his body stilled completely, his whipcord muscles bulging. *"I will never let you go, Lizvetta!"* He remained motionless inside her, his face a mask of strain. "You are *mine!*" he roared, with his eyes aglow, his gaze pinning hers. "Mine! Ah, gods, you are . . . *mine* . . ."

Ecstasy lit his features.

His seed boiled forth in a rush. His hips surged forward in an uncontrollable fury, pistoning between her legs. Scorching jets of semen pumped into her . . . his body pouring into hers . . . over and over. . . .

Once he'd filled her with his heat, he finally collapsed over her. *"Lizvetta,"* he groaned dazedly.

She clutched him close, pressing kisses to his damp temple, his sweat-slicked neck. He lingered inside her, still softly thrusting.

As their hearts pounded together, she experienced that closeness with him that she'd once known and then missed.

"It's only beginning, love," he promised, his shaft stirring within her. . . .

At the end of the night, after countless bouts of sex, he squeezed her against his chest—hard. But it felt good to her.

"Do you know how long I've wanted to hold my Bride like this?" Brushing his lips against her hair, he murmured, "You will never want for anything again, Elizabeth. The world is yours for the taking."

Again, she felt protected. *Safe.* Her lids began to grow heavy. But she didn't want this to end, feared she'd wake tomorrow, and all this would be a dream. "I'm so sleepy."

"My beautiful girl, dawn nears. And all good vampires are to bed."

She eased up, arching a brow at him. "Then you'll stay awake."

Cupping her face, he lightly covered her mouth with his, tenderly licking her fang, giving her one last taste of blood.

The sweetest good-night kiss. Then back into the secure cradle of his arms.

So why did she still feel a shadow of misgiving? Why did she feel like she had in fact just sold her soul to the devil—and there was a no-refund policy?

No, no. What woman wouldn't love this god, this decadent lover with power and money, who seemed to worship her body?

If he told her he loved her right now, she'd say it back. And she'd mean it.

But he hadn't said it. And he'd never told her he was sorry for everything he'd done to her.

I'm Lothaire's fool. . . .

Lothaire had exactly zero kingdoms under his control. None of his vendettas had been carried out and all of his plans had been upended.

Yet a languorous relaxation spread through him. His lips continued to curl of their own accord.

The satisfaction he felt from stroking Elizabeth's hair as she slumbered against his chest . . . indescribable.

He'd pleasured her with his body, stoking her need, then sating it. He'd fed her with his blood until her skin was warmed. Now she slept deeply—while he safeguarded her with the strength he'd earned through eons of survival.

Of course she loved him. He knew she'd been about to tell him earlier. So her loyalty was his. . . .

Indescribable.

Lothaire had taken great pains to rehearse that transformation wish, and the ring had done exactly as bidden. Which meant that tomorrow he would give her a gift no other male could offer.

When she absently worried her bottom lip with one of her adorable little fangs, he sighed.

The Enemy of Old fucking *sighed*.

Dear gods, it'd finally happened to him.

Happiness.

Then his own fangs sharpened. *I will kill anyone who tries to take this feeling away from me.*

51

At twilight, Ellie woke with no grogginess. One second she was asleep, the next awake. Weird.

She found Lothaire gazing down at her with a disconcerting tenderness, his tousled hair hanging over one of his eyes.

If he'd been gorgeous before . . . Lothaire looking well loved was *breathtaking*.

In a gravelly voice, he said, "Good gloaming."

A vampire version of good morning? "Uh, you too."

"How do you feel?"

Mentally? *The jury's still out.* Body-wise? *Amazingly good.* Though she refused to admit it.

Ellie didn't want him thinking he could continue to get away with this high-handedness where she was concerned. If she was going to make a vampiric life—*oh, dear Lord*—with him, she needed to nip this behavior in the bud.

She shrugged. "I feel okay. It's definitely different." She had no twinges, despite their aggressive sex.

But I also have no craving for my usual waffles.

"What are you thinking about?"

"I miss food." With a pang of sadness, she rose, feeling his eyes on her body as she never had before.

Palpable. *Possessive.*

"I'll be your breakfast. I've replenished out of the refrigerator. Come, Lizvetta, you love the way I taste. And I know just how you prefer to tap my . . . font."

So smug. She gazed at him in the bed—it looked like a murder scene. The mattress was shredded. By her claws? Blood was everywhere.

She flushed to realize she'd never offered him her own blood. Did that make her a selfish lover?

He followed her gaze, seeming proud of the destruction. He cast her a self-satisfied smile as if he'd just won an argument. And for some reason his fangs were so . . . incredibly . . . sexy.

Her mind seemed to blank. *Lick them, feel them in me.* She rubbed her tongue over one of her own.

That sinful vampire could make her a mindless sex slave if she let him.

She shook her head hard, then strode into her bedroom to throw on some clothes. She didn't trust herself to be naked around him.

When she opened her closet, she broke the knob clean off the door.

"You'll get used to the strength," he said, suddenly behind her. As she gaped at the doorknob, he added, "It's not a bad thing to be strong."

With a swallow, she set the knob on a shelf and painstakingly began to dress, careful not to destroy fabrics that felt as flimsy as cobwebs.

Lothaire gazed on with an enthralled expression, as if he'd never seen her naked before—or maybe he just didn't want to let her out of his sight. "Admit it. Vampire sex is better."

Atomic blast. "Doesn't matter. Lothaire, we need to talk."

"We will." He reached for her, drawing her close, until she could feel his erection like a steel rod against her. "After we spend again, and you feed from me once more. Dorada will return at midnight, but afterward, I have a surprise for you—"

"*Now.* Please get dressed."

Seeing she was serious, he shrugged. "I'm feeling very magnanimous right now."

The victor. If he'd been arrogant before, now he was insufferable. It chafed as never before.

He traced away. When she returned to his bedroom, he emerged from his closet fully dressed. Just as they had so many times before, he sat at his desk, she on the settee.

"Tell me, Elizabeth. What can't wait until later?"

"Lothaire, you can't make decisions for me again."

"Of course I can."

"No, we start this thing as equals. Say it."

"I can't say that. Whereas you, my love, retain the ability to lie, I do not."

"What was that?" She'd misunderstood him.

"We are *not* equals, Elizabeth. I have thousands of years of knowledge over you. The bloody wisdom of ages."

The room seemed to rock.

"You are my Bride, my most cherished possession, and I am your mate and technically your sire. I will make decisions for us, and you will trust me to know what's best."

"How can you say that?"

"You didn't want to be a vampire, but you ended up loving it."

"Loving one night of it. The rest remains to be seen!" She tried to tell herself that he just didn't know better than to say these things. As Balery had explained, Lothaire was emotionally insensitive because he'd never learned how to—or why he might—behave differently. *Be patient, Ellie.* . . .

"Lothaire, promise me you'll never take my choice away again."

"I'm going to take care of you for the rest of my life, doing whatever is necessary to ensure your safety. If that includes making decisions for you, then so be it."

Her lips parted. She was now a vampire, and he was *still* treating her like shit.

It's never gonna end.

An eternity of living with this arrogant ass?

"No, Lothaire, this bullshit stops *now*! Or I'm leaving you. Do you understand me? I don't *have* to be with you—and I'd rather be alone than be constantly treated like a child."

"Your blood is still high. This will ease in time." He gave her an indulgent look. "I'll forgive these rash words for now."

She sputtered, "*Forgive?* Let's talk about who should be forgiving who."

"Whom," he corrected.

"Shut up! I'm in the right here. Remember all those things you did to me? Threatening my family? My mother and brother? Sending my ass to prison? You never once apologized to me. You never once asked forgiveness—from *me*. You just commanded your pet to get over it. And only *after* you recognized that I was your Bride, once the lightbulb had *finally* flickered on in your thick head."

"And you told me you would get past these things!" he snapped. "You vowed it."

"I—*lied*."

He looked stunned, as if this possibility had never occurred to him. "Then you've already betrayed me!"

"Did you think I'd just shrug off everything in the space of a couple of weeks? I couldn't—especially when you hadn't changed whatsoever! And all of that went on *before* you turned me into a blood-drinker against my will."

"Making you a *blood-drinker* should negate any offenses against you!" he yelled, shooting to his feet. "You should be even more beholden to me. I toiled for years to find that ring! I risked my life again and again—and I do not court death lightly!"

"I never asked for this." To be Lothaire's "made" creature, to be his possession. "I never asked for you!"

"You told me you accepted this thing between us, that you accepted me. I took your words for truth and trusted them. I trusted *you*!"

"You lied, too," she cried. "You told me I'd never regret this. Right now I do, with all my heart! It's becoming crystal clear that this will never work between the two of us."

At that, his furious expression transformed into a cruel smirk. She despised that look. "One problem. You've fallen in love with me. You won't be able to live without me."

He thought he had her at his mercy; she ached to hurt him as much as he continued to hurt her. "No, I haven't fallen in love with you."

After last night, I have completely fallen in love with you. But as ever, she didn't want him to know of her feelings, didn't want to give him yet another hold over her. Besides, love *didn't* conquer all. If she'd learned one thing growing up in a hardscrabble community, it was that sometimes love wasn't enough.

"And again, you lie to me," he said, but she thought she saw a flash of doubt in his eyes.

"Love or not, I'd decided to give us a chance. But you're *ruining* it. You're ruining everything with your arrogance and selfishness—*everything*!"

He seemed to not even be listening to her, his mind seizing on one thing: "You *do* love me. It's obvious. Even if you hadn't told me—oh, how did you put it?—that 'what we feel between us isn't something that everyone experiences together.' "

"Didn't I tell you that the night I realized you were truly gonna kill me? What wouldn't you have said in my shoes?"

"We end this now, Elizabeth. You're acting foolish."

"Of course *I* am the one acting foolish. Never you. Because I'm demonstrably your inferior! Isn't that how *you* put it? How could I ever love someone who treats me like a dog? You expect me to have tender feelings for a man who captured me, tormented me, was secretly planning to destroy my soul. What do you think that would say about me? Would *you* want a woman who allowed an asshole to treat her this way?"

"If you haven't been falling in love with me, then what have we been doing for these three weeks?"

"*We? I* have been *surviving*! And I did whatever it took."

In a quietly ominous voice, he said, "That's all this was to you? A ruse?"

"How could it be anything more? Tell me, Lothaire, I want to know. Convince me why I should love you."

"Because any other female would! Yet you *feigned* affection for me?" His eyes blazed with wrath.

It . . . frightened her. Which only made her madder. "Always in the back of my mind I thought of all you'd done."

"Will you do whatever it takes to survive once more? You have no idea how to trace or get blood. You are completely dependent on me. If I have to use your thirst to keep you as my captive, then I will."

Any trust she'd managed to feel for him had just been violated—beyond repair.

She felt her lips drawing back from her own fangs, felt them sharpening as memories assailed her. *"I've decided to let you go to prison this eve." "I'll kill your family with delight. . . ."*

The fear and frustration that had built and built now boiled over. "I never want to see your face again."

"Too bad, Elizabeth. You're stuck with me. Not for a few decades, not for centuries. You're tied to me forever. That girl and boy offspring you talked of? They'll come from me—or no one."

"I'm *leaving*!" She turned toward the door, striding down the hall, flinching when she recalled those things chasing her the night before.

"Leaving me?" He traced in front of her with a mocking laugh. "Even if you could get through the boundary, where would you go?"

She strode around him.

"Where could you go that I wouldn't find you?" He followed, taunting her, even though her feelings were raw, her nerves frayed.

They were now in the living room where he'd brought her that first morning—straight from the injection bench.

He'd thrown her around, shoving her to the floor. "Where would I go?" she asked. "How about the same place my family went—where you couldn't find them! Eventually, I will get free."

She thought she saw a flare of alarm in his eyes, but his own aggression quickly overran it. "Resign yourself to the fact that you will never see them again! They are dead to you, just as you are to them."

"What's that supposed to mean?"

"They believe you died in that prison escape, shot to death by a guard. They will never know the truth, *pet*."

And with that, her mental rubber band . . . broke.

Instead of checking out, I'm gonna lash out.

She snatched up a vase, hurling it at him. "I hate you! Only a fool could ever love you!" Then a lamp. "Ugly on the inside!" She swooped up the decorative sword she'd threatened him with that first day. "Why don't you try throwin' me across the room now!"

In a snide tone, he said, "Hag called you feral before. Hag had seen *nothing*."

"I'll kill you!"

"You'd never hurt me. Deny it all you like, but you do love me. Use your little sword to convince me otherwise, or accept that you're mine forever." Again he laughed.

His laughter flayed her, cut like a knife. Wild with confusion, she raised the sword, wishing she could cut him back.

When he advanced on her, she cried, "Get away from me! I can't . . . I can't be here now! Just leave me be!"

"You can't be here? And yet, I'm not letting you go."

"I told you to stay away! I'll swing!" Red covered her vision. Literally. Bloody tears. *Dear God, I have blood for tears now. Can't see.*

"You could never wield that blade against me. Now, stop acting like a child, and put it away before someone gets hurt."

She screamed with fury, but she could *still* hear his laughter.

Can't stop screaming . . . sword hilt crushed in my grip . . . blindly swinging the blade—

The laughter stopped. Was that a thud on the floor? She swallowed, dizziness engulfing her.

That had *not* just been his body? *The bastard's messing with me, tricking me.*

She rubbed her eyes, again and again, and saw . . .

Horror.

Lothaire lay on his back, head lolling at an angle to his body. His neck was cleaved through, his spine severed. . . .

Her fingers went limp. The sword clattered to the floor.

Knees buckling, she collapsed beside his body. *I . . . killed him?*

More tears came as she threw herself over his motionless chest. *No, no, no!* He was invincible—*nothing* could take him down. Least of all her. *What have I done?*

She hadn't even been close enough to reach him. *How, how, how?*

Anguish replaced her rage. Even after everything, she'd never meant to hurt him like this—to . . . kill him. Just because she didn't think they could live together didn't mean she hadn't felt love for him. *I wasn't anywhere near him!*

"He's not g-gone," she sobbed. "He's not. C-can't be." Ellie rose up, mindlessly tearing at her hair. Her blood-filled eyes darted—

She froze. *The ring.* "I w-won't *let* him be." She shot to her feet, sprinting for the safe. "I'll bring him b-back."

"You won't be doing anything," a voice said from behind her.

Ellie whirled around. A woman with long black hair, pointed ears, and small fangs stood beside Lothaire's body. Off to the side was a hulking demon, watching the scene intently.

"Who *are* you?" Ellie demanded. "How did you crack the boundary?"

"The Valkyrie about to abduct you. Inside information from a soothsayer."

"Try to keep me from what I aim." Ellie snapped her fangs. "I dare you to."

With a speed matching Lothaire's, the raven-haired female charged Ellie, her fist taking her unaware.

Ellie spun on one foot, blood spraying from her mouth before she fell to her knees. The woman was upon her at once, binding her wrists, then shoving a blade against her throat.

"No! Let me go!"

"You are a former human, then? I bet that took the smug bastard down a peg." She signaled the demon. "Deshazior, now."

At once the demon traced forward, gripping Ellie's arm. He could teleport her out of here in an instant.

Away from Lothaire.

"No, don't touch me!" Ellie hissed, struggling with all her new strength, but she couldn't break the demon's hold. Now pleading to the Valkyrie, she cried, "I have to get to the ring! I'm beggin' you! I'll bargain with it, just listen to me!" The female was immovable. To the demon, Ellie screamed, "No! Don't do this—"

He began tracing with both the Valkyrie and her. Just before they disappeared, Ellie twisted around for one last glimpse of Lothaire.

The vampire she *had* fallen in love with. *I killed the man I loved.*

But I'm gonna bring him back. . . .

An instant later, the three of them appeared in front of a sprawling mansion with red-robed ghosts flying around. Lightning streaked the misty nighttime sky, shrieks sounding constantly.

Have they taken me to a Valkyrie coven? She needed to figure out where she was, and then come up with an escape plan. *Got to get back to the ring before Dorada arrives.*

As the Valkyrie hauled her toward the front entrance, Ellie's mind whirred with ideas. She could force the demon at sword point to trace her back! Then she could heal Lothaire, could take them back in time if she had to.

Get free. Find a sword. It isn't over. Her new claws bit into her palms until blood dripped. *Have to escape! Lothaire's lying there . . . dead.*

When the female began shoving her up the porch steps, the demon gave a teasing bow. "Until we meet again, Carafina."

"No!" That was her ride back! Ellie flailed against the woman's unyielding hold, but he'd already disappeared.

After matter-of-factly offering a lock of her hair to the flying ghosts, this Carafina stiff-armed Ellie, sending her sailing through the front doors.

Ellie whirled around. "Let me go, you bitch!"

The Valkyrie's eyes were violet, glimmering eerily. "I'm the only thing protecting you from my sisters now."

Inside, pointed-eared females were all over the place—gazing down from the second-floor landing, lining the walls. Though each of them was startlingly beautiful in her own way, they all had claws and fangs and moved with an otherworldly grace.

As her captor forced Ellie deeper within, one Valkyrie said, "We're allowing a leech to walk unaccosted through Val Hall?"

Val Hall—the Valkyrie stronghold! In *Louisiana*.

Oh, God, how can I get back to New York? More useless tears spilled, but she was able to blink them away faster. *It still isn't over!*

"Where did the Enemy of Old find a *female* vampire?" another asked. "Oh, gross, I hate it when leeches cry!"

A third quipped, "Then why do you always make them do it on the battlefield?"

The group laughed.

Get back to Lothaire, get back to Lothaire. But Ellie was weakening by the moment, her mouth dry with thirst. From her tears?

"Did that bitch just check out my neck?" a short redhead snapped. "'Cause it is *on* if she's ogling me for food."

When they entered yet another room, Ellie saw even more Valkyries lining the walls. A golden-eyed one sat at the head of a long dining table—with a *bat* perched on her shoulder. "Welcome, Ellie Ann Peirce Daciano. I'm Nïx the Ever-Knowing, and I'll be your soothsayer tonight."

So this is the notorious Nïx. "Why have I been brought here?"

"Cara the Fair, your Valkyrie/Fury abductor for the night, plans to ransom you to Lothaire for information. You see, he took Cara's twin sister—our queen, Furie—and imprisoned her."

Cara gave Ellie yet another shove, her violet eyes turning silver with emotion. "Your lover chained her to the bottom of the ocean so she could drown over and over till the end of time! He did this six decades ago!"

Had *flames* just fanned up around Cara's head?

Nïx murmured, "Easy Carafina, your wings begin to show."

Wings of fire? Ellie was too distraught to care. She bit out the words, "You're too late. He's *dead*."

"What?" Nïx cried, looking genuinely upset. "I didn't see that!"

"I-I beheaded him." Blood bubbled up from her stomach as nausea washed over her, but she choked it back down.

Someone along the wall murmured, "A vampiress beheaded the Enemy of Old? I can't decide if I should gut her or get her autograph."

Ellie whirled around with a hiss.

Cara told Nïx, "He's not dead. His Bride left a sliver of tendon. Not a complete decapitation. He'll rise again."

Hope leapt in Ellie's heart. "He'll . . . he'll *live*?" Again her new claws dug into her palms.

"Come closer, Elizabeth, and let me see for certain," Nïx said. When Ellie eagerly did, the soothsayer seemed to peer inside her mind. After what felt like hours, Nïx pronounced, "Lothaire is very much alive."

"You swear?"

"Often. Though not as much as foul-mouthed Regin. I try not to in front of Bertil." She petted the bat.

"I meant—will Lothaire live?"

"He will."

For some reason, she trusted this crazy Valkyrie. If Nïx said he would live, then Ellie would believe. She sagged with relief.

Cara snatched her up. "And once he heals, he will come looking for you. Until that time, you'll be kept here," Cara said. "There's no escaping Val Hall. If you try to trace from here, the wraiths will prevent you— violently."

Ellie was hardly listening. *I didn't kill him*, her mind chanted, *I didn't kill him*.

Nïx added, "You'll be a political prisoner of sorts."

He's coming for me. Never would Ellie have expected to be so excited over the prospect.

Then she frowned. *Would* Lothaire come for her? Would he forgive her? At one point in their fight, he'd looked homicidal. And that had been *before* she'd nearly decapitated him. Of course he would know that was an accident.

She was his vampire Bride; he'd *have* to come for her. Reassured, Ellie finally gazed around at the room.

Though she was beyond relieved that Lothaire would live, she couldn't feel happiness.

Imprisoned yet again?

52

As if from a great distance, Lothaire heard beings murmuring in . . . Dacian?

Where am I? He'd sleep-traced again? *Why can't I open my eyes?* Every muscle in his body tensed, his first frantic thought for Elizabeth.

—"He's maddened enough," a deep voice said. "But his mate as well?"

—"At least the curse will be ended," a female said.

—"True, Mina, but isn't Lothaire merely a new curse?" a male said dryly. "Perhaps we should have left him in York."

—"Shall I say *I told you so* sooner, or simply more often?" another male said in a slurring tone. "And it's *New* York. Evidently, there's a difference between the two."

Blyad'! They *were* Daci. They'd captured him. *Where is Elizabeth?*

Then memories of her swept over him. The last thing he recalled was her screaming, her eyes black with rage as she'd wielded a sword. She'd *swung* at him.

Then the bite of the blade. *She . . . she nearly cut off my head?*

Gods, she'd lied to him, feigned love for him, and tried to kill him! He'd wondered how many times he could have a sword at his neck before one struck true.

He'd never thought he'd have to worry about his own Bride dealing the blow.

Again, I am betrayed.

With difficulty, he eased his hand to his throat, felt a bandage. Why would the Daci bandage him?

"He's waking at last."

When Lothaire managed to lift his lids, he found himself in bed in some palatial room.

The scent of fresh blood carried on the air. Light streamed in through the open window and fanned over his arms, but he didn't burn. Blurred figures stood by his bed.

He tried to rise. Couldn't.

As his vision adjusted, he saw three tall, dark-haired males, all similar in looks, and a short, fair-haired female. Each dressed in old-fashioned clothing.

Another massive vampire sat at the desk, boots propped up on it. He was drinking from a flagon—what smelled like alcohol-infused blood. His appearance was more modern than the others', his eyes a glacial blue. *As mine used to be.*

The Dacian from the Bloodroot Forest! "Where am I?" Lothaire grated, his throat burning as if he'd swallowed a poker.

"Castle Dacia," the seated one said. "I'm Prince Stelian. Standing are the Princes Trehan, Viktor, and Mirceo, as well as Mirceo's sister, the lovely Princess Kosmina."

She nervously gave a formal curtsy.

"A *female* vampire?" Lothaire hadn't seen a full-blooded one in centuries.

"Ours have been safe from the plague here."

Lothaire narrowed his gaze at Stelian. "You were at Helvita that morning."

"That is correct. We were endeavoring to save our queen from Tymur's men. Since you had—what's the modern term?—*dropped the ball.*"

"Queen?" Dizziness rushed over Lothaire.

"Welcome to your kingdom, my liege. You are our ruler now. Newly restored." He raised the flagon in a mock toast.

"How? I've conquered nothing, have waged no war on you."

"The royal family has chosen you to be our ruler. Almost unanimously, only one holdout."

"Why would you do this?" Lothaire demanded, coughing blood. "Why not take the throne yourself?"

"Here, Uncle Lothaire," the female said, rushing forward with a jewel-encrusted chalice. "Drink this. It has healing herbs—"

Lothaire backhanded the cup against the wall, splattering scented blood. *"Uncle?"*

Stelian exhaled. "Technically, you are our cousin. But the younger Mirceo and Kosmina call us elder cousins 'Uncle' in quaint tradition."

"Answer my question!"

Trehan said, "As Ivana the Bold died, she cursed her family to war and backstab until you were made king, until we all vowed allegiance to you."

"My mother was no witch."

Stelian waved that away. "Perhaps she played on the intrigues already at work. This was before our time. In any case, six generations were wiped out by assassinations and civil wars. Finally we decided to investigate you, to see if you would make a good ruler." He swigged, saying under his breath, "Before we all killed each other."

The three standing males shot looks at Stelian. He merely shrugged. "Lothaire will find out all eventually."

Viktor said, "We studied you, but decided you were too crazed to rule anything."

At Lothaire's scowl, Mirceo hastily explained, "You insisted on appearing at the outskirts of our kingdom, half-dressed, bellowing for someone to 'fucking fight you.'"

Kosmina gasped. "Language!"

Patting her hand, Mirceo continued, "And you also challenged *Serghei*, who's been dead—"

"Dead!" *My vengeance is no more?*

Mirceo nodded. "For more than a millennium."

All these years Lothaire had wasted, hell-bent on delivering retribution. To a male who no longer existed.

Trehan said in a measured tone, "Not to mention the fact that you looked as though you intended to consume that Horde leader in the forest. Yet then you settled in with your Bride, and you grew more lucid. We decided to vow allegiance to you and your queen."

Lothaire tensed even more. So Elizabeth *had* been the key to his throne. Hag's prediction had proved correct. Too bad Elizabeth had tried to lop off his head. "Where is"—*that bitch*—"she?"

He'd throw her in the dungeon of this castle, condemning her to yet another jail.

Blyad'! Why didn't the thought give him pleasure?

Solely because she was his Bride?

He despised that fated tie to her! And now they were blood-bound as well.

But even with that union, Elizabeth had felt nothing for him—had been violently intent on getting away from him—while he'd lowered his guard. . . .

"After the attempt on your life," Stelian said, "she was captured by a Valkyrie named Cara the Fair."

So Carafina took my Bride. Elizabeth was within the walls of Val Hall. Those lightning fiends would terrorize her worse than he ever could. His female had wronged him, and now she would pay.

Lothaire wanted to laugh.

Yet his bitterness staggered under the weight of another feeling.

Loss. *All I feel is . . . loss.*

"And La Dorada?" he asked. "Did you have a run-in with her?"

"Her ring has been returned, your transaction completed," Stelian said, adding against the rim of his flagon, "Gods help the poor souls in that book."

Lothaire already mourned his ledger, his squandered fortune. He would start a new book! Perhaps he and Dorada could trade debts like baseball cards. . . .

Kosmina cleared her throat. When all eyes turned to her, her face turned bright red. "W-we fear Queen Elizavetta is behind the guard of the Ancient Scourge. Th-there's no way to circumvent them." The chit was socially inept, more backward than he'd ever believed Elizabeth to be.

"Your *uncle* knows a way around the Scourge," Lothaire grated with disgust. "But I won't be using it."

Carafina thought to force him to reveal where her sister was? Everyone assumed he knew—simply because he'd been the one to sink her in the first place.

Perhaps I oughtn't to have chosen a seabed with frequent seismic rifts and a strong current?

When he'd told others he had no idea where Furie was, he'd spoken the truth.

To this day, Lothaire couldn't find the Valkyrie queen, despite Hag's help. Even if he could, he would never ransom Elizabeth. *"Ugly on the inside!"* she'd screamed. *"I could never love you!"*

She truly hadn't fallen for him.

For *him*.

Which indicated that she was an idiot. He had no time or patience for them.

Damn you, Elizabeth, why . . . ?

Stelian tsked. "Feelings stung because of one measly beheading?"

They knew she'd done this to him? *I'll kill them all—*

"She left an eighth of an inch of tendon," Stelian added. "Plenty for regeneration."

Lothaire narrowed his gaze at him. "You're the one who voted against restoring me."

"That I am. Seemed wise then, and even more so now that you've lost your queen."

"I haven't *lost* her."

"I'm no expert with females"—the others rolled their eyes at that—"but I believe an attempted decapitation communicates the need for some *space*."

Lothaire didn't like this Stelian smart-ass.

In an innocent tone, the Dacian asked, "Isn't that the modern term for it?"

Viktor said, "We've already assembled a party to negotiate with the Valkyries. If that fails, I will happily lead the siege." Black flickered across his irises, as if the idea of a war aroused him.

So this one likes to fight. "*Dis*assemble it. Carafina can rot waiting." At the male's incredulous look, Lothaire said, "I don't want my Bride retrieved."

Mirceo said, "Whatever happened between Queen Elizavetta and yourself should be subordinate to the good of the crown—"

"Do not speak her name again," Lothaire murmured, "or it will be your last utterance."

Mirceo's lips parted in surprise. "If this is what you . . . command, my liege."

"Not used to taking orders, are you, Mirceo?" Lothaire gazed at them one by one. "You all assume that I *want* your kingdom? Perhaps I prefer the fucking Horde!"

Another gasp from Kosmina, with more furious blushes.

Stelian said, "Go to the window, look out."

Uncaring of his nudity, Lothaire did. With a choked sputter, Kosmina traced away, while Mirceo chuckled. "There *are* garments for you, Uncle. Take care not to set a new fashion."

At the window, Lothaire stared out, agog. *Why did Ivana ever leave this place?*

He was in the fabled black stone castle of Dacia, the one circled by fountains of blood.

The magnificent structure sat high upon some rocky vantage—from here, he could survey a kingdom that stretched on and on, before fading into a mist on the horizon.

Soaring caverns rose above; cobblestone streets wound through the fog below. The architecture was old-fashioned but ornately constructed with carved stone.

At the top of a high cavern, a giant prism diluted the sun's light, shining it over the entire kingdom—muted rays that illuminated all, but didn't burn. Not even a vampire's skin.

And everything I see is . . . mine.

When he could manage words once more, he informed them, "My coronation will be held as soon as my throat heals. I will accept your vows of fealty then."

This was truly happening—the imbeciles were inviting *him* to rule this fantastical kingdom.

"Very well," Stelian said with unconcealed disappointment. "Will you take a new regent name?"

A vampire tradition. Lothaire's own uncle Fyodor had taken a new name when crowned by the Horde—one which meant *rule without end.*

Ah, not quite, Uncle. "No. I've done too much PR with the name I have. I'll be known as King Lothaire, the Enemy of Old."

He'd still have his vampire war, but the sides would be changed. *I'll use the Daci to lay waste to the Horde.* He had no problem reversing himself; he switched alliances with ease.

And then he would be done. He'd have everything he'd ever wanted. Then he'd know happiness.

I knew happiness before. But she stole it from me.

With one swing of her sword. Of all the blows, of all the torture, that strike had hurt him the worst.

Why, Elizabeth . . . ?

Fists clenched, he ordered them, "Leave me to dress."

Leave me to relish the idea of my Bride trapped in a hellhole filled with malicious Valkyries. Arch-Fury Carafina would terrorize her. Belligerent Regin would have her throat. Would Nïx save Elizabeth, or let nature take its course?

I hope the latter. Perhaps he should send his female *a parting gift*, as she'd once said.

Yes, to inform her that I'm now a king, and have forsaken her.

The princes traced away one by one, with Stelian muttering, "A red-eyed king who spurns his Bride. Gods help us all. . . ."

53

This is a kill-or-be-killed scenario, leech," Regin the Radiant, a glowing-skinned millennium-old swordswoman, told Ellie in a baleful tone. "So raise your weapon and prepare for your end. 'Cause I'm about to take your head."

Ellie yawned. Ten days of this was getting *old*. "Girl, I don't wanna play video games anymore."

Regin's berserker mate, Declan, had been having meetings with some other berserkers concerning the Accession, so Regin had been hanging here every couple of days, glowing on the couch, playing games with Ellie.

At first, Regin had been excited to meet her because Ellie had done what Regin had dreamed of for centuries. "Buy this leechly leech assassin a mug of the thick stuff! Took down Lothaire? No shit? Describe it second by second in a breathy voice. . . ."

The only thing the Valkyries hated more than vampires in general was Lothaire in particular.

Of course, Regin would have *succeeded* in "collecting Lothaire's head and fangs."

Yet after a couple of days, Regin had realized that Ellie still had feelings for the Valkyries' archenemy: "*Not* cool, hillbilly, not cool."

Why hadn't he come for Ellie yet? From time to time, Nïx had visited, keeping her informed—even if she wasn't always coherent. Through Nïx, Ellie knew that Lothaire was indeed recovering and had been invited back to Dacia to rule.

Serghei was no more. Lothaire had become a king.

Just as he'd always wanted.

Ellie had gone through so many emotions when thinking about him— guilt, anger, longing.

Was all forgiven? Hell no! She was still furious at him. That didn't mean she wasn't pining for him to rescue her. Ellie knew he could—she believed he could do just about anything. But after nearly two weeks, she had to wonder if King Lothaire was ever going to reclaim his queen.

She'd asked Nïx, "If he's healed, then why hasn't he come for me?"

"Who?"

"Uh, *Lothaire*."

"Not ringing a bell . . ."

"Can I send a message to Dacia, to explain what happened?"

Eyes bright with anticipation, Nïx had cried, "Who are we sending a message to . . . ?"

Now Ellie told Regin, "We'll play tomorrow. Besides, isn't it time for my cup of dinner?"

Regin's amber irises flashed silver with ire. "I am *not* your blood go-fer." She gave a shriek that hurt Ellie's sensitive ears. "Suck my dick, Vampirellie—*suck* it."

Pissed, Ellie drilled her knuckle into Regin's arm with all her new vampire strength. Nïx had told her in the beginning, "If any of my half sisters step out of line, *go mountain* on them."

Ellie had learned there was no other way to deal with Valkyries. If they liked females who took zero shit from them, it was just a matter of time before she was Ms. Popularity here.

"Bitch!" Regin screamed. "You can only skate by on Lothaire's take-down for so long."

Nïx had told everyone that Ellie had attacked Lothaire on purpose, and the near decapitation of one of the Lore's most feared villains had made Ellie *a creature with which one did not fuck.*

"Bring it, Regin, any day of the week."

"Next time I will *brangit.* And your blood is in the microwave, slore." Then she stomped away.

Apparently, this was how Regin treated all her friends.

Ellie shrugged. Each of the Valkyries was eccentric in her own way, from the vacant-eyed Nïx to the daunting Cara—who was part Fury, a breed of warrior females that even the Valkyries gave a wide berth.

Though many of the dozens who lived at Val Hall were wary of Ellie's vampirism, she thought she was growing on them. When they forgot themselves, the Valkyries were kind of *fun.*

They were all half sisters, basically a big family unit, with all that came with a family of this size—feuds, cussing matches, favoritism, and unwavering loyalty.

In a way, Ellie was right at home here.

She sighed. But she still missed her own friends—Balery and Thad—and her own family. . . .

Ellie's gaze dropped to the couch, to Regin's *forgotten cell phone.* Her eyes went wide. After ten days of browbeating her captors to let her make a call, Ellie still hadn't persuaded them.

As carefully as she would cradle an egg, Ellie collected the phone. Did she dare call her family, let them know she was alive?

She'd just started talking herself out of it when she realized she at least had to tell them they could safely come out of hiding now.

Besides, she still refused to accept that she couldn't see them, that she'd never return to her mountain.

Though she understood Lothaire's caution about mixing immortal strength with human frailty—Vampirellie never met a doorknob she didn't break—she believed she could train herself to control her strength.

And what of the warning that she should never needlessly reveal the Lore to humans? Well, her family had had their blinders pulled off long before now. First with Saroya, and then with Lothaire.

If the gods wanted to punish Ellie, she'd remind them that hosting Saroya in her body for six years was *time fucking served*.

On that thought, she dialed her mother's cell. "Mama? It's me. Ellie."

"Oh, Lord Jesus in heaven, I knew you wasn't dead! They told us you'd been shot in some prison escape, but I knew you still lived! Why ain't you come home?"

Ellie could hear the bafflement in her mother's tone, understood it. If she was alive and out of jail, then she ought to be home—end of story. "I will in the future. Sometime. But it's . . . complicated, Mama. And really hard to believe."

"Well, let me see if I can't keep up and keep my eyes in my head."

Where to begin? So much had happened. How much should she reveal to her mother? "First, tell me how Josh is doing."

"Josh is getting even more rambunctious, unruly, and willful, so naturally the family's proud as all get out—"

Valkyrie shrieks sounded in the next room.

Mama cried, "What in the hell was that?"

"The TV! Let me turn it down." She sped to the door, closing it and locking it—by breaking the knob. *Shit.* "How's everyone else doing? How about you?"

"Oh, honey, we're all managing just fine," she said brightly. *Too* brightly.

"Tell me how bad it is, Mama."

An exhalation into the phone. "We're scraping together mortgage payments each month, but Va-Co's holding our feet to the fire, girl."

Ellie's fangs sharpened, violence simmering inside her.

"All our men are back in the mine."

"*What?* But they swore they were done with that. What about Ephraim's store?"

"In this economy? All closed down. It was either the mine, or we'd lose the mountain. Most of your cousins are just happy for the work."

"I'm gonna figure out a way to send you money, okay?"

"Ellie, just tell me about you. Start from the beginning."

She nibbled her lip. "Remember that red-eyed demon everybody saw that night?"

"The one we're hidin' out from? The Mothman?"

"That'd be him. Only he's not a demon or Mothman, and you don't have to hide any longer. He'll never hurt you." Lothaire could never break his vow not to harm her family—she'd seen firsthand how binding those vows were.

"Then what *is* he?"

After a hesitation, Ellie admitted, "He's a vampire. He's the one that broke me out of prison. His name's Lothaire Daciano." Merely saying his name brought on a pang. *You took my name the instant I claimed you. . . .*

Mama sputtered, "V-vampire? Oh, Ellie, you're about to give me a heart attack. Are you sure?"

"I'm sure—I've seen him drink blood."

"Jesus! Did this . . . vampire hurt you? Are you with him now?"

"He came to be protective of me, took me traveling over the whole world. He'd thought that Saroya freak was his mate, but it turns out I was."

"Is Saroya still killing?"

"She's gone, Mama. Forever."

"You're cured! Why didn't you tell me that first?"

Because I was cured of one thing only to become afflicted with something else—something you might have an even harder time accepting. "Um, it hasn't really sunk in that I'm free of her."

"Are you still goin' with that vampire feller? Or do I need to send our menfolk to collect you?"

"No way, Mama! Unless you want them all killed. Besides, I'm not with him at present. I kinda got nabbed by some of his enemies. A bunch of gals. They're very decent though," Ellie quickly added. "I get all the food I can eat"—*blood I can drink*—"and we watch soap operas together. I've got my own room"—which used to belong to some kind of ice princess—"and they treat me real nice."

Not that Ellie relished being a prisoner, but until she could figure out all her new powers, being in a protected, sunless environment wasn't all that bad.

Every hour here she was learning more about the Lore, and the girls were good company. *Never kicking my ass much more than I kick theirs.*

One of the first things she'd learned? Fighting was kind of fun when you never stayed hurt from it for long.

"I don't mind it here at all, really." In a way, she was grateful to be in Val Hall. Because for whatever reason, Lothaire hadn't come to get her.

Deep down, Ellie knew she had nowhere else to go. That knowledge was terrifying.

"They're teaching me all about vampires"—*myself*—"while I wait to see if Lothaire will come ransom me."

Nïx had been a lifesaver, hooking Ellie up with the same tracing tutor who'd taught Thad—though Ellie wasn't allowed to see or communicate with the boy himself. Thad was too loyal to Lothaire, and the Valkyries feared he'd divvy information about her to their enemy.

The tutor, a halfling vampire/Valkyrie named Emmaline MacRieve, was utterly lovely, with bone structure to die for, petite fangs, pointed ears, and long golden locks. She'd been genuinely encouraging when Ellie had started to trace. Well, to *waver*. Though Ellie hadn't quite gotten the hang of it, she practiced every day.

But she could tell Emmaline was keeping her distance, and something about the halfling kept tugging at Ellie's memory, making her wary as well.

Emmaline had probably had some kind of bad personal experience with Lothaire. It seemed like everyone in the Lore had a story to tell about that vampire.

"*If* he ransoms you?" Mama demanded. "I thought you said he's protective of you. Why wouldn't he?"

"We kinda had a falling out. But I'm confident he'll come 'round." *Please come 'round, Lothaire!*

"What is he like?" Mama asked, lighting a cigarette. "That blood-drinker?"

"He's tall, handsome, rich as the day is long." And quite the celebrity.

In the mortal world, Lothaire would've been a heartthrob actor—who'd merely committed an average of a couple of murders a day, for millennia.

As "the Bride of Lothaire," she'd gained some notoriety as well, among Loreans curious about the death-row mortal who'd somehow survived the turning to vampire. When no other female on record had.

"He's also a powerful king among his kind," Ellie said. "Famous in his circles." *Infamous for his underhanded ruthlessness.*

Yes, Ellie had heard all about his misdeeds, knew everyone in the Lore considered him a diabolical fiend. But in the end, she'd decided that while he might be a fiend, he was still her guy.

She sighed again. Was he *hers*? She wondered that every minute of the day. Would he never come to collect her?

In her mind, what it boiled down to was that they had a lot of work to do on their relationship; now that she wasn't *roidal* with new vampire rage, she was ready to dig in.

As long as he comes and gets me, I'll kick his ass into shape, but we'll work it out.

Either it was taking him a long time to heal—or he'd decided not to come for her.

Surely an immortal of his advanced age would be mature enough to discuss their differences.

"What happens if he *don't* come, Ellie?"

Good question. "I'll figure something—"

"Yo, why's this door locked?" Regin yelled from the hall. "Who the hell is Vampirellie talking to?"

"Mama, I gotta run! But I'll send money when I can."

The door came splintering down, revealing Regin, glowing like phosphorescence. "You don't even know how dead you are, leech."

"Love you, Mama, love everyone, talk soon!" She hung up the phone. By accidentally crushing it—

Regin launched herself at Ellie.

Ellie braced for impact, closing her eyes as dizziness overwhelmed her. Waiting . . .

Then came a crash at the TV console. Regin hollered, "Imma be fucking you up!"

When Ellie opened her eyes, she was across the room and Regin had just collided headfirst with the TV.

I traced? Finally! That dizziness—when had she felt it before?

In the fight with Lothaire! *Had I traced even then?* No wonder she'd reached him with that sword swing.

How she wished she could explain that to him!

For now, she had a pissed-off Valkyrie to deal with. But Regin could never catch her now that she could vanish! "What's the matter, lightning bug? Forget how to change the channel? Ha-ha-ha, Valkyrie, you can't catch me," Ellie taunted in a singsong voice. "Hillbilly on the run, on the ruh-hun!"

When Regin vaulted the sofa, Ellie traced once more, but Regin anticipated her reappearance and barreled her to the floor.

"Ow!"

Then Regin proceeded to show her true colors, making Ellie punch her own face. "Why are you hitting yourself? Huh? Vampire, stop hitting yourself."

"Vampire?" Nïx questioned from the doorway, her hair wild, her gaze unfocused. That rabid bat of hers perched on her shoulder, heatedly flapping its wings, as crazed as its owner. "In Val Hall?" Her amber eyes grew silver, the colors swirling. A weird electricity began to crackle in the air.

Every one of Ellie's heightened immortal senses screamed *DANGER*. Surely not from Nïx?

Leaving the bat behind, the soothsayer attacked, backhanding Regin, sending her across the room.

Before Ellie could react, Nïx had her knees shoved into Ellie's shoulders, pinning her with freakish strength. Hair straggling over her wan face, Nïx murmured, "Helen paid with a broken heart. Furie paid. Emmaline—"

"Nïx! It's me, Ellie! What are you doing?"

The soothsayer canted her head like an animal. "You don't know where Furie is . . . ?" Lightning blasted outside, thunder quaking the house.

"Nïxie, *easy*!" Regin clambered over, yanking on her sister. "We were just fucking about." But even Regin was no match for Nïx's power.

Finally, Nïx allowed Regin to heave her away, both of them landing tangled on the floor. The soothsayer blinked in bewilderment. "What has happened?"

Ellie cried, "You're askin' me?" Then regretted her tone when Nïx suddenly looked exhausted, sickly even.

Her bat waddled toward her, hopping on her arm, seeming to soothe her.

"What the fuck, Nïx? You're a regular shit show these days!" Regin disentangled herself from her sister, shooing the bat away. "You went all *Ride of the Valkyries* on Vampirellie."

Nïx frowned at something unseen to Ellie, then sighed sadly. "And I fear between the two of us, I'm doing the better. . . ."

54

King Lothaire, the mad king.

He rather liked the moniker, heard it often said in the sentence: "What has the mad king done now?"

Not because he'd lost his sanity, but because of his behavior—rarely sleeping, wandering the streets at all hours, plotting to send his new subjects into war with the Horde at the earliest opportunity.

This twilight, Lothaire was holding court. He sat upon his gilded throne, decorated with gold-dipped skulls. His design. If he'd had a queen, her throne would have been similar. Of course, her skulls would be *daintier*.

But he had no queen.

The royal cousins who acted as his council knew to gauge his sanity, opening the court on nights when Lothaire seemed more lucid and composed.

For the last three weeks, those kinds of nights had been surprisingly frequent.

He and Elizabeth had exchanged blood, which meant he had an unbreakable tie with her mind. Unlike the one with Chase, the link to his Bride was keeping Lothaire relatively sane.

A blessing—because he refused to let anyone believe he suffered due to his "regicidal Bride."

Lothaire was *not* to be an object of pity. How many times had he made fun of heartbroken males? How many times had he sneered to them, "Aww, did we masturbate through the tears last night?"

As fate would have it, the tie to Elizabeth meant he could survive without her. He no longer needed her; luckily, he no longer wanted her.

Lying to yourself, Lothaire?

When he intoned to the court, "I will see my council, alone," subjects scattered as if they were on fire. It was time for a meeting with the royals, now that he knew them intimately—from routinely spying on them. "Clear the gallery. Including you, Hag."

She glared, no doubt wishing she'd never accepted her position as royal oracle.

After his coronation, a formal affair that was farcically mired in tradition, Lothaire had traced to Hag's for a potion—to erase Elizabeth from his memory completely.

The fey's home had been deserted, looking as if it hadn't been lived in for a hundred years. No scents lingered, no footsteps in the sand leading away from the entrance.

He'd traced to the nearest town to make a phone call, stealing a cell phone from its distracted owner—some fuckwit who'd been saving orphans from an inferno or some such—then dialed Hag's number. "Where the hell are you?"

"Away. I don't want to get in the middle of you and Elizabeth."

"The middle!" he'd roared, regretting that he'd struck Hag's name from his ledger. "If you're not with me, you're against me—there is no *middle*! You're *my* goddamned soothsayer."

"And some of your enemies have discovered our connection. I'm being pursued, as we speak, by the king and queen of the rage demons. They seek my aid to find you—as well as the queen's sister, who's been missing since the breakout on the prison island. Good luck to them with the latter," she'd said cryptically. "Mariketa the Awaited, Portia the Stone

Sorceress, and many more nip at my heels. In any case, your business is concluded, your tasks complete."

"Not all of them." One left. He still wanted the Horde crown, still planned to deal that retribution. "You're to be my new royal oracle. You won't be found if you're within my realm."

Since she'd arrived her attitude left much to be desired. Even now she glared at him before leaving the room.

Once he and the five royals were alone, Lothaire took his time studying them. All were unmated.

Trehan was blooded, but had no Bride to show for it. Mirceo was the youngest of the males, only thirty, and would soon freeze into his immortality, losing all sexual ability. His heartbeat was erratic—and slowing.

His sister, Kosmina, was too immature to even contemplate a male of her own.

Lothaire had no idea whether Viktor's or Stelian's heart beat. They both used an old spell to cloak it. Which Lothaire found intriguing.

Viktor would probably have no time to rut anyway, since all he did was fight. *I've met ghouls who were more peaceable.*

And of the sixth royal, the hidden one they didn't think he knew about? *My investigation continues. . . .*

With a bored air, Lothaire turned to Stelian. "None of my subjects asked a boon of their king?"

The big vampire shook his head. "They fairly much live in fear of you."

"Whyever is that?" he asked blandly.

Grinning, Mirceo asked, "How are you finding your accommodations, Uncle?" He was the head of the castle guard. He liked Lothaire, found him amusing because he was unpredictable.

As I once found Elizabeth.

"They're adequate," Lothaire answered, not a lie, though his sitting room was the size of a ballroom. If he weren't a puzzle master, he could get lost in his labyrinthine new castle. "Why, Mirceo, I don't believe your heart has beat much since you've come in." Not more than one thundering spurt. "And you no longer need to breathe?"

The young vampire stifled his stricken expression. "Unfortunately, this is true, Uncle." He acted stoic about it, but in secret, he was out each night frantically screwing anything that moved, as randy as Lothaire had been in the same situation ages ago.

Just last night, Mirceo had been happily tonguing a female's breasts while a male suckled him—until poor Mirceo had . . . lost enthusiasm.

"Fear not," Lothaire said, "you probably won't even notice that it seems like everyone else in the world but you is constantly fucking like animals."

With one comment, Lothaire could make both Mirceo and his prudish sister deeply uncomfortable. Like bowling a spare.

Stelian quickly changed the subject. "You've been traveling a great deal." As the oldest of the royals, he was the Gatekeeper, the most powerful position after king. Stelian was the one who decided who would enter or leave Dacia, and he alone taught his people how to use the mist to go out undetected.

He'd seemed surprised—and disgruntled—that Lothaire had learned to control it so easily.

But Stelian was quick to add that only *he* knew all the esoteric powers of the mist.

Give me time.

Nevertheless, the Gatekeeper must have been doing a damned fine job if even the *Book of Lore* hadn't tagged Dacia. From his spying, Lothaire knew that Stelian was easygoing—until someone tried to leave without authorization.

Then? Even Lothaire had raised a brow at his chilling response.

"I do travel much," Lothaire agreed. To shore up his sanity even more, he often returned to his apartment and took Elizabeth's scent into him, burying his face in her silk nightgowns, her pillow.

Though it wasn't the same as touching her, her scent—coupled with their blood tie—was enough to get him through most nights.

He wondered what the Daci would think of their new king if they found out he carried his Bride's lingerie in his pocket at all times.

But then, what maddened vampire king *didn't* carry his queen's lingerie in his pocket?

"The capital is boring," he told Stelian. It was—even though other species were welcomed here. Provided they never left.

Which meant there were nymphs to take care of randy young vampires like Mirceo.

"You *do* remain within the mist when you go abroad?" Stelian asked. "Unseen by all?"

"How else would I be able to return?" Lothaire-speak. He'd ordered Hag to devise a beacon for him alone—because sometimes Lothaire liked to be seen.

Part of him wanted to outlaw the mist completely, to make his subjects announce themselves to the world. Otherwise, Lothaire was just the king of a realm that no one knew existed.

In other words, he was the tree in the forest that silently fell—when no one was around to be crushed.

But the cocooning mist did protect the Daci from invasion and plague. Plus, with every excursion, they were basically all out spying, which he wholeheartedly endorsed. . . .

His impetuous cousin Viktor said, "I understand that you observed our soldiers sparring. What did you think of them?" He was a general, and justifiably proud of his battalions.

The army was honed, disciplined, and masterful with swords. In fact, the Daci were obsessed with all medieval arms—maces, throwing daggers, whips, battle-axes.

As soon as a Dacian wielded a weapon, a coldblooded single-mindedness suffused him. Already ruled by logic, he became even more focused, able to predict his opponent's moves.

Much as I do.

"The soldiers were a shade too worried about martial honor," Lothaire answered. All that skill and might—and yet they waged no wars but among themselves? "Not to worry, Viktor. I'll see to that. In any case, they will serve me well enough in my war against the Horde. Unless you're concerned about the defense of my *hidden* kingdom."

Viktor tensed, clenching his fists beneath the table. Blooded or no, he had a brash, querulous nature that ensured he was a loner among the reserved and logical Daci.

And Lothaire's fair "niece"?

Though Kosmina was twenty, she'd been sheltered by the overprotective male royals to a damaging degree.

Apparently, Lothaire's naked male body had been the first she'd ever seen.

Pity, Mina, that you'll forever find all others lacking in comparison to Uncle *Lothaire.*

Yet though she was so ignorant of sex and sin as to be childlike, Kosmina was a killing machine, a mistress at arms with blazing reflexes.

Half simpering schoolgirl, half lethal assassin.

Lothaire had noticed that her ears were pointed, compliments of some fey ancestor—who'd also gifted her with that uncanny speed. He asked her now, "And what is your function? Or do you exist only to be coddled?"

Face hot, she stuttered, "I-I . . ."

Lothaire talked over her, saying, "I understand you have never ventured outside of Dacia, wouldn't know an automobile if it hit you in the face, which it might—if you're not, say, *familiar with fucking cars.*"

Her eyes went wide.

He should send her forth from Dacia, dispatching her to investigate a particularly rambunctious covey of nymphs in Louisiana. "Kosmina, you are distantly related to a female called Ivana *the Bold.* Act like it."

Covering her mouth with her hand, she traced away.

Lastly, he turned to his cousin Trehan, an assassin in charge of an elite band of killers. He was the most dignified of all the cousins, the most "Dacian" of them, and so the least amusing to spy on. He often stared off into nothing, doubtless thinking about whatever Bride had blooded him, then left him.

Lothaire steepled his fingers. "Ah, Trehan, only a female could make you look like that."

"You would know," he replied icily.

While Mirceo was out glutting himself in every murky corner of Dacia, Trehan always traced back to his apartments alone, spending his lusts into his own hand, often multiple times in a night—while Lothaire rolled his eyes in disgust.

Yet don't I do the same?

Not for long; Lothaire had decided that after this meeting, he would reacquaint himself with other females.

He was an all-powerful king, and he'd definitely read interest as he'd walked the cobblestone streets of his realm. Evidently, his subjects still enjoyed *pretty on the outside.*

Yes, an all-powerful monarch was about to commence his hunt for a bevy of concubines. So where was the happiness?

Lost.

He now knew what he was missing, because he'd felt it briefly—even before he'd had his crown.

Lothaire had concluded that each being had a unique key to his or her happiness. *Mine was Elizabeth.* Because of her actions, she'd robbed Lothaire of his key.

His fangs sharpened. He'd killed others for less. *If you're not with me, you're against me. . . .* His instinct was to punish, his mind seizing on revenge.

"My liege?" Stelian said, brows raised. "What revenge are we contemplating this eve?"

Have I spoken aloud? "We'll resume this at a later date," Lothaire bit out, then traced to his suite, pacing from one side of his bedroom to the other.

All he'd wanted was to suffer no more betrayals. He hadn't even desired Elizabeth's love, not particularly. But he had believed that her loyalty would follow it.

Why had he been unable to win her?

In the past, any female he'd bedded would follow him around for years. But not his Bride, the one he'd wanted above all others.

She didn't want me back. And I can't understand why.

As he tried to solve the puzzle that was Elizabeth, his mind would race through their past interactions. *I never told her how I felt. But for fuck's sake, I tried to die for her. She knew me better than anyone; she was clever enough to figure out my feelings.*

Maybe I ought to have told her she was clever . . . ?

He remembered deeming Saroya so arrogant that she would never suspect someone might not desire her. He remembered feeling as if there was a lesson inherent for him.

I was so arrogant I never realized Elizabeth wouldn't desire me as I did her.

Most nights he kept himself busy, but in the lulls he could *feel* her, could perceive her presence across their blood tie. Though he'd tried to delve into her emotions, the distance was too great, and he could barely discern his own, let alone another's.

All he knew was that she felt no fear. So she must be safe.

What am I going to do without her?

When he managed to sleep, he reached for her again and again, aching for her with both his body and his soul.

He despised her for that!

His heart pained him as nothing had before, made him want to howl with misery. A sharp, stabbing agony flared with every beat.

"Elizavetta!" he roared to the ceiling, clawing at his chest. He hated that his heart beat for her alone, that she'd brought it to life. . . .

Brought me *to life.*

Like an animal chewing off its own trapped, rotting limb, Lothaire dug at his chest.

55

P ackage!" someone cried from downstairs.

From Ellie's temporary room, she heard what sounded like a dozen Valkyries speeding down the stairs.

—"Who's it for?"

—"Gotta be me!"

—"Shut up!"

—"No, *you* shut up!"

Ellie sighed, still marveling at how acquisitive her Valkyrie jailers were. She'd seen them stealing clothes in complex heists, sword-fighting over jewelry, pouncing on each other to wrest away new weapons.

Now that she'd learned how to trace, Ellie considered teleporting down there and scooping them all, but she didn't have the energy. Her appetite had deserted her. *Not to crave food—or blood?* But compared to the rich flavor of Lothaire's dark, dark blood, the bagged stuff was nauseating.

It'd been over three weeks since she'd been brought to Val Hall, and still she waited for him to come rescue her.

In that time, Ellie had forgiven Lothaire for turning her into a vampire. Though she occasionally felt like a circus freak—with her eyes growing black and her fangs sharpening for seemingly no good reason—being a vampire wasn't too bad.

On occasion, she even liked being this strong. Such as when pummeling mouthy Valkyries.

Ellie had forgiven him for a lot of the things he'd done, once she'd realized that what Lothaire said and what he did didn't always mesh.

Though he'd mocked her for being a lowly mortal, he *had* tried to burn himself to death in order to save her life—and she'd been mortal at the time.

Their last day together, he'd behaved like a tyrant, ridiculing her; yet in the hours before, he'd made love to her as if he *cherished* her.

When he'd said they weren't equals, that didn't necessarily mean he thought she was stupid or worthless. He'd told her, "Bullshitting Dorada? I couldn't be prouder, Lizvetta."

Again, she'd kind of been mortal still. . . .

At times, Ellie would dream the briefest taste of his memories, seeing their night of lovemaking from his point of view. Or she'd experience some kind of intense connection to him.

But his thoughts and emotions were always so frenzied, impossible to unravel for a novice like her.

All she knew was that she missed him so much, that it felt like grief—

"It's for the vampire!" someone yelled from downstairs.

Ellie shot to her feet. From Lothaire? Who else?

Light-headed, giddy, she traced down to the crowd, throwing elbows to get through to the center.

There was just no other way to deal with Valkyries.

Did Lothaire want her again? Was he even now trying to free her? "Let me have it!"

With a casual hiss, one of the younger Valkyries surrendered it.

The elegant packaging was stamped with some royal-looking seal, addressed to her from *Lothaire Konstantin Daciano, Sovereign of Dacia, the Realm of Blood and Mist.*

Ellie tore open the box, casting everyone an excited grin. Off went the top—

Her fingers went limp. The package dropped to the floor, jostling its contents. A bloody black heart tumbled out.

When it settled at her feet, she shoved her palm over her mouth to keep from vomiting. *Why would he do this? How . . . ?*

The crowd parted for the steely Cara, Nïx trailing in her wake.

"Read the note, vampire," Cara ordered.

With shaking hands, Ellie collected the crisp parchment.

Elizabeth,
With my compliments.
You will never get your claws into another one of mine.

Rot in hell,
L

Nïx clasped her hands over her chest, sighing, "He gave you his heart. That's so romantic. So much better than a candy heart. Those get stuck in the fangs, you know."

"He's not coming for you," Cara said in a disbelieving tone.

Ellie shook her head, numb. "No, he's not."

"Then you're not leverage." Cara's violet eyes flashed. "Your usefulness has ended. Nïx has advised me not to kill you. So you're on your own."

"You're freeing me?" *You're kicking me out?*

"Why should I keep you here?"

Because I have nowhere else to go! Ellie couldn't live with her family. She had no close friends but for Thad and Hag, and their loyalties were first to Lothaire.

Ellie had become a vampire . . . *for no reason.* She'd be all alone in *his* world. He didn't even want to talk to her, to discuss what had happened, much less to *work* on their relationship.

He'd abandoned her to . . . the Lore. After he'd taken her from her family.

At that thought, all her rationalizations about him disappeared. That bastard! *Gonna live in this world, Ellie? Then get hard, get mean.*

Take care of your own business.

Lothaire had told her, "It takes bold strokes to live in the Lore."

She could be just as crazy as all these freaks. *I'm Appalachian!* She would *go mountain* like they'd never seen!

Ellie whirled around on Nïx. "Can I get a package back to him?"

She saluted Ellie, chirping, "I'll see to it myself."

Driven by searing rage, Ellie faced Cara. "Give me a blade."

Whatever Cara saw in her expression had her tossing a knife. Ellie clutched her fist around the hilt.

Then, to the sounds of a shocked chorus of Valkyries . . .

—"Oh, come on, the vamp won't actually do— DUDE! She fucking did it!"

—"Ellie's *my* best friend."

—"I liked her before I even met her—you hate her compared to how much I like her."

—"She'll never pay cover in the Lore again."

. . . Ellie made Lothaire a heartfelt gift of her own.

❖

"Is he sane today?" Stelian muttered as he and the other royal males traced into the council room.

They'd asked to meet with Lothaire tonight to *evaluate* his new rule.

Yes, his coherent and stable nights had been surprisingly frequent; tonight wasn't one of them.

Lothaire rubbed his tongue over a fang. *I've got your evaluation.*

In the council room, there'd once been an ornate round table, indicating equality among those seated.

He'd had the table destroyed, replacing it with a rectangular one. A throne dominated one end. No chair at the other.

And if Lothaire got any pushback on his redecoration, there'd be no council at all.

He was actually getting pushback on other things. Stelian was often too drunk to be afraid of Lothaire and so foolishly spoke his mind. Mirceo usually thought Lothaire was kidding, believing he could jest with his uncle.

Without his Bride, Trehan cared not whether he lived or died. Viktor longed to battle his king, taking every offense in the mean spirit with which Lothaire intended it.

Kosmina adored her new "foulmouthed but well-intentioned uncle." Because, as she put it, "Perhaps we aren't meant to understand him. Perhaps he's as much a puzzle as he is a puzzle master."

Hear, hear, Kosmina. But I'm still sending your ass to Louisiana.

Maybe the royals needed to witness a demonstration of Lothaire's unmatched power. As yet, they merely thought him a besotted fool who'd been laid out by his female.

Still reeling . . . After weeks in Dacia and numerous days of dreaming, Lothaire still had none of Elizabeth's memories. His consciousness seemed to sidle at the very edge of them.

He knew that vampires never saw anything in their visions from which they couldn't mentally rebound.

What lies in Elizabeth's memories that could scar me worse than I already am?

Stelian cleared his throat. "Before we get started, we'd like to talk to you about your queen."

Lothaire steepled his fingers. "Obviously, I have none."

Mirceo said, "You're a monarch with a Bride, my liege. That means she's our lady, and we serve her. Right now, she's a target for your enemies."

An eighth of an inch of tendon. "I don't bloody want to hear this!"

Stelian said, "If for no other reason, you require your Bride for heirs."

"I need none. I plan to live—and rule—forever." So heirs were unnecessary. But what about simply having children? He'd grown pleased at the idea of offspring with Elizabeth. *Yet another thing she stole from me!* He narrowed his eyes. "You scowl, young Viktor? My ruling for eternity doesn't delight you?"

The towering vampire stood, his fists balled. "Your agenda is not what we envisioned, *Cousin*. You seek to plunge us into a new war and believe we should reveal ourselves to all in the Lore? This will no longer be *Dacia*."

With his quiet intensity, Trehan said, "We vowed allegiance to a king *and* a queen."

Viktor added, "We swore to protect Queen Elizavetta—"

In a flash, Lothaire lunged out of his chair, tracing forward to slam Viktor's head against the table. "I told you never to mention that name to me!"

Viktor freed his sword and launched a strike, but Lothaire caught the blade, squeezing it. "If you're not with me, you're against me." His blood gushed over Viktor's disbelieving face. "You've erred for ill." Lothaire gave a brutal yank, hurling the weapon from him.

When the others drew their own, Lothaire swept through the room with a speed they couldn't comprehend. Claws bared, he disabled his opponents—rending a tendon in a dominant arm, slashing a hamstring. . . .

Back to Viktor. He palmed his cousin's head. "Now," he grated as he began crushing Viktor's skull. "Do we all concede that we do not fuck with Lothaire? That I might be your relative, but I will *always* be the Enemy of Old?"

Stunned, reluctant nods all around.

"Above all things, I am your *king*." He stared each one of them down as they fought to catch their breath or stanch a bleeding wound. "You obey *me*. Your undivided allegiance is to *me*. Vow this."

Unlike Elizabeth, they'd be bound to him. *But I'd wanted her loyalty more than anyone's, more than anything.*

Once each royal had made his vow, he released Viktor, who crumpled to the floor. "Lothaire endeth the lesson."

They dragged Viktor away, then traced from the room, all but Stelian, who clamped a gushing arm. "You've earned a lifelong enemy in Viktor."

"I've earned respect!"

"Viktor's too much like you to take the lesson you set out to teach him."

Lothaire absently licked the gash in his hand. "Then he'll soon perish under my rule."

Stelian shook his head. "Now that political ambitions have been neutralized among us, your cousins are a good and true lot. They could unite as a family once more, if you would but lead them."

"You've missed the point, Stelian. They might be good and true." Lothaire bared his fangs. "But *I* am not."

Hag strode in then, clad in conservative Dacian garb—stained with hot-pink and neon-green potions. "We need to talk, Lothaire." She'd told him she'd address him as *sire* as soon as he called her Balery.

Or when hell froze over.

"What is it, *Hag*?"

"I don't know what, exactly when, or how—but the first threat to your kingdom looms . . . soon."

56

"W here am I gonna go?" Ellie asked Nïx as she scratched at her new bandage. She and the Valkyrie, who seemed lucid today, stood on the front porch of Val Hall, waiting for the sun to set.

Though most of the coven had wanted Ellie to stay, Cara had put it simply: "She lingers; she dies."

Despite being penniless, with only a single change of clothes, a hoodie, and a quart of blood packed in a grocery bag, she would heed Cara's decree.

"It was never supposed to go like this," Ellie told the soothsayer. "How will I feed myself or protect myself from the sun? How do I make a living?"

Nïx's palms flew to her cheeks. "I meant to teach you how to join the typing pool!"

"I'm serious, Valkyrie! I can't exactly use my degree to get a job. I don't even have an identity I can use. Hey, maybe I can go to New Orleans, get a job in a Lore shop somewhere?"

"I suppose this would be a bad time to tell you that many beings will kill you on sight just for being a vampire. Werewolves, Furies, berserkers, and witches would try to do you in before they ever got around to figuring out who you are and why they should fear you. I've been sending out memos, but these things take time."

"Why would Lothaire cast me off like this? *'Rot in hell?'* What was *that*?"

"I know, right! Over one near decapitation? Unfortunately, he's still stewing—could stew for decades. Time doesn't mean the same thing to the very old. Think of it this way: Lothaire has lived so long that three weeks would feel like scant hours. His internal clock is telling him he's been away from you for an afternoon."

"So I should just wait for him to see reason? After that package, why would I want to be with the unbalanced undead?"

"Well, don't forget that he came to me for help to save you. Considering that he loathes me—thinks I betrayed him—this was huge."

"*Did* you betray him?"

"Yes. Often." She shrugged. "Sometimes you have to be cruel to be kind."

"I don't follow—"

Nïx shoved her into the front yard, into the light of a blazing afternoon sun. "Flap your wings, little butterfly!"

Ellie traced back in; the wraiths tossed her back out. She hunched and hissed, but her skin . . . wasn't burning.

"What is this, Valkyrie?" She stared at her unmarked arms. "How is this possible?"

"Did you hear Lothaire when he made his wish to turn you?"

Ellie shook her head slowly.

"He's exceedingly bright. Surely he would have phrased his wish to, say, 'make Elizabeth a vampire with all their strengths and none of their weaknesses.'"

Lothaire had told her he had a surprise for her. He *had* listened to her when she'd told him how much she would miss the sun.

And he'd given her a gift no other man could.

All the sunrises for eternity.

Unfortunately, she'd all but beheaded him before he could present his offering to her.

She raised her face to the light, still in disbelief. *I'm truly free.*

After years of captivity, of answering to others, she could go wherever she liked, do whatever she pleased. She could travel the world—without fear of burning.

But Lothaire's selfless gift—after all, he could never enjoy it with her—only reminded Ellie that there *had* been a chance between them. When tears welled, she dashed them away, embarrassed for Nïx to see.

Needing her family, if only just to watch them from a distance for a spell, Ellie collected her bag and hastily waved good-bye to Val Hall, to the wraiths, to Nïx.

"Adieu, Queen Ellie!" the Valkyrie called.

"Thank you for everything, Nïx." Ellie shrugged into her hoodie, pulling it over her head, just in case someone happened to spot her. Then she traced to the woods near her mother's trailer.

The forest blanketing the mountain was old growth, the pines and hardwoods so dense that sunlight barely reached the moist ground—not that she had to worry about that any longer. As she strolled along familiar paths, she gazed up, watching the taller treetops rake a steady ridgeline breeze.

Her senses were so acute now. Here, she could smell the very earth. The sound of the cicadas was like a roar in her ears.

Every time she stepped on green pine needles, their crisp scent erupted. A bite of evergreen.

Like Lothaire's scent.

Don't think about him, Ellie! Look forward, never dwell.

From the edge of the woods, she spied her old trailer, finding it dingier than ever in the daylight. The aroma of cooking food carried from within. Though no longer appealing to her appetite, it smelled like home.

How would she ever be able to leave this mountain again? She knew she couldn't stay, but where could she go?

Ellie briefly considered living in one of the exotic locales Lothaire had taken her to. *And how exactly would I get blood from Bora-Borans—*

Oh, there was Josh! He played with some of his cousins on a broken-down, rusted swing set.

Look how much he's grown! His dark hair had more of an auburn tint than hers did, but their eyes shared the same color.

How she'd missed her baby brother! As she watched him, she got lost in memories of him as a chubby toddler, recalling how he'd barreled around the trailer like a Weeble, always leading with his stubborn chin.

Those tears of hers gathered and spilled—

"Hands where I can see 'em, or I'll blow your head off!"

Uncle Ephraim. In the woods behind her.

She froze. *Oh, my God!* So much for not making contact with her family.

And he was such a quick trigger, she wondered if she could even trace away before a bullet plugged her. *Trace away to where, Ellie?*

"Hands up, I said!"

She dropped her grocery bag, raising her hands. "It's me, Uncle Eph. It's Ellie." She eased around, then uncovered her head.

His weather-beaten face paled, his wide jaw slackening as he lowered his gun. "Ruth!" he yelled in the direction of the trailer. "Ruth, come quick, your daughter's losing her eyes!"

Ellie cried, "What?" Oh, the tears! "Wait, I'm not losing my eyes! Don't call her—"

Too late. Mama came charging out in her house slippers, nearly tripping down the steps. "What is it?" She shoved her thick red hair out of her face, tossing a cigarette.

Ephraim covered Ellie's shoulder with his callused hand. "Just stay calm, girl, and we'll get you to a hospital fast as lightning."

"I'm fine. This is just how I cry now." As if that made *any* sense.

But when her mother reached them, she took one look at Ellie and shook her head sadly. "Ellie Ann, are them tears? What'd that feller *do* to you?"

When Josh came bounding toward them, Ellie whirled around. "Send him down the mountain. I don't want him to see me like this!"

Mama headed him off, shooing him back to his friends, then said to Ellie, "You best come in."

She nodded, and the three of them trudged to the trailer in silence. Inside, once her mother got a closer look—her gaze darting over Ellie's tear tracks, black claws, and small fangs—comprehension dawned.

"Oh, Ellie," she murmured, "don't you know that when you lie down with dogs, you get up with fleas?"

She knows what I am! How would she react? *Will she shun me? Be disgusted?*

"Don't mean I ain't gonna love your flea-bitten hide."

Ellie wanted to sag with relief. When Mama opened her arms, she was tempted to run to her, but stopped herself. "I can't be hugging anybody yet. I'm kinda strong-like."

Ephraim gazed back and forth between them. "Ellie, I think you got a heap of talkin' to do."

Nodding gravely, she sank onto the living room's shabby couch, unleashing dog fur and dust motes to float through the sunlight streaming inside. Then she began to outline her new abilities and immortality, her need for blood. . . .

Once she'd finished, Ephraim appeared dazed. "Gonna have to ponder all this awhile. But the fact is: you're a Peirce. No matter what you got turned into. And we do right by our kin. So just tell us if you're gonna need"—he swallowed—"to drink or anything. I'll hunt, help out where I can."

Mama crossed her arms over her chest, huffily leaning back in her recliner. "I want to know more about the vampire that did this to you."

So Ellie told them about Lothaire as well—leaving out the mind-blowing sex, of course—summing up with: "And then he gave me his heart in a box and told me to rot in hell. He didn't even want to talk about what had happened, just sent me a kiss-off!"

"I'll kill him," Ephraim grated, his eyes glinting, which made Ellie choke up all over again. When he saw her blood tears, her uncle vowed, "I'll kill him dead to rights, Ellie Ann. He sets one foot on our mountain and he's a dead sumbitch."

57

"Yਯou have a visitor, Lothaire," Hag called.

"A *visitor*? In my supposedly hidden kingdom?" He bared his fangs at Stelian, who merely raised his brows. "By all means, show in my uninvited guest."

It was Nïx, carrying a small gift box.

"How did you get in here, Valkyrie?"

She peered around, golden eyes wide, then whispered, "Get in *where*?" Her hair was windblown, and she had dark smudges under her eyes. She wore a crinkled peasant blouse, a long flowing skirt—and one boot.

"You're getting worse." Why didn't he have the energy to hate Nïx as she deserved to be hated? On the island, she'd told him, "There won't *be* a next match, vampire." Because he couldn't be bothered?

"You *were* getting better," she said. "Before. Not so much now."

"If you're here to negotiate Elizabeth's release, save your breath." *An eighth of an inch. Took my goddamned happiness away.*

"I'm not. I'm only a messenger from Elizabeth. You sent her your heart in a box, and she responded."

At once, he traced to Nïx, snatching the package from her. As Lothaire lifted the lid with a sense of dread, Nïx murmured, "Hint: it's the middle one."

Elizabeth's fragile finger. Seeing it severed like this brought on a visceral reaction—pain shooting through his own hand, radiating throughout his regenerated heart.

He closed the lid with a swallow, sentimentally pocketing the package.

"You gave her your heart, and she gave you the bird." Nïx sighed. "Songs will be written about this."

Stelian laughed, choking on his mead.

Then Elizabeth truly does hate me.

Don't give a fuck.

"My coven went wild over this, by the way," Nïx said. "Absolutely adored that feisty vamp. If I don't find our queen soon, they'll probably put her name on the ballot."

So much for their tormenting Elizabeth. The Valkyries had never seen her coming.

"And now your queen is on to the next chapter of her eternal life."

Which is, which is . . . ?

No, don't care! Don't—

Damn it! He seized Nïx's arm, then traced her to his private suite, high in the castle. Too late, he remembered the state of his rooms. Since he'd allowed no one inside to clean, they were in . . . disarray.

"Remodeling, vampire?" She surveyed the area, taking in the furniture he'd destroyed and the wall he'd punched so many times it'd finally collapsed.

All because of Elizabeth!

Nïx frowned. "I liked it the way it was before."

"*Before?* Naturally, you've been here?"

She shrugged. "So you don't want to know what your Bride is up to?"

Can't lie. "I haven't come for her, have I?"

She strolled to the sitting room window, peering out. "Understandable. They say even *you* are frightened of her. And by *they*, I mean *me*. But the rumor's catching on. You'll thank me for that later," she promised, sauntering to his desk and rooting through papers. "It must have taken you days to regenerate a heart. All that pain . . . If only I could find a male so romantic."

"Romantic? It was to mark the end of our relationship. Keep her at Val Hall forever, if you like."

"Oh, no. She's gone. Whereabouts unknown."

His gut tightened. The cloaking tattoo around her ankle had faded with her transformation. Would Elizabeth be safe outside of the wraiths' guard?

Who was he kidding? She was a vicious female—a vampire who'd taken *him* down!

"Ellie did mention something about seeing the world."

He wanted to tell Nïx, "I couldn't care less," but his throat burned on the lie. "You do know that there's a bounty on her head?"

"The one Kristoff posted?"

"Kristoff?" he bit out. *The Gravewalker will be receiving a visit from me*—

"He's on walkabout currently. He'll be back at Oblak in a few weeks. If I remember, I'll be sure to let him know you'll be calling on him."

"Do whatever you like," he snapped.

"Fear not, very few Loreans would target Ellie. After what I've told everyone she did to you? Plus, they know better than to use her as leverage—since you seem not to want her."

Don't I? He still reached for her in his bed, only to find himself clasping nothing. Upon every wakening, he roared with frustration, shaken anew that she wasn't with him.

"You can keep up the façade, Lothaire, pretending how wonderful it is without her. But we both know you miss her."

"Perhaps I simply miss a female—*any* female. I wager I'll be the one vampire who will forsake his Bride and enjoy others."

Starting *today*, he would. His plan to install concubines had been delayed by his regenerating heart. Then he'd lost enthusiasm for the idea because his new heart hurt worse than the other. But no more delays.

Nïx examined her claws, as if his statement was the height of absurdity. "Do you know how many times I've heard that?"

He traced in front of her, slowly backing her toward the wall. "Ah, flower, would you like me to demonstrate how quickly I've forgotten her?" he asked, voice dripping with innuendo.

In a breathless whisper, she said, "Yes. Kiss me, Lothaire."

He quirked a brow. *Could any male turn her down?* Nïx was stunning—and apparently willing. He brushed her tangled hair back from her face.

I always knew she wanted me. What female wouldn't?

Elizabeth. *Because I'm ugly on the inside.*

Ignoring thoughts about his Bride—and his contentious past with Nïx—he leaned in closer . . . closer. He grinned as he imagined Elizabeth finding out about other females in his life, discovering that he was bedding scores of them without a thought devoted to her.

Not a thought. *I'll kiss Nïx—and it will be better than with Lizvetta.*

Better than the night he'd first claimed his Bride, helping her take him inside her body? Better than the night he'd turned her? When she'd kneaded his flesh with her little claws as she'd fed from him?

The way his heart had beat in time with hers . . . the way she always ran circles around him . . . the way her chin would jut stubbornly, her gray eyes fierce . . .

Just before he reached Nïx's lips, he froze.

Better with the Valkyrie? *Fool, it can't be better.*

Rage erupted. *"Ahhh!"* he bellowed. "It's her! That bitch has ruined me!"

He punched the wall beside Nïx's head; she *yawned.*

"You knew this would happen! You knew we'd never kiss. Yet you said I defied foresight."

"Doesn't take a soothsayer to see how much you ache for her, Lothaire. She's your missing puzzle piece. You'll never be complete without her, no matter how many ethereally gorgeous Valkyries you bed."

Elizabeth is *my happiness,* he thought again. "I could hate her for what she did to me."

"Because of one unsuccessful beheading?" She tapped her claw to her chin. "Wow. I never thought you were such a pussy. I'm rethinking our friendship."

He bared his fangs once more. "It's not about my neck! She *betrayed* me." She'd feigned affection for him. For *him*. "I've had enough betrayal in my life. From my father, my uncle, from *you*."

"Me?"

"Don't play coy, Valkyrie. I know of your treachery. You warned Stefanovich of my impending attempt on his life. He *listened well*."

She shrugged nonchalantly. "I did tell him—but only after I explained to you that I intended to do exactly that. I repeatedly told you to be patient, to trust me, but you wouldn't listen. You set out anyway."

"You were my oldest friend! I never thought you would truly contact him."

"I acted for your greater good, to turn your fate in a different direction, before tragedy struck."

"Tragedy?" He turned to pound his fist on his desk and it shattered into splinters, papers flying. "What could possibly have been worse than what occurred? I suffered six centuries of hell because of you! Do you know what it was like in that grave, to have insects boring inside my own living corpse, picking at my flesh? No idea when it would end . . . the blood tree growing *within*." He lurched on his feet, memories threatening to overwhelm him. "It . . . *fed*. I prayed for death. Anything to make the pain end!"

"If Stefanovich hadn't caught you, then you wouldn't have your Bride."

Inhale for calm. Exhale. Draw from the tie with Elizabeth. "What are you fucking talking about?"

"Have you never wondered why I would *betray*"—Nïx made air quotes—"you?"

"Because we are natural enemies. Instinctively you despise what I am. It was only a matter of time."

She perched on the study's window seat. "If you hadn't been caught by Stefanovich, you would have died in the Horde invasion of Draiksulia."

"There was no Horde invasion of the fey plane."

She snapped her fingers. *"Exactly.* You, as well as all our Valkyrie allies, were spared. From just a whisper in your father's ear."

His lips parted.

"And had you perished then, you never would have made contact with Saroya—who would have killed even more while in Elizabeth's body, leaving no time for an attempted exorcism." Nïx's vacant golden eyes shimmered. "I saw your Bride's alternate future as clear as day. One fall morning, Elizabeth did the laundry for her mother, folding clothes off the line. Then she took her father's Remington and walked into the woods alone. She tucked the barrels under her chin. Blood, brain, and bone splattered over leaves."

He flinched.

"I saw it all. Still think me a betrayer?"

I wouldn't have Elizabeth if not for Nïx's actions. He didn't have her anyway! Then his eyes narrowed. "Why did you leave me so long in the grave? You were there the night Fyodor released me—I saw you in the woods."

"My foresight doesn't work with you. I was only able to find you by reading Helen's fate. You know what she became to you."

"Yes." *My aunt.* "An embarrassment."

"Speak ill of my dead sister again, Lothaire, and I'll take my crazy somewhere else."

"Somewhere outside of Dacia?" He waved his arm. "If you could find this kingdom all along, you might have told *me* how! I spent centuries searching. As you well knew!"

"You weren't ready to find it yet. Would you rather have warred with them or become their king by invitation? All it took was patience, which is what I told you again and again. But you never listened to me. *You* broke the trust between us—not me."

"Even after all the antagonism between us, I came to you for help just weeks ago. You turned your back on me and sent Dorada straight to my home! Don't you dare deny it."

"I was hoping Dora would find your addy okay. MapQuest is sometimes hokey."

His fists clenched tight, his shoulder muscles knotting with tension.

"You wanted Elizabeth, and you needed Saroya gone—without breaking your vows."

Nïx had sent Dorada to *help* him?

"My plan was brilliant."

"And risky." If Elizabeth hadn't thought on her feet . . . *We'd both be dead.*

"Great risk leads to great reward, does it not?" Then Nïx chuckled. "I do enjoy telling Loreans, 'Be advised that your blood debt is now being serviced by La Dorada, effective immediately.' "

He was rocked by these explanations. *My millennia's worth of hatred for Nïx was unfounded?*

Who would be his nemesis, if not Nïx? In the entire Lore, she was the only adversary worthy of him. Which was one of the myriad reasons he hadn't retaliated after she'd betrayed him.

Can always kill her, but can never bring her back. . . .

In a contemplative tone, she added, "You saw Dora when she was jubilant from a long-awaited victory. Most of the time, she's *so* apocalyptic. And now she has evil *and* good pawns to wage her war. I'll have to fix that in the future." Nïx frowned, and suddenly she looked very, very tired. After seeming to count on her fingers, she murmured, "*How* will I remember to fix that in the future?"

At length, she glared at Lothaire. "I'm risking an apocalypse for you, and you don't even want to be with Elizabeth!"

"She nearly *beheaded* me! I've never been closer to death in all my years!"

"So now you're pouting in your castle. After the miseries you've inflicted on legions? You can dish it out, but you can't take it?"

"It's different."

"How?"

He stabbed his fingers into his hair. "It simply is."

"*How?*" she insisted.

"Because I think . . . because I was falling in love with her!"

"Then why isn't she here with you now?"

"It was unrequited!" He'd shocked himself by saying that aloud.

Lothaire Daciano, a king, admitting to falling for a female who disdained him?

"Do you believe that because of her dream memories? Or because of her actions?"

"I can't *see* her memories, Nïx. But I know why—it's because vampires don't see what they can't handle!" *I can't handle knowing she played me.* She'd bested *him.* "Just tell me what I . . . tell me what should I have done differently, to make her love me."

Nïx rolled her eyes. "Where to begin?"

"Fuck off!"

"Why should I help you with Elizabeth, anyway? You've betrayed me worse than I ever did you. Why did you strike out at Furie instead of exacting your revenge directly on me?"

"Where would be the sport in that? You're more crazed than I am! Why can't you find Furie, soothsayer? Is she another blank spot in your visions? I never doubted you would locate her."

"Would that have changed your decision to imprison her?"

"No. I followed my king's orders. You of all people should know why I was bound to obey him in all things."

"In any case, will you help the Valkyries find Furie now?"

"As I told Regin, I don't know where she is."

"But you did once, Lothaire. You are the one who chained her to the bottom of the ocean."

"For your interventions in the past, I should be honor-bound to help you," Lothaire said. "Alas, I have no honor."

Her face fell. "I can't help you like this. You're more eaten up with hate than I'd ever thought, and more ignorant about females than I'd ever imagined. I'm wasting time I need for other things." She turned to leave.

Behind her, he called, "I drank Commander Webb, Valkyrie. I have his memories. I know you were working for him."

Lothaire also now knew that Webb had probably been . . . reborn. As an immortal.

Before Lothaire had bitten him, the wily bastard had popped a sample of blood, like a cyanide capsule. As Webb died, he'd had the blood of an immortal running through him, one so powerful that even Lothaire had been overcome after drinking it.

Webb would rise, as gods only knew what.

Perhaps I ought to tell Chase all the dark secrets I've learned about his surrogate father, to relieve some of his guilt.

And to prepare him.

But Lothaire was still Lothaire, and blood tie or not, Chase was still a dick. *I don't give without receiving.*

Yet hadn't he with Elizabeth?

Nïx turned back to him, her face marred with fatigue. "I wasn't working with Webb, I was *using* him."

"How would your allies feel to learn of your connection to him? Through Webb, you sent a witch to the island. Hell, you sent your own sister. I wonder why you gave him *my* name to add to the capture list. Yet another betrayal."

She tilted her head at him, her eyes gone silvery. "Had to catch you before you used the ring, Lothaire. One more second and you would seriously have rewritten the wrong female. You do not even want to contemplate what would have happened to your Bride if Saroya had been made a vampire, with the ability to trace. . . . And more, I needed you on the island for six purposes: Wendigo extermination, saving Thaddeus's life, giving Chase blood to stabilize him until his berserkertude took over. I forgot the others," she said with growing agitation. "No matter. Your takeaway: sometimes you have to be cruel to be kind."

"So after this night, am I supposed to feel beholden to you? Do you expect me to just turn off my animosity toward you?"

He couldn't even if he wanted to. She was right; he *was* eaten up with hatred.

"I *see* Furie drowning, but can never find her. She is my sister! And you wouldn't spare me that?"

Perhaps I ought to tell Nïx where I left her. . . .

But there was more on the line. "You and I both know to whom she's bound. Sinking her was also strategic."

Nïx looked dejected. Lips moving silently, she hugged her arms around her chest.

Understanding hit him. *In order to help me tonight, she has hurt herself in whatever way.* "Nïx?" She was weary, bewildered, hardly the malicious being he'd thought her for so long.

In Old Norse, she asked him, "How will I remember the apocalypse?" Her voice was haunted, her slim frame shaking. "There's so much to see, to remember, so many faces . . ."

For all that the memories had been shadowing his thoughts, visions of the future had been obscuring hers. He'd played his one Endgame; apparently, she'd been playing *thousands*.

"*How?*" she cried. Lightning flashed, bolts *inside* the great caverns of Dacia for the first time in history.

In the streets below, screams rang out. Thunder rocked the entire kingdom, echoing until rubble quaked. *The unknown threat Hag spoke of.*

"Calm yourself, Valkyrie!" He grabbed her shoulders, giving her a jostle.

She thrashed against him harder, and two more bolts speared down in rapid succession. Like detonations. She could topple the castle!

"Phenïx, calm yourself!" He lifted her into his arms to trace her away—

At once, the lightning ebbed. Seconds passed. A muted scream here and there. Disaster averted.

"*Phenïx?*" she whispered up at him. "No one calls me that but you. Everyone who used to is dead. They're all dead."

He exhaled a gust of breath. "They always die before us, don't they?"

"Without fail."

"When was the last time you slept?"

"Not since I saw you on the island."

That had been several weeks ago. "Why? The shrieks at Val Hall keep you up?"

"I like to drift off to the sound of shrieks. No, it's because someone always needs my help. Loreans are incessant, skulking around the manor, with their languishing hearts and unfulfilled desires. I can feel them ache, like a bad tooth I can never yank free."

"You need a male to keep those beings at bay."

"You have *no* idea."

He muttered a curse, then said, "You may rest here this eve." Tracing to the sitting room couch, he gently laid her down. "I'll keep the Loreans away for one night."

"It is blessedly peaceful here, high in this castle. White queen and black king can call a draw for a time. . . ."

My enemy, my onetime friend. Why had she continued to help him? With a brusque "Good night," he tossed a blanket over her.

But she said, "Stay. Just till I fall asleep."

After debating a few moments, he sank down, resting his back against the couch, his arms stretched over his bent knees. "Why do you want *me* here?"

She yawned widely, as the young did. "We can watch each other's backs in shifts, as we used to do."

Though it did feel like times past, he said, "You still can't trust me. I'm considering cutting your hair when you sleep, just for keys past the Scourge."

"Naturally. Talk to me about other things."

"About what?"

"Anything."

Another exhalation, then he spoke his mind. "I feel . . . old." He knew she could sympathize. When they'd been friends, he'd once confessed to her, "Phenïx, you are the only one who understands the truth: Eternal life alone is naught but an eternal punishment."

"Lothaire, I've met dirt younger than we are."

He scrubbed his hand over his face. "I didn't feel old when I was with Elizabeth. I felt like a young vampire, just starting out with her. The world was ours for the taking."

"I envy you that feeling."

After several heartbeats, he admitted in a low voice, "I'd go back to the grave if it would force Elizabeth to love me."

"Oh, Lothaire," she sighed, patting his shoulder. "I tried to help you with her. I watched out for her at Val Hall. I showed her that she could walk in the sun."

"Was she excited?" He twisted around to face Nïx. "What did she say? Did she mention me?" Though Lothaire had long sworn never to bestow a gift with no thought of a return on his investment, he finally had. *I gave Elizabeth the sun.* He'd wanted her to know that happiness, even if he, himself, could not—

"Ellie was . . . sad."

"Sad?" he bit out. He'd never understand females! "Did she *never* speak of me?"

"In the weeks that you ignored her, humiliating her with every day that you didn't retrieve her? Honestly, Lothaire, if she'd brought you up to anyone . . . *awkward*."

He glowered at the ceiling. Silence reigned.

Damn it, Nïx was going to fall asleep and leave him alone and unsettled, wondering how he'd made Elizabeth sad—and whether he should give his Bride another one of his black hearts in penance.

With a scowl, he gruffly said, "I'm not a pussy, you know."

"Then dream her memories," Nïx whispered, before drifting off.

58

After several days back in her childhood home, Ellie still hadn't acclimated.

As she mended socks, she gazed around the trailer, trying to see it through Lothaire's eyes.

Mama was at the stove, frying up chicken for when Ephraim and the others got home from the mine. A singing Big Mouth Billy Bass was proudly mounted on the wall. Porcelain dolls that screamed "QVC Christmas Sale" lined a shelf. Two lazy hunting dogs, Bo and Bo Junior, dozed at her feet.

Lothaire probably hated animals. He'd find it all tacky and shuddersome.

She shrugged. Even compared to the luxury of the apartment and the grandeur of Val Hall, she liked it best here. Though it no longer felt like home.

Because Lothaire isn't with me.

Mama glanced over at her. "If you're hankerin' for that vampire, you just cut it right out, Ellie Ann Peirce."

"I believe my last name is Daciano, actually."

"The hell you say! I could kill that monster for what he did to you."

"He's not a monster, Mama. I think he's just misunderstood—"

Josh came bounding inside, running straight for Ellie. "My fort is the best, Ellie!" he told her, clambering over her onto the couch.

He'd been playing in the tree house she'd built him—the one constructed in less than forty-five minutes without a hammer. She'd used her thumbs to press nails into unwittingly donated lumber.

Initially, Josh had been wary of his long-lost sister, as if he'd sensed she wasn't *right* in some way. Though Ellie didn't suppose she appeared all that different—as long as she wasn't hungry or upset—the boy had been standoffish.

Now she couldn't pry him away. Not that she would ever try to. Since he'd taken to latching on to her at all times, she'd had to seriously accelerate her crash course in vampire strength control.

"Josh, I still can't get over how big you are!"

When he made a muscle with his right arm, she curbed a grin and looked dutifully impressed.

"Uncle Ephraim said I'm gonna be over ten feet tall."

"Well, maybe if you eat your greens."

"And Mama said you came back to the mountain 'cause you got a dee-vorce, and if any man comes 'round askin' for you, I'm s'posed to tell him you're dead, then spit on his boots."

With an arch look at her mother, Ellie said, "A divorce? Did she, then?"

Mama shrugged.

Ellie turned to Josh. "Why don't you get cleaned up, and I'll make you a PBJ."

"No crust?"

"Depends on how the finances are doing, honey." At his raised brows, she said, "Ellie's kidding. No crust, promise."

Once he was gone, she told Mama, "I'm going out tonight." For the last week, she'd continually thought about ways she could break into Lothaire's apartment and steal those jewels.

She'd come up empty.

In lieu of that, she intended to go cat-burgling later, anything to get her family out of the mine—

The trailer rocked, grease sloshing out of the fryer. Just as Josh came running wide-eyed from the bathroom, a loud boom followed.

Ellie and her mother locked gazes, knowing only one thing that could set off an unplanned explosion like that.

There'd been another mine collapse.

❖❖❖

Lothaire drifted off shortly after Nïx, his head slumping forward, his eyes darting behind his lids.

At long last, he began to witness a stream of Elizabeth's memories. He feared what he would find, but heedlessly opened himself to her past. . . .

When her father had died, Elizabeth had been grief-stricken, but she'd allowed herself little time to mourn him. Instead, she'd worked tirelessly to scrabble together a better life for her mother and brother.

Lothaire observed example after example of her using her wits to make strides, with work, with school. And she'd known successes, gaining momentum.

Until Lothaire and Saroya had devastated her existence with a year of hell, culminating in a night of carnage.

Prison followed. Lothaire's eyes stung as he experienced the pall of mace lingering in the ward. He felt her pulse racing when she shot upright in bed, awakened by the other prisoners hissing in the dark, moaning, wailing.

Her bottom lip would tremble when she dreamed about her college pennants and her little brother's ruddy cheeks. How much she yearned to watch him grow up!

But in five years, she never allowed herself to cry.

He experienced firsthand her near execution, the IVs sunk into her veins, her "rescue" to a place even more torturous.

He relived his own mocking, as if it'd been directed at him. He'd derided her background and her loved ones, wounding her repeatedly.

If he had, in fact, ever praised her intelligence, then she had no memory of it.

Not only hadn't he recanted his hateful comments, he'd never righted the wrongs.

Lothaire heard her thinking, "Does he still consider me just a "backward and vulgar hillbilly"? He'll probably be embarrassed of me around others. God, that hurts."

No, you are everything to me!

From her point of view, he experienced the night that he'd told her he'd keep *her*, that he'd chosen her. He felt her flutter of hope; later, he felt her misery once she'd comprehended that he would still kill her, would destroy her soul.

In the beginning of her ordeal with Saroya, Elizabeth had accepted that she would die; yet then she'd let herself hope for the first time since the night he'd sent her off to death row.

The dashed hope was the worst.

Elizabeth had told him honestly, "I don't want to live in your violent, messed-up world."

Why *would* she decide to live within the violent realm of immortals—much less choose *him* as her protector amid it?

He'd given her no reason to choose him over her loved ones, simply decreeing that she'd never see them again.

Once he viewed her memories of her family—laughing with them, covering for them, always there to help out—he recognized how ridiculous he'd been to expect her to forget them.

Her family had proved just as loyal to Elizabeth. With no questions asked, two of her cousins had buried bodies for her behind the barn.

I hadn't even thought—or cared—about what had happened to Saroya's victims.

Elizabeth had once told him that her family was a unit, that their mountain was an ironclad support system.

My own family is lacking compared to that. Ivana had been betrayed by her father. Lothaire's own father had tortured him.

The Peirces were invulnerable to deceit and cowardice like that.

But at last, Lothaire wasn't jealous of Elizabeth's devotion to others—no matter how much he coveted it.

Just because she loved her family and was loyal to them didn't mean she couldn't be loyal to him as well.

As long as he never crossed them.

Instead, he'd set events into motion that would separate her from her loved ones forever. He'd robbed her of her family.

Just as Serghei robbed me of Ivana.

In sleep, he began to sweat as he grasped the truth: *I did to Elizabeth . . . what he did to me.*

Lothaire had never seen her memories for a reason—because he couldn't handle the way he'd treated his precious female.

Just when he was about to wake, despairing of ever winning her back, a flash of another memory arose. As he'd slept one night, suffering from some nightmare, she'd gazed down at him with tenderness. Her chest had ached with feeling for him—as his continued to do for her. She'd smoothed hair from his brow, soothing him with soft words.

He'd never known that before. Ah, gods, she *did* love him.

Lothaire could *feel* it burning strong within her. *I could have the loyalty she showed her family. The love—*

He woke with a yell. "Lizvetta!"

I knew she was falling in love with me!

He twisted around, but Nïx wasn't on the couch. He found her sitting at the window, waving down at his subjects. She looked refreshed, her hair combed.

"Elizabeth did love me!" he barked without preamble. "So why would she lash out like that?"

Nïx shrugged, blowing a kiss to someone. "Because she was a new vampire with her emotions running high? Did you say anything that might have provoked her to that kind of rage?"

He rubbed the back of his neck. "There might have been a few choice phrases."

"Plus, she traced just as she swung the sword at you."

"Impossible. She'd only been a vampire for hours."

"She can trace all around the world now."

Unexpected Elizabeth. "I am prideful. But if she can trace without limits, will she go back to her family?" He was unable to think of much beyond getting his Bride back, his mind seizing on one little task: *get Elizavetta.* "What did she say when she left Val Hall?"

Nïx turned to him. "I remember her standing dazed on our front porch. The vaunted queen of the proud Daci was alone, penniless, with her few clothes—all Valkyrie cast-offs, mind you—in a grocery bag. She had no idea what she was going to do or how she was going to feed herself, and feared her family would never accept her. Oh, and she was light one finger."

He yelled in frustration, tracing to punch a fist into a fresh wall. "You tell me these things? You might as well gut me with a blade."

"I'm just telling you so you know why she might be less than thrilled if you show up."

"I felt her emotions, I know she loved me."

"Before you broke her heart."

Long moments passed. In a low tone, he asked, "Am I never to have her love again?"

"I'd hold on to the finger, Lothaire. It might be all you ever have of her."

Family is her key. He threw back his head and yelled, "Stelian!"

When the big vampire traced inside, he gave a courtly bow to Nïx, who smiled absently.

Lothaire wasted no time. "Go and buy my queen's family mountain. Put it in her name. Lie, steal, cheat, or kill to see this through."

Stelian saluted sarcastically. "We have intermediaries who deal with humans. Consider it done."

"And get the mountains next to it, just in case."

"I see we're planning to buy the queen's forgiveness. It's about time."

"Cease. Speaking."

Stelian disappeared.

Nïx nodded approvingly. "Now you're starting to get it, vampire . . ." She trailed off, shooting to her feet, her eyes swirling silver. "Lothaire, something's *wrong*."

He'd also felt a heavy sense of dread. His connection to Elizabeth was clearer now, more so than it had ever been. "What do you see, Nïx?"

Gaze gone wild, she murmured, "Ellie spinning in blind circles, blood pouring from her mouth. Go to the mountain, Lothaire, follow the screams!"

59

"Elizabeth!" Lothaire found her on her knees in a sunlit field, covered in coal dust, holding her hands over her bleeding ears. He was half-tracing, but still the light burned him.

"L-Lothaire?" Tears tracked down her cheeks, more blood spilling from her mouth. She was frail, obviously hadn't been drinking enough, and was newly injured.

Battered mortals lay on the ground all around them.

"I'm here, tell me what's happened."

She shook her head in confusion. She couldn't hear, could barely speak. "Help . . . me. . . ."

He clasped her in his arms, tracing her back to her home.

"No!" she shrieked, thrashing against him. "Back. Go back!"

Lothaire steadied his breathing, struggling to match his heartbeat to Elizabeth's frantic racing. As her heartbeat began to grow loud in his ears, Lothaire briefly closed his eyes—seeing into her mind, speaking directly into her thoughts.

"Shh, shh, love. Calm yourself."

"Take me back! My kin are dying!"

"I will fix this! Show me what's happened."

"I have to get back!"

"I will save any who live. You know *I can do anything. Trust me?"*

Her lips trembled. Another pair of tears streaked down her face. *"Can I?"*

"You alone can trust me." Words in Russian slipped out from his lips: *I will fight any battle for you, crush any adversity. Because you are mine, beautiful girl. I love you so madly that the past before you feels sane. . . .*

"Lothaire?"

"Depend on me. You must, for your family."

At length, she nodded, and he wanted to bellow with satisfaction.

"Then drink." He bit his wrist, shoving the gash against her lips. *"Heal."* When she resisted, he yelled into her mind, *"Now, Elizabeth!"*

She jerked, eyes going wide, then she pressed her lips against his wrist. When she softly sucked, pleasure rippled through him, but he ordered himself to focus, reminding himself that his Endgame was at stake.

As she drew strength from him, beginning to mend, he said, *"Let me see what happened. Show me."*

Suddenly, he saw pandemonium.

An explosion in a mine, dozens of men trapped . . . Elizabeth trying to trace her relatives out as rocks continued to fall . . . She could only take one at a time, quickly weakening . . . Another explosion burst her eardrums . . . A support beam swung down, striking her torso, damaging something internally.

"If more rocks fall, Lothaire, if it catches fire . . ."

"Where should I trace to? Imagine exactly that location." She did. *"Let me see your relatives' faces."*

Images of one after another arose. Twelve men left. Lothaire memorized them.

"Remain here, Elizabeth. Do not leave this place. I will save any who live."

He traced away, but as their immediate bridge broke, he thought he heard her say, *"Make it back to me."*

Two little tasks: find key mortals, get back to Elizabeth.

Inside. Total blackness. The gloom engulfed him, the kind of darkness found only underground. Even he strained to see down here.

The dust stung his eyes and filled his lungs, as if they were compacting with dirt.

He froze in comprehension. He could be buried alive down here.

The earth grinding over me . . .

With violent shudders, he struggled to breathe. A cold sweat beaded his skin.

He'd told Nïx that he'd go back to the grave for Elizabeth. *Here I fucking am.*

No, focus! Two little tasks. Elizabeth would want him once he saved her family. *I could take her home with me, this very day.*

He clenched the first boulder in his way, heaved it to the side. Then another. Yelling with effort, he began clearing his way through the tunnel.

All the while, the ceiling bowed precariously above him, support beams cracking under their burden.

As silt rained over him, he shuddered anew. Focus!

At last, he spotted lights from the miners' helmets. Most of the men were unconscious, but all had heartbeats. With the dust obscuring their faces, he couldn't discern Elizabeth's relatives from the others.

Which meant he'd have to save all of them, and sort later.

The ones still conscious recoiled from him.

—"Who the hell are you?"

—"Your . . . eyes!"

—"What are you?"

He grabbed the men's collars, tracing six at a time, dumping them in that scorching field and quickly scanning their faces to tally the Peirces.

But he still hadn't found the relative Elizabeth secretly loved the most—her uncle Ephraim. Lothaire traced deeper, deeper, straining to see.

Just when he spotted the man a short distance away, Lothaire heard another ominous quake.

He snatched up her uncle and traced him, tossing him into the field before returning. One man was still unaccounted for, a cousin.

Lothaire had saved his Bride's *favorite* mortal; now he was to risk being buried down here for some random cousin? He was tempted to trace away, calling this finished. She'd told him to make it back, hadn't she? He was ready to get back to the business of *them*.

But she trusted him, trusted him to save any who lived. *Loyalty must go both ways.* Though if he demonstrated it in this shadowy hell, then so help him gods, he had better receive it from her—

He scented the spark too late. . . .

***

Lothaire had come to her. Had he come *for* her?

Ellie was healing with every second, his blood like rich, warm rocket fuel compared to the animals' blood she'd been forcing down.

Her hearing was already back, her internal injury mending.

She was no longer petrified for her family—because Lothaire *could* do anything. If he said he would save all who lived, then that's what he would do.

Funny, Ellie—you didn't mind his high-handedness in this.

But immortal or not, if the coal dust ignited down there, he could . . . die. Beset with anxiety—for *him*—she paced/traced, biting her lip.

She couldn't lose him again. Her eyes began to tear up, blood pooling. What was taking him so long? She shivered, remembering the falling rocks, the coal in her lungs—

She gasped. "Oh, dear God." He'd dreamed of being buried in the earth, trapped. She'd tried to sooth his agonizing nightmares.

And yet I sent him into a mine collapse. With a cry, she traced to the triage field.

So many had already been saved. Hasty head count. Every single one of her relatives, some of them badly injured, was accounted for. So why hadn't Lothaire returned?

Then she noticed that one of her third cousins was helping the others, but he had no dust on him. He hadn't been in the mine earlier—yet she'd shown him to Lothaire as one of the missing.

Lothaire is searching for someone he'll never find.

Filled with dread, she traced inside the mine, immediately dropping to her front as flames shot over her. There hadn't been fire before! *Oh, God, oh, God.* She yanked her shirt over her mouth to keep the flammable dust out of her lungs.

If Lothaire had breathed too much of it . . .

Crawling through the blinding drifts of smoke, she scrambled to reach him, struggling to *sense* him as she navigated the arteries of the mountain. He'd said they had unbreakable ties.

Marshal your wits, Ellie!

Once she settled down and concentrated, she seemed instinctively to know where to go, which way around boulders, and her connection to Lothaire grew stronger, like a sound getting louder closer to the source.

Almost there . . .

She found him. "Lothaire! *Leo?*" He was unconscious, pinned under a landslide of flaming rocks, his skin on fire.

When she dragged him out from under the rubble, she screamed. His coal-laden lungs had ruptured wide, his torso exploded outward.

His lids cracked open. Brows drawn, he mouthed, *"Leave me now . . . get . . . out . . ."* His eyes closed. The tension left his body.

Best be savin' your orders for someone who'll follow them, vampire.

60

"Y our mama's coming," Ephraim warned Ellie as she pressed a cold compress over Lothaire's face.

For two days, Lothaire had lain unconscious and bandaged in Ellie's darkened room, with Bo Junior draped across his ankles for most of that time.

That dog had a mean streak a mile wide. Figured the ornery hound would take a shine to the ornery vampire.

After Ephraim had gotten his own head bandaged, he'd helped Ellie clean Lothaire's wounds and get him comfortable, had even poached a deer to feed the man who'd saved his life.

Everyone—including her mother, *especially* her—had changed their tune about Ellie's villainous vampire.

"So let me get this straight," Mama had said, staring in awe at Lothaire's face. Even burned and gauze wrapped, he'd still looked like a god. "The most beautiful man you've ever seen turned you so you can never get sick or die, then spoiled you with jewelry and clothes while takin' you all around the world?"

"When you say it like that, it sounds unreasonable to have rejected him and accidentally nearly beheaded him."

"If the shoe fits, Ellie Ann Daciano!"

"Have you forgotten what else I told you?" Ellie had cried. "He treated me like . . . like you treat *Bo*."

"That dog sleeps in the bed with me, girl!"

"If I was with Lothaire, I'd have to live inside a mountain!"

Finally, Mama had frowned. "Like in a burrow or something?"

"A castle. But that's not the point. . . ."

Now Ephraim muttered, "I've been runnin' interference with her, but she's got her mind made up about that vampire of yourn."

Mama swept in, her brows drawing together at the sight of Lothaire sleeping. "Just look at him," she whispered. "I'll *never* get used to that face."

Ellie almost said, "Wait till you get a load of his eyes."

"Ain't he just the most beautiful thing? Like a fancy museum statue."

Lothaire continued to heal, appearing more and more like the flawless fallen angel Ellie was used to.

Mama rechecked the blankets over the windows, clucking through the room, organizing some of the get-well balloons and teddy-grams that continued to be delivered.

Finally, she took a seat by the bed. "A man that fine wants my baby to be his queen." She sighed. "Queen Elizabeth. You're gonna live forever in a castle, and you can flit around like a *fairy*"—Ellie didn't correct her—"and you're gonna be rich and adored by him."

"Mama, again, we don't know *why* he came back. He might only need an heir or something. Who knows?"

"Why else would that angel have saved all our menfolk?"

"He never said he'd returned for me." Unless he'd said it in Russian. She recalled the emotion in those words, what had felt like a promise. . . .

"You better *hope* he did," Mama muttered angrily.

"I'm just telling you that he's known to be evil. I have no idea what he's plotting."

"We ain't exactly saints around here, Miss Glass House. Sakes, Ellie, when did you get to be so judgmental?"

My mother is disappointed in me for not making my vampiric marriage work.

Though Mama had never even spoken a word to Lothaire, she'd already instructed Josh to call him Uncle Leo.

Ephraim shook his head. "There'll be no livin' with your mama now. You know that, huh?"

"Yeah." *So I really hope Lothaire came here for the right reasons. . . .*

"I'm in the *trailer*, aren't I?" Lothaire rasped as he came to in Elizabeth's bed. He'd just awakened to her sweet scent on the pillow, when the odor of some unlucky varmint frying in the kitchen overwhelmed it.

Now he peered around him—vinyl walls and threadbare linens, freakish porcelain dolls. A spiteful-looking hound dozed over his feet. He rather liked the dog.

Elizabeth crossed her arms over her chest. "It was either here or I could've left you in the mine."

When he saw balloons and stuffed get-well bears with button eyes, he almost preferred the mine.

She rose and clapped her thigh, urging the dog, "Here, boy, get off him."

The beast growled just as Lothaire said, "He can stay."

She sat back down, mumbling, "You two are perfect for each other. He's now yours, by the way."

Then he's ours. "Why are there hideous stuffed bears with my name on them?"

"My whole family loves you now. They wanted to thank you for saving them. You rescued them all, you know."

"And then you rescued me." Saving his life while risking hers. Loyalty rewarded in kind. *But if she ever puts herself in danger again . . .*

She waved that away. "In any case, we've got more casseroles than we—or they—could eat in a month."

"And how do they explain their rescue?"

"My family knows what we are, but they don't tell secrets to outsiders—believe me. The other miners think you're . . . the Mothman."

Lothaire rolled his eyes. "Mothman. Really, Elizabeth? Really?"

She shrugged. "Look, I'm deeply grateful for what you did. But why have you come here?"

"For you. I've gained control of one kingdom. Return with me to Dacia and be my queen."

"Your last word on the subject was that I should rot in hell."

Unexpected Elizabeth wasn't falling into his arms as he'd anticipated, even after he had acted heroic and been valiantly injured. Perhaps he *had* lost her.

"Lothaire, you gave me your black heart and told me I'd never get my claws in another one."

"I'll give it to you anew." He flared his own claws over his chest, about to dig in. "It pains me as nothing has before—"

"No!" She lunged forward, slapping his hand. Hard. "You just mended that skin."

He lowered his hand, grumbling, "My heart doesn't fucking work right without you."

She seemed to soften at that, but then she asked, "Has anything really changed?"

"I've learned I need to consult you in matters, lest you decapitate me."

"Lothaire . . ." she said warningly. "You didn't truly want me, not until I was a vampire. And that hurts."

"When Saroya was cast out of you that night, it felt like someone had injected me with feeling for you. I saw you clearly for the first time, knew you as my Bride with no doubts. *Before* you were a vampire."

"What if there'd been no ring, no way to turn me? Could you have accepted that?"

"Never."

Pain flashed in her expression. "Why?"

"I don't court my own death, Lizvetta. You were mortal, could perish so easily. When a vampire's Bride dies, he is *ended*, back to being the walking dead—*if* he doesn't greet the sun. So ultimately, I'm only as strong as you are."

"That's why you were so raring to turn me?"

He hiked his shoulders. "And the sex is better."

"Ugh!" She threw her hands up.

"Because it's *safer*. Each time I denied my instincts, I feared I'd harm you myself."

"If I'd remained human, could you have felt the same way about me?"

"I would never have acknowledged to myself everything I felt for you while you were so vulnerable. But then, when you'd been turned, you were so strong. . . ." Voice dropping an octave, he said, "You took all my lusts and made *me* weak."

When she nibbled her bottom lip with one of her little fangs, his thoughts blanked for a moment.

"Everything you felt for me?"

"Come, come, Bride. You're exceedingly clever. You must know that I'm in love with you. Now will you return with me?"

Seeming to steel herself against him, she said, "But you told me we weren't equals. That doesn't really go along with my idea of love."

"You traced the first day you were a vampire. You took *me* down with a sword. Most of the Lore lives in fear of you. Your loyalty to your family never faltered, no matter how much I offered you, or how much pressure I put on you. You've much to teach me, Elizabeth."

When she remained uncertain, he said, "I understand how important your family is to you because I remembered how important my mother was to me. These long millennia, I've hated Serghei for taking my family from me—now I've realized I tried to do the same to you."

"And what if we have another falling-out? Will you refuse to talk to me? I longed to tell you how sorry I was for hurting you—until you sent me that awful package!"

"And you gave me the finger in return. Which I can now admit was uproarious." Especially since it had grown back.

"You didn't answer my question. You don't exactly have relationship skills mastered. And we will fight in the future."

"As I said, you're to teach me. Plus, you'll have my memories and know how I truly feel. All you have to do is drink from me every night." He gazed at her mouth, at her fangs readying from the mere thought. "You miss my blood—admit it."

"No!" she gasped, pressing her lips together.

Voice gone hoarse, he said, "Then why are those sexy fangs of yours so sharp?" Raising his gaze to her darkening eyes, he rasped, "Gods, I am going to do depraved things to you back at our castle."

She swallowed. "I-I haven't agreed to go with you."

"Then tell me where I may do those things to my Bride. If we remain here, we'll break this flimsy bed, possibly this entire conveyance."

Chin raised, she said, "You need to apologize for how you treated me."

She's wavering. He checked a look of victory, saying honestly, "I am sorry, Elizabeth. I tried to go back in time with the ring, intending to treat you like a queen from our first meeting." Then he frowned. "You should always tell me whenever I need to apologize."

"Just till you should be gettin' the hang of it!"

"Ah, you're agreed, then? So let's be off." He sat up, going still. "Am I wearing a wife-beater, Lizvetta?" He gaped down. "Oh, come on!"

"I suppose now's not a good time to give you your Skoal hat?"

"Your retaliation is unspeakable. For this alone, you must forgive me for my treatment of you."

"Still high-handed?"

"I *literally* risked my neck just now to say that in front of you."

He saw her lips quirk, but she schooled her expression.

"I told Nïx that I would go to the grave again if it would make you love me. I went to the grave in that mine, ergo . . ."

"Are you trying to make me feel guilty so you can manipulate me?"

He blinked. "Of course. Now, tell me you love me."

"I do, Lothaire. For some reason, I truly do love you. And I will give this a chance," she said. "If you stay here with me."

Ellie had already made up her mind that she'd try living in Lothaire's castle and being a queen of the vampires and all, but this was too funny an opportunity to pass up.

Lothaire swallowed, his gaze flickering over the Beanie Babies on the windowsill and the stuffed animals.

"You could like it here, Lothaire, I just know it!"

With a pained expression, he said, "Those stuffed animals horrify and repel me." He shuddered. "And the aura of pathos in this place is inescapable. You don't . . . you can't want to live *here*. Not instead of a castle with servants to wait on your every need?"

"Sure I could! And then you wouldn't need all those fancy clothes of yours."

He squirmed. "I don't think I can live here. I really don't, Elizabeth."

And because she was so attuned to him, she could feel something akin to panic inside him. "Don't want to even give it a try?"

"Actually, I can't even *be* here for much longer."

She patted his hand. "I know, baby, I know."

"If you know I can't be here, and you won't come with me . . ." His eyes reddened ominously. "You believe we're living *apart*? I tried that; I detested that!"

Then he made a clear effort to calm himself. He opened his mouth to say something, thought better of it. At length, he grated, "I'm purchasing this mountain and the adjoining ones for you."

A breath left her. "Lothaire, I don't even know what to say."

"Come with me back to our kingdom, and I will have a mansion built here for your mother." With great effort, he said, "We could visit, if infrequently."

She leaned down until their faces were inches apart. "We'll visit every weekend, holidays, and NASCAR, vampire." She pressed her lips against

his, sighing from the rightness of it, from the certainty that her life was
with him.

Oh, Lothaire, you're not even gonna know what hit you. . . .

Between kisses, he told her, "If you agree to only Sundays and holidays,
I will buy all your brethren homes." Against her lips, he said, "And you
knew NASCAR was pushing it, Bride."

EPILOGUE

SOME TIME LATER . . .

W e'd snickered behind your back," Stelian told Lothaire in a dazed tone, "amused by how such a young female was managing you." His expression was thunderstruck.

Lothaire knew that look, wore it often himself. "But you understood nothing of which you spoke?" he said, gazing at Elizabeth across the den of their castle apartments. She sat before a hearth fire, laughing with Hag and Kosmina, the royal hound at her feet.

"Correct." Stelian swigged a deep drink of blood mead. "How did she just get me to agree to her family's Christmas visit?"

In a tone both rueful and brimming with pride, he said, "You never see my queen coming till it's too late." Just this evening, Elizabeth had some-how gotten Lothaire to agree to take Joshua—and eight of his cousins—trick-or-treating.

But really. How hard could that be?

Though it shouldn't have surprised anyone, the mortal boy worshipped Lothaire.

I'm acquiring relatives like unspayed cat shifters.

Elizabeth caught his gaze, casting him that mind-scrambling smile of hers. Draped in the jewels he lovingly bestowed upon her, she radiated her contentment.

She'd had no trouble adjusting to this foreign way of life, taking everything in stride. With each foray out into their new realm, she'd readily picked up more of her subjects' language and customs.

And taught them some of her own. The reserved Daci . . . *adored* her, found her refreshing. As predicted.

After excusing herself, Elizabeth traced to sit beside him on the settee. Their hound—which he refused to call Bo Junior—chuffed indignantly, still baffled whenever anyone traced.

As Lothaire took her hand in his, pressing a tender kiss to the back, Stelian excused himself with a wary glance at Elizabeth.

"Everyone's getting along so much better, don't you think?" she asked. She'd long since dreamed his memories of Dacia, and after analyzing Lothaire's relationships with the royals, she'd set about "salvaging" them.

Now that Elizabeth was queen, some of the ice among them all was in fact thawing. After centuries of strife, they'd begun gathering around the den hearth. Still he said, "Would I admit it, if I did?"

"Lothaire-speak?" She quirked a brow. "Well, I think everything's coming along nicely."

Upon meeting Viktor, she'd told the general, "You're the fierce one Lothaire bragged about! No wonder he appointed you to be head of my guard. When he's away, he'll trust me with no one else." The soldier's chest had bowed.

To Mirceo, she'd said, "You could ask Balery to see how long your wait for your Bride will be. Counting down sometimes helps." Advice from a wise queen who'd had grueling life experiences to count down.

She'd told Trehan, "If I can live with Lothaire, then *anything* is possible with your Bride. Can't you give your relationship just one more try?"

With Kosmina, she'd done little managing, admitting to Lothaire, "I don't even know where to start. She might truly need a complete reboot. . . ." *Hello, Louisiana.*

Elizabeth believed that they were all "coming together as a family" or something, and that the reason he felt uncomfortable around them was that he feared he "might grow to care about them."

He'd scoffed, ready to assure her that he loathed his family and didn't want them near, but he hadn't been able to utter the words.

So for now, they invaded his personal space, Dacianos overrunning them.

Despite this, he was happy once more. As he glanced at his exquisite Bride, he thought, *But I guard my key jealously.*

Queen Elizavetta Daciano was his Endgame, always had been.

Would Ivana the Bold have bowed down to her? Yes. But deep down, he knew it no longer mattered.

Each night, when Elizabeth drank from him, their unbreakable bond only strengthened—and with it, his mind continued to hold steady. He would never be completely sane—not a chance of that—but as long as she accepted him, he could manage.

Whenever she slept, she dreamed of his actions from the previous day's span. If he went out on official kingly business, she would kiss him good-bye with the plea, "Don't do anything I'm gonna regret dreaming about, Leo."

Only two pressing tasks remained. He needed to repay Nïx, and he needed to fulfill the vow to his mother to rule the Horde.

He'd decided—with the help of a sucker punch—to assist the soothsayer's search for Furie. Though he didn't necessarily want Phenïx to be his boon companion once more, he didn't like being indebted to anyone.

And when he thought about how much he loved Elizabeth and how inconceivably right it felt to have her by his side, he recognized that he was seriously—grievously—indebted to Nïx.

Now if he could just find the soothsayer to tell her; when he'd traced from Dacia to save Elizabeth, the Valkyrie had vanished.

No one in the Lore could locate Nïx the Ever-Knowing. . . .

As for his final vow to Ivana, Lothaire was torn. Elizabeth had pointed out: "Ivana wanted you to rule the Horde while Serghei ruled the Daci, joining the two kingdoms, right? What would she have said if she'd known you would take Serghei's place as king?"

Good point.

Yet then Elizabeth had added, "Of course, if the crown's just sitting there for the taking, I know my guy is up for the job. . . ."

In order to avoid a large-scale conflict, Trehan had offered to have his assassins eliminate the two other contenders: Kristoff the Gravewalker and Emmaline the Unlikely, the halfling daughter of the Valkyrie Helen and Lothaire's uncle Fyodor—also known as King Demestriu.

Though both Kristoff and Emmaline were legitimate, neither worshipped the Thirst.

Lothaire had put Trehan on hold, but at the ready. With that thought in mind, he told Elizabeth now, "I go to see one of the contenders to the Horde throne this eve."

"Do you have to?"

"I must confront Kristoff"—*that prick*—"to get the bounty on your head revoked."

She grinned. "Plus you just want to see the look on his face when you reveal yourself to him."

"There is that." *Knows me so well.* "Will you remain here?"

"This one time, yes."

"Very well," he said, masking his excitement—because he intended to make a capture this eve. What good was having a dungeon of one's own unless it was utilized?

Would Elizabeth uncover his coup—truly just a paltry one, probably not even a slaying—in her next set of dreams?

His lips curled. Of course. So he "stored" a message just for her: *Admit it, love, you like it when I'm a little bad. . . .*

She gazed up at him. "Just don't forget our new motto, Leo. 'We can always murder them later, but we can't bring them back.' "

"My wise and clever Bride." He cupped her nape, drawing her close. "You are everything," he said simply.

With a contented sigh, she pressed her mouth to his, giving him a kiss that almost landed her back in their bed.

Somehow he broke away, murmuring at her ear, "When I return, be wearing red silk."

Her irises flashed black, her gaze smoldering. "I'll make sure you'll be . . . pleased."

"Saucy chit," he teased lightly, even as his body tightened with want. *Must make this fast. . . .*

⊰※⊱

Lothaire teleported to Mt. Oblak, the Forbearer seat, and unsheathed his sword. Half-tracing into the Gravewalker's chambers, all but invisible, he found Kristoff gazing out the open window, his sand-colored hair blowing in the breeze.

The male's dark blue eyes were clear of bloodlust, but he appeared preoccupied as he stared into the night.

Dreaming of his future Bride? Of the father he'd never known?

Lothaire remembered peering down at Kristoff as an infant. All those ages ago, Lothaire had loomed over his cradle, bent on murdering Stefanovich's true heir . . . until the fair-haired baby had reached up and grasped at his finger.

As if in recognition.

If Kristoff made one wrong move this eve, Lothaire would remedy his earlier mercy.

Moving like a shadow, silent as death, Lothaire placed his sword against Kristoff's neck, *"Hello, brother. . . ."*